Dear Dick

You are a true inspiration. I look forward to our continued work together —

MW00852567

Andrew Eustace Anselmi

THE AUTUMN
CRUSH

A NOVEL

INKWATER
PRESS

PORTLAND • OREGON

Copyright © 2015 by Andrew Eustace Anselmi

Cover and interior design by Masha Shubin

Images (BigStockPhoto.com): Red Wine Bottle © sumnersgraphicsinc. Red Wine
Glasses © Igordutina. Vineyard in Bright Yellow Sunset © Anna Omelchenko.
Scroll Work © Ozerina Anna.

This is a work of fiction. The events described here are imaginary. The settings
and characters are fictitious or used in a fictitious manner and do not represent
specific places or living or dead people. Any resemblance is entirely coincidental.

Anselmi, Andrew Eustace.
   The Autumn Crush / by Andrew Eustace Anselmi.
   pages cm
   LCCN 2014911072
   ISBN 978-1-62901-120-2 (pbk.)
   ISBN 978-1-62901-121-9 (Kindle)
   ISBN 978-1-62901-122-6 (ePub)

   1. Italian Americans--Fiction. 2. Italian American
families--Fiction. 3. Legal stories. 4. Detective and
mystery stories.   I. Title.

PS3601.N5554A98 2014   813'.6
                  QBI14-600132

Publisher: Inkwater Press | www.inkwaterpress.com

Paperback ISBN-13 978-1-62901-120-2 | ISBN-10 1-62901-120-7
Kindle   ISBN-13 978-1-62901-121-9 | ISBN-10 1-62901-121-5
ePub   ISBN-13 978-1-62901-122-6 | ISBN-10 1-62901-122-3

Printed in the U.S.A.
All paper is acid free and meets all ANSI standards for archival quality paper.

3 5 7 9 10 8 6 4 2

Praise for *The Autumn Crush*

When the brilliant days of summer and toil have passed,
and the colors of the fall are upon us.

To my wife Soledad,
my family,
and all those new Americans
who have achieved sustenance,
yet struggle to earn respect in the place they call home.

Contents

I.

Arraignment

On any other day, it would not have been such a spectacle to see Guy Bennett sitting at a large wooden table, lawyer at his side, before a crowd of ravenous cameras and onlookers. Scenes like this – be they shareholder meetings at which Guy pitched the acquisition of a new company, black tie dinners where he was honored for his charity, or presentations before Congress on the virtues of American competitiveness – had become commonplace. Guy had grown accustomed to being the subject, the audience his object.

But for Guy, this day would be like none before it. For it was now the public's turn to deliberate over him, granting the business mogul his day in court for what The People had already decided was his calculated double murder of his long-time friend and business partner, Vito Petrozzini, and Petrozzini's wife Lena. The normally debonair and vibrant Bennett sat disheveled in his chair, his body drained of life, save the disdain his eyes shot at a press corps as eager to report his demise as they had been to hail him a future governor. Guy had spent a lifetime catapulting his family into the limelight; overexposure was beginning its wither.

Respite from the glaring cameras and cutting whispers of one-time friends came when Joe the bailiff approached the table. Joe was a middle-aged African American whose first son, unbeknownst to Guy, had been a recipient of a college scholarship fund Guy established for students in the inner city. Joe had always wanted to thank Guy personally for what he had done for his son, but never had the opportunity. Using as pretext the replenishment of the already filled pitcher beside Guy, Joe leaned over and offered Guy a handkerchief for his sweating brow.

Guy paused momentarily before accepting the stranger's offer and pat-drying his forehead; Guy was not used to random acts of kindness toward him unless the giver was looking for something in return. Guy looked into Joe's eyes, and extended his hand to return the cloth. "Thank you, sir," Guy whispered.

The bailiff placed his hand on top of Guy's. "You keep it. If you need anything else, I am assigned to this courtroom and my name is Joe." Joe interrupted Guy's stare with a gentle smile. "The Judge is about to come out." Two knocks echoed from inside the door to the Judge's chambers, and Joe instructed the courtroom, "All rise."

Judge Alfred Masterson III entered through the door and lumbered toward the bench. Guy saw in Judge Masterson's neatly combed gray hair and groomed mustache a man who, under the auspices of public servant, had become judge and steward to a community that had long ago bestowed his family enough wealth for generations. "Order, order," directed Judge Masterson as he slammed the gavel that his grandfather had handed down to his father, and so on to him. "The first case before us today is that of *The People versus Bennett*."

After Guy and his lawyer identified themselves for the Court, Judge Masterson read the charges. "Mr. Bennett, The People have accused you of two counts of criminal homicide and one count of burglary, charging that on March 31 of this year, you did purposely and knowingly cause the deaths of Mr. and Mrs. Vito Petrozzini inside their home. Do you understand the charges?"

Guy responded respectfully, "I do, Your Honor."

Judge Masterson marveled at the packed courtroom. "Before I ask Mr. Bennett how he pleads, Mr. Prosecutor, have The People offered Mr. Bennett any plea bargain?"

The assistant District Attorney assigned to the case was the fair-haired and sturdily built Thomas Straid. In part, Straid had been chosen for the case because of his success in parlaying his own humble origins and contempt of wealth and power into an impressive string of convictions against influential businessmen, government officials, and members of organized crime. More to the point, however, everyone knew that Straid harbored a seething dislike of Guy and the Bennett family, and would spare no effort in pursuit of conviction. Hardly able to contain his appetite for the plot that now held Guy captive, Straid stood up in order to look down at Guy. He brandished the sharp tongue that had earned him a reputation as one of the best, and at times, most ruthless prosecutors in the state. "Against my own wishes, The People offered Mr. Bennett single life imprisonment, but the defendant thinks that is beneath him. Apparently, his life as a murderer deserves more respect than the two he took. Perhaps Mr. Bennett thinks he can donate a new wing to the prison system and walk away."

It took Judge Masterson four slams of his gavel before he was able to quiet a crowd that overflowed into the corridor. "Order, order." After restoring the control he so relished wielding, the Judge admonished the prosecutor for his remarks. "Mr. Straid, we are all upset about the deaths of Mr. and Mrs. Petrozzini, but I would ask that you refrain from histrionics. This is a court of law, and I should not have to remind you that the defendant is presumed innocent until proven guilty."

Having achieved his intended effect, Straid turned and smirked at his audience.

The Judge followed, "So I take it that The People will be seeking double life imprisonment?"

Straid resumed an unflinching demeanor. "The People will, Your Honor. I might add that were it not for our esteemed liberal governor overriding the legislature when it voted to bring back capital punishment, The People would be seeking the death penalty."

"I trust that you will leave politics out of this case entirely."

"Of course, Your Honor."

The Judge turned to Guy. "Mr. Bennett, have you rejected The People's offer?"

Guy bit his lower lip. He studied the hard brow of a judge who, with his restrained elocution, would not hesitate to administer the full force of the law. A chill ran through Guy's veins as his mouth moved for him. "Yes I have, Your Honor."

Judge Masterson leaned back. "Very well, how do you plead?"

Guy drew a deep breath and exhaled. "Not guilty, Your Honor." The courtroom, flush with cameras shuttering, hissed like a viper.

Straid nodded at Joe the bailiff and the officer beside him, as he again sprang to his feet. "Your Honor, given the heinousness of the crime and temptation the defendant might have to hop on one of his private jets, The People request that bail be denied and the defendant be remanded to the county jail pending trial."

Judge Masterson raised his sinewy hand to hold off Straid. "Let's address one item at a time, Mr. Straid. The arrest was on Saturday in Mr. Bennett's office."

"In his skyscraper in Manhattan, Your Honor," Straid interjected.

"Please do not interrupt me," the judge smiled, placing his hand flat upon his elevated desktop.

"Understood, Your Honor," answered Straid.

The judge continued. "As you know, you have 144 hours from Saturday's arrest, April 1, to obtain a grand jury indictment. Assuming you are successful, I would like to set a July 5 trial date, which is approximately four months from now. Will The People be prepared to proceed at that time?"

Keeping his focus on the next day's headlines, Straid held his chin high. "Your Honor, The People are prepared to commence trial next week. We have the knife found at the crime scene on the night of the murders, a shovel and plastic bags from Mr. Bennett's car trunk with the Petrozzinis' blood on them, and the forensic experts who will be able to identify both the defendant's fingerprints on the knife, and that the victims' vicious killings were at a time when Mr. Bennett confessed he was at their home." Straid licked his lips. "We also have two members of the board of directors of Mr. Bennett's company, Northern Industries, who can attest to the escalating feud between the defendant and Mr. Petrozzini regarding control of their corporation." A rush of adrenaline carried Straid further. "And most importantly, Your Honor, we have Mr. Bennett's…"

Well after the appropriate time for doing so, but appearing to do Guy a favor, Judge Masterson cut off Straid before the prosecutor could continue his tirade. "I take it from your recitation that The People have no objection to a July 5 trial date?"

"No objection, Your Honor," Straid stated flatly, grateful for the airtime he had been given.

Judge Masterson turned to the defense. "Does the defendant have any objection to a July 5 trial date?"

Guy's lawyer restrained Guy from standing, and rose to address the Court. "Your Honor, the defendant is anxious to have his day in court so he can be acquitted of the charges against him. We have no objection."

Judge Masterson rejoined, "Very well. While I have you standing, Counselor, what is your position on The People's request that the defendant be denied bail and remanded to the county jail pending trial?"

Guy's attorney leaned forward, with his fingertips pressed red against the table. "As I stated earlier, the defendant is eager for his day in court and therefore has no interest in fleeing the jurisdiction. The defendant requests that a reasonable bail be set so that he can spend these few months at his home with his wife."

Waiting until he was certain that Guy's lawyer had stated his position fully for the record, Judge Masterson gave a pregnant pause before ruling. "The gravity of the charges is such that I cannot in good conscience allow the defendant to remain free prior to a trial that is only four months away. I will therefore exercise my discretion and remand Mr. Bennett to the county jail pending indictment. If no indictment is returned within the required time, Mr. Bennett will be free to go home. Bailiff, if you will please take Mr. Bennett away."

After surmising that the sobbing woman in the crowd was Guy's wife, Joe the bailiff altered his routine of immediately whisking away the defendant. He instructed his rookie accompanying officer to instead turn Guy toward the gallery so that he could take one last glance at his wife. When the rookie started to object, Joe the bailiff glowered at him. "Do as I say."

Guy savored the fleeting sight of his wife Marie as she fell into the arms of their daughter Lisa, who could not even bear to look at Guy. As Lisa's husband ushered the two women away while issuing Guy a glare, Joe rotated Guy toward the path to his dark confinement.

So was all dignity lost from an otherwise extraordinary life.

II

A House in Whitebridge

T hree fall seasons before Guy Bennett was arraigned, life was his oyster. Driving his plush black Mercedes-Benz toward his home in Whitebridge, New York, on a crisp autumn Saturday morning, he was a page out of storybook America – the place schoolteachers, historians, and politicians have gilded through the ages. Born of Italian immigrant parents who ran a grocery store by day and delivered coal at night so that their first American son could receive a college degree, Guy had everything the new Americans of the early twentieth century had ever thought they were entitled to after only one generation of toil – a beautiful and wholesome wife, three children educated in the best private schools, majority ownership of a construction and real estate empire, and a lawn in the affluent suburb of Whitebridge. The starting gun for the American dream sounded early for Guy, who, as the first born in a new country, responded by running the course diligently and honestly, and earning a place in the winner's circle by the ripe age of fifty-two.

Yet, despite all his achievements and possessions, the sum of which could be divided generously among ten men, Guy's big ambition still eluded him; while running the race and pushing ahead, he had developed a lust for a seat among the select and quiet few in the spectating crowd who sat in judgment over Guy and those who would follow. Guy had amassed the trophies of one well-defined dream only to be burdened by the intangible allure and rewards of another, an obsession to be colleague to those who lead, shape, and define. He wanted his Italian American family to be envied and revered, beyond derision as "wops," "dagos," or worse yet, as part of the Mafia. Guy had a particular distaste for being associated with organized crime just because he was in construction and successful.

It was in pursuit of this mistress that Guy moved his family to a sprawling Tudor style mansion in affluent Whitebridge. Perched safely beyond the shadows of New York City's skyscrapers and the din of its streets, Whitebridge was a well-ordered community of doctors, lawyers, and investment bankers more concerned with the green of its grass than with the gray of vacant lots that plagued urban neighbors. It was a club-like and homogeneous elite dedicated to the preservation of the old order rather than the creation of a new one.

For Whitebridge, the recent arrival of the Bennett family was still a novelty that did not altogether fit; Guy sensed as much as he entered his long driveway. The name Bennett read well alongside light posts engraved with Stoddard, Caldwell, and Hayes. The difference was in what happened behind the discriminating oak doors. It was in the unbridled passion that permeated every fiber of Bennett being: their food and drink, the way they argued and drew strength from one another, and the lingering Old World Italian traditions that Guy was not yet ready to relinquish.

So it was on this promising Saturday morning. As Guy's neighbors packed their cars dutifully for weekend retreat amidst brilliant foliage, Guy was bringing home crates of grapes he had purchased for the annual Bennett winemaking, a ritual Guy and his family referred to affectionately as the "autumn crush."

Guy's anxious approach to his garage, through which he would pass to sort the grapes, was interrupted by the eye contact he made with a neighbor, Chauncey Stoddard, as Stoddard and his family marched to and from their Range Rover loading their country wares. Although Guy was uncomfortable with small talk and might otherwise avoid it, he knew that the rules of Whitebridge etiquette required that he roll down his window for a brief exchange.

"How are you, Chauncey?" asked Guy.

"I am well, Guy. Please, call me Chaz."

Always keenly attentive to his environment and the processing of its details, Guy speculated to himself about the long history of privilege and careful breeding implied by Stoddard's nickname, his lantern-shaped jaw, and the fading dahlias that adorned the Stoddard front walk.

"Headed anywhere special?" queried Guy.

"Catherine and I are taking the kids to Mountain Echoes."

Too proud to admit his confusion as to whether Mountain Echoes was a town or a resort, when in fact it was a creative arts festival open only to the invited few, Guy exited curtly with a hedge. "I hear it's beautiful. Enjoy."

Returning to thoughts of wine, Guy entered his multi-car garage, where two of his eldest laborers, Fernando and Giuseppe, were readying the press for the green and white grapes they had purchased for Guy in the City. Guy was now in the world in which he was fluent as master and creator. Speaking to Fernando and Giuseppe in the hybrid Portuguese-Italian-English he had developed over the last thirty years since he and his partner Vito Petrozzini first inherited the duo from their fathers – along with a pick, shovel, and truck – Guy cracked his signature august smile and asked *"I grape, son buon?"*

Giuseppe shot back. "Boss, *molt' buon*. The best. We pick ourselves the way you ask and La Signora she like – nice and sweet."

Guy shifted his grin to Fernando, whose skin was weathered by years of service to Guy. The stocky man responded softly, *"Sí,* boss. *El mejor* – the best."

Guy walked to the rear of his Mercedes, summoning the two to follow. Like a pirate opening his treasure, Guy inserted his key in the car's trunk, and turned it. "Yes. This year, my wife chooses white wine. *E i grape* that you bring, *son buon*. But, I went to *la citta* myself this morning to pick up a few red grapes – *i rossi* – so we can try to make cabernet sauvignon."

Fernando and Giuseppe raised their eyebrows in disbelief; winemakers in their own homes, they knew how difficult it was to master the cabernet, a rich and mature red wine that demanded years of careful attention before its full body and rich aroma could be uncorked and decanted. But these two old men knew Guy as well as anyone, and had seen him excel most when the challenge was greatest. Their eyebrows subsided, and envy set in, as they helped their boss ready a vintage that they might not live to taste.

Guy paid the men for their overtime efforts, wished their families well, and gave them the bags of used Bennett family clothing his wife had set aside for their families. Fernando and Giuseppe thanked Guy repeatedly, and went humbly on their way. As Fernando and Giuseppe backed out of Guy's driveway in a company-owned pick-up truck, they waved to Guy's first son Albert, who was approaching in his shining new Jaguar.

Albert blew his horn repeatedly as he drove proudly toward his waiting father. After pulling the Jaguar to a stop, Albert jumped out of the car and presented his father with a heavily taped red box. Always eager to impress his father, Albert spoke coyly but hurriedly. "Hey, Pop. It's filled with twenty-five refugees from Castro's army that a partner from my firm had smuggled into the country." When Guy looked puzzled, Albert grabbed his father by the shoulder. "Dad, they're Cuban cigars. Your favorite – Cohiba, Churchill size. The partner gave them to me for writing a winning brief for a big client. We can smoke them with the wine at lunch."

But Guy was more concerned with his own mother and handicapped father, whom Albert had transported to the house in the back seat of his car. "Great, we'll smoke them with your brother Edward when he gets here. But first let's help your grandfather out of the car."

Disappointed by his father's lack of enthusiasm for the booty of cigars, Albert reached for his grandmother, Philomena, as Guy tended to his father.

Guy's father Dante was a strong and proud man who, thirty years after suffering the stroke that crippled him, nonetheless had difficulty accepting his handicap. He leaned heavily on his cane. Speaking in his still broken English, he directed, "Don't worry, Guy, I be okay. Help-a you mamma bring-a da plates inside; they too heavy for her. She has-a homemade ravioli and biscotti. Then get me a shirt and pant to wear so we can start crush-a da grapes."

Despite his father's order, Guy persisted. "C'mon, Dad, I don't want you to fall."

Dante's temper flared, as he pushed his cane forward, his step precarious, "I will no fall. Help-a you mamma."

Guy acquiesced and grabbed the ravioli and biscotti, trailing closely behind his father.

III.

The Autumn Crush

No sooner had Guy and Albert disembarked Guy's parents than Guy's wife, Marie, arrived home with their younger son, Edward. Edward had flown in from his third year at Harvard Law School just so he could be with his family for the Autumn Crush. Jeans frayed and sporting a rumpled tweed jacket, Edward grabbed his bags packed with dirty laundry and stepped quickly toward Guy. "Morning, Dad. Are we ready to commence the annual Bennett Autumn Crush?"

Guy responded with in-kind enthusiasm. "Eeeeed-ward, this is going to be a great batch. But we won't be able to enjoy it for a while because it's going to be a cabernet sauvignon. Throw your law books in your room so we can begin God's work."

As Edward turned to the house, Albert emerged from within. Though their feelings for one another were profound, the two brothers were never much for smiling hellos or the standard "How are you?" Too superficial, not enough spice. Instead, their private lexicon was playful barb, competitive one-upmanship.

Seven years separated the two brothers. Albert was thirty years old and Edward twenty-three, placing them in two sharply different generations. Albert was a young Baby Boomer, born in the '50s during the American High, when the country's potential seemed limitless.

Edward was an elder member of what was derisively referred to as Generation X, that much smaller group of young Americans who grew up in the '70s, waiting in line with their parents for gasoline, and learning theories about the destructive winds and long winter that would follow an attack with nuclear bombs. The Baby

Boomers liked to dismiss Generation X as a deadbeat bunch of underachievers; Generation X loved to point to the selfish motives that propelled their seniors' every act and proclamation.

The gap between them was typical of the many differences that Albert and Edward loved to exploit at every turn. Staring at the uneven sleeves of Edward's jacket, Albert commenced the joust. "Well, if it isn't my little socialist brother. Do you and your young Hegelian friends at Harvard wear that sackcloth you call a jacket in order to summon the spirit of your mentor Karl Marx? Or is this merely a showing of solidarity with your poor and oppressed brethren?"

Not to be outdone, Edward attacked his brother's bloated figure. "Well, it is obvious that the fall harvest has been good to you. I would say you are a biscuit away from royal weight. Who is your new tailor, Omar the Tentmaker?" Looking around, he added, "And where is our lovely sister?"

"Has the rarefied Cambridge air deprived your brain of oxygen? Lisa Marie has never helped out at the Autumn Crush – this is men's work!"

"Maybe that's just one of many changes that those of us who aren't stuck in Old World ways need to institute," Edward fired back.

As Guy finished unloading the red grapes, he redirected his sons' attention. "C'mon guys, get changed, we have a lot of work to do. Albert, help your grandfather to the backyard."

Guy was proud of his backyard. Large enough to buffer the neighboring estates of Whitebridge, Guy had landscaped an elegant blend of Italian countryside and English understatement, the latter having become a guiding principle in his life. In its far corner was a cobalt blue-tiled pool, at the foot of a Roman columned cabana with a marble-topped bar. Guy's gardens were dominated by Japanese willow and rhododendron, with a sprinkling of ivy, lamb's ear, chrysanthemums, and asters. The forest that hemmed the yard's rear was lined with a chipped stone walkway that led to a small pond with a shrine to Guy's favorite saint, Francis of Assisi. Guy and his wife Marie had purchased the life-like miniature of St. Francis from a local artisan while honeymooning in Assisi.

Too impatient to wait for his sons, Guy finished unloading his red grapes to a small shaded area of the backyard that had become a shrine in its own right, the site of the annual Autumn Crush. Guy began removing the grapes delicately from their stems. He held them to the sunlight and sang the opera arias of Giuseppe Verdi and Giacamo Puccini that were thundering from his outdoor speakers. Even the birds seemed to be singing along with Guy. He thought to himself that these were prize grapes indeed, which would please even the most discriminating palate once they matured beneath the cork of their tinted green glass.

As Edward walked down the porch stairs toward his father, he complained with a smile, "Dad, do we have to listen to fat Italian men sing about the woes of their polygamous ways while we make wine? Can't we listen to Bruce Springsteen or Eric Clapton this year?"

Guy waited until he finished singing the chorus of "La Donna è Mobile" before jesting, "You little uncouth barbarian. Why don't you go back to your ivy-covered walls and play with your books? Get down here and start picking the grapes to the melody of the soundtrack from heaven." Not missing a beat, Guy picked up the next verse and a handful of new grapes.

Guy's father, Dante, who with grandson Albert at his side was a few paces behind Edward on the back porch, overheard the exchange. Dante stopped at the top of the steps and planted his cane to look to the sky. With a glint in his eye, he lent his aged voice to his son, as the aria reached crescendo. *La donna è mobile, qual piuma al vento – muta d'acce-e-e-nto, e di pensiero* [The woman is fickle, like a feather in the wind – she changes in word, and in thought]."

When the two finished their brief duet, Dante began his descent of the porch steps to the backyard, abandoning his cane, using the railing instead. "*Bravissimo*, Gaetano," he yelled out to his son, and continued, "Whas a-matta wit-a you boys, Gaetano? Day no unda-stand-a beautiful music?"

Albert followed his grandfather closely, and gave him back his cane at the bottom of the stairway.

"I don't know, Pop. These guys are going to lose all the traditions unless we teach them." Guy placed another crate of red grapes on top of the card table he had set up for the occasion. He instructed Edward to turn the handle on the grape crusher, and ordered Albert to help him remove the stems from the new crate.

Dante steadied himself with his cane, as he prepared to lecture the boys. "Nessun Dorma" from Puccini's *Turandot* floated gently through the air.

"Ah, 'Nessun Dorma.'" He closed his eyes to take it in. He opened his eyes and exhaled. "Opera, ees a speerit dat comes from da soul," the eldest Bennett told his grandsons as they continued to feed the steel crusher. "Ees like-a da rose in weenta or rain on a sunny day. Ees about contrast and emotion."

Edward, who was not as steeped in Italian tradition as his grandfather, father, or even his brother Albert, challenged his grandfather politely. "But Grandpa, how can I appreciate it if I don't even understand the words? Besides, most operas end in death anyway."

The old man listened, all the while grimacing while shaking his head slowly. He paused, then in scratched voice answered. "Eduardo, dees ees why you wrong-a. Opera has-a no reason. Ees pure beauty. Eet no need-a da esplanation. Justa listen."

Guy filled in, as his father's thoughts seemed to wander to another place, "Edward, even the stories are beautiful."

Edward was always game for a provocative exchange, no matter who was on the other side. "Oh yeah, well what's this one about?"

As the choir singing "Nessun Dorma" subsided into strings and Luciano Pavarotti began the first verse, Guy began his ode to opera. "This opera, son, is called *Turandot*, named after a Chinese princess whose affections no mortal was able to obtain. It's Pop's favorite," he smiled at his father. Gesturing with a hand motion that Edward should resume cranking the crush, Guy continued. "It was Giacomo Puccini's last opera, which he never finished before he died."

Using a technique he had learned around the family kitchen table before it was taught to him formally in his legal training, Edward interrupted with a question to break his father's train of thought. "Dad, I didn't ask you about the history, I only asked you about the song."

This subject was too dear for Guy to get rattled. Instead, he responded, "Son, weren't you the one who always regarded history as prelude and postscript, the best explanation of that which comes before and after it?"

Humbled by his father's eloquence, yet unable to restrain himself, Edward quipped, "I am beginning to believe the old adage that history is nothing more than the final fiction. Anyway, please continue. I'm listening."

Guy explained, "Puccini's friend, the great conductor Arturo Toscanini, had another composer complete the third act based on the sketches that Puccini left behind." Albert reached around his father gingerly to pick up the next crate of grapes, so that Guy did not have to stop. Guy reflected on his grape-smeared palms. "And while conducting the opera on opening night, Toscanini laid down his baton abruptly in the middle of the third act." Guy caught his breath. "He turned to the crowd and said, 'The opera ends here, because at this point the maestro died.'"

"He just stopped?" Edward asked Guy incredulously.

Albert charged in support of his father. "Respect!!! Respect, you little socialist idiot. The respect of one friend to another, from conductor to composer. The respect you should have for Dad, Grandpa, and our Italian traditions."

Displaying an insatiable appetite for argument with his brother, particularly when the elder challenged his loyalties, Edward was dismissive. "First of all, we're American. As for this guy discontinuing the opera midstream on opening night, sounds to me like he was trying to create his own opera at the expense of his dead friend. A cheap trick if you ask me. What was the dead guy's name? Jack Pacini?" Edward asked, tongue-in-cheek. "I played baseball with a guy named Jack Pacini. He used to put Vaseline on the ball to make it move. Maybe they're related."

Guy stepped in again as referee, and began relating the story of *Turandot*. "As I told you before, Turandot was a beautiful, yet icy princess, whom no man was able to woo until a young prince named Calaf appeared with his father near the walls of Peking." Guy signaled to his son Albert to remove the grape crusher from the plastic garbage can it was placed atop, so that the boys could clean some of the excess debris, and Guy could use his special three-legged stick to compress the grapes to the bottom of the can.

Guy pushed the grapes with his staff. "Calaf originally wanted to see Turandot so that he could curse her, because although her father, the king, promised that she would marry the first male of royal blood that solved three riddles presented by her, she sentenced to death all of those who failed to solve the riddles."

Edward muttered, "Sounds weird to me. No trial before they were executed? Did these guys even have a lawyer? Where's the due process in this kangaroo – or should I say – panda bear court?"

"Ed-ward," Albert glared.

"But when Calaf finally saw the princess," Guy explained, "he too was taken by her beauty, and became intent on solving the riddles, despite the risks, so that he might take Turandot's hand in marriage." Albert and Edward finished cleaning the grape crusher and placed it back on top of the garbage can. Guy lifted a new crate of red grapes on top of the card table. "When Calaf eventually solved the riddles, Turandot was so grief-stricken at the thought of marriage that Calaf gave her an option if she could accept a challenge: Turandot did not yet know his name; if she could guess it by the morning, he would die and she would not have to marry him. Turandot instructed the entire kingdom that no one would sleep – 'Nessun Dorma' – until she found out the prince's name."

As Pavarotti's voice began to rise, Guy chased it wistfully. "And this was the prince's heroic response." Guy then stopped what he was doing and thrust his right arm upward.

Ma il mio mistero è chiuso in me,
il nome mio nessun saprà!
No, no, sulla tua bocca lo dirò,
quando la luce splenderà!

Guy translated for his sons, "Calaf proclaimed, 'But my secret lies hidden within me, no one shall discover my name! Oh no, I will reveal it only on your lips, when daylight shines.'"

Taken by the moment and the music, but too proud to admit it, Edward asked meekly, "It's beautiful, but how did the story end?"

Guy sobered and resumed picking the grapes. "At this point, Calaf's father, and a beautiful young slave girl who had accompanied Calaf and his father to Peking, were dragged into the palace to reveal Calaf's name. Turandot threatened to torture the slave girl, who herself had long been in love with Calaf, if she refused to tell the secret. As Turandot waited for a response, the slave girl took a knife from one of the soldiers and killed herself so that she would not have to betray the man she loved, and her prince could win. The subjects of the palace left in awe."

Again appalled by the story, and unimpressed by the beauty that resounded from the outdoor speakers, Edward stepped up his own challenge. "I don't know whether to think this slave girl was the real hero of this story or just plain stupid – she kills herself just so her master can have his ego massaged and get his rocks off?!"

Albert weighed in. "This is a beautiful story. Why are you trying to spray-paint graffiti all over it? Maybe you should go rub your lava lamp and decide how best to organize your little proletariat revolution."

Guy thrust his arm into the air to finish the fairy tale. "But in the end, despite the odds, Calaf is victorious." Guy held up his finger. "Quiet, here it comes." He took a deep breath and joined Pavarotti for the triumphant last line of the "Nessun Dorma" aria. "*Vincero* [I will win]. *Vinceeeeeeeeeeeeeeeero*!"

When his father finished singing the final high notes, Albert applauded, "Bravo. Braaaaaaavo!"

Edward rolled his eyes. "That was great, Dad." He had to keep himself from smirking. "I can't wait to hear how the kids turned out."

Albert threw a wad of grapes at Edward that hit him in the face.

Stunned, Edward smiled at his brother as he reached slowly to arm himself with a handful of the miniature purple grenades.

Albert returned the smile, and the battle began.

Returning from a momentary lapse during which his thoughts seemed to wander, Guy's father Dante sighed. "Ees-a too bad. Da world has-a become so complicaded. They used to be a time when-a no one would question. Ever-body was 'appy. Like-a when me and-a you Uncle Francesco use-da sit e lissen to da opera in da town square."

"Tell these boys, Pop."

"We joost-a sit e lissen, wit-a mamma e pappa and ever-body. One-a time, da greatest tenor of dem all – Enrico Caruso – sang in da town-a square. It was filled wit-a people. Up into da hills. No more-a. Now is a time-a to quest-a every- ting! Joost-a like Edward. Nobody lissen to nobody."

"Pop knows."

Dante surprised Guy, with an unexpected turn from proud to somber. "Maybe Edward ees-a right. Maybe ees-a betta dis-a way. I just weesh me and Francesco could sit in da square again and-a lissen to Caruso sing-a."

Guy put his arm around his father, "Don't worry, Pop, we will all be with Uncle Francesco when we go to Italy next month." Guy then lightened his father's mood. "Besides, everyone knows that Luciano Pavarotti is the greatest tenor of all time, not Caruso."

Dante squinted. "You wise-a guy."

As Guy and his father Dante shared a tender moment, Guy's wife stepped out of the kitchen and onto the back porch. Her real name was Maria, but Guy's brisk move through country clubs and symphony boards over the years had elided the final "a." The velocity of the journey's wind left Guy's wife with the plain and more convenient "Marie."

With her chestnut-brown hair glistening under the autumn sun, however, it was unmistakably "Maria" who stood above. Her high cheekbones, sharply defined chin, and subtle olive skin were the gifts of generations of uninterrupted provincial Italian lineage. As she stood with gravy-stained apron fastened between her still shapely hips and bountiful breasts, even Guy could not help himself. He drew closer, and called out to the woman with whom he had fallen in love over thirty years earlier. "What is it, Maria, *mi amore*?"

Guy's mention of his wife's real name perked her smile, prompting her to return the favor. "*Andiamo,* Gaetano, *mangiamo.* C'mon, boys, it is time to eat!"

Guy yelled for Albert and Edward, who were both covered with the juice of the red grapes they had thrown at each other. "C'mon, guys. Albert, help your grandfather."

"I no need-a da 'elp," muttered Dante.

IV.

A Page in History

After washing, the men gathered in the large kitchen, the inner sanctum where Marie thrived as priestess, creating and consecrating, along with Guy's mother Philomena, her cornucopia of Italian delight. Philomena brought to the table the first course – a beautiful array of Prosciutto di Parma, water-soaked mozzarella, sopresatta, roast beef, and sun-dried tomatoes – all covered with a generous coat of virgin olive oil.

Guy raced for the loaf of hard-crusted Italian bread he had purchased in the Bronx early that morning. "No matter how sophisticated these people in Whitebridge think they are," Guy explained to the congregation at the table, "you still have to go to Nick's in the Bronx to get a decent loaf of bread. The kind that's burnt on the bottom."

Grandmother Philomena warned. "Boys, don't-a fill up-a on da meat. You mamma still has a da ravioli wit meatball e brasciola. "

The boys waited until their grandmother headed back toward their mother at the stove, before tearing away wildly at the bread, filling it with meat, and adding a dash more olive oil for good measure.

As Guy tore a piece of bread for himself, he exclaimed proudly, "Albert and Edward, this is a great time for our family. Albert is already a successful lawyer and married with two beautiful children, and Edward, you are about to get your degree from Harvard Law School." He turned to his father. "My Ivy League son. Hey, Pop, we've come a long way, haven't we? From the fields of Aquino, Italy, to Harvard Yard. God-damn!!!"

Guy continued, "And now, my first son Albert is considering a run for the United States Senate, the most elite club in the entire world."

Edward swallowed quickly. "You're finally ready to do it, eh bro? And to think, you waited until you were thirty years old. I guess you are now content that your mountain of money is high enough for you to understand better the people you have screwed to get there."

"Very funny, Karl Marx," Albert responded. "In all seriousness, little brother, Dad and I have been talking about it for a while, and if we make a run for it, we want you to be my campaign manager, to be my eyes and ears. You have experience in political campaigns, and you're family. I trust you more than I do any of those high-paid glossy consultants from inside the Washington Beltway, with their focus groups."

"Fellas, I'm flattered, but I promised myself I was done with politics. The great American experiment in Democracy is failing. Politicians no longer serve their constituents. It's all about self-preservation in the hallowed halls of Congress, convincing the people through cheap gimmicks like school prayer and 'English only' in the schools. That decentralizing the government is somehow improving the country's lot. It's like Plato's Allegory of the Cave."

Albert bit into his sandwich. "What are you babbling about now, Karl Marx?"

Edward restrained himself from eating. "American politics is like Plato's Cave. The politicians are the puppeteers in the cave manipulating shadows on the wall. We – the idiots who are chained to the wall and can't see anything else – accept the shadows as the real issues. I don't know. Maybe it's the media that keeps us chained to the wall and fixed on these shadows of truth. Whatever it is, the whole thing is broken and I don't want any part of it. I want to go somewhere where I can really help people, without having to worry about the 'spin' in the newspaper the next day, or whether the story 'has legs.' I want to work in a place where nobody notices what I am doing except for the people I am helping."

Guy smiled and turned toward Albert. "I told you he would be perfect. He's got just the fire you need to win this thing."

Albert laughed back. "Yeah, all we need to do is muzzle him from making public statements. Otherwise, ol' Senator Joe McCarthy may rise from the dead and finish what he started almost forty years ago."

"As always, you guys are not taking me seriously. Albert, even though we both are Democrats, we disagree on fundamental issues like affirmative action and a woman's right to have an abortion."

Albert responded with a controlling air that had always irked Edward. "We are brothers, we will work it out."

"Besides, guys, I am about to take a job as a public defender. I plan to spend a couple of years in the New York office."

Guy lost his smile. "I don't understand. You will graduate at the top of your class at Harvard Law and be able to name your price. What do you want to do? Help the poor? Help acquit the Blacks in the city who are killing each other?" Not wanting to lose his focus, Guy cooled. "Well, whatever you do after you graduate is your decision. But if your brother needs you next year to help him run for the Senate, you will be there. In the meantime, I will introduce him to some of my influential friends. You know, the power brokers. But you are going to help Albert win this thing. I didn't work all of these years for nothing."

Everyone continued eating quietly, as they always did after one of the children was scolded.

After a momentary silence that echoed with suppressed passion, Guy began again, "We have some other good news, boys. Vito Petrozzini, Jr., has asked your sister Lisa Marie to marry him. They will be married some time next year."

In a rare exercise of defiance, it was Albert who now challenged his father. "Talk about giving away everything you ever worked for. Your partner's idiot son, who couldn't spell the word cat if you spotted him the 'c' and the 'a,' will take over the business that you never let Edward and me join. *That* makes sense."

Guy looked to his wife, "Marie, listen to this."

"I know," Marie responded sternly.

"How many times do I have to tell you boys that your mother and I put you in the best schools, we traveled the world with you, just so you wouldn't have to get into my business. If you guys were in my business, people would call you tag-alongs. They would make jokes about you being in the Mafia."

"Vito should have done the same thing," piped up Marie. "There should be no family in business."

Guy sighed, "My partner Vito and his wife took a different approach. They wanted Vito, Jr., in the business. It was the same thing with Vito Senior and his father Adamo. They never really left behind the ways of the Old World. The son takes over the father's business so the father can rest. Well, we are on a different course."

"What course might that be?" asked Albert snidely.

"I have given you guys the liberty to debate foreign affairs and help shape the world I sweat in. I have lifted you to a place higher than mortal money making. I want our family to be like the cabernet that we are making today – rich, refined, and appreciated everywhere. I want us to earn a page in the history books."

"Which chapter?" quipped Edward. "The 'Fall of the American Empire'?"

Guy returned to the specific subject at hand. "As for your sister marrying Vito, Jr., you have nothing to worry about. He has always been loyal to his father, who has forever been loyal to me." Guy looked over at his own father. "True, I was not happy when my father forced me to make Vito my partner, after I had built the business myself."

Dante grumbled. "I owed hees-a father a debt-a."

Seeing that he had made his father uneasy when it was not his intention to do so, Guy slapped Dante on the shoulder and addressed his sons. "Vito Jr. loves your sister dearly, and she will need someone who can provide for her as she raises a family. There aren't too many young men like that anymore."

Relishing the sparks between his brother and father, Edward added kindling. "I don't know what the big fuss is all about. Vito, Jr., is a decent guy who is obviously in love with Lisa Marie. Just how much more money do you need, big brother?" After filling his plate with a couple of ladles of the ravioli and meatballs that had just arrived, Edward prepared his family for some news of his own.

"This really neat girl I have been dating at school made us some pretty labels for the wine."

Guy removed the string from a piece of sauce-covered beef brasciola. "Sounds great, Edward, what is she?"

Even though he knew full well that this was his father's way of inquiring about a person's ethnicity or religion, Edward queried back in order to establish a foundation for the argument that he knew would follow. "What do you mean 'what is she'? She's a beautiful female law student with whom I will be working next year when I go to the Public Defender's Office. I think I'm serious about her."

Guy gnawed some meat from the bone he was holding with both hands. "Edward, don't play games with me. You know what I'm asking. What is she? Irish? German? You're not dating another Black girl, are you?"

Edward looked down before mustering the courage to shoot a glance at his father. "She is Japanese."

"She is what?" Guy asked incredulously. "Are you vying for U.S. Ambassador to the World? What is it with you? Do White girls bore you?"

Edward responded in a voice that was just above a whisper. "Her name is Nancy, and her mom is Japanese. Her dad was an American GI stationed in Japan after World War II. They came from Japan in the late '40s."

Upon hearing the revelation, Edward's mother Marie yelled from across the kitchen where she was still preparing lunch. "You're dating a Japanese girl? Guy!"

On cue, Guy wiped the oil from his hands with a napkin. "It's not that we are racists or bigots, son. It's just that this girl Nancy and you are from two completely different cultures. She is probably not even Christian, much less Catholic."

Edward took a sip of wine, a Bennett vintage from years past. "As a matter of fact, she is Catholic. She goes to church every Sunday."

Guy wiped his mouth. "Still, she's different."

Edward raised his voice. "I think you're being a racist."

"No, son, just a realist."

Sensing a free shot, Albert smirked. "Dad, I don't know what you are getting all excited about. Edward's kitchen table will be just like this. The only difference is we would be sitting on pillows eating raw fish." He laughed out loud, "And drinking wine made of rice instead of grapes."

Guy was not amused by Albert's humor. "That will be enough from you."

Dante appeared about to instruct Guy on the matter when the discussion was interrupted by the ring of the phone. When Marie answered, her loud response in Italian suggested that the call had come from Italy. Her questions and somber tone made clear that something was wrong.

Guy asked excitedly, "What is it, Marie? What happened?"

"That was the church rectory in Aquino, Italy. Uncle Francesco has taken a turn for the worse. His condition is critical. He may pass any day now."

Guy extended his arm across the table toward his trembling father, Dante. "Don't worry, Pop. We'll get the next flight out of here." He then turned to his wife, and issued orders. "Marie, call the airline. Albert, the taxi. Edward, go pick up your sister at Vito's, and everyone pack their bags. We are going to see Uncle Francesco."

Without asking a single question, everyone did as they were told.

V.

Flying First Class

A blond, blue-eyed stewardess, wearing a country smile and pin engraved with "Sandy," rolled a cocktail cart down the aisle of the Alitalia airbus that was cruising toward Italy with the Bennett family aboard. Only first-class tickets were available on such short notice; otherwise, Guy and his family traveled coach as a rule, where Guy felt most comfortable despite the lack of space for his large frame. Guy thought it dangerous to stray too far from his parents' humble origins, even when it came to relatively minor matters like airline tickets.

Guy sat next to his father, with his mother and wife across the aisle. He tried to console a still shaken father who had always worked hard for his children but found it difficult to express his emotion for them – particularly when it came to his only son Guy, of whom much was demanded.

"Pop, why don't you have a glass of wine? It may taste like kiddie grape juice compared to our home stock, but it will still make you feel better. Before you know it, we will be with Uncle Francesco. He is going to be all right."

As he always did in matters that could affect his slowly deteriorating health, Dante looked to his wife Philomena for counsel; she was busy whispering prayers to herself, passing her right index finger and thumb methodically over a set of black rosary beads. Seeing her husband's glance only in her mind's eye, Philomena reached across the aisle to clench Dante's hand in her own. Though the doctors told her that even a small glass of wine could aggravate her husband's diabetes, she knew that the nourishment of the cup was far greater than any prescribed medicine. Philomena nodded her approval without interrupting her novena.

The red wine took hold of Dante, as he sipped it slowly to savor its effect. Within moments, the old man grew nostalgic, pondering the fantastic journey of his own life and that of his family in the United States. He gripped his cane as a king would his staff. "I don't-a know if I ever told you, Guy, but-a you mamma and me, we were very lucky to 'ave a son as smart and 'ard working as you, who 'as done-a so much and can take care-a us like-a dees."

Not familiar with such an open display of affection, Guy became embarrassed. He looked down at the armrest that separated him from his father. "Don't be silly, Pop. I think the wine has already made you drunk."

"No, I mean eet, Gaetano. When I first leave-a Italy to come to Ameriga ova seesty years ago, I was treated like-a cattle in da bottom of da boat, countin' da minute until a sailor man would come around wit a canteen of wata. I joost-a wait, and dream of United States wit its wide-open fields."

"And your dream came true, Pop," said Guy, as he sipped more wine.

Dante raised his cane slightly, and planted it with conviction. "Now I fly-a first class after my son, he press a few buttons and da lady, she serve me a glass of wine dat-a my papa and me would 'ave to work all day to make if we want-a drink a year aft-a."

"And you know what, Dad?" Guy's body pumped. "We've only just begun. After we get Uncle Francesco better, we are going to make Albert a United States Senator. And if we ever get Edward's head out of the clouds and screw it on straight...who knows? We might even have a Supreme Court Justice. From farmers to framers in just two generations!"

"Yeah," Dante uttered as he rested his cane on the floor, "we 'ave come a long way and 'ave-a many miles left to travel." He closed his eyes. "But wit-a you son Edward, you can no poosh-a too 'ard. Otherwise, ee may do what-a you want, but his speerit will run away – far away."

Before his son could respond, Dante began a gentle but steady snore.

Taking advantage of the extra space afforded him in first class, Guy negotiated his way around his father without waking him, and covered him with a blanket from the overhead compartment. Guy then made his way back to his children. Lisa Marie and Edward were giggling together on one side as they often did, while Albert sat alone on the other; the seat next to Albert was empty of his wife Victoria, who against her husband's wishes and after a bitter argument with him, decided to remain at home with their children.

Guy gripped the seats on both sides of the aisle. "How are we doing, kids?" As if they ever had a choice as to whether to make the trip, he thanked them. "Your mother and I appreciate your dropping everything to be with Grandpa and Uncle Francesco. It's too bad Victoria and the kids couldn't make it, Albert; it would have been nice having everybody together in Italy."

Albert defended the state of his household. "Her migraines were acting up again and she thought it was too much strain to bring the kids. Besides, she is in the middle of trying to write a novel, and her father has finally been able to arrange a meeting with a literary agent that she would rather not cancel."

Guy tried to put a favorable spin on what he and his other children had long known was really a case of marital discord between Albert and his wife, a rift that was growing wider because of Albert's political pursuits and flirtatious smiles. "I think it's great that Victoria is trying to write a novel. The Bennetts need a place among the literati."

Edward would not be quite as generous as his father, whom he found to be infinitely shrewder and more aggressive in his business than in addressing his children's shortcomings. It bothered Edward that his brother had married Victoria Kirby for money and power rather than love. Victoria was the daughter of Giles Kirby, a Wall Street dealmaker who was the managing partner of an old-boy investment banking firm named Webb Investments. With the combined financial resources of his own father and Giles Kirby – plus the access to the Establishment that Giles had inherited but Guy was still struggling to attain – Albert would not have to worry about many of the traditional obstacles that stand between a candidate and the seat he covets. Edward vowed to never make such a bargain when marrying; neither the means nor the end were worth it, and his passion for love and life would never allow it. His passion for Nancy would never allow it.

Nor would Edward's strong feelings give way to diplomacy on the matter. "Yeah, Dad, we all think it's great that Queen Victoria has descended from her throne to write a novel. Who knows? By time we return she may have completed a modern *Gone With the Wind*. Did she grow up on a plantation? I always thought that Scarlett O'Hara was her favorite American hero."

Albert gulped his champagne, and leaned his head back. "That's 'heroine,' little brother. I am surprised that our Ivy League sibling would commit such a gaffe. Perhaps you will get sharper once your ideas and rhetoric are tested in the real world."

"Hero, heroine, whatever. But I forgot, the Queen's migraines are acting up again. So if the load gets too heavy, maybe she will just commission someone else to write her novel. She is good at that. And God knows she will cater the most talked about book-signing party in all of Whitebridge, once her novel is finished."

Albert's smile acknowledged his brother's wit on a topic that made him uneasy. The tension came more from the appearance that he was having marital problems than from the problems themselves. Albert looked to his father for an ally and fired back at Edward. "Listen, samurai warrior. At least my wife does not wear a kimono with a dragon stitched on it, or walk ten paces behind me. Does your girlfriend Nancy and her family have a god, or do they just sit and meditate? Maybe someday you can use Victoria's literary agent to write a book of your own. You can call it *Zen and the Art of Lawyering*, and dedicate it to your little geisha girl."

"Your listening skills were never very good. I told you that she's Catholic. She probably goes to church more than you do."

Guy stepped in. "Don't worry about Edward. He will marry whoever he loves, and that will be fine with all of us. All I can say is that I have a business friend, Vincent Giovine, who has a daughter named Donna who keeps asking about Edward." Guy hit Edward over the head. "She is a big redhead. I'm just worried that she's too much woman for you."

Albert pretended to almost lose his mouthful of champagne with laughter.

Guy looked over at his daughter. "But we should be talking about your sister, Lisa Marie. Have you boys congratulated her on her engagement to VJ, as we plebes at work call him?"

Albert took a third glass of champagne from the stewardess, tipped her with an inviting glance from his sparkling blue eyes, and drew a short sip. "We are all taking bets on how long it will be before Vito Jr. controls the company and Northern Industries becomes a subsidiary of VJ Enterprises International." He then laughed out loud. "I guess it will take some time, because first we have to teach VJ that a subsidiary is not some kind of sandwich or naval vessel."

Edward could not help himself from joining in Albert's laughter, at the same time embracing his sister and kissing her congratulations. "Now the real queen will take the throne." Just as Lisa Marie was returning the favor to Edward's cheek, he continued, "Let's just hope she is not marrying the court jester instead of the king."

Lisa Marie slapped her brother Edward on the shoulder. "Daddy, tell them to stop."

"Don't listen to these two idiots. Between them, they have not known a single hard day of work. I built my company through blood and sweat – something they only see in the movies – and it is not going anywhere. VJ is a hard worker from good stock who wants only to make Lisa Marie happy and raise a family. Just because he doesn't argue about Plato or St. Thomas and his Proofs does not mean he is a dummy. I gave you guys that opportunity; his father did not."

Guy softened his tone and looked upon his daughter. "This trip will be extra special for you, Lisa. This is the first time that you will be visiting Aquino, the small town that your grandfather and VJ's grandfather, Adamo Petrozzini, left from together to come to America. It will be a first time for all of us, for that matter. Your grandfather never let any of us go back to visit Aquino."

"Why not, Dad?" asked Edward.

"I don't know, son. I can't count how many times we have been in Italy with your grandfather, within ten or twenty miles of the place, and he has refused to go back. He never even wanted to talk about it, so I never pushed. Yet, he would always go on and on about the happy times he had there growing up as a child, with his brother Francesco and little sister Annunziata, who died of polio after he left."

"He left his family behind?" asked Lisa Marie.

"That's what I think it is – the painful memory of leaving his family behind and feeling that he did not do enough to keep his poor little sister from dying. I bet he sees her face every day." Guy helped himself to a sip of champagne from Albert's glass. "I don't know. Anyway, sit back and relax. With the seven-hour time difference and a lot of driving between Rome and Aquino, we have a long couple of days ahead." Judging by Guy's somber demeanor, it was apparent that even he did not want to discuss the matter further.

"It's not difficult to relax in these seats, Dad," remarked Albert. "How come we never went first class before?"

Guy's spirit lightened. He challenged his son. "Because we are not there yet, son, and I have to keep you guys a little hungry so we can get there. Leisure and comfort always come before the downfall. You can travel with your family in first class after you become a United States Senator. Now get some sleep."

Hours later, the pilot announced that the plane was about to arrive at Leonardo DaVinci International Airport in Rome. Dante opened his eyes to the morning Italian sun, stretched his arms, and turned toward Guy. "Wow, what a deeference between dis-a treep and when-a me and Adamo cumm-ma ov-a from de udder side."

What a difference it must have been, Guy thought to himself. What a difference, indeed.

VI

A Sister Left Behind

After hustling through customs and renting two cars, the Bennetts wended their way through the Italian countryside to Aquino. Guy and Marie drove Guy's parents in one car, while Albert followed with Edward and Lisa Marie in the other.

The children spoke little during the car ride. While Albert worked the wheel and Lisa Marie slept, Edward marveled at the landscape that led to the province of Aquino. With its pregnant soils laced with rows of olive and fig trees, tended by old men on mules, this earth spoke to Edward with an eloquence and wisdom that places like Whitebridge would never attain during his lifetime. This land was no longer in a state of becoming; it already was what it had long been and would always remain. No condominiums or strip malls would ever grow from it – just a rich and bountiful fruit. Before even meeting any of the people who lived in the region, Edward had a taste of its wholesomeness and tradition.

When the clan finally reached Aquino, however, all wonderment and anticipation screeched to a halt. Albert woke Lisa, stunned by what he saw. Instead of medieval arches along cobblestone streets, there were cold concrete buildings, constructed with a dated modern style. Instead of hearing children playing or wives bartering in open-air markets, the Bennetts were greeted with an eerie silence.

"Dad must be lost again," gasped Albert. "This looks like a has-been town in America."

"I think this is it," said Edward, as he saw his father stop his car to park. "This is Aquino. Just like when I went to Mom's town. Completely different."

When the children got out of the car wearing a confounded look, their grandfather spared them the embarrassment, and answered the question he knew they wanted to ask. "Eet was not always like-a dis." Guy studied his father's cane, as Dante continued to speak through his own glazed stare. "Eet was-a beautiful when I left wit Adamo. Beautiful fountains ever-where and piazze way ever-body talk and sing-a. Aft-a de war, day change-a ever-ting wit-a con-grete. Day call it progresso."

"Sure seems like progress to me," said Albert, as he slid his finger across a building's wall, causing debris to fall. "Grandpa, they should have called you and Dad before they did anything."

"Some-a-time, when you rush-a make-a some-a-ting new, is worse-a dan da ole."

"You see, punk," sneered Albert, "Grandpa agrees with me."

"I am sorry that these people ruined your postcard picture of this place, Albert," shot Edward. "But maybe they prefer to have heat and running water."

"They should preserve the old town," rebutted Albert, "keep the old ways."

"Francesco take care-a. He rebuild-a da ole church-a, *Il Gesú*, in da ole town. Ee 'as to get-a bett-a, so dat *Il Gesú* can get-a bett-a. *Andiamo* [Let's go], Gaetano. Let's find Francesco, inzide dis-a church-a dat look-a like-a post office. Ee probably sneak outta bed to light-a da candle."

The others remained by the cars as Guy escorted his father to the front of the new church, a simple wooden frame stripped of ancient adornment.

"Does it bring back any memories, Pop?" asked Guy.

"No, dis-a church was no 'ere when I leave-a. Day make-a dis-a church as part of da progresso."

"What do you remember?" asked Edward.

"I no rememb-a much." Dante half-smiled as a young couple sped by on a Vespa. "Or maybe I joost no want-a rememb-a."

As they entered the new church and blessed themselves with holy water, Guy and his father found a modest but spiritual interior.

A nun knelt in prayer at its altar. "*Aspetta* [Wait], Gaetano. You stay 'ere. I go ask-a da Seesta where ees Francesco."

Dante's slow procession up the small church's aisle, clutching his cane, was betrayed by his quickening heart and racing mind. His eyes were fixed on the nun bowed in prayer, whom he suspected was his cousin, Theresa. During Francesco's few visits to America and frequent letters to his older brother, he described to Dante how Theresa – the object of every young man's desire when she was growing up in Aquino – had become like a sister to him after Dante left and little Annunziata died of polio. The young Francesco and his cousin Theresa were inseparable; their parents often joked that they would someday intermarry like the royal families of Europe, though they knew that their faith would never allow it. When Francesco shocked the family with the news that he was becoming a priest instead of running the family vineyard, it was not long before Theresa followed and became a nun. She had been at Francesco's side ever since, teaching at the church's school and cooking for the church priests.

Dante reached to place his hand on the knelt woman's shoulder. He looked to the crucifix for strength before beholding his cousin, one of the many young faces he had left behind, as a nun. Speaking in his native Italian dialect, Dante whispered playfully. "Excuse me, Sister. I am from out of town. Can you tell me where I might find my brother, Father Francesco? He said…"

Theresa lifted her head from her clasped hands, and turned. Her piercing eyes and dimples sucked all of the breath from Dante, and extinguished his charade.

Tears welled up in Theresa's eyes. "Is that you, Dante?" A small bead rolled down her soft cheek. "We have been praying for this day. You are just as handsome and playful as when you left." Theresa's warm embrace was so strong that for a passing moment, Dante was able to drop his cane, and wrap his weakened arms around her heavenly bodice.

Guy stood silent in the back of the church, fighting his own goose bumps.

Sister Theresa reached down to retrieve her cousin's cane. Dante reassumed his grip, and gave back to the nun her distance.

The nun began speaking in rapid fire. Her words seemed to flow faster than the movement of her generous lips. "It's incredible, Dante. We almost lost Francesco a couple of days ago. His heart seemed gone. The doctor said that his condition was hour to hour. And you know your brother. He is just as stubborn as you. With what little strength he could gather, he forbade us from bringing him to the hospital. He refuses to leave until the new church is open for the people. The masons and painters have been working all day and night so he can see it before he..."

Theresa looked at Guy, who was still waiting obediently by the fountain of Holy Water at the entrance. "And when he heard you were coming with your family. Words cannot describe the transformation. I don't think I am imagining it, but it has been as though we are witnessing a miracle."

Dante looked down at his cane, and smiled wistfully. "Francesco is the miracle."

"You know what I mean," the nun continued, as she placed her hand over his, holding the cane. "Every hour he asks whether you have arrived. Where is your family? Your wife and children?"

Trembling in a crossfire of emotions, Dante turned to Guy, who was growing anxious to enter his father's world. Reveling in the tongue to which he was born, Dante continued in an Italian his son understood. "Son of mine. Come here and meet your cousin, Sister Theresa."

Still having no idea who the madonna-like figure before him was, but always the consummate diplomat, Guy recalled the broken Italian he heard from his parents as a young boy. "Sister Theresa, what a joy! Father has told us so much about you."

"How beautiful," sighed Theresa as she stroked Guy's right cheek with the back of her cupped right hand. "Truly his father's son."

His cheeks reddened, Guy looked to his father. "Let me go get Mom and the kids."

Sister Theresa grabbed Dante by the arm and addressed her young cousin in their shared tongue. "Your Uncle Francesco is still sleeping, and you are probably hungry. It has been a long trip. I have prepared lunch for everybody in the rectory next door where you will be staying. Pull your car around the side. I will walk your father over. Dante and I have a lot of catching up to do. He still has to tell me about his lovely wife, Philomena, whom I have yet to meet."

After being introduced to their cousin Theresa in a flurry of kisses and exchanges the children could barely decipher, the Bennetts assembled around a large wooden table. The smoked aromas emanating from the kitchen hinted at a feast. All of the Bennetts, including Guy, were amazed by Sister Theresa's wealth of knowledge about them. She peppered them with questions, as she leafed through a scrapbook with their pictures: the wedding day of Guy and Marie; Albert's law school graduation, a first for the family in America; Edward hoisted on his teammates' shoulders after a football championship; news articles written by Lisa Marie when she was the editor of her college newspaper.

Without thinking about the possible language barrier, Lisa Marie blurted out in English, "Sister, I don't understand. We have never even met you. How do you know so much about us?"

Guy warned his daughter, "Lisa. Sister Theresa is not one of the nuns from your high school. We are in Italy. She speaks Italian, not English."

"No wor-ry, Guy," Sister Theresa uttered in broken English. She moved to the front of her seat. "She ees okay. I practice English weet da children een my class." Sister Theresa locked Lisa Marie's eyes into her own. "Day always ask-a me about Ameriga. And I tell dem about my *cugini*. Cugini ees da word for cousins, yes?"

"Yes, cousins," answered a mesmerized Lisa Marie.

"I tell dem about my cousin Dante, de brudda of Padre Francesco, who write many time and always send-a da picture."

"What could you tell them?" asked Lisa Marie.

"I tell dem 'ow Dante leave Aquino to go to Ameriga. And how his son, Gaetano, bring-a da whole family over da white-a-breedge to a town wit big 'ouses, pretty flowa and fancy car."

"Yes, Whitebridge," said Lisa Marie, with an incredulous smile.

"Ees-a long-a breedge, White-a-breedge? 'ow long eet take to cross? Da children always ask-a me."

"Sister, Whitebridge is actually not a bridge that leads to the town," responded Lisa Marie politely. "It is the name of our town."

"Da way Dante esplain in da lett-a, I always see da whole family crossing big white-a-breedge to get to a new plaze. How you know dat da town was no named after a white-a-breedge a long time ago? Maybe da first breedge built to reach-a da town was white."

Everyone laughed.

"And Lisa Marie, everybody, please no call-a me Seesta. I'm a you cousin – call me Theresa. Or how you say in Ameriga, Terry?"

The laughter grew louder this time, enough to pull a smile from Dante's stern face.

Drawing a quick breath, Sister Theresa continued. "I always tell da lit-tle girls in school about-a my cuz Leesa, who work-a in da big-a city and make-a more money dan de man-a." As usual, Sister Theresa had the entire crowd enthralled by her charm and vigor. "Because in Ameriga, anyone – man o woma – can do whateva day want-a."

"'I am not sure that a woman should be able to do whatever she wants," interjected Guy.

"Dad," pleaded Lisa Marie, "what about my journalism classes? You know that's what I really want."

"I'll tell you what you want," smiled Guy. "You are twenty-six years old and you want to get married and you want to have kids." Guy straightened. "Lisa Marie is engaged to marry Vito Petrozzini, Jr., the grandson of Adamo Petrozzini, the man with whom Dad left Aquino."

"Yes, I know. I meet Adamo grandson, Vee-Jay, when Adamo bring-a da family to Aquino every summ-a. He ees a nice-a-boy."

Guy wanted to finish his point without seeming to question Sister Theresa's wisdom or authority. "But what you don't hear about in Aquino is the divorce rate of working women. Particularly, the so-called successful ones."

"But dees es why Adamo and Dante left Aquino to go to Ameriga. So dat da children and grandchildren can do what day want and 'ave ever-ting. Lisa ees a good-a girl. She can be good-a wife, motha, biz-a-ness-a persa o writ-a."

"First she has to learn to cook as well as you," remarked Guy as he received from Sister Theresa a bowl filled with meat covered by smoldering red gravy. "What do we have here?"

"Rabbit. I know you no eat-a eet much in Ameriga. But, Francesco tell me eet was all-ways Dante's favorite."

"Did she say 'rabbit'?" Edward stage-whispered to his older brother, as he took the bowl from him. "As in the Easter Bunny?"

Albert looked down at the bowl, and suppressed a laugh. "I think so, bro. Dig in, ears and all."

Everyone overheard the exchange. Sister Theresa shared a snickering smile with Lisa Marie, and asked the young men, "Was-a matt-a boys, you no 'ungry?"

Albert spoke for himself and his brother. "No, Sister. Excuse me. I mean, Terry. It's just that our stomachs are a little unsettled after the flight. It was very windy."

"I t'ought I 'ear Alberto tell Eddie dat ee was so 'ungry, ee could eat-a da cow. Da rabbit ees much-a more small, no?"

Sister Theresa smiled again at Lisa Marie, encouraging her to be adventurous and fork some of the cooked rabbit into her plate. "Try it, Leesa, you like."

At the same time, Sister Theresa summoned Marie Bennett and her mother-in-law Philomena. "*Andiamo*, Maria e Philomena. We see if we can no find som-ma medicine for da boys' stomach-ache."

A moment later, the three women emerged from the kitchen outfitted in aprons and armed with steaming ceramic bowls. Marie assured her sons, "Don't worry, boys. Sister also knew that *fettucine ammatriciana* with meatballs and sausage was Guy's and Albert's favorites. Do you feel better now?"

"Only if you are Guy or Albert," joked Edward, as he and Albert emptied the bowls into their plates. "I must say, however, that I feel my stomachache subsiding."

Guy chuckled, and wiped his mouth after swallowing a meatball. "How is Uncle Francesco?"

"I tell you fada, when I call you Saturday, Francesco, ee almost die. But when ee 'ear dat you come-a to see 'im, ee start-a look and feel bett-a. Da dottore no can esplain, but ee say Francesco still needa da rest. But Francesco say we 'ave to bring 'im wit you to open da church."

"What do you mean open the church? I thought Dad and I found you in the church."

Sister Theresa turned to Dante, and asked him in Italian, "You no tell-a dem?"

Dante shrugged his shoulders, closed his eyes, and tilted his head to the side.

"Like I tell-a you befo'e. Dante write-a many time to Francesco, and ee send-a da photo of da family. But ee also send-a lott-a money to rebuild-a da ol' church, *Il Gesú,* and da piazza in front-a. Da men 'ave been workin' to finish da church so dat Francesco can bless eet tonight-a, and dedicate da piazza in front to da see-ster of Dante and Francesco, Annunziata, who she died of polio aft-a Dante leave for Ameriga."

"To think," Guy frowned, "and today our doctor can prevent it with a vaccine."

Dante grew impatient. "C'mon everybody. 'urry up and fineesh-a you food so we can see Francesco."

VII.

A Holy Man Ailing

Wanting to Dance the Tarantella

The Bennetts finished the meal without their usual banter, and followed Sister Theresa down a narrow hall into a tiny room. The clan huddled around Father Francesco's bed, which was supported by a cold cement floor. The quarter was decorated with nothing more than a single small window and bedside dresser with a bible. A bare lightbulb hung from a wire, flickering upon the crucifix over the priest's head.

Guy whispered to his father, "Dad, why didn't you ask me for money for Uncle Francesco so he could at least have a room where he could fit some furniture?"

Dante whispered back. "Ee told me 'is room was like-a 'eaven. I no t'ink ee would-a-lie. Ee ees a priest!"

Father Francesco opened his eyes, and moved his parched lips slowly in Italian. "Brother. Is that you? You must be tired. How was the trip? Have you eaten?"

As the frail old priest struggled to sit upright in his bed, Sister Theresa firmed his single pillow behind him.

Dante responded in Italian. "Don't worry about us, little brother. We are fine. How are you?"

"I am well. Very well. And how is the family?"

"You remember Philomena?"

"Of course. How can I forget the face of the woman who stole my big brother's heart? I always said that if he did not meet you, he would have become a priest and returned here to work with me."

Philomena leaned over and kissed Francesco on the forehead. "We have been praying for you, dear Francesco. You are the only person who your brother talks about more than his son, Gaetano."

On cue, Guy shook his uncle's hand, kissed him on both cheeks, and reintroduced his wife to him.

Francesco grabbed a hand each from Guy and Marie, and held them inside his own. "The pride and joy of Aquino in America. I still tell people about your wedding day." He smiled at Marie. "Do you remember when we danced the *Tarantella* together? You didn't know that priests knew how to have some fun, did you?"

Marie leaned over and kissed the priest. "I look forward to doing it again."

Father Francesco turned to Guy's children, raised his frail arms jubilantly toward them, and addressed them in English. "My neffews and-a-niece. Alberto, when you become Sen-a-door?"

"Not yet, Uncle," Guy interposed, "we still have some work to do."

"Ees okay. Alberto ees a good-a boy. Eef ee 'as da brain of Gaetano, da 'eart of Maria, and da luck of Dante, ee will be presidente."

The crowd laughed.

"E Eduardo, how you? You granfadda tell me dat where you study law – 'arvard – ees-a spesh'l, because ivy grow on da wall. What you do when you grad-ate, sell da ivy for you-self?"

The laughter continued.

"Or you go in business wit you brudda?"

"No, Uncle Francesco. Albert is going into politics. I don't think the country would be safe with two of us running the place. We would never agree on anything."

Uncle Francesco smiled, and looked at Guy, who shrugged.

Albert followed, "Yeah, instead, Edward is going to defend criminals."

Confused, Francesco asked his brother for a translation of what Alberto told him. As he began to understand, the priest's eyes widened.

Even in a far away place before his pious uncle, Edward felt compelled to defend himself from his brother's jabs. "What my big brother means to say, Uncle Francesco, is that I am going to work as a Public Defender. The Public Defender is a government agency that provides legal representation to the poor, to criminal defendants who can't afford a lawyer of their own. I will be one of their lawyers."

Father Francesco shot his brother a quick question, to which his brother replied "*Si.*"

"Dees sound-a like a good t'ing, Eduardo," Father Francesco told his nephew, as he pulled open the top drawer of his bedside table. He reached for a dusty little book with pages tattered from multiple readings. "No lissen to any-body or any-ting except-a you 'eart." Father Francesco handed the book to his nephew.

Although Edward did not understand Italian, he could surmise its contents from the title, and the solemnity with which his uncle presented it. "A book about Saint Francis?" Edward asked, as he received the text humbly.

"*Si*, ever-body laugh at San Francesco when he want-a help da poor. And ever-body den, just like-a now, t'ink all da poor are crim-i-nal. In dis-sa life, we all on trial, da way day teach-a you at 'arvard."

"Let's hope he's learning something at that place, considering all the money I am paying," laughed Guy.

Father Francesco continued, "And we will be judge by 'ow we 'elp-a doze around us. Doze who 'ave da least need-a da most 'elp-a. Doze who 'ave da most-a, must give-a."

Edward offered back the book of St. Francis.

Francesco refused. "You keep-a da book. It make-a you strong – so you can 'elp-a da weak."

"I can't, Uncle Francesco. It is your book. I don't speak Italian. I won't understand it."

"I t'ink you understand all-ready."

"We will let him be Saint Francis for a while," Guy assured his uncle, "but eventually he will have to support a wife and children. Pop always told us in Italian, '*se i soldi non entrano dalla porta, l'amore vola via dalla porta.*'"

"What does that mean, Dad?" chirped Lisa Marie.

"If money does not enter through the door, love jumps out the window," jested Guy, with his father and uncle laughing heartily along with him.

"*Senza I soldi,*" quipped Dante, "*il prete no canta il mis.*"

The three men laughed again, Francesco the heartiest.

"What did Grandpa say?" asked Edward.

His mother translated, "Without money, the priest does not say mass."

As the air in his musty room seemed to lighten, Father Francesco looked into his brother's eyes. "T'ank you, ever-body, for come-a da see me. You are all-ways in my pray'rs."

He then looked to Lisa Marie. "And 'ow about-a my lovely niece, Lisa Marie?"

Lisa Marie blushed. "I just got engaged to be married to a man named Vito Petrozzini."

"I know Vito, his fadda Vito, and *his* fadda Adamo. Afta you and Vito get married, you come-a to Aquino for visit. By den, maybe I be strong enough to say da mass en *Il Gesú.*" He smiled at Marie. "And danz-a da *Tarantella* like I do wit you mama."

Sister Theresa stepped in and pulled Father Francesco's bed cover to his chin. "For now, no *Tarantella,* you need-a da rest so you can bless-a da church tonight. I will have Padre Bernardo show everybody da town while I clean 'im up and get ready for tonight."

"That's a great idea," echoed Guy. "We are all anxious to see where Dad grew up with you, Uncle Francesco, and Adamo Petrozzini."

"I think I'll stay behind and help Theresa," said Lisa Marie. When Guy gave his daughter a puzzled look, Lisa Marie responded defiantly. "You were the one who said I need to have Sister Theresa teach me to cook."

Marie pulled her mother-in-law Philomena by the hand. "C'mon, Ma. We'll stay with Lisa Marie and Sister Theresa."

"*Molto bene,*" replied Sister Theresa. "I go find Padre Bernardo."

VIII

A Vineyard Lost

Children of Aquino

F ather Bernardo was tall and bookish looking, with horn-rimmed glasses resting upon his large nose; though his physique was awkward, his presence was poised. There was only a faint trace of accent in the otherwise fluent English he had learned while studying in an American seminary. He had been looking forward to the opportunity not only to meet the family of his mentor, Father Francesco, but also to speak with them about America while explaining Aquino.

Standing beside his compact Lancia automobile, Father Bernardo greeted the Bennett men without introduction as they walked out of the rectory. Under the fading southern Italian sun, a cock crowed in the distance, and a small dog limped in front of the Bennetts. "How is everybody? My name is Bernardo." He clicked his heels together. "I am your tour guide."

"Did Father Francesco import you from an American church?" retorted an impressed Guy. "Your English is impeccable."

"In fact, he exported me to America to study in a seminary in Minnesota. Just when I mastered the art of staying warm and having fun, he imported me back. I think it is a form of clerical mercantilism." The men were taken by Bernardo's command and wit, and the young priest knew it. "Where would you like to visit first?"

Guy shook his new friend's hand. "Take us to where it all began. The Old Town."

Bernardo opened the passenger side door. "Very well. Shall we? The back may be tight but I think we can squeeze."

The men drove an asphalt road, around a few sharp turns, until they reached the cobblestones. As Bernardo negotiated the Old Town's narrow turns, a plaza's wall clock stood frozen, with one arm broken and its carved Roman numbers barely legible beneath the grime. Around another corner, a bell tower tolled no more. Empty bottles were everywhere.

"This must be the Old Town," exclaimed Albert.

"Yes it is," answered Bernardo.

"Look at these buildings. This is what I was expecting. These must be hundreds of years old," said Albert excitedly.

A pigeon pecked away at crumbs in the unkempt hair of a woman sleeping on a bench. Beneath the doorway of what was only a facade, an unshaven man stuffed money in a woman's bra, as he pressed up against her.

"Who lives here?" asked Edward.

"The poor people," answered Bernardo. "Those who can't afford the new city."

"So it is literally a tale of two cities," said Edward, "to quote a famous English novelist."

"Very cute, Mr. Dickens," snapped Albert.

"Yes, they are like two cities," explained Bernardo. "And Father Francesco is determined to bring the church back to this one, to the poor, to the place where he and his brother Dante used to play."

Dante stared out the window, and was startled by a toothless man extending his hand for money. The car sped by before Dante could reach for his pocket.

"Francesco has done a remarkable job. Obtaining funds from the government, supervising construction, and even carrying pails of cement himself, all to rebuild the old church and its piazza. Unfortunately, I think it is the strain of it all that put him in the bed you found him."

"Bennetts have always been hard workers," said Guy.

"Thanks to Francesco's hard work and the generosity of people like his brother, the two cities are almost one again. Francesco wants to make the old church, *Il Gesú*, the center again, the heart of all of the people of Aquino."

"Da way eet was-a," uttered Dante.

"We are all so excited that you made it for the blessing," beamed Bernardo.

"Father Francesco is a priest, father, builder, and mayor – all rolled in one," exclaimed Guy as he and his sons absorbed the grand plan that the young priest was recounting.

Dante was speechless, gazing without a blink at the impoverished remnants of the town he left behind.

"To attribute Father Francesco the mere sum of those titles would underestimate his power and influence," waxed Father Bernardo. "He taught the people of Aquino real faith in God, not the kind that lurks in the darkness of fear, but grows from love of self and neighbor. The kind that opens like a flower's petals when it first feels the light of day. Parents have named their children after him. It was because of him that I became a priest." There was a sparkle in Father Bernardo's eye. "His power can move mountains." Father Bernardo snapped himself from the sermon he had inadvertently commenced. "I am sorry. I was getting a bit carried away."

"It is quite all right," assured Guy.

"Would you like to walk through the Old Town?" He stopped the car, and pointed down a winding street, encroached by shadows. "This is Via Della Valle, the Way of the Valley. The church, *Il Gesú*, is just down there."

Dante said nothing.

"Father Francesco told me you also wanted to see the family's old vineyard," followed Bernardo, offering an option.

Dante accepted the offer. "We shood-a go see da vineyard. I rememb-a ees far. If we go late, it be dark-a and can no see nut-ting."

"Very well, we will go to the vineyard," said Bernardo as he up-shifted the car. "You will see the church in all its glory tonight." A few turns more, and Father Bernardo shot out of the Old Town onto a dirt road. He made a left toward the vineyard. "How are things in the United States?"

Guy replied. "You tell him, Albert."

"We have our problems, no doubt. But it is because we are the most diverse nation in the world, and ours is the only system open enough to confront and discuss our problems. We will resolve them. We always do. The country is just a bit overweight. It needs to get back to the basics – hard work and self-reliance." Albert grabbed Dante's headrest in front of him to brace himself. "No different than what it took Grandpa to succeed when he came from Italy."

Father Bernardo pulled abruptly off the dirt road, having almost passed his destination. "Here we are. The old family vineyard."

"It can no be," exclaimed Dante. "Da vineyard ees much more far. Dis is too close."

"Maybe it seems closer than when you and Father Francesco traveled the road by horse and cart in the hot sun. This is it, I assure you." He came around and opened the door for Dante. "Welcome back to the fields."

Dante was unsettled. As he stood upright, a passing car nearly hit him, distracting his thoughts. With Guy at his side, he peered over a fence, upon barren grounds where grapes once thrived, but grew no more. He could see some of the wooden stakes around which his and his father's fruit wrapped its way. Beyond the stakes, there was a collapsed trellis that used to provide his father cool shelter from the sweltering heat. He wanted desperately to grab a pick and shovel and spring life from the baked soil. He walked to the chain lock on the fence's entrance, and pulled. It would not open."

Guy moved swiftly toward his father to keep him from falling. "Careful, Pop. It's locked."

"Bernardo, what 'appened to the vineyard?" asked Dante.

"Your brother ran it for a long time, even after becoming a priest. In fact, for a while some of the young men, including myself, helped him harvest the land so he could use the profit for the church. But when he started rebuilding *Il Gesú*, the work became too much."

"Yes. Dis I know," replied an impatient Dante. "But ee never tell me who ee sell it to."

"He sold it to Bruno Petrozzini, the first son of the man with whom you left Aquino, Adamo Petrozzini. I thought you knew."

"No. We neva 'ear much about Bruno afta he left 'ome when ee was-a young."

"Oh, yes." Bernardo responded studiously. "Bruno became a wealthy businessman raising cattle, making wine, and trading leather in South America. I think he lives in Buenos Aires, but I am not sure. He is very private, to himself." Bernardo kicked a pebble. "Anyway, when he found out that Father Francesco was selling the vineyard, he said he had to have it. He offered more money than Father Francesco was going to ask, without ever once seeing it. I don't think he has even visited since purchasing it."

"He must have really wanted this dirt," smirked Albert, as a passing wind rattled the fence.

"We believe that he bought the land as an act of charity, without intending to use it. He asked Father Francesco not to tell anyone. Like I said, he is a private man. But being that he is practically family, and it was your vineyard, I guess it is all right for me to tell you."

Edward looked at Dante. "Grandpa, did you used to work on the farm?"

Dante asked his grandson to repeat the question, then answered. "Every day until da day I leave for Ameriga. Francesco and me used to work dis-sa farm wit our fadda aft-a school da way you play you baseball and football. We would work, and if it got too 'ot, my fadda would rest under de trellis. I loved dissa farm. It was because of dissa farm dat I leave-a."

"Why? How do you mean?" inquired Albert.

"Nev' mind, ees a long story. We need-a go back to da town, I'm-a tired."

It was clear that Dante wanted no more of the vineyard. The men retreated to the car.

On the short car ride back, Edward continued to barrage Bernardo with questions about current life in Aquino, while Guy and Albert asked about the past. Dusk set in as they re-entered the Old Town.

"Any special requests to see in the Old Town?" asked Bernardo.

Dante tried to use the impending darkness as a pretext for adjourning the visit. "Maybe ees too dark. We come back-a tomorrow."

Guy put his hand on his father's shoulder. "C'mon, Dad. You

were the one who always said sundown was the best part of the day. That special light that makes everything prettier. When work is behind and the mystery of the night awaits."

Having talked his father into submission, Guy turned to the young priest. "Bernardo, can you take us to where Dad and Francesco lived?"

Without hesitation, Bernardo made a sharp right turn and spoke above the rubble and dust. "This, to your right, was the corner grocery store that Sister Theresa's mother and father ran while they were alive. They did very well. Apart from Dante and Bruno Petrozzini, Sister Theresa's parents were the wealthiest natives this town remembers. I'm sure that their small fortune is very little compared to what you enjoy in Whitebridge. But it was enough to send their son – Theresa's brother Beppino – to university to become an engineer, which is not a privilege enjoyed by many people in this town. Unfortunately, Beppino, his wife Vicenza, and their children died in a car crash on the autostrada."

"Everybody need-a move so fast-a," lamented Dante. "What a-shame."

"That's a sad story," said Edward.

"Dis town is filled wit sad story," replied Dante.

"And this is the house where Dante, Francesco, and their younger sister Annunziata were born," pointed Father Bernardo as the car stopped in front of an abandoned single-story home. "I will let Dante explain this one."

The troop deployed once again, and Dante kicked his heavy legs through the debris. "We 'ad many good-a time in dis-sa 'ouse." Using his cane to bat away a scurrying rodent, he went to a stack of crates, where the family's kitchen table once stood. "Dis is da kitchen where we eat in da morn', before we go to da farm, and again at-a night-time. Where we eat and play cards wit Papa – we could-a never beat 'im." Off the top of one of the crates, Dante picked up a used syringe. "What is this?"

Albert grabbed the syringe from his grandfather, without explaining that it was used to inject heroin. "Here, Grandpa, I will take care of that."

After a confused pause, Dante resumed his journey, to a set of broken rusted pipes that protruded from the wall. "Dees was-a da sink-a. Annunziata, she 'elp mamma wit da dish." He let slip a smile. "She wipe-a wit her little hands-a."

"Where did you sleep, Pop?" asked Guy.

Dante veered gingerly four steps to the right of the kitchen, careful not to trip upon the strewn remains of his past. "Dis is where me and Francesco sleep. Annunziata sleep in da room next door."

Albert turned to his brother. "This house could not have been more than twenty feet long."

"If that," returned his brother. "I think it might have even been shorter than your attention span."

Dante squinted. "And on de udder side a de kitchen, is where mamma and papa sleep." The old man reflected. "Now, eet all seem-a so small. Back-a den, papa's chair, da radio, da bed – day were so beeg-a. Ees 'ard to believe dis is da same 'ouse. But I know it ees. What I can no see, I feel." Dante faced his audience, his mood becoming increasingly upbeat. "Bernardo, take us to da church. Let me see if Francesco know how to build da way me and Gaetano build in Ameriga."

With new vigor, Dante insisted that they walk the three blocks to *Il Gesù* and the piazza in front, where he and his family would go at night for conversation with neighbors. The setting sun waltzed on Via Della Valle and the withered buildings along the way, bringing back memories that Dante had long suppressed: a young boy ringing the bell on his bicycle as he passed with bread in his basket; a paneless window within which a blacksmith pulled from the fire his last iron of the day; elderly women draped with black veils, exchanging gossip as they walked home from evening mass. Dante closed his eyes and shook his head to clear it. When he opened them again, yet another image came: Dante's young sister Annunziata playing jump rope in the piazza, while Adamo Petrozzini described tales of success in America to a small group of his and Dante's friends. The shadows set in further on Via Della Valle.

A few steps more, and the narrow passage opened to the full view of the piazza. Bernardo looked at Dante and Guy, and extended his arm and open hand proudly toward *Il Gesú*. "Have you ever built anything like this?"

Before them stood an amber-white rock, risen from the refuse. Among the engaged pillars of the first level were three doorways, all cast from bronze, the tallest in the center. Between the pillars of the tapered upper level were deep recesses. Fanciful side buttresses supported the roof, which had a solid gold cross atop it.

The painters and masons filed out of the church. As the last of them locked its tall center door, Guy responded. "No, I can't say we have ever built anything this magnificent. Bridges, highways, tunnels, and skyscrapers – yes. A church with such beauty – no. I don't know of a parish in America that could afford something like this. The cost of labor alone would be prohibitive." He pointed to the gold cross that shone in the setting sun. "That would have been gone in a day."

"You're exaggerating, Dad," smiled Albert.

"How did Francesco do it?" marveled Guy, as he stroked the cornerstones of *Il Gesú*.

Bernardo folded his hands in front of him, beneath his clerical cloak. "It wasn't easy. But with the financial support of people like your father and Bruno Petrozzini, it became a possibility. There is also one important difference between building a church here and in America. These men whom you see walking out the front door, they have come after their normal jobs and on weekends for free – for love of God and Francesco, in no particular order."

Albert laughed. "Just like you always told us, Dad. The labor unions have ruined American productivity."

Instead of taking his brother's bait and mouthing a comeback, Edward's attention was diverted elsewhere. He turned his head to listen. "Father Bernardo, what is that noise? It sounds like someone is singing."

Father Bernardo smiled as he peered over the broad Bennett shoulders, and down the bends of Via Della Valle. A flicker of light came around a curve, followed by a hymn. "Someone is singing. It appears that Francesco decided to start the blessing a little early. I guess he could not wait."

Three generations of Bennett men shuffled around to see the light, growing larger, and the melody, sounding sweeter, marching from the distance. As the light grew brighter and the singing louder, they could discern Sister Theresa pushing Father Francesco in his wheelchair, with a woolen blanket over his legs. Philomena, Marie, and Lisa Marie walked beside them holding candles. Ten men fell in line holding lit torches; their sights forward, they raised their flames high. A trio of violinists followed, walking and playing with eyes closed, rapt in their devotions. Rows of townspeople – men, women, and children – kept coming around the corner, all carrying a candle, each illuminating a different face, dedicated to the same calling. In the middle of the troop, an angelic maiden, with olive-butter skin, sang out into the darkening Via Della Valle:

> *Ave Maria! gratia plena*
> *Maria, gratia plena,*
> *Maria, gratia plena*
> *Ave, Ave! Dominus, Dominus tecum*

> [Hail Mary! Full of grace
> Mary, full of grace,
> Mary, full of grace
> Hail, Hail! The Lord, the Lord is with thee]

As the torches fended off the night, the maiden continued her song:

> *Benedicta tu in mulieribus*
> *Et benedictus,*
> *et benedictus fructus ventris*
> *Ventris tui, Jesus.*
> *Ave Maria!*

> [Blessed art thou amongst women,
> and blessed,
> and blessed is the fruit
> of thy womb Jesus,
> Hail Mary]

The townspeople joined the maiden in the next verse.

Guy turned to his sons, his eyes welling. "The 'Ave Maria.' Isn't it beautiful?"

By the time Guy turned back around, his father was racing toward his approaching brother. Dante moved his feeble heavy legs forward, jabbing his cane hard into the ground, to get closer to Francesco.

The singing kept up, the whole town supporting the olive-butter maiden in the "Ave Maria." "Pop," called out Guy, "what are you doing? You can't..." He hurried after his father.

Dante drew closer to his brother. Suddenly his legs felt light.

While Sister Theresa wheeled him, Francesco raised his hands off his lap, palms to the sky, to applaud Dante's miraculous walk. "Bravo!"

Dante's smile widened, his pace quickened. No longer needing the cane, he threw it aside.

"Bravo," mouthed Francesco again, just steps away.

Just then, Dante's legs gave way, their strength spent. He began to stumble.

Francesco assumed the wheels of his chair, moving them faster, escaping the grip of Sister Theresa and leaving her behind.

Dante reached out, knowing he was on his last step.

Francesco thrust a final turn of his wheels, and broke his brother's fall, catching Dante in his lap.

Guy and Sister Theresa reached the knotted brothers at the same time. They dared not touch Dante, as his head was buried in Francesco's chest, his arms draped around his brother's shoulders, his legs limp to the ground. His head and shoulders bobbed in Francesco's hold.

The procession stood in place to wait, its "Ave Maria" continuing to crescendo:

Ave Maria!
Ave!
Ave!
Ave!

Guy put his hand on Dante's shoulder, to comfort his father while he cried.

His shoulders still bobbing, Dante lifted his face from Francesco's chest and turned toward Guy. His face was dry of tear, his grin as wide as all outdoors. He was laughing – laughing as gaily as he ever had.

"Pop," Guy joined with a giggle, "what is so funny?"

Dante did not answer. He just kept laughing, as he braced him against his brother's legs, and back to his feet.

"Here, Pop," extended Guy, "your cane."

Guy waved off his son, pushing away the cane. He worked the armrest of the wheelchair, and then its backing, until he was at the handles.

"Dante," chimed Sister Theresa.

"*Posso farlo* [I can do it]," responded Dante. He began wheeling his brother the rest of the way. The two were one, pulling and pushing: Francesco was Dante's cane, Dante his brother's keeper.

The maiden rang out in solo again, drawing the rest of the procession out of the Via Della Valle and into the square.

Sister Theresa directed Dante and the rest of the Bennetts to the head of the square, atop the steps to the church. With their backs turned to the risen church of *Il Gesú*, the Bennetts beheld the townfolk filing into the center. The ten men with their torches spread themselves evenly around the piazza, their swirling fires revealing the square's restoration: to the left and in the rear, a statute of Giuseppe Garibaldi, the great unifier of Italy, on his war horse; on the right side and forward, a cast of a young woman, her toga slipped off the shoulder, holding fruit behind her, peering seductively around a column; palm trees and just-painted benches, planted among freshly laid bricks; at the center, a simple white marble fountain, spouting water from a natural spring, before a monument to the Crucifixion.

The townspeople each assumed a place in the square, facing *Il Gesú*, making room for all who emerged from the Via Della Valle. As a breeze swept through, tossing their hair and tussling with their dresses, the light of their candles was unwavering: small children accompanying a middle-aged woman, whose premature lines marked the loss of a husband and father; an older man with hard jaw and brown skin, seared in the fields; a young couple, with eyes bulging and wide. These were the faces of Aquino – worn and hopeful – separate and one – their candles' light staying night's darkness.

When the singing subsided into the evening air, Father Francesco addressed the crowd; Father Bernardo translated for the Bennett children. "Tonight, we come together to celebrate a new beginning that we, guided by faith, have created. Our church has risen from neglect, a place of worship where before there was only despair."

Father Francesco reached over his right shoulder to grab the hand of his brother, who was still standing behind, leaning upon his brother's wheelchair. "I want to thank my brother Dante for his support in our mission. Without him, this night would be dark and cold." The priest looked toward the stars. "When we were young boys, we played in this square with some of you, and our little sister Annunziata." The priest choked momentarily on his words.

Dante looked down.

After a brief pause, Francesco's words came again. "The Lord called for her early, and she went without protest. She left us, but her spirit remains." The priest took a deep breath to draw some composure from within. He smiled. "The only condition that my brother placed on his assistance was that after we finished the church and piazza, we would dedicate the piazza to our sister Annunziata, whose smile through days of pain was an inspiration to us all." The good father raised his holy hand before his face, and made the sign of the cross. "God bless our new church, *Il Gesù*, and its playground, 'Piazza Annunziata Di Benedetto.'" He looked to the sky, which was chock full of stars. "May Your light always shine upon those who fill this place."

Father Francesco nodded at Sister Theresa, and looked to Dante. "On behalf of all of Aquino, my brother, we would like to present a gift to you."

Sister Theresa summoned a group of teens to the natural spring fountain, in front of the monument to the Crucifixion. As they scurried, she organized them in two rows facing the Bennetts, and distributed to each of them a sheet of music. While the Bennetts stared puzzled, the townspeople smiled and whispered, well aware of what was unfolding. Sister Theresa stood at attention before her young singers to elicit the same.

But the night would not permit Sister Theresa every detail of the moment. Just as the nun enforced silence upon the new piazza, she was interrupted by the pitter-patter of a tiny girl, running across the square's new brick. With candle in hand, the child inserted herself at the front and center of the choir. The girl looked up at Sister Theresa, who leaned over and caressed her small head. Sister Theresa lit the child's extinguished candle, then stepped aside to lead the group in song:

> Amazing grace! How sweet the sound
> that saved a wretch like me!
> I once was lost, but now am found,
> was blind, but now I see.

Guy pulled his wife Marie closer to him. "Uncle Francesco must have told Sister Theresa that this was Dad's favorite song, and had her teach it to the kids in English." He kissed her on the head. "I am so glad he lived to see this day."

A sobbing Lisa Marie joined her parents' embrace. "I have never heard anything so beautiful. They sound like angels from heaven."

Albert turned to Edward. "I have to get my wife to write about this."

"Don't bother. No one would ever believe it."

Dante was riveted by the little girl in front of the choir that launched into its third verse:

> Through many dangers, toils, and snares,
> I have already come;
> Tis grace that brought me safe thus far,
> and grace will bring me home.

Whether by an amazing grace or guilt for a dying brother and long-lost sister, Dante had finally come home. The singing warmed the old man like the blue knit blanket his mother pulled over him as a boy before bidding him good night. He was safe, in a place where no one or nothing could hurt him. As Francesco and the others wrapped themselves in the comfort of the warm calm, Father Bernardo gestured to Dante, encouraging him to address the crowd.

Dante cleared his rusty throat. Unable to formulate the appropriate words in his head, he surrendered his native Italian tongue to his heart.

"For many years, my family and I have lived far away, at a distance not easily traveled. Today, I see many of you for the first time, but somehow your faces are familiar. We were not always together." His voice trembled. "But, we were conceived in this place and took our first breath from it." Dante paused, and called out to the gathered crowd. "We are all children of Aquino."

The crowd burst with pride and joy. The ten men planted their torches in the ground, providing light for a festival. The church bells rang.

Amidst the jubilation, and from his perspective atop the church steps, Dante thought he saw the water spring higher from the fountain at the center of the piazza, reaching like a hand, lifting the bowed head of the Son of Man from the monument Crucifix. As the living water raised the head of sorrows slowly, Dante saw a smile spread across Jesus' face. The Lord's content could not be for him, Dante thought to himself, but must be for Francesco and his flock. The spirit filled him all the same. The Christ's smile went away, and He bowed back his head of sorrows.

Like siblings reunited with their brother, the townspeople swarmed Dante and his family, anxious to catch up on old times and create new ones. A man with a cane showed Dante a cracked picture of them standing together proudly in the square, just before Dante left Aquino. Adamo Petrozzini's cousins gave Philomena a string-wrapped package to deliver to their relatives in America. With the help of Father Bernardo, the town's youth asked Guy's children about everything from rock-n-roll music to the Grand Canyon.

When Edward put his arm around Albert and told the crowd

that his brother would one day be a United States Senator, a young boy asked if they could all visit the White House when he became President. Everyone laughed, and so it went through the night.

IX.

To See a Father Weep

The Bennetts eventually retreated to the church's rectory to sleep for the few hours that remained before dawn. Albert and Edward bunked together in a small room, in iron framed beds. In the midst of undressing, Edward placed in his bag the book about Saint Francis that his great-uncle had given him, and reminisced about the night. "You know, bro. You really do have to go to a far-away place and have a stranger tell you who you are. Being with Father Francesco and those people today made everything so clear, including what I said about you becoming Senator. You know I will be there for you."

"I never doubted it." Albert dusted his sheets and climbed into bed. "And you know that I am only kidding you about your liberal views and your new girlfriend. What's her name?"

"Nancy."

"When we get home, maybe Victoria and I will drive up to Harvard and take the two of you out to dinner. Victoria may seem selfish to you, but trust me, she is not all that bad. Our situation is complicated. It's partially my fault…"

"Albert, stop. You don't need to explain anything to me. I am your brother." Edward turned off the light, and got into bed. "Speaking of siblings, that's one thing – jeez, there were so many – that I did not understand about tonight."

"What's that?" asked Albert.

"Well according to Father Bernardo, Father Francesco dedicated the piazza to his and Grandpa's little sister."

"Yeah, so?"

"I thought he called her Annunziata Di Benedetto. Our name is Bennett."

Albert clapped his pillow. "Sometimes I wonder about you. All these years, you assumed that Bennett was our original name? Does Bennett sound Italian to you? Grandpa changed it from Di Benedetto after he left this town."

"I guess I never thought about it. You were always better with that stuff, you know, the details of tradition and all the silliness that goes with it."

"You were the guy who went back and found Mom's town."

"That's true. So why did Grandpa change our name?"

"The same reason Mom and Dad never taught us Italian when we were kids. They wanted us to be accepted as Americans, not made fun of as mandolin-playing greasy immigrants. America was built by WASPs for WASPs, without much room for guys named Di Benedetto."

"So grandpa hid our real name, kind of like that prince Dad was describing yesterday in that opera, written by that guy Pacini. What was it called?"

"*Turandot.* If you took a little more pride in our Italian heritage, you would know."

"But I thought we were American."

Albert laid his head on his pillow, and closed his eyes. "Good night, brother."

Meanwhile, Guy lay restless in his bed down the long corridor, pondering every detail of the evening. While his wife Marie slept, he got up and went to the rectory kitchen to have a glass of milk. He opened the refrigerator to find only a bottle of wine, a wedge of aged provolone, and some bread. He grabbed the wine and bread, searched until he found a drawer with a knife, and sat for a snack. Instead of tiring him, the small meal whetted his appetite for the night.

With nowhere to go and hours more before his mind would let his body sleep, Guy decided to call his partner, Vito Petrozzini. It was still late evening in the United States, and Guy had to speak to someone.

"Vito, can you hear me? It's Guy."

"Guy, where the hell are you calling from, Italy?"

"Yeah, Vito. You would not believe..."

Because of the delay in the transmission, Vito spoke before he heard what Guy was trying to say. "How's your uncle?"

"He's great. Vito, you wouldn't believe what happened tonight. They blessed the church and new piazza that they rebuilt, and dedicated the piazza to my father's sister."

"I remember seeing them rebuilding *Il Gesú* when Lena and I visited last summer. It's a beautiful town, isn't it?"

"Yeah but it's the people, Vito, you never told me about the people. They held candles in the piazza and sang 'Amazing Grace' – in English."

"They did what? I must have heard you wrong because I thought you said they held candles and sang for you!"

"You heard me. And I met your cousins. Anyway, I'll tell you all about it when we get back. Anything happening at home?"

"Well, I hate to disappoint you, Guy, but you've only been gone a day, and we haven't had any candlelight vigils." The two shared a laugh. "I was going to call you yesterday about a call I got from our office on Friday."

"What about?"

"Mohammad from finance called me at home late Friday."

"Mohammad? Who is Mohammad?"

"You know, the new Indian guy we hired a couple of months ago to help restructure the company's stock and real estate portfolio."

"Okay. I remember, the little Indian guy. What did he have to say?"

"He reported that just before the market closed on Friday, there was some large quantity buying of our stock."

"And?"

"And nothing. That's it."

"Well at least somebody still believes that Northern Industries is a great company. I am telling you, Vito, I have a feeling we are going to turn the corner this year and get back on track."

"I do too. Get back safely, we have a wedding to plan."

Finally ready to retire, Guy hung up the phone and headed back to his room. While walking the narrow hall, however, he overheard his father whispering to his Uncle Francesco. Guy peeked through the slight opening of his uncle's door, and saw his father sitting at his brother's bedside speaking to him in Italian. Guy listened closely, eager to hear another verse from this glorious reunion.

Dante grabbed his brother's bedpost and raised his voice slightly. "I understand. But why did you have to sell it to Bruno Petrozzini. And why didn't you tell me?"

"Brother, how was I to know? You never told me. Besides, I promised Bruno I would not say anything."

Dante clenched his lips, and covered his face with his hand.

Francesco pulled Dante closer. "Don't worry, Dante. The Lord will watch over you."

Dante rested his head on Francesco's chest, beneath the gentle touch of his brother's hands.

For the first time ever, Guy saw his father weep.

X.

1920

Leaving the Fields

Father and son were busy cultivating silence in their fields of grapes when a train passed nearby. The locomotive's whistle was the pair's alarm, telling them that it was 4 p.m. – time to quit work early and head home for dinner. Dante Di Benedetto wiped the sweat from his eyes to view his last harvest of succulent blue-red grapes, hanging heavy beneath the cover of their leaves. It was September of 1920, and the air was rife with the sounds and smells of uncertainty and change.

Dante looked to his father, Eustachio, whom his family and friends referred to as "Stas." Without saying a word, they gathered their tools and walked to a stone shed. Under the shed's hot tin roof, and behind its wooden door, was the only place Dante felt he could speak freely to his father, as equals after a hard day's work.

But that privilege had been taken away two weeks earlier, when Dante stood firmly upon the shed's earthen floor, and suggested to Stas that the family should buy more land and diversify their vineyard by growing olives and wheat. Stas's unequivocal yet predictable "no" was the cue for Dante to tell his father he was no longer interested in farming, and would be leaving for America with his friend, Adamo Petrozzini. The heat of the argument that followed scorched any words that remained between father and son. Two weeks and hours of painful silence later, the day of Dante's departure had arrived.

Dante and Stas entered the shed, where a table and two

benches awaited them. They each pulled a dry shirt and pair of pants from the pegs along the wooden wall, and assumed their separate benches. They set themselves to change their clothing.

While Stas concentrated on his bootlaces, Dante stared at the shed's open door, inching back and forth in the arid afternoon breeze. The rusted hinges creaked.

Stas grabbed from the table the empty wooden pail in which he carried his and his son's lunch. He looked briefly at Dante, who was still buttoning his shirt, then exited briskly from the small house. Dante followed, locking the door behind him.

As Stas and Dante walked the dirt road that led back to their hometown of Aquino, other farmers were still grooming their vines. Nearly everyone who farmed in or around Aquino grew grapes; the profits were modest but certain for a people who believed that God gave this land to make His wine. The farmers of Aquino needed only enough to survive until the next harvest. The Lord would take care of the rest.

A young man clipping a vine called out. "Dante, good luck in America. Save some for the rest of us."

The boy's father recognized Stas, and chided his son to return to work.

The well-wisher was but one among Dante's admiring fans. At 5'9" with muscular physique and undulating black hair, Dante already cut a handsome figure at the age of seventeen. His personality was no less engaging. Dante could tell a story like none other, keeping his listeners – young and old alike – curious and howling throughout the night. His stage was Piazza Gesú, which unfolded in front of the church in Aquino. As of late, he had entertained the town's youth with stories about America, using the license his popularity lent him to replace fact with fiction. Apart from his native charm and charisma, Dante's stories were intoxicating because he wanted to believe them as eagerly as did his audience.

Dante waved to the young well-wisher without breaking his gait. Continuing down the dirt road, he and his father came upon the old cemetery. Stas knelt to say a prayer, as was his custom. Dante dirtied his knees to join his father, but was anxious to get home; he sneaked short glances to see whether his father had finished paying homage. Finally, the old man unfolded his hands to make the sign of the cross upon his forehead, chest, and shoulders. Dante hastily did the same. They resumed their walk, careful to keep the silence between them.

After what seemed an eternity to Dante, the town of Aquino was in sight. A tiny bead among the hills of Southern Italy, Aquino was preserved in the wrap of tradition. Its streets were narrow and paved with cobblestones that were hand-placed individually and grouted with cement. The church of *Il Gesú* and its piazza were the center of both the town and its congregation's lives, relegating Town Hall to the mundane shadows. The people lived slowly yet heartily. Stas and Dante passed through the piazza, stopped again to make the sign of the cross in front of the church of *Il Gesú*, and turned right onto the street where they lived.

A tall woman, brown eyes red with grief, filled the frame of their home's open doorway. Antonia Di Benedetto relieved her husband of the empty pail he was carrying, and took her son by the hand. "Come. The food is ready. Let's eat."

Dante's little brother and sister, Francesco and Annunziata, were already propped in their seats, waiting for what was to be their last meal with him. At age ten, Francesco was seven years younger than Dante. Annunziata, the youngest at eight, had become increasingly frail in recent months. Though their mother had explained to Francesco and Annunziata that their brother was going to America, they still did not understand why Dante was leaving. Perhaps they were too young, or maybe no one except Dante really knew why he was going away.

With everyone sitting, Antonia poured soup into each of her children's dishes. "Dante, I have packed your Sunday suit, two pair of winter underwear, and three pair of socks. The shirts are the ones your uncle bought when he worked in Rome." She proceeded to serve Stas, but remained focused on her son. "And I fit the blue blanket that I knit you for your thirteenth birthday..." A mother's tears fell into the soup she was serving her husband.

Before Antonia had completed her round, Stas began saying

grace. "Thank you, Lord, for the food that you have given. Bless this family, keep it safe from danger, and give it strength in all its endeavors. May your fruit continue to be plentiful. Amen."

Antonia dried her eyes, and dinner began.

"How far is America?" piped little brother Francesco.

"It will take two weeks by boat," answered Dante.

"Will you be home for Christmas?" asked Annunziata.

Dante looked into his little sister's eyes. They were growing weary with what Dante believed openly, over the violent protest of his parents, was the onset of the devastating disease of polio that was ripping through the region. On several occasions, Dante urged his mother and father to send Annunziata for treatment in Rome. They dismissed his theories and advice, reminding him that they were his little sister's parents, and God would take care of Annunziata, whatever the affliction.

Dante responded to Annunziata's question. "I don't know, but I will always be thinking about you. I will send you boxes of sweet American candy, so long as you keep smiling." He tapped her on the nose. "Always smile."

The corners of Annunziata's tiny mouth hopped with excitement.

Stas tore a piece of bread with his hands; it was his way of demanding that attention be shifted back to him as patriarch and protagonist. "Antonia, pass the meat." As Antonia reached for the rack of lamb that she had been preparing all day, Stas broke the two-week silence he had imposed upon his son. Without looking at Dante, he took control. "I have written a letter to our cousins in America to tell them you are coming." He reached into his pocket and pulled out an envelope. "Their name and address are written inside. You can live with them. Use the money in the envelope to pay them rent for the first three months. After that, you are on your own."

"Thank you, Papa. But you keep the money. You will need help in the fields when I leave."

Stas grumbled through his eating. "Take it. Francesco is already working hard; he will do fine in your place." He swallowed. "Besides, the money is not for you. It is for our cousins."

Dante raced through his meal, barely chewing.

Her eyes still mourning, Antonia forced a smile. "Slow down, my son. This may be the last decent meal you have for a while."

"Don't worry, mama. I will be fine. Where is my suitcase? My train for Naples leaves in half an hour. Adamo is probably already at the station."

Antonia began picking up the plates. "Your bag is in your room. Go get ready while I clean the table."

Every night in bed for the past two weeks, Antonia had cross-examined her husband about his argument with Dante in the shed. Like a stubborn witness, Stas gave his wife answers only bit by bit. From the start, Antonia knew in her heart that she had to let go of Dante, but continued to muse desperately about why her husband and son could no longer work together in the fields of Aquino.

Antonia stacked the dirty dishes in the kitchen sink. "Did you even ask him about his idea for buying more land?"

"Antonia, I told you, this is not about him wanting to grow olives and wheat. He wants to leave, and he needs an excuse. Whatever it is, he needs to get it out of his system. It is early September now. I promise you he will be home by Christmas."

"I hope so. He is still so young." Her tears welling rounder and heavier, Antonia collapsed into her own embrace.

The little family walked together to the Aquino train station. Annunziata was on Dante's shoulders, alongside Francesco, who was struggling with both hands to carry one of his big brother's bags. Stas wore his jacket and Sunday hat, Antonia a black sweater draped over her shoulders.

The silence screeching inside her head, Antonia made small talk about the train schedule. "The train should arrive in fifteen minutes. They are usually on time."

Dante engaged his mother, but could not bend his father's forward march stare. "Yes. It may even be early."

When the Di Benedettos arrived at the station, Adamo Petrozzini was already waiting with his parents on the train's platform, dressed neatly in a jacket and tie. Like Dante, Adamo was eager to go to America, but his reservations were many more. Adamo was closer with his mother and father, who owned Aquino's only butcher shop; the lamb that the Di Benedettos had just eaten came from the Petrozzinis' store. His family being of better means, Adamo's memories were richer. At bottom, Adamo was not as well equipped as Dante to uproot his life; he did not have the lion's heart of his friend and leader, nor the strength to sever the cord of tradition.

When Dante reached Adamo on the platform, he pinched the knot of his friend's tie between his thumb and forefinger, and whispered in his ear. "Nice outfit. Where are you going, to a funeral?"

After exchanging pleasantries with Mr. and Mrs. Petrozzini, Dante continued a few paces along the platform, so that he could be alone with his family. Setting his luggage in front of him, Dante took his sister Annunziata down off his broad shoulders, and sat her upon his suitcase. He held her sallow face between his hands. "You be a good little girl while I'm gone. Do what Mama says. And remember, always smile. No smile, no candy." He kissed her on the head, and turned to Francesco.

Dante grabbed his little brother around the waist, and hoisted him above his head into the constellations. "You, little man. Work hard with father in the fields, and watch over your sister." Dante placed Francesco back on the platform, removed his own silver crucifix necklace, and placed it over his little brother's head. "This is now your cross. Wear it well."

Dante took a slow step toward his mother; before he could land another, he thrust himself upon her. "I love you, Mama."

"My son. Take care of yourself. Write us as soon as you arrive. If you get cold, the blue blanket will keep you warm. We love you."

The bell on the tracks began ringing; Dante's train was pulling into the station.

Dante stood square with his father, each looking into the other's eyes. There were so many things that Dante wanted to say, but could not in such a short moment. His thoughts and emotions collided, rendering him speechless. When Dante finally shook his father's hand and bid him farewell, his words were muted by the approaching train. Just as well for both of them; the right sentiments would come later, once the wounds healed. Their eyes spoke for their mouths; both Dante and Stas hoped they would be together again, but neither had the strength to say it.

Dante waved goodbye to his family, and called for Adamo, who was still deep in the embrace of both his parents. "Let's go, Adamo. America's streets of gold are waiting to be danced on by those fancy shoes of yours."

The two boarded the train and settled into their seats. As the train pulled out of the station, they lowered their windows to wave a last goodbye. Through Dante's window, Stas and Antonia stood next to one another, with young Annunziata cradled in Antonia's arms. Francesco jumped and waved excitedly, as his new crucifix bounced off his chest. He continued to jump and wave until the train and his brother disappeared.

XI.

❧❀❧

Chasing a Fisherman's Horse

One-Way Tickets to Marseilles

The conductor asked Dante and Adamo for their tickets, and the young men closed their windows.

Adamo handed the man his one-way ticket to Naples. "Sir, how long before we arrive in Naples?"

The conductor punched the ticket. "At 6 a.m."

Adamo continued. "If we sleep, will you wake us when we arrive?"

The conductor laughed out loud. "Sure. Would you like me to also read you a bedtime story?"

Dante ended his friend's embarrassment by presenting his ticket to the conductor. He then rummaged through his bag for an apple and knife. He cut the skin of the apple slowly with one hand while he held it with the other, the way his father had taught him in the fields. He gave a piece to Adamo. "Okay. Here is the plan. After we arrive in Naples, we need to go to the waterfront and find an agent who will book our passage by boat to America. Once we get on the boat, the next stop is New York."

"It's that simple?"

"It's that simple. Get some sleep."

While Adamo slept, Dante reclined with his eyes wide open. Despite his bravado with Adamo, he knew the journey would not be simple. Nothing in life was. For with every change, there are many ripples – some intended, some not, some good and some bad. But Dante also knew what his friend needed to hear. Propelled at once by fear and excitement, Dante's mind would not allow his body to rest that night. It was a curse and blessing he would carry, and be carried by, for the rest of his life. And little Annunziata – if only he could have brought her with him.

Throughout the long night, Dante stared out the window where his family once stood, and upon the eastern horizon, willing the sun to rise. As the sky lightened from deep black to majestic blue, he knew that Naples was not far.

When the sun began to bulge, Dante poked his partner. "Hey, Adamo. I think we are almost in Naples." He scraped through his bag again, this time fetching some hard salami and provolone, and sliced enough for two. "Here, have some. We are going to have to hustle once we arrive. How did you sleep?"

Adamo began the day with a yawn and stretch. "Very well. How about you?"

Dante lied about his restless night. "Like a baby. I would probably still be sleeping if the sun was not so bright."

"Napoli," the conductor cried out.

The boys hurried to finish their salami and provolone so that they could assume the aisle with their suitcases.

Through the pushing and shoving, Adamo called back to Dante. "Let's follow everybody else. They must all be headed for the waterfront and America."

Dante and Adamo rode the crowd as it wound like a serpent through the station. The boys' feet barely touched the ground. Anticipation, the energy of life – if only it could carry them straight to America.

But once they reached the streets, the crowd dispersed, some walking, some getting on buses, others ducking into a café for morning espresso. Dante and Adamo were alone. There was no clear passage. Dante grabbed Adamo by the shoulder. "Let's go, let's start walking. We will find the waterfront ourselves."

The streets of Naples would not be so obliging. After a few optimistic minutes, the neighborhood grew hard. Two policemen chatted on the sidewalk, while a T-shirted man kicked violently at a boy who lay crying in the streets. When Dante peered into an open doorway, he was propositioned by a woman whose breath and half-naked body were spoiled with liquor.

"We are not in Aquino anymore," Dante told Adamo. "We better stay close together."

The morning sun began peeling the darkness from the streets. In the distance, Dante noticed a man crossing an intersection in a small horse-drawn cart, carrying what looked like a fishing pole and net. "Let's catch up to that guy. I bet he is a fisherman. He must be headed to the waterfront, or at least know how to get there."

Dante and Adamo ran with their bags in hand, yelling ahead with whatever breath their lungs would spare them. "Hey, you in the cart. Wait. We are looking for the waterfront. Can you help us? Wait!"

The horse accelerated to a trot. The boys picked up their pace to chase the fisherman's forward hunched back, to draw closer to the clatter of his pole, net, and gaff. Dante sprinted ahead of Adamo, and reached the cart's side. He shouted again to the fisherman, who was in the middle of his morning cigarette. "My friend and I are going to America. We need to find the waterfront. Can you tell us where it is?"

The fisherman and his cigarette would not separate, the burning ash holding firm as the wheels of his cart kept turning.

"Where is the waterfront? I must find the boat to America." Nearing exasperation, Dante called again. "Are you deaf? Where is the waterfront?"

The fisherman pulled up on his horse's reins, bringing his cart to a halt, at a crossroad.

Dante pulled up beside him.

The fisherman turned his body left, in the seat of the cart. He looked over at Dante for the first time, the young man's body swelling with sweat and frustration. The fisherman withdrew the cigarette from his mouth, blew a puff of smoke, and smiled. "No, my young friend, I am not deaf. But I wonder if your running and yelling at me has caused you to lose your senses. Take a deep breath. What do you smell?"

Dante inhaled. "Salt?"

The fisherman assumed his cigarette again, saying nothing while studying his billow.

Impatient, Dante looked at his watch, and back at the man again; he could taste the salt of his own sweat rolling off his cheek.

The fisherman sat patiently in his cart.

A boat's horn sounded from Dante's back. The fisherman smiled again, and pointed with his hand that held the cigarette. "Now, look behind you."

Dante turned quickly. He saw a harbor, with two large boats emerging high. The horn of one of the boats sounded again, startling Dante. Embarrassed, he returned the smile to the fisherman. "I am sorry. Thank you."

"For what? I haven't done anything. I am just on my way to work, enjoying my cigarette."

"Thanks anyway."

"Have a good trip." The man finished his cigarette, extinguished it on his seat, and cast it into the street. "Listen to your senses, not your emotions. Especially in that new country you are headed to. I hear it's big, and easy to get lost in." The man prodded his horse, and the cart pulled away.

When Dante and Adamo reached the harbor, there were thousands of people, each part of a clamoring voice and chaotic line to the two ships that sat majestic in the Mediterranean blue. Adamo was nearly knocked over by two men who were fighting for a ticket that was being offered by a third. "I don't think I have ever seen so many people in one place at one time."

"Me neither," replied Dante. "Let's find the booking agent. His address is 31 Via Del Mare." Dante put his bags down for a moment and looked around, trying to separate himself from the madness of the mob. He pointed across the street. "There it is, Via Del Mare. Let's go."

Inside the office at 31 Via Del Mare, the anxiety of the crowd was even more arresting than it was by the ships. The room was packed tightly with the stench of fear and perspiration. Dante read from a flier that detailed how easy it was to get to America. "I told you, Adamo. All we need is our passport and 1,000 lire. It says so right here."

When Adamo did not answer from behind, Dante turned to find his friend entranced by an infant boy, sucking hard from the large brown nipple of his mother's bare breast. Momentarily, Dante too was stricken by the woman's soft round face, and bountiful white bosom, as she fed her baby.

Dante whispered into Adamo's ear. "Stop staring. You are embarrassing her. Unless you are waiting to take the baby's place, leave the woman her peace."

Adamo smiled at the teen mother, and took a step forward in line.

After waiting inside the office for four hours, Dante and Adamo reached the booking agent's desk. They each presented 1,000 lire inside their passports. The man looked up, shaking his head. "Not enough. You need your military papers stating that you have completed your mandatory one year of national service."

Adamo became agitated. "But sir, we have never been in the army."

"Then you can never go to America. Next."

Dante slammed his fist on the agent's wooden desk. "Wait a minute. We left our families miles away, traveled all night, and spent most of the day in this pig sty just so you could tell us we can't go to America." Dante thrust the flier into the clerk's face. "Where does it say that in your little brochure? We are not leaving until you give us the ticket."

The mustached agent, pot belly sitting heavy upon his rarely used thighs, sneered at young Dante, whose muscular chest argued forcefully through the open buttons of his shirt. "Impossible. It is against regulation. Leave before I call the police and have you thrown in jail."

As Dante lunged forward and cocked back his arm, a middle-aged man dressed in a white suit stepped between Dante and the clerk, placing fifty lire on the desk. "No need to call the police. They are with me."

The agent took the money, and stuffed it into his coin-filled front pant pocket. "Very well. Only because they are with you. Otherwise, they would be on their way to jail."

White Suit ushered Dante and Adamo away from the desk, and back to the street where a group of other young men were waiting with their bags. "Do you want to go to America with these boys?" he asked them.

"Yes" they both answered.

"Do you have 200 lire?"

"What for?" followed Dante.

"I thought you just said you wanted to go to America," replied White Suit.

Dante refused to stand down; the day had already been far longer than even he had expected. "We do want to go America. We like to know how we are spending our money before we give it away. If you haven't noticed, we are not packed for a vacation."

White Suit softened. "Okay, then listen. In exchange for 200 lire, I have given each of these boys a one-way ticket to Marseilles, France. Boat passage from Marseilles to America does not require military papers, and costs only 900 lire. So what I am offering you will cost only 100 lire more than if you left from here. Do you want the one-way ticket to Marseilles?"

Dante looked at Adamo, who shrugged a lukewarm approval. Dante handed White Suit 400 lire. "Give us two tickets."

XII.

A Stuffed White Pony for a Girl With Black Locks

Luggage in the Rack

The pack of young men, twelve in all, started back toward the train station where Dante's and Adamo's search had begun hours earlier. None of them was a day over eighteen years old; nor were they anxious to talk through the beating Neapolitan sun. Their slow sliding steps across the cobblestone reflected the worry of a journey that had hit an unexpected bump, about which each of them was too proud to speak.

Dante could hear the trepidations and second thoughts rumbling through the boys' minds. As was his talent, Dante filled the silent void. "Nothing to worry about, guys. If things don't work out, there are enough of us to build a ship of our own."

The group didn't respond, some of the boys looking puzzled, others annoyed at the newcomer's babble.

With his impeccable timing and masterful delivery, Dante then served the punch line. "We can start by ripping the shirt off that fat ticket agent at Via Del Mare, and using it as our sail."

A few of the boys smiled.

Dante looked to the frowns he had not yet lifted. "We will tie him to his chair in the middle of the boat, and give him his shirt back after he blows us to America."

Everyone laughed, and the rest of the walk was spent embellishing the image of the obese agent heaving his wind into a makeshift shirt-sail.

Spirits high, the boys arrived at the station at 3 p.m., two hours before their 5 p.m train to Marseilles. Dante inquired at the ticket window, and led his new team to the track where the train would run. The boys sat on their bags, forming a circle around which they could share food and conversation. Dante took out his salami and provolone, while another boy grabbed his bread, and another fruit. They ate busily, enjoying the chitchat as a garnish to their meal.

"If only we had the blessed grape in the bottle," sighed Dante as he sat gripping bread in his right hand, salami in his left.

A tall skinny boy sitting opposite Dante joined in his lament. "I hear they don't even drink wine in America. They don't drink anything. It is illegal."

The mouth chewing next to him swallowed a hard crust and spoke. "I guess their priests really can change water into wine. Or maybe they just use milk during mass."

Dante cut a piece of provolone for himself. "In America, you can get anything you want so long as you have the money. Everything is either made there, or you can pay somebody whose job it is to get it there for you. If it is illegal, you can probably pay somebody for that too. In that way, it is no different than Italy."

"I will have my wife send me Italian wine," exclaimed a heavy-set boy sitting next to Adamo.

Adamo turned to him. "You're married?"

"Yes. And my wife is pregnant."

Adamo's face was pulled by a look of shock. "Then how could you leave them?"

Heavy-Set responded coolly. "You left a family behind, didn't you?"

Adamo frowned and bent his head to one side in tacit admission.

Heavy-Set continued. "I left the same way you did. For the same reason."

Another boy, whose face seemed lost behind his oversized spectacles, spoke out. "When I get to America, I am going to study to become an engineer, so that I can build bridges and highways. That is what fascinates me most about America. While Europe is busy fighting about boundaries that separate its small countries, America is always building more bridges and highways, bringing people together instead of driving them apart."

Dante smiled. "That's an interesting way of looking at it. It sounds like you have thought a lot about your plans in America."

Spectacles responded. "Haven't you? How else could you travel such a distance?"

Dante's rugged body fell limp. For the first time, he realized he had no plan; he had been so consumed by the argument with his father in the shed that he never took the time to think about an agenda or grand ambition for his new start in America. Get away – he just had to get away.

Never comfortable on the defensive, Dante resorted to compliment to free himself of Spectacles' firm grasp. "Of course I have made plans. I am just not as poetic about them as you are."

Dante stood up and turned to Adamo. "I am going to take a walk. My legs are getting a little cramped."

As Dante walked along the tracks, he thought to himself soberly about where the rails might lead him. He couldn't farm in New York, and he knew nothing else. His education was basic, and he had never been much interested in books. He was destitute of everything except his charisma, wit, and handsome looks. Spectacles was right; he needed a plan. But there was not enough time; it was difficult enough leaving Aquino and getting to America. Remember the words of the fisherman – listen to your senses and not your emotions; once in America, take the time to make a plan. Not just any plan: to be worthy, it had to be a grand design that included a family and soaring vision – a house, a car, children who would go to college...

Before he could even begin fantasizing about the wings of such a dream, Dante's thoughts were interrupted by the bell of the locomotive rolling in from the distance. It was time to leave and go again.

The twelve dusted the crumbs from their clothing, collected their bags, and boarded the train. As the rest of the boys entered through the rear, Dante pulled Adamo ahead to a separate car. "Let's go. We have a better chance of finding a seat without them."

Walking attentively through the train's aisle, Dante and Adamo found two empty seats. No sooner had they sat down than the conductor asked for their tickets. "Sorry, guys. You cannot sit with these tickets. They are for standing room only."

"The guy in the White Suit didn't tell us that," Adamo complained to Dante. "This train ride is thirty-six hours long."

Dante laughed. "Don't worry, this is probably the least of our problems. We will make the best of it. C'mon, we will find a quiet spot in the aisle where we can sit on our suitcases."

Like soldiers in a minefield, Dante and Adamo stepped over and around other single men and huddled families in search of their space. Just as it appeared that a spot could not be had, the doors of a passenger compartment slid open, and a shirt-sleeved shoulder, braced with suspenders, reached out to retrieve two bags that filled the aisle. Dante and Adamo hustled to the clearing, and squatted with their suitcases.

Brushed and bumped by passersby, and feeling as though only his suitcase and a thin floor separated him from the scrape of the tracks, Dante grew restless. He needed a sense of control. "I am going to see if I can find the other guys, to see how they are doing." He instructed Adamo. "You stay here and watch the bags."

Dante trekked toward the back of the train where the other boys had entered. As he passed over them, he studied the menagerie of faces that were jammed in the aisle: a baby crying to be fed, an elderly woman knitting to pass the time, a young couple sleeping peacefully in each other's arms. They were families struggling for something better, whose only luxury in life was the ability to pack all their worldly possessions into a few small bags. Though Dante could feel the pain of their plight, he rationalized to himself that he and they were the brave injured, fleeing from the debris of a crumbling Old World. Those who were smart enough to go to America, he thought to himself, would be made whole again, flourishing in the new country's abundance of sunshine and opportunity, feeding off its milk and honey. Milk and honey – the tasty muse that pulled Dante from the bitter vineyards of Aquino.

While passing from one car to another in search of the other boys, Dante noticed an old man crying alone. "Excuse me, sir." Dante reached down, and placed his large hand on the old man's shoulder. "Are you okay? Are you lost? Is there anything I can do for you?"

The old man looked up with his tear-filled sagging eyes. "My wallet. I had all of my money in it. Everything. It's gone."

"Did someone steal it from you?"

"I don't know. It's gone. I have nothing. Nowhere to go." The old man hid his wet face behind his wrinkled hands, and continued to cry.

Dante crouched, pulled the old man's fingers gently, and gave him a cloth to wipe his face dry. "Did you have it with you when you got on the train?"

The old man's short breaths and sniffles slowed. "I think so."

"Are you sure?"

"Yes. I must have." The old man hesitated, then pointed with his right index finger. Because I remember taking my wallet out of my pocket when the conductor asked for my ticket."

Dante smiled, proud of the progress he was making with a man decades his senior. "Do you remember what you did after you gave the conductor your ticket?"

"Yes," the old man said, anxious to get to Dante's next question. "I put it in my pocket and opened my suitcase to get a piece of cheese."

Dante told the man to open the suitcase to see if it had fallen inside. The old man loosened the frayed rope that tied shut his overstuffed suitcase. He rifled through his belongings – food, some clothing, a bible, and a framed picture of a young family. When he reached the bottom, he sighed with disappointment. "Nothing."

"Okay, all right," Dante sputtered as he thought about his next line of inquiry. "Did you move anywhere else on the train after you gave the conductor your ticket and ate the cheese?"

The old man paused, desperate to come up with an answer.

The poor fellow, Dante thought, must be losing his memory.

The old man's eyes grew wide. "Yes, yes." He pointed to the door ten feet away. "I went to the door to have a cigarette. I did not want to bother the young woman next to me with her children.

They were so small. One was a little boy, the other a girl. They were sleeping in blankets on their mother's lap. They looked like my son's children. He lives in Rome. I am on way to see him. He's so good. My wife died last year and..."

Dante focused the old man back on the wallet. "What happened after you went to the door to have the cigarette?"

"Let's see. I had just started smoking the cigarette when the conductor came by and asked again to see my ticket. I became nervous because I had already shown it to him. I was afraid he might try to kick me off the train, and I would have no place to go." The old man squinted, looked around, and lowered his voice to a whisper. "You never know these days. Even the train conductors are like the police. Very strict, and not always fair. The Fascists are right. We need more order, less crime. But not everyone can be a policeman. Otherwise, there will be more confusion and crime than if there were no policemen at all. Who will watch them?"

"I agree," replied Dante. He started to realize that it was probably no coincidence that the old man, with his failing memory and wandering thoughts, had lost his wallet. "What happened after he asked for your ticket again?"

"I pulled out my wallet and showed it to him." Before Dante could ask the next question, the old man continued. "After he saw the ticket, he told me that I could not stand by the door. I don't know why. I wasn't bothering anyone. I was just smoking my cigarette in the corner so that I would not wake the two children sleeping on their mother's lap. They looked so comfortable. I tried to explain this to the conductor, but he did not want to listen. He seemed more concerned that his shiny badge stay pinned straight on his jacket."

Dante interrupted. "Then what?"

"He wouldn't move until I did as he said. So I hurried to put my wallet and ticket back into my pocket, and come back here so that he wouldn't get angry and throw me off the train." The old man gave Dante a puzzled look. "What does the conductor have to do with my wallet?"

Dante gestured toward the door. "Let's go."

"Where are we going?"

"Back to where that conductor gave you a hard time. That is where I think you dropped your wallet. If you're lucky, it is still there."

The old man followed Dante docilely to the door.

Dante inspected both sides of the aisle next to the door, and reached behind the last seat in the car. He pulled out a black leather wallet that was wrapped with rubber bands. Dante smiled. "Is this your wallet, sir?"

The old man wiped his eyes with the cloth Dante had given him. His lips curled with joy against his aged gums. "Yes, yes. That's it." He took the wallet from Dante, and ripped off the rubber bands. "I must repay you for your kindness. Where are you headed?"

"America."

"Tell me, how much money do you need to get to America?"

Though the offer was tempting, Dante refused. "Nothing. All I ask is that you promise me you won't let people scare you just because they wear a uniform. And I am not going to move until I see you put the wallet back in your pocket."

"Very well," the old man answered as he deposited the wallet back into the vault of his inside jacket pocket. He pulled Dante by the sleeve. "But come here. I have something for you."

The old man brought Dante back to the place where he had been crying like a child moments earlier, and presented him with a quart of wine. "Take this. I made it myself. You will never find anything this good in America. I guarantee it."

Dante thought for a moment about his father and the fields of Aquino. He pushed the quart back politely. "I can't."

The old man grew stern. "It is yours. If you refuse, I will be insulted." When Dante accepted, the old man smiled. "Enjoy it."

No longer concerned about the other boys, Dante hurried back to Adamo to share their first new fortune. As he approached Adamo, Dante gave his friend a shouted whisper. "Adamo. Look what I have."

Adamo's eyebrows jumped into his rippling forehead. "Where did you steal that from?"

"I did not steal it. An old man gave it to me."

"Let's go. Nobody on this train gives away anything for free."

"I am telling you. I did not steal it." Dante sat on his suitcase, took a swig from the quart, and began enjoying his two favorite pastimes – drinking wine and telling a story. He and Adamo imbibed until Adamo passed out, into a peaceful slumber.

Dante rode the train through the evening darkness, stopping at several small towns along the way. With each new passenger came a cool breeze that dissipated quickly when they took their place among the many, overcome by the collective odor of the crowd. Dante felt that he and Adamo were getting closer, yet he knew there were many miles and days ahead. Night – the peaceful harbinger of things good and bad, the inscrutable quiet before the dawn.

The train made an extended stop in Rome, allowing the passengers time to get off and stretch. While Adamo went out to use the bathroom, Dante remained behind with the suitcases. He was becoming weary, and was finally falling into a light sleep. As he dozed, he felt a hand on his shoulders. Startled, he looked up. It was the old man.

Suitcase in hand and ready to get off the train, the old man held a large bag. "I wanted to find you before I left. Please take the food inside the bag. It is of no use to me now. My son is going to meet me at the station. He will take care of me. He has been so good to me since my wife died last year. His heart is big like yours. We have always been so proud of him, as I am sure your mother and father are proud of you." He handed the bag to Dante. "Have a good trip."

Dante marveled at the treasure trove of hard salami, cheese, and fruit inside the bag. "Thank you, sir. Thank you very much. This is really not necessary."

Before Dante could give back the bag, the old man started walking away, passing Adamo, who was returning from the bathroom.

"What's in the bag?" asked Adamo.

Dante opened the bag to reveal its contents.

Adamo pulled out the roll of hard salami. "Where did you get this?"

Dante smiled.

Adamo rubbed the night sand from his wine-filled eyes, and

held his hand up to silence Dante. "Don't even bother. Let me guess. The old man?"

"Yes."

"I am going back to sleep. Tell me when we get to Milano."

As the train pulled out of the Rome station and headed to Florence, Dante fell into a sleep so deep that he did not even wake when the train stopped in Florence and Milano, emptying itself of several passengers, and taking on many more.

When the sun rose, so too did Dante. He opened his eyes to find that while he was asleep, the props on the stage around him had changed. A spot in the aisle in front of him had become vacant. A set of expensive leather bags had been placed in the overhead racks; a family of four with a girl of mature beauty and tender air had assumed one of the nearby compartments. Dante studied the girl's curly black locks, broad shoulders, and majestic nose as she snuggled close to her mother. Her thick black eyebrows led the charge for her coffee brown eyes; her breasts rushed against her white dress. Her lips were full and soft, her chin cleft faintly. Though her age was yet tender, she was the most sensual creature Dante had ever seen.

Never shy about his own masculinity, Dante thought to himself about the pleasures of touching her lush red lips with his own, pressing his muscular chest against hers. The young girl perceived Dante's devouring carnal stare, and teased his appetite with a smile. Dante poked Adamo in the ribs. "Adamo. Wake up. Look at this one. She and her family must have boarded in Florence. I bet she is royalty, a real princess. Maybe they are Medicis."

Adamo, who was one year older than Dante, already had a steady girlfriend in Aquino whom he had promised to marry. He suppressed the tingle of the young traveler's inescapable beauty. "Don't be silly. If they were worth anything, they would not be next to us."

Ever persistent, Dante returned. "That is why they have seats."

Adamo reached into his bag for a comb to straighten his disheveled hair. "She is too young for you, Dante."

"Bologna," cried the conductor. "The train will stop here twenty minutes before continuing to Genoa."

With the train's wheels at a standstill, Dante's turned quickly, as he schemed about how best to get the young girl's attention without interference from Adamo. Even though Adamo had a girl-friend, Dante knew that his friend's competitiveness and old-fash-ioned self-righteousness might try to step between Dante and the young girl's radiance – a deliberate slip of the tongue, a not so inadvertent fumble – just enough to break the rhythm of Dante's pursuit. The trick was to be able to approach her alone; Dante knew that Adamo did not have the nerve to initiate contact.

"You're probably right," Dante smiled to Adamo. "She is too young." Dante reached into his pocket for some change. "This time I will go outside first while you watch the bags. I need an espresso. Do you want one?"

"Sure."

Dante hurried out of the train, but before exiting, tried to steal another smile from the young beauty by saying "Hello."

The girl turned away, clinging to her mother's stern arm.

His spirit heightened by the challenge of the mild rebuff, Dante continued his plot on the outdoor platform. There were two stands outside the station – one selling espresso and trinkets, the other newspapers. There was no line for the espresso, but several people waiting for the news. Perfect. Dante would bring Adamo an espresso, and ask that his friend return the favor by buying a paper. While Adamo stood in line for the news, Dante would have the time he needed to capture the maiden.

"Two espresso please," Dante asked the young boy at the espresso counter.

"Four lire," the young boy responded matter-of-factly. With a towel strewn over his shoulder and a pencil tucked behind his ear, the boy businessman's poised service was the accelerated matura-tion of an entire generation in Italy, children more fluent in sur-vival than playful banter.

As Dante downed his shot of rich black espresso, he noticed a small white stuffed pony among the trinkets for sale. "How much for the horse?"

"Five lire," answered the boy businessman as he wiped clean the counter.

"Five lire? For a tiny horse?" Dante gestured with his fingers. "For that kind of money it should gallop."

The boy businessman closed the deal by handing the pony to Dante. "Give me four lire."

Dante paid, tucked the pony under his shirt, and ran back to the train.

The boy businessman shook his head and smiled, as he continued to wipe the counter.

Dante handed Adamo the espresso that he brought for him. "Why don't you take a few minutes outside, get some fresh air in your lungs?"

Adamo outstretched his arms and yawned. "Yeah, I guess you're right. I need some cold air to wake up."

Adamo downed his espresso and made his way down the aisle. Dante called out. "Adamo. Grab a newspaper while you are outside. We should see what's going on."

With Adamo gone for at least five minutes, Dante had the opportunity to make his move. The girl was still attached to her mother, their legs crammed on top of their large suitcase; the baggage must have been too heavy for the family to lift into the empty overhead rack. The girl's white dress lifted just below her knee, revealing the feminine muscle of her calves. Dante could no longer restrain himself; he needed a way to impress the mother, so that he could hear the girl's voice and feel her breath. The suitcase. He had lifted barrels twice its size back in the vineyard in Aquino.

Dante dusted his pants, pushed back his hair, and approached the family. He smiled first at the object of his desire, then addressed the mother. "Excuse me, madam. But I could not help noticing how uncomfortable you must be with your legs on top of that suitcase. Is there anything I could do to help?"

The father responded sarcastically. "Maybe if you found three friends – all bigger than you – the four of you could lift it into the luggage rack."

The young girl smiled at her father's humor.

Dante looked into the girl's smiling brown eyes, then to her father. "May I?"

"Be my guest."

In one motion, Dante squatted, thrust the bag above his head, and placed it into the rack. He smiled as he wrung his hands in victory. "Just call me when you need to take it down again."

Impressed by Dante's ox-like strength, the girl's mother engaged him. "Thank you. What is your name, young man?"

"Dante Di Benedetto."

"And where are you from?"

Dante looked at both the mother and father to be polite. "A small town you have probably never even heard of. It's called Aquino."

"Of course we have heard of Aquino," replied the mother. "My name is Marietta Ponte, this is my husband Pietro, and our daughter Lucia. In fact, there is a young man from near your town who is very interested in taking our daughter Lucia's hand in marriage."

Lucia slapped her mother on the arm and blushed.

Slightly taken aback, Dante persisted. "But I thought you got on the train in Florence."

"No. When everyone got off the train in Florence, we found these seats. We are from the same province as you."

Dante turned toward Lucia's locks, lips, and eyes. "Well then, I guess congratulations are in order on your marriage. He is quite a lucky guy."

The mother looked at her husband. "Not yet. We are on our way to America. We have no idea what awaits us." She looked into her child's eyes. "She is still young. She is only seventeen."

The father asserted himself. "And where are you headed?"

"Same place. America. Jersey City to be exact."

Content that he might be able to close a conversation that had already gone on longer than he would have liked, the protective father answered. "Well, we are going to live in Brooklyn. I hear that it is very far from New Jersey."

Dante would not be deterred. Instead of ending the chat, he defied the father's challenge and pulled young Lucia back with the hook of his eyes. "Are you excited about going to America?"

Lucia shrugged her broad shoulders. "Yes, I am excited, but I am also a little scared. We have no family, and I do not speak any English."

"Don't worry, you will be fine. You are much prettier than anything America has to offer, and probably twice as smart. People will make it their business to learn what you have to say."

Lucia giggled, but would not take her brown eyes off Dante. He had made contact, struck a spark.

Adamo joined the group, with newspaper in hand.

Dante introduced Adamo. "These are the Pontes, Adamo. They are going to America, just like us."

"That's great," stated Adamo, who then broke the flow with a bit of news. "I was just reading in the paper that the police threw a group of guys in jail in Naples for trying to get on a boat to America without first serving in the military. Boy are we lucky..."

Dante interrupted before Adamo could halt his pursuit. "Yes, we are lucky...that our opportunity to go to America came after we served in the military." Dante changed the subject with another lie before the Pontes could inquire further. "We are meeting one of my cousins in Marseilles, France, and going to America to live with his family. Are you also leaving from France?"

"No. We are leaving from Genoa," answered the mother.

"Well, enjoy the rest of the train ride, and call me if you need help taking the bag down from the rack." In his hurry to end the conversation and get Adamo out of the way, Dante forgot about the stuffed pony he had stowed in his clothing for Lucia.

As they walked away, Dante punched Adamo in the arm. "What did you do that for, you idiot?"

Adamo smiled wryly. "What? What are you talking about? I did not do anything."

"You know what I am talking about. You were about to say how lucky we were because we have not been caught, even though we did not serve in the military. If I let you finish, you would not only have ruined my chances with Lucia, but would have us visiting the prison in Genoa."

"What chances with Lucia? You really are a dreamer. In ten

minutes, she will not even remember your name." Adamo stuffed the newspaper into Dante's chest. "Here, read about it for yourself. I am going to find the other guys."

As the train pulled out of the Bologna station, Dante sat back on his suitcase and read the newspaper Adamo had fetched, *Il Popolo d'Italia*. Adamo was right. The government was cracking down on young men trying to leave the country without serving in the military. Security and order suddenly were becoming a priority in a country where government was never paid attention, much less respect. Social currents and political tension were growing violent in Italy, and there was no clear arbiter to decide the outcome.

Though these issues and terms were not much part of conversation in the fields and piazzas of Aquino, they were becoming the subject of increasing concern everywhere in Italy. Dante continued to read the front page of *Il Popolo d'Italia*, drawn by the fiery rhetoric of the newspaper's publisher, Benito Mussolini, who only one year earlier had founded Italy's Fascist Party, *Fasci di Combattimento*, with but tens of followers in a small room in Milan. Despite his own electoral failure in November of 1919, Mussolini's support was growing, as was his zeal for social unrest.

On this September day in 1920, the thirty-seven-year-old Mussolini aimed the dagger of his words at all sides in the laborer takeover of factories that began at the Romeo works in Milan in August, and soon precipitated the worker seizure of several other factories in the Lombardy and Piedmont regions. A former Socialist now leading the Fascist movement, Mussolini at once applauded the workers' efforts in the takeovers and scolded the presiding government for not ending the dispute earlier. Dante read Mussolini's polemic. "A legal system centuries old was shattered. Our legal system of yesterday was this: the article labor on the part of the workman; salary on the part of the employer; and there it ended." Further along, Mussolini wrote that if the Government cannot act, "we invite the citizens, and especially Fascists, to prepare with all means to destroy the Bolshevik plans of the Socialist Party."

Mussolini's words were melodic, but their meaning was elusive. Dante could not tell whether the writer and his Fascists sought to lead the laborers toward better wages or protect the businessmen from further revolt. Dante was even less certain what he himself thought, and began to feel a headache. Perhaps the old man who dropped his wallet was not losing his faculties, but was instead suffering the same confusion and anxiety that seemed to afflict the entire country, and now Dante.

While Dante was still reading, Adamo returned in a huff. "The guys."

Dante folded the newspaper. "What about them?"

Eyes bulging, Adamo followed. "They are gone."

"What do you mean they are gone? They can't be. The guy in the White Suit gave us all the same deal. They are going to the same place we are – Marseilles."

"Not anymore. I looked all over for them. When I could not find them, I asked an old lady in the rear compartment if she had seen them. She said they were sitting near her until the train stopped in Bologna. They got off the train there and never came back, and their bags are still on the train. The police must have caught them. What are we going to do? The police will find us next."

The two boys crouched slowly onto their suitcase-seats. Dante's chest and stomach started dripping a cold sweat. He whispered. "Don't worry. We will be fine. So long as there are only two of us and we remain quiet, the police won't bother us. We are almost in France." Dante unbuttoned his shirt to cool his perspiration, and realized that he still had tucked away the stuffed pony he bought for Lucia. He held the pony against his mouth, and gazed wistfully at Lucia, whose smile-traced face slept on her mother's shoulder. Dante felt so close, yet so vulnerable. If someone like Spectacles could be caught, so could he, unless his cunning was somehow smarter than Spectacles' intellect.

When the train arrived in Genoa, Dante turned to Adamo. "Quick. Grab your bags and follow me."

"Why?"

Dante snapped back. "Follow me."

Dante moved quickly to reach Lucia and her parents before they exited the train.

As Lucia's father reached to retrieve the suitcase that Dante lifted earlier, Dante interceded. "Allow me, Mr. Ponte. I promised I would take it down for you. I am good for my word." He handed the bag to Lucia's father, who grunted a "thank you" before making his way from the train, commanding his family to follow.

Mrs. Ponte was not in as much of a hurry as her husband. "Dante, I thought you were going to Marseilles to meet your cousin. Why are you getting off here?"

Dante responded sanguinely. "Adamo and I are just trying to find a seat for the rest of the ride."

Mrs. Ponte smiled. "Well by all means, take ours. And thank you for helping my husband. He sometimes does not like to admit that he is not young and strong like you anymore." She stroked Dante's unshaven face with her worn hand. "Might we see you in America?"

Dante's voice rose. "You bet."

Mrs. Ponte turned to her daughter. "I will meet you outside. Don't get lost."

With Adamo hovering unshakably behind, Dante gave Lucia the stuffed pony. "I know you have to leave, and it sounds like you already have a boyfriend, but take this. I bought it for you in Bologna. When we get to America, I will find you, and we will ride a real horse together over the fields and across the rivers. Until then, keep this as a reminder."

Adamo muttered over his friend's shoulder and into his ear. "Didn't you say she was supposed to marry another guy? Are the three of you going to ride on the horse together – over the fields and across the rivers?"

Dante elbowed Adamo in the stomach, knocking the wind from his friend's lungs. He stared intensely into Lucia's eyes. "Wait for me. I will find you in Brooklyn."

Just when he thought he had created and controlled the exchange, Lucia kissed Dante on the cheek and ran out of the train.

As Dante stared at the space still warm with Lucia, Adamo slipped into the Pontes' seats. "Riding together over fields and across rivers. That is one of the best lines I have ever heard from you. What do you say, cowboy, why don't you take a seat?"

The conductor entered their car to make an announcement before Dante could respond. For theatrical effect, the conductor touched his cap and tweaked his curled mustache. "Ladies and gentleman, we will be stopping here for forty-five minutes so that we can change lead cars. The electric train, sent to us by our friends in America, will pull us over the mountains to the French border. You can either sit and relax, or step outside for an espresso. Thank you, and enjoy the ride." The electric train the conductor was so proudly referring to was the Westinghouse E550, an oddly shaped locomotive imported by Italy from America to traverse the heavy gradients and tunnels surrounding areas like Genoa. In a country ever struggling for national unity, Italian kings and heads of state had been obsessed with the development of railways linking the country.

Dante pulled himself out of his dream-like stupor, and addressed Adamo. "We can't sit down."

"Why not?"

"The border guards will find us before we reach France. We can't take a chance."

"So what are we supposed to do?"

Dante pointed to the overhead luggage racks. "Wait a minute until these people get off the train, and then get in the rack."

"You are crazy."

Dante smiled at the last weary couple straggling off the train. Once they were gone, he pulled down the shades to cover the surrounding windows, and cupped his hands as a step for Adamo. "Here, quick. Before anyone gets back on the train. Nobody can see us. There is enough room for us to get in the racks and hide behind our bags." Dante catapulted a resistant Adamo, threw the bags after him, and climbed into the rack. Once they were squeezed into place, Dante snickered to his friend. "Leave a little space for air so you don't suffocate."

Dante and Adamo lay motionless in the racks as passengers old and new started taking their places in the train. A man with small eyes and simple attire first settled into one of the two seats beneath Dante and Adamo. He placed his suitcase in the rack, banging Adamo on the head. The other seat was assumed quickly by a middle-aged man, dressed smartly in a three-piece woolen pinstriped suit. He inserted his suitcase next to the bag that shielded Dante.

After the two men were seated, Dante peeked through a gap in the overhead rack and saw the man with the small eyes reading the newspaper, while the other pulled a shining gold watch from his vest pocket and wound it repeatedly. Shortly after the train left the Genoa station, the frail hands that held the newspaper dropped, and Small Eyes began to sleep. The large hands that wound the gold watch kept at it in methodical turns back and forth. Once he was finished, Gold Watch placed his timepiece back in his vest pocket, and reclined in his seat. As Gold Watch stared toward the overhead rack, a smile started spreading across his otherwise steely face. Afraid he might be detected, Dante moved slowly away from the gap.

Dante and Adamo lay quietly in hiding, as the American electric locomotive pulled them slowly to the French border. Gold Watch's loud ticking kept the boys from sleeping. Dante began counting the ticks to keep his mind occupied. With each tick, Dante thought to himself, he was one second closer to America. Slow and sure, the American electric locomotive kept pulling.

When the train stopped hours later, Small Eyes awoke. He looked past Gold Watch out the window. "I wonder why we are stopping here."

Without hesitation, Gold Watch responded. "This is the last stop before the French border. The lead car has to be changed again, and border guards will be getting on the train to check passports and luggage."

Puzzled, Small Eyes shook his head, pretending to understand when he did not. "Oh, I see."

Dante's heart started beating rapidly. If the border guards asked to see Small Eyes' and Gold Watch's luggage, Dante and Adamo would be found. Dante's ears were filled with the thumps from his heart, intermittent with the ticks from the Gold Watch. Thump-tick. The border guard drew closer, the sound louder. Thump-tick, thump-tick. Through the crack, a view of Gold Watch sitting silent and content, a cacophony – tick-thump, tick-thump, tick-thump...

A border guard reached Small Eyes and Gold Watch, and asked

Gold Watch for his passport. After the young guard studied Gold Watch's passport to his satisfaction, he asked him to pull down his luggage so that it could be searched. Gold Watch removed a leather billfold from his jacket pocket instead, and held it open for the young border guard to read.

The young guard's smugness deteriorated quickly into embarrassment. "Signore Mestrone, I am so sorry. If I knew it was you, I would not have…"

Gold Watch held up his large right hand. "Don't worry, I know that you were only doing your job."

The border guard looked at Small Eyes, and back at Gold Watch for instruction. "Don't worry. He is with me."

The guard apologized again to Gold Watch, bowed, and moved on.

Small Eyes was completely baffled. "What just happened?"

Gold Watch explained. "I wanted to save us both the trouble of pulling down our heavy luggage. So I showed him my badge. I am a retired border guard captain."

"Oh. I see."

Dante's heart slowed, and he soon fell asleep to Gold Watch's suddenly sweet, ticking serenade.

Dante's ears were silent until hours later. A pair of large hands shook him gently on the shoulders. "Wake up. It's time to go. Wake up."

Still half asleep, Dante responded without opening his eyes. "Papa, I don't want breakfast. I will meet you in the fields."

The hands shook him again, this time with more force. "I am not your father. This is the last stop. If you do not wake up now, you will either be arrested, or find yourself in Italy again."

Dante's body jerked, waking up Adamo, and his eyes popped open. It was Gold Watch. Dante defended. "Leave us alone. We have not done anything. We are visiting a relative in France."

Gold Watch smiled. "I am not going to do anything. I just wanted to tell you that the train is in Marseilles." Gold Watch's smile widened. "May I assume that you are visiting your relative in Marseilles before boarding a boat to America?" Gold Watch helped the boys as they crawled out of the overhead rack and onto the floor.

Dante dusted off his clothing. "How do you know we are going to America?"

"I knew as soon as I sat back in my chair and saw you peeking through the overhead rack. That is why I showed the border guard my badge – so that he would not check the luggage and find you."

Ever suspicious, Dante continued. "Okay. So how many lire do we have to pay you so that you do not turn us in? We do not have much."

Gold Watch placed his large hand on Dante's, as Dante leafed through his wallet. "I do not want your money."

Seeing an opportunity to assert himself in a harmless situation, Adamo stepped in. "So then what do you want?"

Gold Watch gripped each of the boys by the shoulder. "I want you to have a safe trip to America, and once you are there, kiss the Statue of Liberty for my son. Like you, he always dreamed of going to America. He would have gone, but he never returned from the War."

Guilt weighed heavily on the back of Dante's neck. "I am sorry, sir." He lifted his brow. "But maybe your son did not die. Maybe we will see him in America."

Gold Watch clenched Dante's chin. "I wish you were right. I think he would have liked you."

Dante looked at Adamo, and smiled. "Could you do us one more favor? The last time we were looking for a port, we got lost. Can you tell us where the port is in Marseilles? We cannot really afford to get lost again."

Gold Watch roared with laughter. "You are quite the young travelers, aren't you?" Gold Watch put one arm around Dante's shoulder, and pointed out the train window with the other. "Go straight for four blocks, and then make a left. You can't miss it." Gold Watch then picked up his bag, and started getting off the train. "You better hurry if you want to see that relative of yours before the boat leaves."

XIII.

Balvina Gavroche

Following Gold Watch's directions, the two boys ran to the port. Once they arrived, they lowered their bags in awe before the boat that bore both French and American flags. Dante put his arm around his friend. "This must be it. Our ticket to America."

Adamo replied. "Speaking of tickets. Don't you think we should buy them first?"

"You're right. The guy in the White Suit never told us where we could find the booking agent here, did he?" Dante noticed a bar nearby echoing with the voices of other men. "Let's go to that bar and ask. I could use something to eat anyway."

The boys picked up their bags and walked excitedly to the bar that had no name. It was dark and filled with sailors – hard men, unshaven and dirty, sitting in small groups hunched over their drinks, inhaling each other's smoke. Dante and Adamo approached the bar meekly, and laid down their bags. The crowd quieted, and the bartender stared at the boys without speaking.

Dante looked at Adamo, cleared his throat, and addressed the bartender in Italian. "We would like two plates of macaroni, please."

The bar exploded with laughter. A thin man drinking alone at the bar stood on his seat above Dante and Adamo, and yelled to the audience in French through his yellowed and crooked teeth. "They want a plate of macaroni. Who is going to tell them they got off at the wrong stop?" The crowd laughed in unison. Crooked Teeth turned the back of his ear forward with his forefinger, and shouted again. "Shhh. Quiet everyone." He lowered his voice. "I think I hear their mother calling. I recognize her voice. The last time I was in Naples, she asked me for more after I was done with her."

As the mangy crowd continued to laugh at the boys' bewilderment, the bartender pulled Adamo by the collar, and spoke to him in broken Italian beneath the surly din. "There is an Italian place two blocks away named Rico. Get out of here before they stop laughing."

The boys rushed out of the bar, and Adamo held his forearm up against the late afternoon sun. "Nice going, genius. God knows what they were saying about us. Judging from their looks, they were probably wondering how we might taste for dinner."

"How was I to know they don't speak Italian? Let's find this place Rico that the bartender told us about."

The air that filled Rico was clearer, its chairs filled with men and women eating their dinner. Adamo and Dante approached the bar again, this time to address a sturdy barmaid who was busy stocking her shelves. Dante spoke again for the two. "We were told you serve Italian food here."

The barmaid turned and wiped her hands with her apron. To the boys' delight, she spoke in Italian. "What would you like?"

Adamo salivated. "Two plates of macaroni. And bread. Lots of bread, please."

The woman called the order to the kitchen, and turned to the boys. "That will be six francs."

The boys looked at each other, and Dante pleaded. "But we only have lire. We can't..."

The woman placed two glasses of water in front of Dante and Adamo, and put the boys at ease. "Don't worry. You can pay me in lire. I will send it to my family back in Italy."

The barmaid wiped the counter, and struck up conversation with the boys as she studied them through her sad and dark-bagged eyes. "What brings you to Marseilles?"

Sensing he had found a friend in the foreign port, Dante answered the barmaid. "We are going to America. Do you know where we can find an agent to buy our tickets for the boat?"

The barmaid tipped her head toward Dante's left, where a woman, her smooth skin at odds with streaks of gray in her hair, was drinking soup from a bowl that she held with her sinewy dirtied hands. The woman finished pouring hot broth down her long throat, then turned to Dante. While looking at him, she wiped her brown moled cheek, still wet with soup that her small mouth could not contain, with the thin dress that covered her rounded shoulder. "My name is Balvina Gavroche," she spoke in Italian. "I am the ticket agent. Tickets to America will cost you one thousand lire each. The boat leaves tomorrow at 7 a.m."

Dante responded politely. "Signora. The man in the White Suit who sent us here from Naples told us the tickets would cost only nine hundred lire each. And we did not know the boat was going to leave tomorrow. We have no place to stay."

Balvina Gavroche showed little sympathy. For her, everything was business. She tore a piece of bread from the plate that the barmaid placed in front of Dante, and chewed violently. When she finished, she continued the negotiation. "Very well. Give me nine hundred lire each, and you can work here tonight for the extra one hundred, as well as a place on the basement floor to sleep."

The barmaid crossed her hands as if to pray, and pleaded with Balvina Gavroche. "Madame Gavroche, please don't take their pay from our share. My husband and I need the money."

Balvina Gavroche threw back a healthy gulp of red wine to break up the dry bread in her mouth. "Don't worry, Giovanna. I will not penalize you and Salvatore. You can use some help for one night. But with four extra hands, I expect you to serve that many more people in my restaurant tonight."

Although Giovanna the barmaid was probably old enough to be Balvina's mother, she continued to comport herself as a servant. "Of course. Thank you, Madame Gavroche. You are very kind. Thank you."

Balvina Gavroche smirked at Dante. "And you?"

Beneath Gavroche's boorish ways and gruff demeanor, Dante began to sense a face robbed of its beauty not so long ago. He stared at her high and smooth forehead, draped with thin black and gray hair that could not have been combed but with a stroke of her bare hand, falling over deep inset eyes, whose blue-green color seemed to wane from the wash of tears shed in the dark. And the mole on her cheek, limp and faded, when it should be lighting up a smile. Dante began to feel a strange magnetism to the brutish exterior that protected the young girl beneath it all. He replied. "Yes, Madam."

"Where is your nine hundred lire each?"

Dante hit Adamo on the arm, collected the money, and handed it to Balvina Gavroche. She placed the money in her brassiere and got up from her bar stool. "See you bright and early tomorrow morning, boys."

Dante held out his hand. "What about the tickets?"

"You will get them tomorrow morning, after you have earned them. If you are late, they will go to the highest bidder."

Dante and Adamo gobbled two plates each of the hot macaroni and pork ribs that Giovanna served them. When they finished, they wasted no time putting themselves to work in the restaurant, picking up orders from Giovanna at the bar, and delivering them to the restaurant's many patrons. They worked as if they were playing a game, animated by the thought that their departure was finally in their grasp. It was not until hours later that the last customer finished his meal, and Giovanna locked the door for the day. The worn and weary boys slumped into the hard wooden chairs at the last table they served.

Giovanna returned from the door with a proud and unpracticed glow. "You boys did a great job. I do not remember the last time we served so many people." She retrieved a bottle of wine and three glasses from the bar, and joined the boys at the table.

Dante looked up. "Thank you. Are you going to have a glass of wine with us?"

"No. The third glass is for my husband Salvatore. I always serve him a glass of red wine at the end of the night, before we go to bed."

A short bald man emerged from the kitchen, wiping his hands on his apron as he spoke. "Giovanna. What are you doing? We have a mountain of dishes to wash."

Giovanna filled the three glasses with wine. "Come sit down, Salvatore. You have not even met Dante and Adamo. They worked very hard. I think we did more business tonight than we have in the past week. You and I can wash the dishes tomorrow, after the boys leave."

Salvatore sat down at the table shaking his head. "Giovanna, you are too soft. Those dishes will take hours to wash." Salvatore tilted his glass of red to his mouth, extending his right pinky finger toward his wife as if to touch her. He turned to the boys. "Where are you going tomorrow?"

Adamo chirped up. "The United States of America. We leave on the boat in the morning."

"Where are you staying tonight?"

Giovanna explained for the boys. "Madame Gavroche said they could sleep on the floor downstairs."

The grumpy man sneered. "She must have been in a good mood. Has a new boat full of sailors come into port?"

Giovanna scolded her husband. "Salvatore!"

Salvatore defended himself. "Ever since her husband left her, Balvina Gavroche has turned away from God. She should spend less time drinking with men, and more time looking after her son. That boy would be in jail had she not sold herself to the chief of police. We do all the work in this place, while she runs around with men and keeps half the profit. The least she could do is take care of her son."

Giovanna looked down at the table. "Salvatore, it is her restaurant. And she did take us in when no one else would."

"I know, I know. It has been a long day. I just feel bad for her boy. He needs parents."

Dante tried to change the subject. "What about your children? Where are they?"

Giovanna choked up, and a small tear filled her eye. Salvatore placed his hand on top of hers. "We do not have any children. We prayed for many years, but children never came. That is why we left Italy to live here. The pain became too much." Salvatore smiled at his wife. "We will go home someday. Our families write to us all the time telling us how much they miss us."

Giovanna then spoke. "I am fortunate to have Salvatore. He is a strong and loving man. Poor Madame Gavroche has no man. She is alone in a crowd with her child, deserted."

Dante did not want to interrupt the tender moment that was

being shared by husband and wife. He rose slowly from his chair. "It has been a long day. I think Adamo and I should get some sleep. We have to wake up early tomorrow morning."

As her husband continued to hold her hand and sip his wine, Giovanna instructed the boys. "The basement is through the kitchen. I will be down in a few minutes with some blankets and pillows."

Dante lifted a quick smile. "Don't worry. We will be fine. Take your time."

After Giovanna set the boys' makeshift beds, Adamo went to sleep instantly, his head clear. Dante tried to do the same, but could not. While his head spun with thoughts of the perils ahead, a rat ran across his feet, startling him fully awake. After calming himself down, he slept lightly on the cold basement floor. He did not want to miss the boat, and have Balvina Gavroche auction off their tickets to the highest bidder.

Sometime after midnight, Dante was wakened by the smell of a burning cigarette. He sniffed and called out into the darkness. "Who is it?"

The sound of two measured footsteps came from above, and a figure emerged.

Dante whispered. "Signora Gavroche. What is it?"

Balvina Gavroche crouched next to him, and whispered with a breath thick with smoke and wine. "It is about your tickets. You must come with me right away."

"I will wake Adamo."

"That will not be necessary. Come with me. Alone."

Balvina Gavroche led young Dante out of the building, to a port side area behind the restaurant. She faced Dante square, and slid his hand beneath her dress atop her bosom. As her nipple grew hard under Dante's touch, Gavroche turned her head away to blow a puff of smoke. She could feel Dante's youthful energy charging her breast. "How badly do you want to be on that boat?"

"What are you talking about? What are you doing?"

While Dante trembled, Gavroche eased his back onto the dirt

ground. She straddled Dante on her knees, and laid her burning cigarette on a brick next to his head so as not to waste it.

"Signora Gavroche…"

She placed her finger over his quivering lips to still them. After peeling off Dante's shirt and loosening his pants, Gavroche licked the salt from his body until he was erect in the moist Marseilles air. Gavroche lifted the skirt of her dress, and consumed Dante within her hearth.

As Gavroche moved slowly with poise, Dante turned his head to focus on the cigarette burning on the brick. His thoughts were with Lucia, with whom he had dreamed of being forever just one day earlier. He had to save himself, as he had been taught by his parents and village, both of whom he had abandoned. The image of his church pastor flashed through his head. Dante clenched his jaw, and hardened his stare at the burning cigarette.

When Gavroche began to ride him more rapidly, Dante could not resist looking up at her. She ripped open the blouse of her dress, and let it drop to her waist. A medallion of the Virgin Mother clung to her sweating breasts. Dante fought to pull back the pleasure, but Balvina would not be denied.

The full moon shining brilliantly in the night was swallowed by a passing silver cloud. Dante's virgin thrust threw back Balvina's head, causing her to cry out in ecstasy, him to lose his breath. A fishing boat's bell rang faintly in the distance, as the odor of dead catch wafted from the shore.

While Dante breathed heavily with eyes closed, Balvina buttoned her blouse and retrieved her cigarette still burning on the brick next to Dante's head. When Dante opened his eyes, Balvina was standing at the water's edge, smoking her cigarette with arms crossed, staring out upon the sea. Without thinking about it, Dante dressed himself and walked to Balvina's side.

Balvina blew a puff of smoke into the sea. "Don't believe what they say about me. I am not a bad woman. My husband left six years ago to avoid the war, and I have not seen or heard from him since. I know he will be back. In the meantime, I must live."

Balvina threw the cigarette into the sea, and turned to Dante. She held one of his cheeks, while she kissed the other. She pulled back with a smile. "I will always remember how I was your first."

Before Dante could stage a protest, Balvina started walking away. "Get some sleep. The boat leaves in four hours."

Though a fortnight of ebb and flow awaited him in a ship's steerage – and decades more after that – Dante Di Benedetto, without plan or preconception, had traveled his passage.

He was seventeen years old.

XIV.

Voices From a Black Box

Paying a Premium

Two boys from a small town in Italy, just off the boat that brought them, stood awestruck in the middle of New York City, with little more than their wits and a suitcase each. They stared as passersby looked down upon them from the imposing altitudes of their Model-T Fords, Briscoes, and Templars, while others rushed by foot to get their copy of the increasingly popular tabloid, the *New York Daily News.* Two men, dressed smartly in suit and hat, stood together on the street corner, next to Dante and Adamo.

Eyes popping, Dante gasped as he caressed the rear wheel guard of a passing Ford. "Adamo, someday we will drive a car like that, shiny and new. Maybe we will have two for each of us, one for the week and another for the weekend."

Suppressing a yawn, one of the two men on the corner responded to the other, as he studied the stock prices listed in the newspaper he was reading, tapping the brim of his hat as he spoke. "I don't care what the experts say. I think Baldwin Locomotive and U.S. Steel are still good buys."

Adamo chided Dante at a nervous pace. "Forget about shiny new cars. You are crazy. First we have to find jobs. What will we do? You are a grape farmer in a country where wine is illegal, and I am a butcher in a city that probably already has one on every corner. We don't even speak English."

The other of the two men on the corner muttered to his friend from the side of his mouth, so as not to expend too much energy.

"Ruth hit another home run last night. I guess he is worth the $125,000 the Yankees paid the Red Sox for him. What I would do if I had that kind of money to invest in the market. We would be standing in the Hamptons right now."

Dante gave Adamo his signature vise-like grip on the shoulder. "We need to find my Uncle Carlo and get out of these clothes. This country has already been waiting too long for us."

One of the two men on the corner used his handkerchief to dust his lapel. "I heard the police arrested another group of Reds last night. Damn Bolsheviks should learn to keep to themselves." He then clapped his hand with the rolled newspaper he was holding in the other. "What do you say we meet at T.J.'s at 7? Since Prohibition, his homemade gin has been the best in town. It's so good, he is thinking about giving up his regular job." He downed an early laugh with his friend. "See you there at 7?"

"Right-o."

Dante and Adamo walked into a young country that, like them, was working through its own adolescent insecurities and yearnings; yet, despite its vulnerability, it would take years of labor and assimilation to understand and conquer even a small corner of the new land. It was evident in the crowded streets, where thousands of people, some with dark leathered faces and coarse clothing, brushed with those whose fair complexion was protected from the sun by a fashionably cut hat and veil. Horse-drawn wagons carrying produce from the docks drove alongside new cars making their way to Wall Street and the shopping districts. Young boys in stylish suspenders and knickers accompanied their glove-handed mothers to the market, where they purchased their food from miniature men their same age. Amidst the frenzy were sailors returning home victoriously in uniform, carrying their blue cloth bags proudly over their shoulders. In the event the flow of humanity became too heavy or the threat to the tenuous order too great, policemen buttoned and badged in imposing gold were planted at every other corner.

As the two walked south on West Street, Dante's mouth was drawn open by his accelerating step, while the rest of his body swelled with excitement and sensory overload. "This is it, Adamo.

We are finally here. For a while, I thought we would never get off that boat. I can't wait anymore. Let's ask someone how to find my Uncle Carlo in Jersey City."

Dante stopped a woman who was walking toward them, her long hair pinned beneath her hat, one of the stitches on her hemmed skirt undone. He spoke in Italian. "Excuse me, can you tell us how to get to Jersey City?"

Understanding nothing other than that Dante had mentioned Jersey City, the woman placed her soft pale hand on Dante's shoulders, and mouthed words through her wet painted lips that he could not understand. Dante stared at the woman's lustered lips as she smiled and called for two policemen from across the street. Having discharged her duty, the woman removed her ivory hand from Dante's shoulder and pushed on, leaving a sweet fragrance in her wake.

Adamo chided Dante. "How many times do I have to remind you that we are not in Italy anymore? These people do not speak Italian." The policemen started walking towards Dante and Adamo. "Now look what you've done, you jackass. As soon as they hear us speak Italian, these two cops are probably going to throw us in jail."

Dante talked himself out of the momentary spell the woman's paint and perfume had cast over him. "Well…then…maybe you would like to speak to them in English." He turned and looked Adamo directly in the eye. "I keep forgetting how many different languages you know. Stay quiet. I will find out from these cops how to get to Jersey City without getting us arrested."

Dante and Adamo knew that for all of its attractions, America had not embraced Italian immigrants with open arms. Though it had not yet reached its full notoriety in the United States, the arrest of Nicola Sacco and Bartolomeo Vanzetti in May of 1920 for a robbery and murder in Massachusetts had already resonated throughout Italy, including Aquino. Like visitors in another person's home, Dante and Adamo knew that they had to be polite and circumspect, particularly when dealing with men in uniform. But Dante refused to be intimidated, for he believed that the only meat law enforcement preyed upon more than disrespect was fear. Now that the policemen were upon him and Adamo, Dante would not shy away until he got what we wanted. This time, he did not speak. Instead, he pulled out a piece of paper with his Uncle Carlo's name and address on it, and folded the paper so that only the address, not the name, was visible. He presented it to one of the policemen.

The policeman read it with squinted eyes and showed it to his partner. His overfed face looked down from beneath his hat and over his badge. He spoke to Dante slowly, in a patronizing manner. "Yeah, so what? If you are asking me whether I have ever been to this address, the answer is 'no.' I can barely even read it."

As Dante and Adamo looked at each other confused, the two policemen shared a chuckle at their expense.

Dante grabbed the piece of paper back from the policeman, and gestured to Adamo that he needed a pen. The policemen were confused. Adamo pulled a pen out of his back pocket and gave it to Dante, who circled "Jersey City" on the piece of paper, and inserted a question mark next to it.

The policeman's partner spoke. "Jack, I think he is asking us how to get to Jersey City."

The policeman pointed downward to the street repeatedly, and spoke loudly to Dante and Adamo as if it would help them understand him better. "This is West Street and Fiftieth." He then pointed south. "You have to walk twenty-seven blocks to the Lackawanna Ferries on Twenty-third Street." The policeman opened his mouth wider and spoke slower for more volume. "The Lackawanna Ferries. Twenty-third Street.""

The boys continued to stare blankly at the policeman, who, frustrated by the communication gap, took the piece of paper and pen back from Dante, and wrote "Lackawanna Ferries" underneath the address. He showed Dante what he had written, and pointed south again. "Lackawanna Ferries." He held up two fingers from his left hand, three from his right. "Go to Twenty-third Street."

The boys bowed their heads in thanks, first Dante and then Adamo, before making their way.

The policeman who gave the instructions to the ferries turned to his partner. "Probably just off the boat. Where do you think they came from?"

"I don't know. But they sure did smell. Don't they have soap in Europe?"

Bouncing steps ahead, Dante threw his suitcase upon his shoulder, as he and Adamo headed for the ferries. "Nice guys, but the one seemed a little dumb. I have always heard that Americans are not as smart as Italians."

The two new arrivals walked south toward the Lackawanna Ferry Terminal, acclimating their eyes and ears to sights and sounds they had never before seen nor heard. The apartment houses that lined West Street were built very simply: three- to four-story buildings laid of red brick. The first floor of each building was a store that showcased an array of prizes for purchase. Inside every doorway, block after city block, there was something to buy: fresh meats, bread, fruit, clothing, paints, and hardware. And just beyond them in the background were mammoth towers, scraping heights to which Dante and Adamo had never paid homage except to beg mercy from southern Italy's oppressive sun. Other buildings still in progress were scaling even higher.

Dante pointed to one of the buildings that was being riveted, hammered, and sawed by no less than one hundred men. "I guess this is what the kid with the spectacles was talking about in Naples. I bet he wishes he was here with us."

"Yeah. I wonder what happened to those guys. They probably went home after they got thrown off the train."

While Dante and Adamo pushed downtown toward the Lacka-wanna Ferry, a salesman shouted from within a growing audience, as he fiddled with a dial on a small black box, set on a card table. The black box had attached to it a copper wire, and a cord with a headset at its end. The salesman held the ends of the headset apart. Voices cames through the headset, albeit faintly. The crowd drew close to listen, forming a huddle around the salesman and his black box. Dante and Adamo joined the huddle, Dante mumbling quietly to Adamo. "Jesus Christ. I think I hear voices. Where are they coming from?"

Adamo pointed to the salesman. "It's probably him. I think I see his lips moving."

"It can't be. He is talking at the same time as the other voices."

Adamo stood on his toes to look behind the salesman. "Maybe there is another guy back there doing all the talking."

Dante extended from his toes to join Adamo. "No one."

Suddenly, the salesman turned toward Dante. He grabbed Dante by the hand to pull him next to the black box. He looked at Dante, then addressed the audience. "Ladies and gentleman, I have said enough. I will let this handsome young man show you the wonders of this magnificent new breakthrough, the crystal radio. Young man, if you would please tell everybody your name."

Dante looked around. All eyes were on him. The town square in Aquino had trained him how to handle audiences, but never without understanding the script – he was always the narrator, and never the prop.

The salesman inserted some humor into the moment. He stage whispered for everyone to hear. "What's the matter, son, does the cat have your tongue?"

Dante's heart raced as he looked from one laughing face to the next, until he found Adamo telling him in Italian that the salesman wanted him to say his name. "*Il tuo nome. Il tuo nome.* Dante, Dante!"

Dante smiled and thrust his arm into the air, clenching his fist. "Dante!"

The salesman moved the dial, and invited Dante to do the same. "Very well, Don. If you will just turn this knob for me." The salesman moved his hand away from the knob to spread apart the ends of the headset, nodding for the huddle to listen.

Reading the salesman's body language rather than his lips, Dante guessed correctly and started rotating the knob slowly, liberating a battery of voices from the black box. While continuing to turn the dial, Dante peered at the faces watching him, their mouths agape. Dante too was amazed, but sensed a ripe audience. He rotated the dial further, and moved his mouth for the huddle as the black box spoke through the headset, adopting the voice as his own. The huddle began to smile. When he reached a female voice, he continued to move his mouth while making feminine gestures, pushing his hand against the back of his head, buckling his left knee inward, and twinkling his eyes. The huddle roared with laughter, and stepped back to applaud.

The salesman dismissed Dante in order to regain the audience's attention and pitch his sale. "Thank you, Don." He wrested the radio back from a still entertaining Dante, and barked to his customers. "Step right up, ladies and gentlemen, and place your order for this wonderful new breakthrough, the crystal radio. Get 'em while they last."

When Dante rejoined Adamo, his friend asked, "Where the hell were those voices coming from?"

Dante glowed. "I don't know, but this country is going to love us. Let's go."

After about one hour of walking, Dante and Adamo reached the Lackawanna Ferry. There were eight slips in all, some filled and others empty. People on foot, trucks, cars, and horse-drawn wagons jockeyed to get a good position on the ferries. Dante drew a deep breath, and took his first stab at the English language. "Jair-c Cit-y?"

A red-haired ferry clerk fixed his blue eyes on Dante. "We can hear you. You don't need to shout. Over there, slip number 5."

Dante did not understand a word the red-haired clerk uttered, but was able to follow the point of his freckled finger. There was a crowd around the booth at slip number 5, and Dante and Adamo eventually muscled their way to the front.

This time, Adamo pushed his rugged friend aside, and spoke for the two of them. "Jer-sey Cit-y please."

The woman inside the booth shook her head "yes." "That will be ten cents each, sir."

Dante reached into his pocket and slapped one lira on the small wooden counter.

"American money," the woman smiled. "You're in America."

As Dante and Adamo stood flustered, there were anxious calls to move from behind. The redheaded clerk was watching; he stepped up, and thrust four fingers before their faces. He took four lire each from Dante and Adamo, reached into his own pocket to give two dimes to the woman in the booth, who in turn issued Dante and Adamo their tickets.

As Dante and Adamo walked the gangway, the woman in the booth called out to the redheaded clerk. "You turned another trick, didn't you, Red?"

"Let's just say those two guinea-wops paid me their price of admission to the U.S. of A."

XV.

Liberty Green

Ice and Coal

The ferry took almost a half hour to cross the Hudson River. The boys had barely settled on board and caught a rear glimpse of a giant statue of a green woman in the water, standing tall holding a torch, when the ferry docked in Jersey City. There was a surge for the dock. Once again, Dante and Adamo were speechless in search of an unknown destination, this time Uncle Carlo's house, at 550 Atlantic Avenue.

Studying each house number as he went, Dante stopped finally when he read a gold stenciled "550" on the windowed doors of a row house. He lowered his bag to the sidewalk, and unfolded the tired piece of paper that contained the address, its edges frayed and print faded from repeated readings and showings during the journey. As Dante looked at his little treasure map, a bead of sweat fell upon the barely visible text. His eyebrows sprouted confirmation, and a content smile streamed to his ears. He stuffed the now useless piece of paper back into his pocket, and threw his thick arm around Adamo's narrow shoulder.

"We made it, buddy. This is it."

Neither boy moved, as they gawked at the grandeur of Uncle Carlo's house. Though ordinary through any American set of eyes, the coffee-colored steps seemed wide and inviting to its visitors, each rising confidently to the tall front doors, made of thick wood, a precious commodity back home. The doors were painted light green. The facade was auburn brick, its windows and threshold embellished with concrete moldings, each also painted a light green.

Adamo spoke first. "This is incredible, Dante. Your uncle's house is beautiful. And look, the door is the same green color as that big statue of that lady we saw from the boat. I heard one of the Italians say it is called the Statue of Liberty. That must have been what the guy on the train wanted us to kiss for his son. That statue was something else, huh?"

Dante looked starry eyed. "I guess I really didn't notice when we were on the boat. For some reason, this looks better than the statue. This is real."

"I've never seen that color green before," Adamo said while gawking at the door. "It's so pretty. I wonder if it has a name."

Dante opened his mouth wide with a smile as he stared at the house. "If that tall lady in the water was the Statue of Liberty, I guess it's called liberty green."

"Are you sure this house belongs to your uncle, and not to some president or king?"

Dante pointed down the row of houses beside Uncle Carlo's. "You saw it on the way in, you see it now. They are all the same, block after block. In this country, everyone can live like a king, and paint their doors liberty green. And this is only the beginning. Come on. Let's meet my Uncle Carlo the king and get something to eat inside his palace. I am starving."

Dante and Adamo walked up the coffee stairs and knocked on the liberty green door. When no one answered, he pounded harder. A woman approximately thirty years old, amply set and pregnant, opened the door wide.

Dante addressed her in Italian. "I am Dante from Aquino, Stas and Antonia's son. This is my friend..."

Before Dante could finish his sentence, the woman wiped her hands dry on her apron and hugged each boy with a kiss. She spoke hurriedly in Italian. "Dante, Adamo, welcome. I am Connie, Carlo's wife. We have been waiting for you." She pulled back from her embrace, and looked at both of them. "I am sorry I didn't answer the door at first, but I didn't hear you." She turned to the doorbell and pushed it, creating a buzzing sound in the front hallway. "All you had to do was push the button."

Dante shook his head at Adamo, realizing that even in the simple act of entering Uncle Carlo's house, his new surroundings confounded him. As his pregnant aunt hauled the boys' bags into the house, Dante pushed the button, laughed giddily at the buzz, and looked at Adamo.

Adamo shrugged his shoulders. "I don't know."

A young man a few years older than Aunt Connie stepped into the hallway, standing slight, beaming beneath his thick coiffed hair. He continued the welcome in Italian, slower and deeper. "Dante, my nephew, you are late. Where have you been?" Without any need for introduction, Dante's Uncle Carlo threw his thin arms around Dante's barrel chest. "Welcome." He turned to his wife and seven-year-old son, who had scampered behind him. "Connie, bring them some food. Anthony, help your cousins bring their bags to the extra room."

The three men and Anthony sat around the kitchen table, which was covered within minutes by Connie's generous servings of bread, salami, pasta, rice, and homemade wine. Carlo peeled his suspenders off his shoulders, and uncorked a large green glass jug of red wine. Without asking, he poured a tall glass for Dante and Adamo, then filled his own before lifting it for a toast.

"To..."

Eyes begging, young Anthony stood on his chair and thrust his empty glass in front of his father. "Papa?"

"Okay," replied his father. He bent over and held his index finger and thumb an inch apart. "But just a little bit, and only in this house. The police can arrest you for drinking this. They will throw you in a room with mean men, and you will never be able to eat your mama's pasta again."

Uncle Carlo reassumed the toast position. "To one hundred years of health, happiness, and family." They each took a gulp of the thick red.

Anthony coughed from the alcohol, jolting a penny from his shirt pocket onto the table.

Uncle Carlo laughed, picked up the penny, and again raised his glass. "Thank you for reminding me, son. How could I forget?" He held the penny like a priest would a Eucharist at mass. "And to fortune. To one hundred years of fortune as well."

Dante stood smiling and raised his glass higher. "To fortune."

As Uncle Carlo passed the salami and peppers, and his wife doled out the pasta and rice, he polled the boys about the journey. "So what took you so long? Your father's letter said that you would be here days ago. We were starting to think maybe you had second thoughts and decided to go home."

His mouth dripping, Dante chomped through the bread and peppers so that he could respond. "No. No second thoughts. This is where we want to be. It is just that the trip did not go exactly as planned."

"Was there trouble?"

Dante looked at Adamo to keep him silent, then spoke slowly. "No trouble." Dante squelched any curiosity his uncle might have about the journey by catering to his ego. "Adamo and I are amazed by your house, Uncle Carlo. What can we do to be as successful as you? It's probably too late for us already. There's not enough time."

Uncle Carlo sat proudly at the head of his table of plenty and his wife's serving hands. "I have worked twelve hours a day for years building my barbershop business. I started by sweeping the floors and just watching the old masters cut the hair of other men."

He waved his fork like a maestro would his baton. "The way they combed it."

He picked up his knife and glided it slowly beneath his chin. "And then finish with a smooth shave. They treated their work like art, and made their customers feel like men."

Uncle Carlo resumed eating. "That is how I made it in America. I watched, learned, and then did it myself. Who would have thought that I would own a business in the United States? I don't even speak English. You are both welcome to join me at my barbershop. You can start as I did by sweeping the floors."

Adamo spoke up immediately. "I would like that if you need the help."

"Absolutely. What about you, Dante?"

Dante looked down at his bowl of pasta. "That all sounds great, Uncle Carlo, and I am grateful. It's just that I am used to working outside, and…"

Uncle Carlo interrupted. "You do not need to explain to me, my nephew. Your mother and father warned me that I might have a problem keeping you inside four walls for an entire day." He tore with his hands a piece of bread for Dante, then shook it between Dante's face and his bowl of pasta. "I have already spoken to my friend, Ruggiero Cuorduro, who owns the largest ice and coal delivery business in Jersey City. He has four sets of horse-drawn wagons. He is originally from Naples. He told me he could use some extra help. It involves a lot of hard labor."

Dante's head shot up from his bowl. He grabbed the bread his uncle offered. "Does he really need someone?"

"You will have to be at his barn down the road at 3:45 a.m., and when he says 3:45, he means it."

"I will be there."

Uncle Carlo stuffed his mouth with rice. "Well then let's hurry up and finish eating so that we can go tell Cuorduro you would like to work for him."

Dante and Adamo inhaled their meal, the sooner to enjoy the dessert of the evening's brisk autumn air.

XVI.

❦

An After-Hours Tailor

As Dante, Adamo, and Uncle Carlo walked up Atlantic to Bergen Avenue, Dante felt as though the entire city was built specially for him. The freshly cut lines in the sidewalk, the gas that sputtered light into the street lamps, the horses that pulled an oncoming streetcar – it was all for him. Dante was the center. Everything else radiated from him, because of him.

Dante noticed that his uncle was carrying a brown paper bag. "Uncle Carlo, what do you have in the bag?"

"A pair of pants that need to be fixed. We are going to drop them off at the tailor. That's where we will meet Cuorduro."

Dante looked incredulous. "But it is after 8 o'clock."

Uncle Carlo smiled. "That's okay. Tonight is the night the tailor stays open late."

The three walked another block until they reached a storefront window with a name inscribed in it: Ventilli Tailors.

Uncle Carlo knocked on the front door. When no one answered, he knocked again.

Dante pressed his face up against the window. "Uncle Carlo, are you sure that tonight is the night this store is open late? It looks dark."

"I am positive. Just wait."

The door opened, and a bald man appeared with a tailor's ribbon measure around his neck. "Carlo, how are you?"

Carlo introduced Dante and Adamo. "Mario Ventilli, I would like you to meet my nephew Dante Di Benedetto, and his friend Adamo Petrozzini. They just arrived from Aquino." Carlo held up the paper bag and smiled. "And they need a pair of pants fixed. I am sorry we are late."

"Of course. Come in, come in."

Mario closed the door behind them, and pulled down the shades. He led the trio to the middle of the room, and lifted a door that was built into the floor. A carnival of light, smoke, and laughter erupted from the opening. Mario grinned. "I do my best work downstairs."

Uncle Carlo gestured for the boys to proceed. Dante and Adamo walked gingerly down the stairs to find a room filled with men drinking, smoking, and playing cards around a table.

Mario yelled from behind. "This is my evening staff." The tailor jockeyed by to assume his empty seat at the table, and invited them to have a drink and join the game. "Come, we're on break. Have a drink with us."

"Uncle Carlo, what is this?"

Carlo whispered back to his nephew. "Since the government outlawed alcohol, this is the only way we can drink together. It's the best thing that ever happened to Mario. I don't think he has sewn a pair of pants in weeks."

Dante noticed that most of the men were drinking red wine, but a few were slugging a gold liquid from tall glasses. Dante grabbed a glass of the gold, and poured another for Adamo from a pitcher. He celebrated out loud. "Adamo, this is great. They even have strega, just like at home." Dante was referring to the sweet yellow liqueur that was popular in southern Italy. The table quieted as the two downed what they thought was strega.

Both boys frowned as if they had sucked bitter lemons. Dante struggled through repeated coughs. "This isn't strega."

A thick dark man sitting at the head of the card table removed a black Oscuro cigar from his mouth, and spoke from his unshaven face. "We don't serve strega at this bar, my young friends. We drink wine and beer. If you are looking for something sweeter, maybe we can get you some candy." The group laughed. The man with the Oscuro cigar continued. "Isn't it past your bedtime?"

Uncle Carlo stepped in to introduce the boys to the man with the Oscuro cigar. "Ruggiero Cuorduro, this is my nephew that I told you about. Dante Di Benedetto. And his friend Adamo."

Cuorduro stood up in front of Dante, almost a full head above him. He blew a cloud of cigar smoke into Dante's face. "It's a pleasure to meet you. But maybe you should be in bed. You are supposed to be at my barn for work tomorrow at 3:45 in the morning."

Dante squinted from the irritation of the smoke, and looked straight back at Cuorduro. "I will be there."

Cuorduro jerked his head toward Adamo. "And what about him?"

Uncle Carlo put his arms on Adamo's shoulders. "He is going to work with me at the barbershop."

"Good. His back does not look strong enough to lift much more than a comb."

Uncle Carlo finished introducing the boys to the rest of the group, then pulled two chairs to the table for them. Cuorduro exhaled his fumes over his pile of winnings, and dealt the table another hand. "Carlo, do they want to try their hand at poker?"

His nose still in a nasty hold from the cigar smoke Cuorduro blew in his face, Dante began to signal that he wanted cards.

Uncle Carlo grabbed Dante by the arm. "No. They will just watch tonight." Uncle Carlo continued to squeeze Dante's forearm, and whispered in his ear. "What are you doing? You don't even know how to play poker. Remember what I told you at dinner – watch, learn, and then you can do it yourself."

Dante had not even started work yet, and he already despised his new boss, Ruggiero Cuorduro. On the way back to the house that night, he asked his uncle, "What is wrong with that guy Cuorduro, and his big black cigar?"

"The black cigar is called an Oscuro. He is always smoking one, even in the morning. I think he sleeps with them. He smokes so many of them we call him Cuorduro L'Oscuro, or simply L'Oscuro. He is a little rough, but very successful. L'Oscuro is a good name to know in Jersey City when you need something done, especially if you are thirsty. If you don't think you can work for him, tell me now, before you begin."

Dante snickered. "No, I will gladly work for L'Oscuro. Someday he'll work for me."

XVII.

Shpeaking English

At 3:15 the next morning, Connie knocked on the door of the room where Dante and Adamo were sleeping. When there was no answer, she whispered, "Dante. Wake up. It is 3:15. You are supposed to meet L'Oscuro at 3:45. You have just enough time for the bread and coffee I made you."

Dante answered groggily. "Okay, Aunt Connie. I will be dressed and out in a minute." Dante pulled his mother's blue knit blanket over his body, and turned to his other side to continue sleeping.

Fifteen minutes later, his Uncle Carlo returned to the room with neither a knock nor a whisper. "Dante. Wake up. You are not even dressed yet, and you are supposed to meet L'Oscuro in fifteen minutes."

Dante sprang from his bed immediately, and pulled off the floor the pants he had laid there the night before. He buttoned his shirt nervously. "Don't worry, Uncle Carlo, I will make it on time. Tell Aunt Connie I will take a piece of bread with me."

Dante ran into the kitchen, where the familiar faces of parental concern awaited him. "Where do I meet L'Oscuro?"

Uncle Carlo finished gulping his second cup of black coffee of the morning. "Up the hill to Bergen Avenue. Make a right. Three blocks to your left you will see L'Oscuro's barn. You better run."

"I will." He kissed his Aunt Connie on the cheek and grabbed a large piece of crispy bread from the table. Dante spoke crudely through his chewing. "I will see you tonight."

Dante sprinted through the fall mist that hung in the still dark night, and began to perspire by race's end. He opened one of the doors to L'Oscuro's barn that was slightly ajar, and was greeted by a waiting ready column of four horse drawn wagons, all but one of them saddled with a pair of men. In the silence, L'Oscuro sat visibly angry with a partner in the first wagon, the left side of his lips hugging his trademark black cigar. He drew the smoldering black beast from his mouth and looked at his watch. "It is 3:55 a.m. You were supposed to be here at 3:45 a.m." L'Oscuro escalated his syrupy voice to a yell. "Didn't you hear me last night when I said 3:45?"

Dante looked down and nodded his head yes. His scorn for L'Oscuro boiled him in more perspiration. The sweat from his pores splattered loudly onto the straw beneath his feet.

L'Oscuro growled again. "Get in the last carriage with Guido before you collapse. You do whatever Guido tells you. He is your boss."

L'Oscuro turned to the rest of his waiting crew. "Let's go. If we are lucky the German will still have ice left for us. If not, no one eats, and you can blame your new friend who likes to sleep."

Dante jumped on the last carriage driven by Guido, as it began its slow trot from the barn. As soon as Dante settled into his seat, he offered his new partner a handshake. "My name is Dante. Dante Di Benedetto. As you can see, I am neither a friend nor relative of L'Oscuro. He just doesn't know me yet."

Guido acknowledged Dante with an overbite and nervous jerk of his head.

Dante was eager to make a friend in the darkness. "Well, it took L'Oscuro yelling at me to find out that your first name was Guido. I would hate to see what I have to do to find out your last name."

The roundish Guido, who was five years Dante's senior at twenty-two, let slip a smile through his simple eyes and large mouth. "Scarpetto." He gave a handshake back to Dante. "My name is Guido Scarpetto."

Dante wrapped his arms across his chest to keep warm. His teeth began to chatter. "Where are we going for the ice that he is in such a hurry?"

"Hans Hauffman's House of Ice. It is run by a German."

Unable to help himself, Dante responded. "Really? Judging by the name, I would have guessed he was from Naples."

They both laughed again, putting Guido at ease. "Yes, the German is very tough. If you are late, he does not care. He does not deal in faces or friendship, only numbers. He's just like all Germans. Very tough. Only numbers."

Dante retrieved Aunt Connie's bread from his pocket reserve, and offered a piece to Guido. "Then it serves him right that he has been sentenced to a life in a house of ice."

Guido spoke proudly of their boss as he accepted the bread. "Luckily, L'Oscuro's numbers are large, and the German is always willing to make an exception for him."

L'Oscuro's caravan of horse-drawn wagons pulled up to the large brown sign painted in cream, "Hans Hauffman's House of Ice." A single wagon was exiting the rear with just two blocks of ice in its bed, and a worker appeared to be closing the front door before L'Oscuro waved him off.

Guido looked at Dante concerned. "For your sake, I hope the German saved L'Oscuro his ice."

The wagons drew to a stop inside the House of Ice, and after one of the laborers inside the House called out "Hans," a lumbering figure appeared from the recesses. Built hardily, with blond hair and shaggy mustache flaked with chunks of ice, Hauffman bore an inescapable resemblance to a walrus. He was not happy, and L'Oscuro knew it.

Out of respect, L'Oscuro removed the smoldering black beast from his mouth, left it with his riding partner, and approached Hauffman with hat in hand. With uncharacteristic meekness, he addressed the German. "'ans…"

The German interrupted L'Oscuro. "Ants? Vut am I, some kind of insect you shtupid guinea?"

He turned to his employee soldiers who had filed in neatly behind him. "Is dis vut da guinea calls us ven he is late? Ants? Do vee look like ants? He and his guinea vorkers – day are dee ants."

The German's troops laughed smugly.

The German approached L'Oscuro, and stood inches away, face to face. "Before you ask me anything, you shtupid guinea, I vant you to say it right – Hans Hauffman's Haus of Ice."

L'Oscuro stared back. "'ans."

The German stamped his foot and yelled. "Hans!"

"Hans." L'Oscuro paused before continuing. "Hauffman's 'ouse…"

The German pounced on his h's. "Haus. Haus, you shtupid idiot."

L'Oscuro finished quickly. "House of Ize."

The German began his interrogation. "Vhere have you been? You know dat dare vere many men already here who vould have gladly taken your ice, and paid more for it? Some of dem were your shtupid guinea friends. I could tell by the shpaghetti sauce on their shirts."

The German's troops laughed again.

L'Oscuro spoke quickly. "I am sorry…" L'Oscuro stopped himself abruptly to concentrate on pronouncing the German's name correctly. "…Hans. It will never 'appen again. It's joost dat today, I 'ave a new boy, and ee was-a late."

The German snapped back. "And dis is my fault?" The German shook his head and pointed to the corner. "Go ahead. Take your ice. I saved it for you. But dis is da last time. Next time, you pay. You should take some of the money I shpared you today, and pay for some lessons to learn to shpeak English, you shtupid guinea."

L'Oscuro thanked the German profusely, and marched to the carriage manned by Guido and Dante, where, back in his native tongue, he gave furious orders to Guido under his breath. "You can help him load the ice." L'Oscuro looked coldly at Dante. "But after that, you are to go the tall one on Bergen Hill, and you are not to lift a single piece of ice. He is to carry all of them."

Guido pleaded in defense of Dante. "But L'Oscuro, the tall one is six stories high, and usually takes three of us. He can never finish it alone in one day. The ice will melt."

L'Oscuro's wagon partner ran over to give him back his cigar. Re-armed with his black beast, he pointed it at Guido's hands. "If I find out that those fingers touched a single piece of ice today, you are done. Whatever melts or is not finished will come out of his pay." He looked back at Dante. "Nobody embarrasses L'Oscuro."

Dante and Guido loaded their wagon with the thirty blocks of ice that were to be delivered to the tall one on Bergen Hill. Each block weighed one hundred pounds, enough to keep a family's food refrigerated until the next day's delivery. En route to Bergen Hill, Guido tried to console Dante. "I will help you. There is no way you can deliver the tall one without another set of hands. L'Oscuro will never find out. He was just upset because the German embarrassed him."

While Dante sponged the sweat off his forehead using his sleeve, Guido reached behind his seat and gave Dante a clean rag. Dante covered his entire face with the towel. "Don't worry about me, Guido. I am not going to get you fired. At this rate, you may be the only friend I have. But tell me, how could the German humiliate someone like L'Oscuro? I thought everyone bowed to the one with the black cigar."

Guido prodded the horses toward the slightly brightening horizon above the hills ahead. "In this country, money is king. There are no dukes or contessas like in Italy. In America, whoever has more money has more power. The German has more money than L'Oscuro, and that is why he can treat him that way." Guido chortled. "But you should have seen the German during the war, he wasn't quite as loud then. Lucky for him, this country has a short memory, especially when it comes to business."

When Guido and Dante arrived at the tall one on Bergen Hill, Guido pointed it out. "There it is, the tall one. Six stories, five apartments on each floor. You won't be able to carry each of the blocks up the stairs before they melt. C'mon, I will help you."

Dante held Guido down by his shoulder so he could not rise from his seat. Dante studied the tall one, and noticed on the top floor an American flag shooting diagonally from the building's side into the air, its pole planted to the building's facade in a heavy metal casing. The flag made a ruffling sound in the cool morning wind, calling for attention. "Those six windows under the flag. Where do they lead?"

Guido squinted. "Those are the windows at the end of the hallway on each floor."

Dante's mind turned. "Where is the nearest junkyard?"

Guido pointed across the street to a man removing a chain from a gate. "Over there. Why?"

"Pull the wagon beneath that row of windows. I will be right back."

Dante returned twenty minutes later with a hooked cable, a large thick burlap sack with ringed holes at the opening, and a pulley. He spoke through his huffing. "The flag." He pointed and swallowed. "I will hook the pulley to the metal casing holding the flag, and slip the cable over it. I will put two or three blocks of ice in the sack, and hook it closed with one end of the cable. Then I'll hook the other end of the cable to the back of the wagon, and all you will have to do is draw the horses forward to lift the sack to the hallway window where I will be waiting. I will unload and deliver the ice on each floor." He smiled. "You will never have to touch a single piece of ice. Just as L'Oscuro ordered. We'll finish early and you will still have a job."

Guido looked at Dante in disbelief. "How did you pay the guy at the junkyard?"

"I didn't. He was Italian, from Puglia. He said I could pay him when I get paid. C'mon, let's hurry. If we get back soon, maybe L'Oscuro will give us a raise – or maybe even one of his big fat cigars."

L'Oscuro pulled into his barn early that day, and found Dante relaxing on a bale of hay. Guido paced nervously beside him. Sensing a victory, but puzzled by the comfort that Dante was enjoying, L'Oscuro dismounted the wagon and approached Guido. "How many blocks of ice melted before he could deliver them? How much does he owe me?"

Guido responded quaking. "None, sir. He didn't lose any."

L'Oscuro tilted his head to the side and downward to get under Guido's scared glance at the ground. "And how many of the blocks did you carry for him?" He shook his finger. "Don't lie. I'll find out the truth."

Dante rose from his hay couch, holding over his shoulder the pulley-cable-sack he had assembled. "He didn't touch the ice. I did it all myself." Dante pulled the contraption off his shoulder to display it. "I put this together. I loaded the sacks with ice. I unloaded and delivered the ice." Dante threw his invention to the ground, and extended his dirty hand. "Now where is my day's pay?"

L'Oscuro reached into his pocket, pulled out a wad of single dollar bills, and placed two in Dante's palm.

Dante shot his head forward toward L'Oscuro. "The deal was three dollars a day. Where is the other dollar?"

L'Oscuro spoke around his black beast. "You did not work the entire day, so you are not entitled to an entire day's pay."

Dante picked up his pulley-cable-sack and started exiting the barn.

L'Oscuro called after him. "Where are you going with that thing? That's mine."

Without turning back to face L'Oscuro, Dante kept walking. "I was going to give it to you after you paid me the three dollars. But now if you want it, you will have to pay me the full three dollars for the day, the additional two dollars it cost me, and another dollar profit." Dante stopped and turned. "If you don't pay me, I quit. And I take my property with me."

L'Oscuro pulled the four-dollar ransom from his roll, and threw it to the ground. "Be here at 3:45 tomorrow morning."

With L'Oscuro gone, Dante scooped up his money, and looked at Guido in delight. "There goes your theory that the guy with more money has all the power. I guess brains count for something in this country." He stuffed the money in his pocket and stood up. "C'mon. Let's go pay the guy from Puglia, and I will buy you something to eat. You pick the spot."

The two new friends walked out into the clear blue sky, the bulk of their day still ahead of them.

XVIII

Passing Through an Iron Gate

A Virtuous Tutor

Dante and Adamo scampered through their initial weeks in America like two children set loose in a candy store. Propelled by challenge and the endless promise of money, their appetite for their new country was insatiable. With Uncle Carlo as their captain and Guido Scarpetto as their third musketeer, they grabbed and consumed as many treats as they could find: going to the Polo Grounds to watch Babe Ruth smash the red-laced white ball with his wooden bat; finding a crystal radio to hear the first radio broadcast, the election of a man named Warren Harding to be President of the United States; poker and booze in clandestine bars; sitting in the movie theater, marveling at the vampish Theda Bara in the film *The Blue Flame*, immersing themselves in the seduction of it all.

But the glitter of the autumn pageant was soon overcome by the cold and dark of winter; realities new and old began to set in. Instead of a playful face-off with the Germans in their House of Ice every morning, Dante and Guido took L'Oscuro's wagon to the rail yards to pick up their day's worth of coal for delivery. Dante hated the black rocks, whose grime inevitably found its way into his hair and lungs.

The days were shorter and quieter, freeing Dante's mind to think more about Aquino, and his little sister Annunziata. Every time the bitter air or coal's soot made him cough, Dante thought of his ailing sister. At night in bed, when he cuddled in fetal position beneath the blue blanket his mother knit for him, Dante thought about Aquino and Annunziata. But he would not allow himself to write to his family – at least not until Christmas – for that would be perceived as a sign of weakness and longing. Based on his family's failure to write him, Dante suspected that his father's thinking was the same.

Instead, Dante began directing his energies toward the conquest of America. If it had not happened already, Dante knew that his time as visitor would soon expire, and he would have to begin cutting his swath as an American. Otherwise, he could easily fall complacent in his small community, achieving little more than an American version of Aquinan success: the financial rewards enjoyed by his Uncle Carlo, or in limited circles, the petty power of people like L'Oscuro and the German, but never a notoriety that reached beyond – a status that would raise his competitive stare above those he perceived as ahead of him, a station that would lift his soul from the mire of fear and envy. Dante had been in America only a short time, but knew that his clock was already running. He craved wealth and influence, and was not willing to wait for either of them.

So it was that Dante convinced Adamo and Guido that, after their hard day's work, they should all start getting lessons in English. Dante asked his Uncle Carlo if he could help find a tutor.

While picking up some clothing from Mario Ventilli, the tailor, Uncle Carlo mentioned it, speaking in their native tongue. "Mario, my nephew Dante..."

Mario interrupted. "Hey, how is he? Things were a little rough between him and L'Oscuro at first, huh?" He cut a thread on his teeth. "I would not fool with L'Oscuro."

"He's fine. He and L'Oscuro are fine now. But you know, the kid is a little crazy. He won't sit still. He wants to learn English. Do you know anybody?"

Mario extended his hands open. "Why does he want to learn English? Tell him to take a look at you and me. We have more money than we ever dreamed of on the other side, and we don't even know how to salute this country's flag without that little card they gave us when we became citizens."

Uncle Carlo shook his head. "I know, I know. I told him he is wasting his time, but he won't listen. Do you know anybody?"

Mario unfolded his glasses, black and thick, from his shirt pocket. He leafed through his handwritten diary of business records. "There is this wealthy banker, I think he is English." Mario found the name in the book. "There it is." Mario struggled to say the name. "Bur-tone Alessander." He wrote it out on a piece of paper. "B-u-r-t-o-n A-l-e-x-a-n-d-er."

"What are you suggesting? That my nephew pays some wealthy English banker to teach him the language? I think you have been drinking too much of your own stuff."

"Of course I am not saying that the banker will teach him English." Mario raised his hand. "If you would let me finish."

"Very well."

"What I was going to say is that this guy loves Italian suits. I think he lived in Italy for a while. Anyway, he comes in about three times a year for me to make suits for him. The problem is, he can't speak a word of Italian."

Carlo interrupted. "But I thought you said he lived in Italy?"

Mario folded his glasses back into his pocket. "I know. Can you imagine? Italian is beautiful. I think these English are savages."

"So how does he tell you what he wants?"

Mario raised his forefinger. "When he comes in for his fittings, he brings his daughter as an interpreter. Her name is Kay. She is finishing high school. She speaks fluent Italian. He sends her to Italy every summer to travel and study." He pounded his chest with both hands. "We run away from the place to come here, and the Englishman pays to send his daughter there for vacation. You have to see her, with her blond hair and blue eyes, speaking Italian. You won't believe it."

"When are they coming in for his next suit?"

"Saturday. I will ask her if she gives lessons." Mario handed Carlo the rest of his garments, and grinned devilishly. "You will drop off more clothes on Wednesday night?"

"Of course."

"We'll be downstairs, as usual, working away."

The contact was made on a Saturday, and after work the following Monday, Dante, Adamo, and Guido marched to Dickinson High School in Jersey City for their first English lesson. The school was a mammoth concrete fortress, four stories high with proud friezes carved into its center portals. There was grass all around, upon which the children stood and played. The great lawn was sliced with a series of long concrete staircases that scaled the hill leading to the school. At the base of each stairway were tall iron gates that served as the only perimeter entry to the otherwise fenced grounds.

The trio approached one of the closed gates tentatively. Dante grabbed two of the bars to the gate with his hands, and pressed his sooted face between them for a better view. From the inside looking out, he appeared a prisoner desperate for his freedom.

Staring at a knicker-panted boy roughly his same age walking carefree with a plaid-dressed young girl, Dante asked the others, "Are we sure this is the high school? It looks more like a monument. We must be in the wrong place."

While Adamo stood silent with eyes wide, Guido responded. "This is it, guys. Trust me."

Dante turned to Guido. "How are we supposed to get through this gate to meet the girl?"

Guido pointed slowly over Dante's shoulder. Dante turned and saw at the top of the staircase a blond young girl, with eyes sparkling blue, smiling in a white dress. Though her appearance was plain, a modest radiance emanated from her long blond hair, along her straight waist and down her slender legs. The boys were thrown aback when her thin pink lips began to speak to them in Italian. "Dante? I am Kay Alexander." She turned to the others with the same white-toothed smile. "And you two must be Adamo and Guido? Are you ready for your first lesson?" She walked down the steps, and with ease pushed open the heavy iron gate. "It is open. Come in. I have a classroom for us inside."

As the boys climbed the steps in single file behind Kay, a group of students began to gravitate toward the blonde and her visitors. Two tall and thin boys, both light haired beneath the cap they each wore, walked alongside Dante, Adamo, and Guido, and gawked at them as if the three were animals in a zoo.

One of them thrust his face toward Adamo jeering him. "And who are you? I don't remember ever seeing you around here before?"

Adamo cowered and looked the other way.

The taunters knew from the confused look on the trio's faces that they had what they wanted – immigrant meal. The other of the duo called out to Kay. "Hey Kay, tell us about your new green-horn friends," referring to them by the generic pejorative that was branded on all new immigrants who were yet unaccustomed to American manners and ways. "Where are they from?"

Kay continued to lead the trio, and responded without looking at the duo. "They are from Italy. Leave them alone."

Kay's irritation served only to entice the duo further. One of them looked to the other. "Brendan, I think we have ourselves some new guinea-wop friends. Maybe we should check their passports. You never know, they might be Reds."

"Good idea, Ned," said Brendan as he moved toward Guido, who was walking in the third spot in the moving procession, behind Kay and the already humiliated Adamo. "Let's ask the fat one." Brendan extended his cap toward Guido. "Excuse me, Mr. Guinea-Wop. May I see your papers?"

Guido looked back at Dante nervously, who pointed ahead so that Guido would keep walking.

Ned moved on to Dante. "How about this one with the black face?" Ned pointed to the soot that was thick on Dante's cheeks and forehead. "He is worse than a guinea-wop. I think he is a Negro-Darkie. Must have come from down South." Ned stepped between Guido and Dante to halt the procession and face his victim directly. "Excuse me, Mr. Guinea-Wop Negro-Darkie. I am talking to you. Where is your passport?"

Kay, Adamo, and Guido stopped and turned, as the small crowd of students looked on. Ned continued the attack. "What's the matter? It's bad enough that you are stupid. Maybe you really are a Negro-Darkie. Or maybe you are deaf."

Although he did not understand the words being leveled at

him, Dante felt assaulted by the mean curl of his perpetrator's lips. Despite his best attempt to harness his anger, Dante had been pushed beyond the limit. He moved a step closer to the taller Ned, moving within an inch of his nose.

A tense silence filled the air.

With the crowd watching, Brendan whispered to his friend. "C'mon, Ned, we've had our fun."

Ned pushed Brendan away. "Don't worry. This guinea-wop has no fight."

Without breaking his glare, Dante slid his suspenders off his shoulders slowly, first the left, then the right. As he rolled up his left sleeve over his bulky forearms, Kay pulled him away and spoke to him in Italian. "Dante, let him be. He is a fool." As she held Dante's shoulders, Kay could feel the rage trembling inside him. She glanced at Ned, and continued her diplomacy with Dante in Italian. "Look at his pants, he does not even know how to zipper them."

Dante peered out of the corner of his eye at the boy's open fly. He smirked.

"What are you looking at, Guinea-Wop-Darkie?" Ned stepped up.

Dante stepped back, and pointed to the boy's open zipper.

Ned's crowd started to laugh.

Embarrassed, Ned pulled up his zipper, speechless. He glared at his followers to silence them.

It was just enough to cool Dante, and Kay sensed it. "Let's go inside and begin what we came here for – your English lessons."

Dante acquiesced, and Kay and her students continued their way to the school.

Ned turned to Brendan. "I told you. No fight in those Guinea-Wops." He poked Brendan in the ribs. "Let's go throw the football."

XIX.

A Crown of Hot Peppers

At their first lesson, Kay gave each of the boys a blank tablet that they were to use for their daily writing exercises. The boys struggled through their classes and homework, reaching for the "h" in words like "house" and "Thursday," and learning to drop their reflexive "a" and "o" from the end of words that Kay translated for them into English. Though arduous for Dante, it was his eagerness to learn, and the anticipation of being with Kay, that made tolerable each day's labor at the command of L'Oscuro and his dreadful coal.

On a snowy Friday afternoon in December, the boys finished their work early before what was to be their last lesson with Kay before the Christmas holiday. Kay had told them to wear their best clothing, and not to make any plans for that night. She had said she had a surprise for them. Dipping into their earnings, they each went out and bought a new shirt, tie, and jacket. Though still a bit disheveled and uneven in attire, the boys felt like millionaires in their new duds. They strode proudly to the school that would not otherwise have them.

From her desk, the teacher directed her students through their exercises. She spoke to them in Italian. "Okay, guys, before we finish I am going to give each of you a letter. You are to repeat for me a word that begins with that letter, spell the word, and use it in a sentence – all in English. We will begin with you, Adamo. We will start in the middle of the alphabet with the letter 'J.'"

With knickers, suspenders, and short red necktie, Adamo rested his chin on his clenched fist that was bolted to his desk by his elbow. "J." He paused. "Jolly. J-o-l-l-y."

Kay smiled as she wrote the word on the chalkboard for the entire group. "Very good, Adamo. Now use it in a sentence."

There was a twinkle in Adamo's eyes. "Eet ees da sea-son to be jo-ly."

"Excellent," rejoined Kay.

Adamo continued. "Fa la-la-la-la-la-la-la-la."

Laughing out loud, Kay went on to Guido. "All right, Guido. The letter 'K.'"

Guido fidgeted to create space in his new jacket, and took off his new cap to wring it. He looked straight up for divine inspiration, and quickly down again. "Ket-tle. K-e-t-t-l-e. Wit- da ket-tle, I make-a my café."

Kay applauded her student. "Great."

Guido matched Adamo with a follow-up. "Some-a-times I use da ket-tle to make-a my cafe black, udder times wit a leetle milk-a."

Kay shook her head in disbelief. "You guys are too much. Now you, Dante. The letter 'L.'"

Due to his competitive nature, Dante's word had to be the best. He wanted to impress Kay. With his bow tie largely knotted and crooked, he stood upon his shiny new shoes. Poised, he uttered, "Liberty. L-i-b-e-r-t-e."

"Excellent, Dante, but you spelled it wrong." She went to the chalkboard and wrote the letter "Y" and pointed to it. "Liberty ends in a 'Y,' not an 'E.'"

Dante pleaded his case to Kay in Italian. "But how can that be? You say it 'libert-e.' The letter 'e.'"

Kay pulled a penny from her pocket and walked to Dante's desk. With her long pale forefinger, she pointed to the front of the shiny new penny, to the left of Abraham Lincoln's profile. "Liberty. L-i-b-e-r-t-y. Now use it in a sentence."

Dante took the penny from Kay, and looked at his friends before addressing her. He held the penny with the same reverence as did Uncle Carlo on Dante's and Adamo's first night in America. "In Ameriga, da money ees liberty."

Kay rolled her lips inward and eyebrows upward. She spoke

in Italian. "Yes...Yes...Bravo, Dante. Brav-o." She stood up and clapped. "Bravo to all of you. You have progressed wonderfully."

Dante nodded at Adamo and Guido, and they all approached Kay together. Dante spoke in Italian. "Kay, you have been so good to us. Spending all this time every day. We have learned so much. We want to show our gratitude." Dante reached into the pocket of his new shirt, pulled out ten dollars and extended it to Kay. "We have been saving this money to pay you."

Kay was touched to the brink of tears. Her father gave her twenty dollars every month as petty cash spending money, but she knew it was worth exponentially more to the boys. She pushed Dante's hand away. "I can't. I do this because I enjoy it. Because I am fond of the three of you. I refuse to take your money." Before they could rebut, Kay stood up with a wide smile. "But I have something for all of us. Do you have any idea why I asked you to dress up today?"

They looked at each other confused.

Kay pulled an envelope from her pocket. She lifted the flap and removed four tickets. "My father gave me four tickets to see *Gianni Schicchi* at the Metropolitan Opera House in New York City."

The boys smiled lukewarmly, still confused beneath their jumbled tie knots and mismatched attire. Although the local bands at home sang the operas of Donizetti, Verdi, and Puccini in Piazza De Gesú in Aquino, they had not heard of Puccini's *Gianni Schicchi*.

Disappointed that the boys were not more excited, Kay thrust the tickets forward in her grasp, her Italian emphatic. "C'mon, guys. *Gianni Schicchi* by Giacamo Puccini. I have four tickets for tonight. I saw it in New York with my parents two years ago when it debuted. It is beautiful. My parents got the tickets through my father's bank, and they don't want to see it again. So they gave them to us."

With the mention of Puccini, the boys lit up, and the air was suddenly filled with elation and giddiness. Dante turned to Adamo, and hit him on the shoulder. Not having previously known the opera himself, Dante pretended otherwise. "Puccini, you idiot. It's his new opera."

Familiar with his friend's tricks, Adamo followed Dante's lead. "Of course. Puccini." He turned to Guido, and hit him. "Puccini."

Guido lifted both of his arms, and his belly shook. "Puccini. The great one!"

While walking the school's polished corridors, Dante started singing the opening line of Puccini's famous aria, "E Lucevan le Stelle," from an earlier work with which both he and Adamo were familiar – *Tosca*. With his deep voice, Dante belted out "*E lucevan le stelle* [And the stars would be shining]..."

They kicked open the school's doors like swashbucklers. The stars were hiding behind the falling snow, into which they marched merrily.

As they walked down the long steps toward the street, however, the two boys who had previously teased them – Ned and Brendan – were waiting with three others. The opera singing ceased. A cold gust of wind blew by.

With his hands behind his back, Ned stepped up to Kay. He looked downward. "Kay, we wanted to apologize for what we did to you and your friends last month. So we made you a little something."

Ned had to keep himself from giggling as he brought his right hand from behind his back. He held a makeshift wire crown that had a green pepper planted upward on each side, the flaming hot variety that only Italians were known to enjoy. "We crown you Kay, Queen of the Greenhorns." Ned turned to his laughing followers, and then placed the crown on Kay's head. "It's made of those nasty peppers that your guinea-wop friends love."

A tear streamed down Kay's cheek as she wore the crown. "You bastard."

When Ned cocked his hand to gesture a slap at Kay, Dante stepped in. In one swift motion, he grabbed the collar of Ned's coat with one hand, and twisted the thick wool into the boy's throat. He spoke to the bully in English. "You no toch-a our friend Kay." With his free hand, he removed the crown from Kay's head by grabbing one of the green peppers. He shook the rest of the crown to the ground, and placed the green pepper in front of Ned's mouth.

"Now you eat-a dis."

Ned stood silently on his tiptoes, quaking under his cloak.

When Ned refused to open his mouth, Dante twisted his woolen collar tighter into his throat. Through the falling snow, the only sound that could be heard was the muffled snap of Ned's top button inside Dante's grip.

Choking, Ned coughed and called out to his troops. "Guys? Where are you? This guinea can't do this to us."

Dante laughed, and turned Ned around to show him that all that remained of his friends were their scared footprints. Dante jerked the tall boy back to face Kay, and again placed the fire pepper to his lips. "Eat."

Ned grimaced his way through three bites beneath Dante's chokehold, his mouth ablaze with the pepper.

Kay finally persuaded Dante to let go. "C'mon, Dante. If we don't leave now, we will be late for the opera."

Dante threw Ned to the snow-covered ground, dusted his jacket, and extended his elbow for Kay. Adamo and Guido joined on Kay's other side. Dante looked down at the fallen Ned. "Now if you weel ex-cuse us, we are going to da o-pera." Dante resumed the aria that Ned had interrupted, and the journey to New York continued.

Once they were gone, Ned shoveled snow into his mouth to cool it.

On their way back from the opera that evening, the trio and the Kay skipped through the snow, their hearts light with music's content. It was the first time the boys had been to an opera house to enjoy the majesty of their native art, having heard it sung only in the open-air piazzas back home. They laughed, sang, and chased each other with snowballs, without a care in the world.

Short of breath to continue to play, Kay stopped running and began to tell a story to keep her boys entertained. "If you think that opera was good, I bet Puccini's new opera will be even better."

Dante packed another snowball. "New opera? What new opera? What are you going to teach us about our country and our Puccini now?"

"When I was in Florence last summer, I heard Puccini was working on a new opera." Kay shoved her hands in her pockets, and looked up at a cluster of stars that was breaking through the clouds. "It's about a foreign prince who tries to win the love of a jaded Chinese princess. It is supposed to be his masterwork."

Dante aimed his snowball at a light post, and picked off the three icicles that hung from it. Impressed with his marksmanship, he looked at Kay. "What's the name of this new opera?"

Kay was still busy looking at the stars. "*Turandot*."

Before Dante could push another breath from his interested smirk, Guido and Adamo smashed a giant snowball over his head. Dante hesitated, but then gave chase to his assailants.

The story of *Turandot* would have to wait.

XX.

A Most Unappetizing Feast

Christmas Eve arrived at Uncle Carlo's, the most sacred meal of the year for Italians on both sides of the Atlantic. Uncle Carlo, his son Anthony, Adamo, and Dante crammed around the family's new dining table as Aunt Connie prepared diligently the hallowed *sette pesci di sette mare* – seven fishes from the seven seas. A bowl full of boiled *gamberi*, the crunchy shrimp that Uncle Carlo's son Anthony loved to eat with his hands, sat waiting at the table; watching the little boy devour it reminded Dante of his little brother Francesco. Next, Aunt Connie served a platter of fried *capitone*, the eel appetizer brought home alive in a sack, accompanied by its smaller fried smelt companion, *pescaril*. As an intermezzo, Uncle Carlo passed around the *scungilli* salad that he had prepared, the slices of boiled conch that were showered with lemon juice, garlic, and oil.

The aroma of red sauce tiptoed from the kitchen. Uncle Carlo and the boys knew that the linguine pasta and three last fruits of the sea were not far behind. When Aunt Connie walked through the dining room door, Dante saw in her the face of his mother Antonia. She brought *calamari* for each of them, a large squid stuffed with breading. She shuttled back with a plate filled with steamed *cozze*, the mussels that were separated from their black shells only after an effort. And finally, Aunt Connie's *baccalà*, the cod that she had soaked in her bathtub of fresh water for the past three days to rid the dried fish of its salt.

Uncle Carlo tried to make conversation with Dante and Adamo, both of whom sat mute. He cut into his stuffed squid. "So what do you boys think of your first months in America? Dante?"

Dante sat with his face against his fist, twirling his linguine slowly around his fork without looking at it. His eyes glazed over. "It's good. But it is cold. I can deal with L'Oscuro, but when it's cold...And the coal. I hate it. It's so dirty. Kay. She is very sweet. I like her."

Uncle Carlo and Aunt Connie conversed without speaking, his raised brow asking her if she thought Dante might be interested in Kay, her quick head shudder responding that he should not pursue the issue with his nephew.

Uncle Carlo moved on to Adamo. "And I know Adamo is doing very well. Everybody at the barbershop has told me how polite and hardworking he is. You will be cutting hair in no time, boy. Just a little while longer lathering and watching."

Before responding to Uncle Carlo, Adamo reached for his cloth napkin to wipe his mouth. By accident, he knocked over a glass of water that spilled on Dante's lap.

Dante yelled at Adamo. "You jackass. Can't you do anything right?"

Aunt Connie interceded with her own white napkin. "Don't worry, Dante, it's just water."

Adamo stuttered. "Unc- Uncle Carlo. I – I was wondering if it would be okay if I worked somewhere else after the new year. I have a great opportunity."

Uncle Carlo sucked a mussel from its black shell. "Of course. What is it? Tell us about it."

Dante dropped his fork and looked on in shock.

Adamo smiled. "I wanted it to be a surprise." He looked at the dumbfounded Dante. "To all of you. I have always loved numbers and finance. Kay asked her father, who said I could work as a clerk at his bank. He said I could help attract more of the Italian clientele from Jersey City."

Dante rose abruptly from his seat.

Uncle Carlo called out, "Dante, where are you going?"

"To my room. I am not hungry. Merry Christmas."

Adamo excused himself politely, and followed Dante to their room, where Dante was sitting on his bed with his blue blanket over his knees. "I thought you would be happy for me. This could be good for both of us. Kay's father deals with a lot of important people."

"Why didn't you tell me before? We tell each other everything."

Adamo sat on his own bed across from Dante. "I didn't think you would care. Besides, I thought you might talk me out of it. I have been doing a lot of thinking, and the kid with the glasses at the train station in Naples was right. I need a plan. I can't live like you, day to day, dealing with each new situation as it comes up. I am not that quick. I need a plan, and this is it. We came here for money. I am going to work where money is made – in a bank."

Dante extended a handshake across the divide. "I am sorry for getting upset. Congratulations. It's just that fat bastard, L'Oscuro, and his filthy coal. I wish he would choke on one of those black cigars."

Both boys laughed.

Dante continued. "You are right. I need a plan too. I have to have a plan." Dante yawned. "But first I need some sleep. You are not going to become wealthy before morning, are you?"

Adamo was glad that his friend no longer seemed upset. "I don't know what you are complaining about. You are still going to be making more money than me."

Dante pulled the sheets down his bed. "Just call me the King of Coal. Merry Christmas, Adamo."

"Merry Christmas, Dante."

Dante was not sleepy; he just wanted to be left alone. Wrapped under his blue blanket, he lay with his face to the wall, straining to make himself cry and purge his isolation. But the tears would not run; his eyes were chapped and dry. For hours, his mind spun with thoughts of the vineyard in Aquino. When he fell into a light sleep, he saw his mother holding little Annunziata in the middle of the field. The sickly girl was crying in Antonia's arms while Stas and Francesco worked the fields. When the image of Stas and Francesco focused, Dante noticed that instead of picking grapes from the vines, they were pulling coal. Black coal. When they looked up at Dante, their faces were caked with soot.

Dante leapt out of his bed, and went to the kitchen to fix himself a plate of Aunt Connie's leftover linguine with *baccalà*. He lit a candle on the table, and sat to write a letter to his family. He would eat three more plates before he finished the letter. Dante brought the letter with him to work the day after Christmas. At the end of the day, he bought a box of candy for Annunziata, and went to the post office to send home the package. To make up for lost time, he sent his first mail home first class.

XXI.

Walking Above the Birds

The Cobbler's Helper

The winter air thinned gradually, and the sun began to share more of its warmth. The boys continued their English lessons with Kay, and Adamo was enjoying his work with Mr. Alexander at the bank. Despite his pledge on Christmas night, Dante never took the time to develop a plan. He was content that the days of black coal were winding down, and he would soon resume the long season of delivering the clear and clean ice. L'Oscuro was not bothering him, and among the other young men working in the wake of the black cigar, Dante had become somewhat of a legend because of his initial defiance. Dante had his audience, and for the first time, a modest amount of money. He was not ready for a change, nor was he inclined to think about one.

Instead, a yearning for female companionship preoccupied him. Though he tried hard to forget it, Dante was haunted by Balvina Gavroche's sweat-bathed breasts descending upon him on the dock in Marseilles, snatching his virginity from him. Conquered by force and taken with pleasure that night in Marseilles, Dante had at once suffered a scar and conceived a need, both of which demanded the attention of a woman. The virtuous Kay was the fair tutor of his tongue, but did not move his spirit; she was his teacher, not his temptress. Dante became obsessed with finding the girl from the train, Lucia Ponte, the one to whom he had given the stuffed white pony.

Early one Saturday in March of 1921, Dante shook Adamo from his slumber. "Adamo, wake up."

Adamo turned over in his bed and groaned.

Dante persisted. "Let's go, Adamo, get dressed. We are going to Brooklyn."

Adamo rubbed his eyes. "Why the hell are we going to Brooklyn?"

"To find Lucia."

Adamo knew exactly whom Dante was talking about, and was surprised that it had taken his friend these many months to mention her. Her beauty was etched in his memory. But he pretended otherwise. "Lucia who?"

"Lucia Ponte. You remember, the girl from the train on the way to France. The one who couldn't take her eyes off me."

Adamo sat up and rolled his eyes. "Oh, of course. That one. You will have to excuse me, there are so many women in your life, I sometimes get confused. How are we going to get to Brooklyn?"

"We will take the ferry to New York. I will pay your way. Then we will walk to the Brooklyn Bridge." Dante fluttered his fingers in the air. "We will walk over the bridge, and we will be in Brooklyn."

"Then what?"

"I will figure that out when we get there."

Adamo climbed out of his bed. "What makes you think she will even remember you?"

Dante buttoned his shirt. "That's the least of my worries."

The boys took the morning ferry to Manhattan, and by noon were walking across the Brooklyn Bridge. For the rest of his life, no matter how many times he had seen it, Dante never ceased to marvel at the magnificence of the cabled span. He took a break to look over its railing. "This is why we came to America, my friend. At home, we would have to wave to each other from either side of the river. There would not be any bridge. We would never have enough money or men. And even if we did, there would probably be a workers' strike before it started." He turned to Adamo. "In America, everything is possible." Dante pushed his two fists inward toward one another. "If they did not need the river, the Americans could probably force the two sides together." Dante pointed to a seagull passing under the bridge. He laughed. "The American bridge has us so high that we have to look down to see the birds."

Adamo was not interested in Dante's diversion. "Where are we going?"

Dante was disappointed that his friend would not fly with him. He started walking. "Don't worry. Follow me."

Dante marched across the remainder of the bridge, and approached an elderly woman propped up by a cane. He mustered the best English Kay had taught him. "Ex-cuse -a- me ma'me. Can you tell me where ees da nearest church-a?"

The woman smiled. "Why certainly, young man." "I recommend you to go to St. Joseph's Church." She pointed. "It's a bit of a walk that way, but if you keep going straight you can't miss it. Follow the noise. The church is on Pacific Street, and the feast of St. Joseph began a few minutes ago."

Dante hurried back to Adamo. "This is our lucky day. Not only are we going to find Lucia, but if I understood the old lady, we also get to celebrate the feast of St. Joseph. I would have never thought they celebrated it here. It must be an Italian church. The priest there will be able to tell us how to find the Pontes."

The boys ran for blocks, Dante a little faster. When they heard the din of a crowd, they sped up. They chased the sound of an accordion around a corner, finding themselves at the foot of a stage cluttered with fixtures of their childhood. A band was at the end of the cordoned street where St. Joseph's Church stood, its drummer beating loudly alongside his brass companions, the trombone and trumpet. The sidewalks were lined with tables of food: macaroni in thick red pomodoro sauce, thin strips of fried beef bracioline rolled in string, sausage and peppers, a block of nougat torrone that had to be chopped, and the St. Joseph pastry filled with custard and cream. The Monsignor stood solemn in his purple robe beside the shrine to St. Joseph that had been built for the occasion, and blessed the faithful who stood in line to pin a dollar on the statue of the patron saint. Everything was Italian without interruption, just like at home. People singing, eating, laughing, praying – all in Italian.

The boys lost themselves in the music and food, and Dante seemed to have momentarily forgotten his mission; Adamo was not about to remind him. Just as Adamo thought that the issue of finding

Lucia was dead and the rest of the afternoon would be filled with the nougat torrone he was gnawing, Dante gave the order. "Let's hurry and finish. We will stand in line to pin a dollar on the statue, and when we get to the Monsignor, we will ask him how to find Lucia."

"What makes you think he is going to know the Pontes? This is a big city. It's not Aquino."

Dante wiped his mouth of the custard from the St. Joseph he had just inhaled. "He is God on earth. He has to know. I will tell you what. If he doesn't know, I give up and we will stay here the rest of the afternoon."

"Agreed."

Dante waited in line for access to the priest. When it was his turn, he approached the statue of St. Joseph with humility, the way his mother and father had taught him in Aquino. As he pinned a dollar to the area of the garment above St. Joseph's heart, he could see the sorrow in the saint's eyes. St. Joseph, the man who fathered the God that Dante worshiped, seemed to be weeping for his lost son. Dante made the sign of the cross, and kissed the patron's cold cement feet before moving on to the Monsignor.

Dante bowed before the Holy One, who placed his large hands on Dante's head. With his stare fixed to the ground, Dante asked his question. "Father, I am looking for the Ponte family. They have a daughter Lucia. Where can I find her?"

The Monsignor shuddered with surprise, and looked down from beneath his large hat. He kept his holy hands on Dante's head so that the boy could not look up at him. "What did you say, my son?"

"Lucia Ponte, Monsignor. I am looking for a young girl named Lucia Ponte. Can you help me?"

The Monsignor smiled to his adoring flock, and mumbled to Dante under his breath. "You can tell me your sins, and beg forgiveness. But don't ask me to help you commit sin." A trombone from the band blew a sour note.

"Let's go, Father, I paid my dollar. Please tell me where I can find the Pontes."

The Monsignor continued his incestuous smile with his congregation, and scolded Dante. "You filthy little swine. Rid your heart of lust, or you will burn in the fires of hell." The Monsignor closed his eyes, and made the sign of the cross over Dante's head. The drummer beat his canvas louder. The Monsignor broke his meditation. "Move on, young man. There is a long line behind you."

"But Monsignor, I wasn't…"

The Monsignor pointed Dante away with his long right index finger.

Adamo was anxious to question the dejected-looking Dante. "Well, what did he say? He did not have a clue, did he?"

Dante did not answer.

Adamo felt bad, and offered his friend some consolation. He pointed across the street. "C'mon, I will buy you a lemonade from that stand over there. It will help wash down the six plates of pasta and St. Joseph pastries you just ate. I am surprised you are still standing."

"Two lemonade," Adamo proudly asked in English, raising his thumb and forefinger in the air.

"Tank you, my friend-a," Dante smiled grudgingly, taking the cup from Adamo. As Dante sipped the lemonade, he looked down at the banner draped in front of the table that indicated the sponsor of the stand. He spat the lemonade out of his mouth, and grabbed Adamo by the shirt. "We found it, look."

Adamo shifted his brow slowly, and his smile dropped when he read the sign. "Happy St. Joseph's Day from Ponte's Shoes."

"Let's go. I have the address. You have had enough to eat," Dante snickered in the direction of the Monsignor, and the boys were on their way to Ponte's Shoes.

After a couple of misdirections and queries to passersby, Dante found the window that read "Ponte's Shoes" in silver cursive. The boys peeked through the large pane, with their hands bent around their eyes to shield them from the glare. Dante's heart dropped when he saw an older man behind the counter cobbling a shoe. His words were staggered. "That's not Lucia's father."

Realizing the same, Adamo hit Dante on the shoulders. "There are probably one hundred Pontes in New York. C'mon, let's go back to the feast."

As Dante continued to stare in disbelief through the window, a young girl emerged from the back room with a box wrapped in brown paper. It was Lucia. Dante's smile erupted. He pounded Adamo on the shoulder. "It's her, it's her. Lucia. She came out for me."

Dante bustled through the door. As the young girl retreated to the back area, Dante called out her name. "Lucia."

Lucia's broad shoulders and thick black curls turned to face Dante. She spoke in English, as she always did when addressing a new customer. "May I 'elp-a you?"

Dante slapped his hands on the counter where the old man was working, startling him. He kept to the native tongue. "Lucia, it's me. Dante Di Benedetto, from Aquino. I helped your father with his bags on the train." Dante looked over at Adamo in a panic. "Don't you remember?"

As he surveyed the silence, Dante noticed that next to the area where Lucia was wrapping boxes was the white stuffed pony Dante had given her on the train. He lit up and pointed. "I gave you the pony."

Lucia's bluff was called, and she rewarded Dante with a shy smile. "Oh yes, yes. I remember you, Dante."

The older man behind the counter intervened on Lucia's behalf, gripping her wide shoulders. "Are you all right? Do you want me to throw this guy out of here?"

Lucia responded courteously. "I am fine, Uncle Aldo. Dante and the other boy, Adamo, are friends from back home. Mom and Dad know them."

Adamo perked up when he heard Lucia remembered his name. He felt he had to say something, but he did not know what. He blurted out, "So are you married yet?"

Lucia alternated her shy yet alluring smile between Adamo and Dante. "No, it didn't quite work out with the boy I was supposed to marry. The distance was too much. Things are different here." She tapped Adamo on the hand. "What about you?"

Adamo knew that he could not lie about how he was still engaged to be wed to a girl back in Aquino, and was too nervous to come up with a clever answer. So he just adopted Lucia's words as his own. "Yeah, things really are different here."

Lucia wrung her hands tightly, and cracked one of her dimples at Dante. "What about you, Dante?"

Dante responded with predictable cool. "I'm just waiting to take that pony ride we talked about on the train." When he got the blush from her that he wanted, Dante broke a boyish grin. "Hey, listen. Adamo and I just came from the feast. Why don't you join us? Last time I checked, Adamo had not eaten all the food."

Adamo finally regained his composure. "They have torrone."

Lucia looked up at her Uncle Aldo with an irresistible pout. "Can I, Uncle Aldo? I will make up for the time Monday."

Uncle Aldo took off his hat and scratched his head. "Very well. But if your parents ask, I don't know anything. So be home early."

Dante, Adamo, and Lucia laughed, ate and sang the afternoon away at the feast of St. Joseph. Little girls in white dresses marched along the procession exalting the dollar-garbed Saint Joseph, while the young boys tried to pull their hair. The band continued to bang and ring its way through every eater's ears, and the Monsignor sold his blessings. Dante, Adamo, and Lucia told story after story about their former life in Italy. It was as though the three were trying to spin one another into their past, so that they could somehow remember being there together. Every bite into the feast's macaroni and sweets was taken with the anxiety and longing of their first seven months in the new country. They ate until the last stand was taken down.

It would leave them filled and heavy for days to come.

XXII.

A Stallion in Full Gallop

As spring bloomed, Dante and Guido began delivering ice again, with Dante spending his Saturday afternoons with Lucia. They would go to the park, walk the streets, and go shopping – anything to pass the time together. Dante was dedicating himself to his new love, without losing sight of his first. Despite the revelry and nostalgia of the feast, and Lucia's commanding beauty, Dante's overriding passion was still America, his chief pursuit to become an American.

One Saturday, Dante surprised Lucia and took her for the pony ride he had promised her on the train when he gave her the stuffed miniature. A fifty-cent trot through Newark, New Jersey's Branchbrook Park was not what either of them had pictured when Dante pledged to ride with Lucia "over the fields and across the rivers," but much had passed since then. Their expectation of America was still grand, but tempered. They both had learned much about the new country, but were still sifting through the differences between it and the old.

Lucia was delighted riding on the saddle behind her handsome suitor, her arms wrapped around his muscled chest. She poked her head over Dante's shoulders as he prodded the horse, its steps restrained and deliberate. "This is so nice, Dante. I can't believe you remembered. I thought about it a lot, whenever I looked at that little pony that you gave me on the train. You know, I never told my parents that you gave it to me."

Dante smirked. "Why not?"

Lucia frowned. "Because my father would have probably taken it away from me. I said that I found it abandoned in a seat."

Dante steered the horse to the left. "Your father keeps a close eye on you, doesn't he?"

Lucia rolled her deep brown eyes beneath her thick brows. "He still wants me to marry the boy back home. 'Strong,' he says. 'He comes from a good family – he will provide you what you need, Lucia, and you will give him many sons.'"

Lucia and Dante laughed, as a breeze blew through their hair.

Lucia tightened her hold around Dante's chest, and laid her head on his shoulders. "I just want to ride horses with you – over the fields and across the rivers."

Dante was silent, his body unmoved by Lucia's grip.

Lucia lifted her head. "What's the matter, Dante? Why are you so quiet?"

As the horse continued the stroll, Dante ran a free hand through his hair. "I'm just thinking."

"About what?"

"My little sister Annunziata. When she gets older, she is going to be beautiful just like you, and my father is going to fuss the same way. If she gets better."

"How is she? Any word from home?"

Dante shook his head. "No. I guess she is doing fine." Dante quickly changed the subject. "I talked to Kay the other day after class. I think I am going to change my name."

"What?"

"You heard me, I am going to change my name."

Lucia stroked the back of Dante's head as the horse continued to plod. "But Dante is such a beautiful name. It's poetic."

A pair of hummingbirds chirped in the distance, and a little boy was skipping stones across the pond.

Dante swiped Lucia's hand from his hair. "I am not talking about my first name. It's my last name. Di Ben-e-det-to. It's too complicated. It sounds like a dish. Like chicken cacciatore." Dante pointed to the sky. "I can see it on the menu. Spaghettini Di Benedetto. That's how my name will make it in lights in America."

Lucia's forehead ridged with confusion. "Why are you doing this? Your parents will disown you."

Dante stiffened. "It's not their decision. Every time I tell people my name in this country, they assume I am nothing more than some wine-drinking peasant that plays the mandolin. Or some menial laborer who works for his pay in guineas. A dirty immigrant without a passport. A greenhorn. I hate that one. Makes us sound like animals, or the devil's cousin. I don't want to have to prove anything. There is not enough time. I want to be an American now."

Lucia retreated from the fire of Dante's oratory. "So what did you and Kay decide should be your new last name?"

Dante clenched his lips together. "Bennett. Dante Bennett."

When Lucia fell silent, Dante jostled her. "And when we get married, you will be Lucia Bennett. Or maybe just 'Lucy.'"

Lightheaded at the mention of marriage and the thought of being Dante's wife, Lucia slapped Dante on the back of his head. "You are crazy."

Against the instruction of the man who rented the horse to him, the young Mr. Bennett whipped his stallion into a full gallop, throwing Lucia's long locks of black hair into the wind that he was creating.

XXIII

Rooting for the American

Bringing His Girlfriend Home

Still under the same roof at Uncle Carlo's house, Dante and Adamo began growing apart in the spring of 1921. Adamo was consumed with his new job at the bank, and the Alexanders had practically adopted him as a son. He ate dinner at their home, and even made extra money on the weekends doing odd jobs for them. People who did not know any better often mistook him for Kay's brother. The irony became that people more often assumed that Adamo was an American, when it was Dante's obsession to be so. Adamo was not interested in name changes or mistress America; he was only along for the ride. His desires were simple: to be comfortable, raise a family, and keep his Italian traditions.

Dante continued to spend many of his weekends with Lucia, without sharing with Adamo the details of his trysts. He knew his friend well, and although Adamo had never uttered a word of affection for Lucia, Dante knew it was there. He had seen it on the train in Italy, and at the feast in Brooklyn. It was evident in the way Adamo perked up when Lucia looked at him, and in the pulled jabs Adamo threw at Dante in front of her. Adamo wanted to compete for Lucia's attention, but knew he did not stand a chance next to Dante's looks and charm. Besides, he was still engaged to be married to a girl at home. Dante barely mentioned Lucia's name in front of Adamo, on the assumption that Adamo already knew of the relationship, but did not want to know more.

Dante was starting to miss the camaraderie of his sidekick. So on one hot night in June of 1921, instead of diving into bed after a long day's work and feeding from Aunt Connie, he initiated conversation with his pal.

"What do you think about the fight next week?"

Adamo looked down as he unbuttoned his shirt. "What fight?"

Sitting on his bed, Dante unlaced his boots. "The heavyweight championship between Georges Carpentier and Jack Dempsey. Right here in Jersey City, at Boyle's Thirty Acres. I pass it every day on my route. They are expecting ninety thousand people, the biggest ever. People are coming from all over the world. Dempsey gets paid $300,000 just for showing up. He will probably knock the pretty Frenchman's head off in the first round, and get home in time to start spending some of his money on a nice dinner."

Adamo challenged Dante's enthusiasm for the event and Dempsey. "I had not really thought much about it, but I am pulling for the Frenchman. He has more class. Dempsey is so loud and obnoxious. It is like a parade every time he is in public."

Dante threw off his boot. "You are kidding, right? The guy is twice the size of the Frenchman. Who cares how he acts outside the ring? He's a real American – strong and unstoppable."

Adamo folded his pants at the crease. "To be a champion, you have to be graceful."

Dante reached under his mattress, and pulled out two tickets. "So I guess that means you don't want to come with me to the fight?"

Adamo's jaw dropped. "How did you get those?"

Dante fanned himself with the tickets. "While you have been counting Mr. Alexander's money at the bank, Guido has taught me how to play poker. I won the tickets from one of his friends last night. People are paying as much as thirty dollars each."

Adamo grabbed for the tickets, and Dante pulled them away. "Say please."

Adamo rolled his eyes. "Please."

Dante handed Adamo his ticket. "I got a ticket for Guido. And for Kay too. She brought us to see Italian art; we will bring her to see American art."

The boys laughed.

Dante continued. "It's on July 2, two days before the Americans go crazy celebrating their independence from the English. They are going to have brass bands, fireworks, everything. We should meet beforehand in front of Ventilli Tailors."

Adamo studied the ticket, with a smile from ear to ear. "Why? Why can't we go together?"

Dante pulled a T-shirt over his shoulders. "Because I have to pick up Lucia." Dante knocked Adamo on the head. "Remember, she lives in Brooklyn?"

Adamo pushed a laugh as he slapped the tickets repeatedly against the palm of his hand. "Of course. Lucia – Brooklyn."

On fight day, leaden skies greeted the multitudes that poured into Boyle's Thirty Acres in Jersey City. People came from every direction: the tube trains herded human cattle under the Hudson River from New York every three and one half minutes, while ferries criss-crossed above; fistic fans jammed into horse-drawn carriages, while dignitaries entered smoothly in their Model-T Fords. Several hundred men and boys slept outside the arena the night before in the hope of getting tickets or sneaking in. The fight was touted as the main event in what was already being billed as the Golden Age of Sports. Anybody who knew or heard about it had to be there, to watch the heavily favored brawny American have his way with the finely groomed Frenchman.

After meeting at Ventilli Tailors as planned, Dante, Lucia, Adamo, Kay, and Guido stepped into the spectacle at Thirty Acres. The streets around the big saucer of an outdoor arena resembled an early morning scene at a circus. There were young boys and men selling flags, souvenirs, peanuts, hot dogs, and all the other trinkets that seem like precious gold in the midst of a mob. The fans who slept outside were doing calisthenics to seek warmth from the morning meadow breeze. There were hundreds of cops and ushers anxious for action. Everything about the day was big, and everyone there rushed through it as if being pulled by a giant magnet.

Dante asked his group to wait as he purchased an American flag. He handed it to Lucia, and taunted Adamo. "We are rooting for the American. Because we are Americans."

Adamo looked at Kay before responding. "You can buy as many flags as you want – Mr. Bennett – but you are still a thick-headed Southern Italian. The smart money is with the smarter boxer – the Frenchman." Adamo glanced at Lucia, who was wrapped around Dante's arm. "I haven't heard Lucia say whom she wants. Let her speak for herself, you loudmouth."

Lucia shrugged her shoulders, and fluttered her long curled eyelashes adoringly at her smiling suitor. "The American – Demp-sey."

Adamo looked over at Guido, who was busy filling his round cheeks with a hot dog. "And you?"

His mouth too stuffed to respond, Guido simply grabbed the American flag from Lucia and waved it.

Adamo scoffed at Lucia and Guido. "Ah, you two have been hanging around him too much."

Dante and his entourage joined the swarm that pressed its way to the gate. Everybody was pushing ahead, even though there were still two hours before the fight began, and their seats were assigned.

Adamo smiled at Dante. "I can barely breathe. Why is everybody pushing?"

Dante responded. "Don't worry. Just do the same, and you will get to the front."

In the distance, Dante noticed two policemen pulling a group of boys from a secret hiding place. As his eyes glazed over, he hit Adamo and pointed toward the incident. "I wonder if the kid with the spectacles is there."

Lucia asked. "Who is the kid with the spectacles?"

Dante smiled at Adamo. "Just somebody we know who likes bridges."

The group crammed into their seats in the giant arena, hundreds of rows from the ring. Each tier was draped with flags and bunting, and a brass band played folk classics. It was the quintessential American event, and Dante and Adamo were right in the middle of it.

During the preliminary bouts, Dante educated Lucia on the sport of boxing, how it is scored, and how it is won. As Carpentier stepped to the center of the ring to meet the champion Dempsey,

Dante gave Lucia her final lesson. "In this fight, the Frenchman will have to knock-out the American to win."

Lucia yelled into Dante's ear through the roar of the crowd. "Why?"

Dante yelled back through his own applause for Dempsey. "Because the American is the champion. To beat the champion, you can't just win. You have to knock him out."

Although Carpentier fought gamely, he never stood a chance against Dempsey's size and strength. The American pushed the Frenchman from one side of the ring to the other, to the savage cries of all but a few of the 90,000 fans in attendance. Dempsey threw successful jabs to Carpentier's head with such regularity that it appeared the Frenchman's nose was attached by a string to the American's fist. Every time the Frenchman tried to counter with a blow to the American's body, it looked as though he were punching a bag of cement. The humidity hung heavy in the air, and quickly began to soak the energy from the smaller challenger. The crowd's hunger burned, and they screamed out for more pain.

"Knock his eyes out, Dempsey," screamed a young boy sitting next to Dante.

"Cripple 'em," begged an older man.

At the end of the second round, with Dempsey in control, a few in the crowd began to chant. "U-S-A! U-S-A!" The shout was proud, but out of synch.

As he clapped and chanted along, Dante looked at Adamo, who was not quite as ebullient about the course of events. He hit Adamo on the arm repeatedly, but was able to provoke only a couple of claps.

The master of the moment then stood up next to his damsel. Dante threw his sweating arms repeatedly toward the sky to the chant of "U-S-A." He rotated himself around to address the rest of the still seated crowd. He gestured for them to stand up with him. And they did. First tens – then hundreds – rose to their feet around Dante to roar in unison, "U-S-A."

The seats rattled beneath the booming cheer. "U-S-A!"

Lucia shot up next to Dante to join the chorus, as did Guido and Kay. At Kay's prodding, even Adamo stood just before the bell commencing the third round rang. In a matter of seconds, Dante Bennett had conducted his first American chorus.

When they sat back down, Lucia whispered something in Dante's ear.

Dante leaned over toward Adamo. "We are going to get something to eat. We will be right back."

Adamo squinted. "But you just ate."

Sweat poured off Dante's face. "What can I say? We are hungry again."

Dante and Lucia were gone for the entire third round, and still had not returned when the fourth round began. Adamo looked over at Kay, who herself was caught up in the excitement, throwing short punches in the air along with Dempsey as he ravaged Carpentier. "Kay, what do you think happened to Dante and Lucia?"

"They said they were getting something to eat." As Dempsey staggered the Frenchman, Kay threw a right jab of her own. "Knock him out, Dempsey." She looked back at Adamo. "Don't worry. You act like she is your younger sister." Kay pointed to the ring. "Look, Dempsey is going to win."

With a crushing blow to the head that shot Carpentier's sweat and blood into the air, the American sent the Frenchman to the canvas. The referee ordered Dempsey to his corner so he could begin the count, and ten strokes later, he raised the champion's hand in victory above Carpentier's still body. The crowd went wild as fireworks filled the air. A loud bang thundered from above, and Adamo still searched for Dante and Lucia. He looked at Kay and Guido. "Where are they?"

But Kay and Guido did not respond; they were caught in the rapture with the rest of the crowd. A large sign in the bleachers, lit with holiday sparkle, announced "Happy Independence Day."

Dante then appeared with Lucia following behind. He offered two hot dogs to his friends. "Here, you want some, we couldn't finish."

Kay and Guido grabbed the hot dogs, and shoved them in their mouths as they continued in the chaotic applause.

Dante followed. "Let's go back to Uncle Carlo's house and tell him all about it."

Adamo jerked his head. "What's for you to tell? You did not even see it."

Dante rushed the group back to the house, anxious to introduce his girlfriend Lucia to his Uncle Carlo and Aunt Connie. As they approached the front door, Dante tried to calm Lucia. "Don't worry. They are very nice. They are going to love you."

When little Anthony opened the door, Dante tried to rile him about the fight. "Anthony, I wish you could have been there. The crowd, the fireworks. Little boys like you everywhere. You are coming with us next time."

Anthony stared blankly at the group, and yelled to his father. "Papa, they are home."

"Bring them in," called Uncle Carlo from the kitchen.

Anthony ran toward the voice of his father.

Dante grinned at Lucia. "He is just a little shy."

Dante ushered the group into the kitchen, where his Uncle Carlo and Aunt Connie were sitting solemnly around the table. Aunt Connie was cradling her infant girl. Dante burst with pride. "Uncle Carlo, Aunt Connie. You know Adamo, Kay, and Guido." He grabbed Lucia by the hand and pulled her forward. "This is Lucia." Dante thought he saw that his aunt was crying as she looked down at her baby. "What's the matter, Aunt Connie. Is little Anna okay?"

Uncle Carlo stood. He spoke in a slow soft voice. "The baby's fine." He turned to Lucia. "It is so nice to meet you, Lucia. We have heard much about you."

Dante continued in hurried excitement. "Lucia lives in Brooklyn. She is..."

Uncle Carlo raised his hand to stop Dante. He looked over at his wife, behind whom little Anthony was hiding. Aunt Connie wiped a tear from her eye. She handed Uncle Carlo a letter, and Uncle Carlo invited Dante to sit. "We got a letter from your parents today. You need to read it."

As he sat down, Dante smiled nervously over his shoulder at Adamo. "I told you they would write. They probably want more candy for Annunziata."

The small crowd did not need to see the letter to know its

content; the kitchen's air was already filled with the pall of tragedy. Dante's hands began shaking as he read through it.

Uncle Carlo spoke in a whisper. "The town doctor did everything he could for your little sister. They think it was polio."

Dante raised his fist in the air, and slammed it in the middle of the kitchen table. "I told them it was polio." He shuddered. "He did not want to listen. He never wanted to listen to me."

Aunt Connie tried to console Dante. "There is nothing they could have done."

"They could have had her treated in Rome," Dante muttered to himself.

"Little Annunziata is in heaven now," prayed Aunt Connie as she made the sign of the cross.

Lucia stepped up to comfort Dante. She placed her hands on his left shoulder. Dante looked at Lucia's long finger that reached just above his speeding heart, smiled at Lucia, and turned to Adamo. His voice was shaking. "Adamo, please take Lucia home."

Adamo peeled Lucia's hands from Dante. "Don't worry. I will take care of her."

XXIV

All In

Over the next two months, Dante plunged into an abyss of grief and self-destruction. With the loss of his little sister, so went the glint in his eyes, displaced by the weight of cynicism and mistrust. Dante cut himself off from the rest of the world, except Guido and Adamo, both of whom he had to see every day, but with whom he shared only a few spare words. He discontinued his English lessons with Kay as unopened letters from Lucia piled on the small night table next to his bed. His routine devolved into work, poker, and heavy drinking. Life became hard and unrelenting, a violent wave to be endured rather than ridden.

On a Wednesday night in September of 1921, Adamo scurried home in search of Dante. Aunt Connie was in the kitchen with little Anthony washing dishes. Baby Anna was beside them in her bassinet. "Aunt Connie." Adamo was huffing. "Where is Dante? I have to speak to him. It is very important."

Aunt Connie spoke slowly as she stacked the dishes that little Anthony handed her. "He went to the tailor with Carlo. He said he had a lot of clothing to be fixed." Aunt Connie grabbed another dish from Anthony. "He has been going there a lot lately. I never knew that he cared so much about how his clothes look."

Adamo kissed Aunt Connie on the cheek. "It is going to take him some time. Don't worry. He will get better." He kissed his fingers and placed them on baby Anna's forehead, then bolted from the kitchen.

Adamo ran to Ventilli Tailors and knocked on the dark window. Mario peeked through the shade, and once he recognized Adamo, threw open the locks that lined the door.

"Mario, is Dante here? I have to speak to him."

Mario looked both ways, and pulled Adamo inside before speaking. "He is downstairs. I think he has lost his mind. He and L'Oscuro are in the middle of a hand. They have bet each other hundreds of dollars. L'Oscuro keeps laughing and Dante keeps drinking. Your friend won't fold. Not even his uncle can stop him." Mario motioned Adamo to follow him. "C'mon. He is about to lose every last penny he has."

Mario ushered Adamo downstairs, where all eyes were fixed on Dante. The young challenger was staring at his nemesis through a shroud of cigar smoke. Dante pushed his remaining chips to the middle of the table. "I see your five hundred, and raise you one thousand."

L'Oscuro counted the chips and laughed out loud. "How do you raise me one thousand dollars with money you do not have?" He hit Uncle Carlo on the shoulder. "There is only five hundred there. I would count it if I were you, to make sure he is not betting your house."

Dante grabbed his uncle's hand as he reached for the chips to count them. He stared down and spoke in a monotone. "The other one thousand dollars is my free labor to you for an entire year if you win. Can you match me, or do you fold?"

Adamo pulled on Dante's shirt. "Stop this madness. I need to speak to you. It's important."

Dante did not budge, his body numb with liquor. "Not now. I'm busy."

L'Oscuro tried to intimidate Dante with mental warfare. He laughed again. "Instead of seeing your bet in cash," L'Oscuro drew from his Black Beast, and then used it to point to his remaining stack of chips, "I will make you an offer. What service or asset of mine do you find worthy of your one year of free labor?"

Dante responded immediately. "Your business."

L'Oscuro choked on his Black Beast's breath. "What?"

Dante placed down his cards and folded his hands. "Your business – the route, the barn, the horses, and the carriages – mean as much if not less to you than does a single year of labor for me." With his hands still folded, Dante pointed to L'Oscuro's unused chips. "After all, you still have those, and plenty more where they came from. If I lose, I will have nothing but the pleasure of working for you for free."

Dante picked up his cards, and threw down a shot of beer. "Of course, if you think the proposition is too steep, you can always fold. Then you would keep your business and all of your other money."

L'Oscuro looked around at his friends' anxious eyes. L'Oscuro never folded when the stakes were high. "I see your year of labor and call." He flipped his cards over. "Three aces." He smiled nervously. "What do you have, little boy?"

Dante looked at Adamo stoically, and turned his cards over one by one. "Four twos." He gathered his winnings from the center of the table. "And my own business."

Dante leaned over the table. "If you want to work for me, be at the barn at 3:45 sharp tomorrow morning." He pulled the cigar from L'Oscuro's incredulous mouth. "And no smoking on the job."

L'Oscuro shot up and lunged for Dante. "You son of a bitch."

While the other men restrained L'Oscuro, Adamo pulled Dante outside. Dante gloated drunkenly, as Adamo pushed him into the dark night. "Did you see that fat bastard's face when I told him to be at the barn at 3:45?"

Adamo closed the door behind him, and turned Dante around toward him. "Yeah, he was shocked." Adamo buttoned Dante's jacket for him. "Dante, we have to talk."

"Yeah, yeah. What about? I'm sorry I cut you off in there. It's just that the fat bastard, he..."

Adamo interrupted. "It's Lucia."

Dante pulled back his gaiety only slightly. "What about her?"

"She and her family are going back to Italy tomorrow."

Dante burped and pounded his chest to relieve himself. "Going back to Italy? She never said anything to me."

"Dante, she has written you a stack of letters higher than the pile of money you just won from L'Oscuro. You have not opened a single one of them. I have seen them on your night table."

Dante extended his arms and looked up at the stars. "Why

would anyone want to leave this country, the land of opportunity?" Dante hiccupped. "This is paradise." He belched out loud.

"She would not tell me why they are leaving. She just said that her family has to go immediately. I think someone on the other side must have died."

Dante smirked. "Oh well. Is that what you came to tell me?"

Adamo looked down at the sidewalk. In the background, a streetlight's flame began to peter out. "There is more."

Dante lifted Adamo's chin. "What?"

"I am going, too."

Dante spoke slowly. "And?"

Adamo bit his lip, and forced out the words. "I am going to ask Lucia to marry me. I want your blessing."

Dante looked up at the sky without saying a word.

Adamo repeated himself. "I am going to marry Lucia, but I want your blessing."

As Dante continued to look up, Adamo tried to explain himself. "You abandoned her after your sister died. Out of respect for you, I waited. But I can't wait anymore."

Dante looked back down, into his friend's fearful eyes.

Adamo braced for a violent blow, clenching his fists ready.

Dante extended his hand in congratulations. "I wish you the best. You will make her happier than I ever could. I always knew you liked her."

"Thank you, Dante." Shocked at his friend's cool response, Adamo relaxed his fists, and put his hand on Dante's shoulder. "You have to get over this and on with your life. Annunziata is not coming back."

Dante smiled. "At least now I have my own business. I can have somebody else deliver the coal." Dante started walking, and waved Adamo along. "C'mon, I'll help you pack. You are not taking everything, are you?"

"I don't know. What do you think?"

Dante swiped Adamo across the head, and the two went back to Uncle Carlo's to spend their last night together.

XXV

The Deal

After the departure of Adamo and Lucia, Dante's drunken grieving worsened without withering. He continued to gamble, and gradually lost everything he won from that September night at Ventilli Tailors. His last day working with ice and coal was when L'Oscuro took back his business with a late night poker hand.

Adamo and Lucia were married in Aquino and had two sons – Bruno and Vito. Adamo worked with his father in the butcher shop, and saved every penny until he could bring his family back to America. It took him five years.

When Adamo returned to Jersey City, he found Dante sobered. He had moved out of Uncle Carlo's house, and settled into marriage with an Italian girl named Philomena. Dante and Philomena had a son named Gaetano, who was the same age as Adamo's second son, Vito. Dante had garnered the patience to learn and save, and was able to scrape together enough money for a two-story house and a used Ford. He painted the car his favorite color – liberty green.

Mr. Alexander gave Adamo his old job at the bank, with a raise. Though Adamo and Dante saw one another occasionally, it was mostly by accident; their relationship would never be the same as the days when they hid in a train's luggage rack, and shared a room at Uncle Carlo's. They were too busy living their separate lives.

Years later, after the Great Depression, Dante finally came up with a real plan, one that had goals to be pursued over years instead of hours and days. He would start a construction company and develop it to the point where he could build bridges and sky-scrapers; he dreamt of someday standing on top of his creations to view the world around him. Unfortunately, Dante was long on vision but short on resources. His small circle of friends was similarly lacking capital; they had all been devastated by get-rich-quick schemes and the crash of the stock market.

Adamo was the only one who had the contacts and savings to help Dante get started. He gave Dante a loan to found his company that the two of them agreed would be called Aquino Construction. The company flourished in its early years, building sidewalks and driveways, first by the handful, then by the dozens. Dante was hitting his stride, albeit later than planned.

Like a bolt of lightning, disaster struck Dante a second time. He suffered a stroke, and became crippled before he ever repaid Adamo. After graduating college, Dante's son Gaetano, nicknamed Guy, assumed the mantle, and Aquino Construction thrived in America's post–World War II prosperity. It was not long before the company was doing small public works projects, and colleagues referred to its captain as Guy. Dante remained in the background, with the support of his cane.

When Adamo came calling on his credit that seemed all but forgotten, he and Dante reached an agreement. Dante told Guy he had to take him to a lawyer's office in Jersey City to finalize the deal with Adamo. Being that they were going to see an attorney, Dante told his son that they needed to wear suits. Guy bought one, and took it to Mario Ventilli for tailoring.

Guy drove his father to the attorney meeting in his brand new Bonneville convertible, the wind blowing through their hair. Guy spoke to Dante in Italian. "But I don't understand, Pop. Why do we have to give the Petrozzinis a share in our company?"

Dante caressed the dashboard of his son's new car. "This is a beautiful machine."

Not knowing whether his father was criticizing or applauding him, Guy responded, "I had it painted your favorite color – liberty green." He repeated, "You didn't answer my question, Pop. I don't understand why I…" he corrected himself, "I don't understand why we need to give the Petrozzinis shares in the company based on a loan Mr. Petrozzini gave you years ago. At the rate we are going, we can have the loan paid back within twelve months."

"I don't want to to talk about it, Gaetano. A deal is a deal."

Guy squeezed his steering wheel to restrain himself from saying more.

Dante broke the uncomfortable silence. "Mr. Petrozzini was there for me when I needed him. It doesn't matter that we can pay him back now. We would have nothing if he didn't help me." He took a deep breath. "You wouldn't be driving this car."

Steaming that his father was minimizing his own effort in making Aquino Construction into the success that it was, Guy pulled the car up to the curb, stopping it abruptly. He looked up at the window. "Thomas W. Sherman, Counselor at Law." He pursed his lips. "I guess we are here."

Dante moved up in his seat, retrieving his shiny black cane from the floor in front of him. "Come around and help me get out of the car."

Guy did as he was told, stomping angrily around the car to open the passenger-side door. He lifted Dante to his feet by his arm. Dante planted his cane into the sidewalk, and braced himself. Guy pulled hard to button the double-breasted jacket of his father's black suit, which was brandished boldly with wide lapels and silver pinstripes. "A little snug, Pop," Guy quipped. "You either need to lose some weight or we have to buy you a new suit."

"In my day," Dante lifted his hand, "I was in better shape than you." He studied his son's physique, emaciated by long days of labor, swimming in his single-breasted brown wool suit. He scoffed. "By the way, that tie is too narrow."

"It's the style, Pop. But neither of us can turn back now. These are the only suits we have." He extended a hand to help his father along. "Let's go."

Dante waved his son off. "I am fine with my cane."

Dante and Guy were shown into the attorney's office by his secretary. "Mr. Sherman will be with you in a moment," she smiled.

"Tank-a you," replied Dante.

"Yes. Thank you," Guy followed.

Adamo and his son Vito were already waiting, sitting plain-clothed in their chairs.

"Why didn't you wear a suit?" Dante whispered to Adamo in Italian. "This is an attorney's office."

"I'm sorry," Adamo shot back, "I thought he worked for us." Never fully comfortable with challenging Dante, Adamo changed the subject. "How is Philomena?"

"Good." Dante swallowed hard on his dried throat. "And Lucia?"

"Very good."

Dante peered down at his cane. "Tell Lucia I said 'hello.'"

"I will. And to Philomena as well."

Dante looked at Guy and pointed to Vito. "You remember Vito – Mr. Petrozzini's son. He's going to start to work with us."

Guy began to boil again. "Of course I remember Vito." He faked a smile at his father. "I just didn't know he was joining us."

"He is good with numbers," answered Dante, as he lowered himself into his chair.

Guy did not jump to help his father.

Seated, Dante exhaled from the strain of bending. "Vito will help us grow the business."

Guy extended his hand toward Vito's to shake it. He repeated his father's words slowly. "He will help us grow the business." Vito's hand inside of his, Guy found his new colleague's grip to be weaker than his own.

"Assuming that it," Vito stuttered, "that growing makes sense. Don't you agree?"

"Of course."

The attorney walked into the room, looking up from the papers he was carrying. His suit was a conservative dark blue, his jacket adorned simply with a perfect pocket square. "Good afternoon, gentlemen. I am Thomas Sherman. Welcome to my office."

He looked at Adamo and Vito. "I have already had the pleasure of meeting the Petrozzinis."

Dante was impressed with the lawyer's perfect pronunciation of the Italian surname.

"You must be Dante and Gaetano Bennett."

"Yes," Dante nodded.

Sherman sat behind his desk. "Just a few questions before we move ahead. Dante and Adamo – do either of you have any debts that have been discharged in the last five years?"

Dante turned to his son.

Guy spoke. "About twenty years ago, Pop bought a piece of land in the swamps of Florida. The deal went bad, but Pop eventually paid his loan."

"I am curious. Where was the land?" the attorney asked.

"A place called Merritt Island. Pop thought it had real potential."

"Interesting. Anything else?"

Both men nodded "no."

Sherman handed a set of papers to each of Dante and Adamo. "Well then, here they are. The corporate resolutions to make Mr. Bennett the 65% owner of Aquino Construction, and Mr. Petrozzini the 35% owner. The documents provide for you, Gaetano, and you, Vito, to succeed to your father's shares."

"Pop, you didn't tell me that…" Guy began to mutter.

"And you make-a Gaetano the Presidente of the compania," he looked at Adamo, "Like we agree-a."

Adamo nodded his accord.

"Certainly," answered Sherman. "One of the resolutions states that Gaetano is to be President, with all executive decision-making power, removable only by unanimous consent of the shareholders, which are Dante and Adamo."

Guy was quieted by the resolution. It was a pleasant surprise to him that not only signified his father's confidence in him and willingness to hand over the reins, but also a guarantee that Guy would forever be in control.

The attorney opened his drawer, and pulled out two fountain pens, giving one to Dante and the other to Adamo. He also retrieved a bottle of ink, placed it on his desk, and unscrewed its top. "Very well, gentlemen. If you will review the documents and execute them, the deal will be final."

Dante marveled at the gold nib on the fountain pen the lawyer handed him. He smiled back at the lawyer, and reached for his best English. "Some-a-day, sir, I hope my son have a lawyer as a son, and that -e." He stopped and tried again. "And that *he* use a nice pen like this when *he* work-a."

"You all seem to be doing pretty well with your company," the lawyer smiled. "But I must say, I find that being a lawyer is a noble profession."

"Yes, eet is." Dante dipped his nib in the lawyer's ink, and sealed his deal.

XXVI.

An Office in the Sky

Going Before the Board

Almost one year had passed since the return of Guy and his family from their momentous visit to Aquino. Seeing his brother Dante and the dedication of the church had bought Father Francesco only a few additional weeks. He died in the winter, and Dante soon followed, unable to make it through another cold season. Those who remained consoled Dante's wife Philomena with the faith that the brothers were finally together again, with their little sister Annunziata, in a place where no one could harm or separate them. A bright spot, and distraction from it all, came with the summer marriage of Guy's daughter, Lisa Marie, to Vito Petrozzini's son, VJ. The partners spared no expense for the gala event, replete with all the trappings and local bigwigs. To those in attendance, the Bennetts and the Petrozzinis had it all, with the Bennetts having slightly more.

When the toasts were done and the confetti was cleared, however, Guy's and Vito's construction and real estate conglomerate, Northern Industries, remained in a stubborn declining state. Forty-six floors above Central Park in New York City, Guy and his partner sat in Northern's boardroom. The company had five floors for itself, those beneath it occupied by old-line law firms, investment banking houses, and insurance companies. Northern Industries' offices were at the top, with the best views of the City. Guy and his father had wanted it that way ever since they decided to design and build the sleek skyscraper. They had named it the Northern Tower.

Guy sat at the head of the long mahogany boardroom table, Vito to his immediate right. An enlarged black and white photo hung on the wall behind Guy's place; it was a picture of him and his father in front of the company's first pick-up truck, with their foreman Guido Scarpetto at their side. The company's entire work force at the time, young Giuseppe and Fernando, sat in the bed of the truck holding a pick and shovel, their faces dirty with the day's labor. The driver's side door was painted with the company's original name, Aquino Construction.

After the company changed its name to Northern Industries and went public on the stock exchange, Guy and Vito made it a policy to confer in the boardroom prior to the quarterly meetings of the full Board of Directors. Even though they had built the company, and as Chairman of the Board and Chief Executive Officer controlled its operations, Guy and Vito still felt like visitors in their New World, the same way their fathers did when they arrived from Italy. The language was the same, but the lexicon and subtle tongues of their white-shoed fellow directors made them feel like foreigners still.

So Guy and Vito made a pact early on that whatever their differences, they would resolve them among themselves and not in front of others. With the company's financial performance faltering, the differences between the long-time partners were growing. Guy wanted to expand to foreign markets; Vito wanted to either simplify operations or sell the company.

Vito leaned back in his soft leather chair, gazing at the picture behind Guy's head. "You know, Guy, one of my biggest regrets was changing the company's name from Aquino Construction. Aquino is where our fathers came from. That's the way the company started. That's the way it should have stayed."

Guy was busy leafing through the company's financials. "What are you talking about? We paid our consultants good money to come up with the name Northern Industries. We could have never gone public as Aquino Construction. We would have been just two more guineas with a construction company. No one would have ever invested."

Vito rocked back. "Yeah, and look where it has gotten us. We were better off when it was you, me, and Aquino Construction, with old Guido Scarpetto cracking the whip. We have so many people now, I don't even recognize the company anymore. If you ask me, most of them are hangers-on, bullshitters. They'll say whatever they think we want to hear."

"Your son VJ seems to have enjoyed the success of Northern Industries," said Guy.

"I don't know why you won't let your sons join the company," Vito defended. "It would be better than dealing with these strangers."

The company's financial analyst, Mohammad Nardeen, stepped through the doorway where Guy and Vito were sitting. An immigrant from India, who had topped off his education with a business degree from an American university, he was holding a folder thick with papers.

Guy waved to Nardeen. "Come in, Mohammad. Do you have the reports I asked you for?"

Nardeen scrambled to the table, laid the reports in front of Guy, and started explaining them to him. "Yes, sir. I have broken down the markets you requested by region, and then by country." Nardeen pulled out the first report, a color chart with graphics. "For example..."

Guy interrupted Nardeen by picking up the piece of paper, admiring it, and showing it to Vito. "Isn't it amazing what our new computers can do? I feel like I am looking at a photo."

Vito grumbled as he leaned his cheek against his fist. "I like the old ones better. They did the same thing in black and white, and were helluva lot cheaper. Another brilliant idea by our overpaid consultants."

Guy waved Vito off. "Don't mind him, Mohammad. He is just in a bad mood. Continue, please."

"Very well, sir. As I was saying, the first report is a snapshot of the regions you asked me to research. For instance, this one is for South America, and it lists the overall growth in construction over the past five years, the average laborer wage, and the governmental stability. Each of the variables is scored on a scale of one to ten. It is followed by individual reports for each country in the region, listing the same information. I have similar reports for the other two regions you requested: Africa and Southeast Asia."

Guy held his fountain pen to his mouth. "Which region and country do you find most promising as a result of your research?"

Mohammad crossed his arms as he remained standing. "It is difficult to say, sir. I think I would choose South America, primarily because of its proximity and cultural ties. The military dictatorships of the '70s and '80s appear to have restored the markets, and made the governments more stable for moderate democracy and growth. The default ratio on government contracts is low. Not as low as Southeast Asia of course, but the contracts are more lucrative, and the costs are lower."

Impressed by Mohammad's wealth of knowledge, Guy prompted him to display more of it in front of Vito. "What about the other regions?"

"Africa has not progressed enough yet where our company could feel comfortable making heavy investments, and the large growth markets of Southeast Asia appear to be already dominated by companies much larger than ours. The density of populations in the region also give me pause; they are much more vulnerable to revolution when growth heats up. I find South America comfortably in between. Specifically, I like Chile and Argentina."

Vito held his palms open. "What about North America? You remember, the United States." Vito mimicked Mohammad to punctuate his point. "Specifically, I like New York and New Jersey."

Nardeen responded matter-of-factly, the way he was paid to. "The labor costs are too high. With the government cutting back on spending, the large public works projects are too few, the profit margins too thin. If my current projections of cash flow and expenditure on domestic projects are true, it will not be long before we have to consider filing."

Vito's forehead creased sharply. "Filing for what?"

Nardeen turned to Vito. "For bankruptcy, sir."

Vito threw down his pencil, and turned quickly to Guy. "What are these projections? And who told him to do them?"

Before the discussion went any further, Guy dismissed Nardeen. "Thank you, Mohammad. We will call you if we have any further questions."

Guy got up from his seat to close the door behind Mohammad. He spoke softly as he returned to the table. "Well, what do you think?"

Vito raised his voice. "What do I think? The question is, what do you care what I think?" Vito grabbed the leaves presented by Nardeen. "South America, Southeast Asia. You and that little Indian are crazy – those are foreign places. They are jungles for chrissakes. Next you are going to tell me we have an in with some of Mohammad's relatives in Pakistan."

"He's from Delhi."

"I don't care if he is the goddamn Green Grocer." Vito extended his arms, and planted his palms on the table in front of where Guy was sitting. "And what the hell was going on with those projections? If numbers like the ones he was describing ever got into the wrong hands or went public, there would be a run on our stock so fast that it would put us out of business before you could generate another one of those silly color reports. No one other than you and me should be talking about numbers like that. And no one, including you and me, should commit them to paper."

Guy raised his hand, and pointed his thumb to the door that led to reception. "Calm down. Otherwise, they will hear you." Guy banged his pen on the Italian marbled border of the mahogany table. "First of all, it is okay for Mohammad to make those projections. If we don't have them, we are playing in the dark. I asked him to do it, and told him that the project was strictly confidential. I trust him. But I understand your point, and I will have him destroy any reports he has regarding our numbers."

Vito raised his eyebrows. "Well, thank you."

Guy smiled and persisted. "But what do you really think about expanding our markets overseas? It is a fantastic opportunity."

Vito got up and went to an easel that held a map of the United States. It was pegged with green thumbtacks that each represented one of Northern Industries' projects. He flicked his finger in the middle of the paper map. "I think there is plenty of opportunity right here in America. Why don't we use our size and resources on simpler projects, like roads and residential building? We can dominate the market."

Guy paced behind his chair. "C'mon, Vito, you are going backwards. We have to have some vision, the kind our fathers had when they came here. They took a huge gamble in a foreign land, but look at the payoff." Guy turned to face the picture of him, his father, and the original crew that hung behind his chair. "Next you are going to tell me that we should concentrate just on sidewalks and curbs, the way my dad did in the '30s." Guy snickered. "Or maybe we should just sell the company and get out."

Vito stared straight back. "Maybe we should."

Guy could not believe his ears. He turned away from the picture to focus on Vito. "Maybe we should what? Go back to sidewalks and curbs?"

"You heard me. Maybe we should sell the company and get out."

When Guy fell silent and turned back to face the aged photo, Vito approached him. "C'mon, Guy. Think about it. We have already made enough money for us, our kids, and our grandkids to have everything they want." Vito stopped next to Guy, who was still staring at the photo. "With the sale of our stock, none of them would have to work another day in their lives. Isn't that what it's all about?"

Vito mistook Guy's silence for interest in what he was saying. Guy was burning inside; he clenched his teeth to keep from exploding. Though he had grown to accept Vito over the years and trusted him, Guy was still resentful of the partnership that his father had forced upon him. The wound became aggravated whenever Vito disagreed with Guy, or tried to forge a different direction for the company.

Guy took a deep breath to extinguish his internal fire, and remind Vito of his place. "No, Vito, that is not what it is all about. That is not why my father started the business, and it is not why I saved it. Money was only the first step." Guy shifted to face Vito. "Money bought us choices, but the goal is to take our company and our families to the next level, to make a difference beyond the walls of our little houses. To be players, not spectators." Guy halved the inches of distance that separated him from Vito. "If you plan to retire or sell out, tell me now. I will have a secretary come in and draft your resignation."

Like a younger brother who had just been reprimanded, Vito hung his head. "Guy, we are in this thing together until the end. You know that. It is just that with all that we already have, it sometimes gets a little frustrating living with this constant pressure. I have not had a good night's sleep in years."

Guy loosened as he returned to his chair. "Tell me about it. I rarely sleep in my bed anymore. I spend half the night in my living room watching television until I doze off on the couch." Guy sat and looked at his watch. "The Board will be here in a few minutes, and they are going to want some answers. I will tell them about our current projects, and the profits we turned from the sale of our real estate holdings."

Vito joined him at the table. "Sounds good so far."

Guy continued. "And then I will just send out a trial balloon on expanding to foreign markets. We will set up an exploratory committee. These guys love exploratory committees. Makes them think they are doing something without having to make any hard decisions they can be sued for." Guy gave Vito a concession for his apparent acquiescence. "We can even have VJ and Lisa Marie take a couple of trips to South America on the company for exploratory purposes. It will be like an extended honeymoon for them."

Vito bit his fingernail. "I guess I can go for that. VJ always complained that your kids traveled more than he did. It always bothered him. I mean, we traveled. It's just that we always went to Italy. My thinking was, why go anywhere else when Italy had everything? I couldn't convince VJ. He would talk about the stories Albert and Edward would tell about your trips to Africa and Australia, and felt like your boys were looking down at him. That really bothered him."

"Vito, you know that's not true. Even before he got engaged to Lisa Marie, VJ was like a third brother to Albert and Edward."

Vito grimaced. "Some travel would be good for VJ. He needs to get out of my shadow a little bit. Maybe you are right. Maybe him working for the company was not such a great idea. I think he feels a little intimidated. He is not like your boys. He is a simple guy, who of course loves your daughter. It is just that he does not have the confidence yet. I don't know if he ever will."

Guy was happy that he had forged the deal with his partner. "VJ will be fine. This is probably just what he needs, a little independence." Guy slipped in the last item on his agenda. "Oh, and there is one more thing I wanted to discuss with the Board."

"What's that?"

Guy's eyes widened. "Albert is going to announce that he is running for the open seat in the United States Senate."

Vito slapped the table. "You're kidding. But Guy, why would he want to subject his family to that mess? The press – they are goddamn animals. They're worse than the labor unions."

A smile snaked across Guy's face. "It was his decision."

Vito lifted a corner of his mouth wryly. "You always said that the United States Senate is the most elite club in the world."

Guy raised his finger to the air. "First, we have to get him there. Marie and I are going to have a party at our house in two weeks so that Albert can make the announcement. Five hundred dollars a plate."

Vito took out his pocket calendar, as if a conflict would absolve him from purchasing tickets. "Two weeks, huh? We'll be here. How many tickets am I in for?"

"Oh, I don't know. As many as you want." Without allowing Vito an opportunity to respond, Guy followed. "Albert's father-in-law, Giles Kirby, has already said he is in for ten."

Vito twitched. "I guess that means I am in for twelve. Fine."

Guy pointed. "You will bring VJ and Lisa Marie?"

Vito retorted. "So long as you are not sending them to Antarctica that night."

The partners chuckled.

Vito leaned forward. "I assume Albert is running as a Democrat. What does the competition look like?"

Guy explained. "We already have the blessing of the state and national Democratic committees. They like his style and resources."

"Who wouldn't?"

Guy completed his thoughts on a subject it was obvious he helped his son pursue. "So it does not look like we will have a problem getting the nomination. The seat has been Republican so long that most other Democrats won't even try. The real challenge is the general election. We think the Republican nominee is going to be the county District Attorney, Thomas Straid. Hard-nosed Irish guy. You know, law and order."

Vito tapped the table. "Aren't they all?"

Guy finished. "So I will see if I can get some of our blue-blooded friends on the Board to buy some tickets."

"Good luck. These WASPs are so damn tight that if you stuck a piece of coal up their collective ass, it would turn into a diamond."

Both men howled out loud.

The intercom in the middle of the boardroom table buzzed. A young female voice spoke. "Mr. Bennett."

Guy wiped the tears of laughter streaming down his cheek. "Yes, Barbara."

"All of the directors are here."

Guy slapped Vito on the shoulder, as Vito continued to laugh. "Send them in, and ask them if they would like any coffee."

The five outside directors assumed their usual seats. To Guy's immediate left was Nick Covitt, a slick Harvard MBA who had taken over a failing regional airline and made it a model for efficiency in the industry. Next to him was Eleanor Whittlesby, the elder heiress to her family's oil empire, who surprised everyone with her business acumen after her father died. Rounding out the left side was Jared Pym, a former Director of Transportation for the State of New York who was teaching urban planning and engineering at his alma mater, Columbia University. On the right next to Vito were Bramford Leach, the owner of a stock brokerage house, and Wall Street corporate attorney David Rothstein, from the firm of DeWitt & Case.

Nick Covitt made small talk with Jared Pym. "So Jared, did you go to the game?"

Pym's thin smile complemented his bow tie and tweed jacket.

"No, unfortunately. I was doing some consulting in Malaysia that week. I didn't make it back in time."

Covitt would not let Pym off the hook. "That's too bad. You might have been able to see how football is meant to be played, Harvard style. I believe the score was Harvard 44, Columbia 3. Didn't we have a wager on the game?"

Pym reached into his pocket and pulled out his money clip. He peeled a dollar bill and handed it to Covitt. "Yes, we did. Here is your dollar. Next time we will bet a free cocktail on one of your airlines."

"And what will I get if I win? An outline of one of your lectures?"

Pym turned to Guy. "I apologize for my colleague's poor manners. It seems that they no longer teach etiquette at Harvard. How are you, Guy? Shall we begin?"

Guy snickered. "A one-dollar bet? I am just glad you guys are on my side."

Bramford Leach cut to the chase. "Guy, the brokers at my place are telling me that the word on Wall Street is that Northern's earnings are down. If we don't watch it, we might become a target for a takeover."

Guy assumed the Bennett poker face. "Nonsense. We have $500 million in jobs pending. Our aqueduct projects in California and Arizona are ahead of schedule, and it looks like we are going to see sizable profits on them. I want to thank Jared personally for his initiative. These projects could lead to more work like them in the future."

Nick Covitt draped his custom-made jacket from London's Savile Row across the back of his chair. "We can talk about the future in the future. What about the present? The shareholders want the now."

Guy tapped his index finger on the table. "Because of the flooding in Ohio and Pennsylvania, we have had delays there. So it doesn't look like we are going to see much cash flow from those states next quarter. And the steel workers in New Jersey are on strike for their eighth straight week. They want more benefits. Getting work done there has been hampered severely."

Nick Covitt kept his focus. "So how do you plan to fill the gap?"

Guy was prepared. "Well, Scalini Realty has done a wonderful job selling off our major real estate holdings, and we should see nice profits on them shortly."

Eleanor Whittlesby raised an eyebrow, as she rubbed one of the pearls on her necklace. "Yes. Umberto Scalini, isn't it? Doesn't he have a place on Mulberry Street in Little Italy, right next to where that fellow got shot through the window while he was eating his spaghetti?" Covitt and Leach giggled at Whittlesby's dry innuendo that Scalini was in the Mafia. "I just hope that our profits aren't going into his marble floors – alongside any of his enemies."

Before Guy could speak on behalf of Scalini, whom the Board knew was a personal acquaintance of Guy, David Rothstein assumed the defense. While the others on the Board were chosen strictly for their pedigree and shareholder appeal, Rothstein had the added attraction of being long-time counsel to Guy, in whom Guy entrusted all his faith on corporate legal matters. "The real estate department at my law firm has had numerous dealings with Scalini Realty, and has told me that they are tops because of their professionalism. I can assure you, Eleanor, that our money is not going into marble floors."

Whittlesby spit a breath from between her wrinkled lips. She looked at Covitt and Leach. "No need to snap, David. I am just telling you what I heard."

Bram Leach stepped into the fold. "Assuming our money is not going into some palace in Little Italy and we see some profits from the real estate, that is fine for this quarter. But where are we looking for next quarter? Wall Street will want to know."

Guy took out his crescent-shaped glasses and slid them low on his nose, the way Jared Pym always did when reading or making a point. He opened the folder that Mohammad had prepared for him. "I am glad you asked, Bram. I had one of our analysts look at three international markets – South America, Africa, and Southeast Asia – for the possible overseas expansion of Northern Industries."

Leach and the others did not expect such a definitive answer from Guy, and were alarmed by its boldness. Leach followed. "And what did you find?"

Guy enjoyed having the upper hand on the Board, and would play it to the finish. "We concluded that there is a real opportunity in South America, specifically Argentina and Chile." Guy cut himself off, anxious to hear the quiver in the Board members' throats.

Eleanor Whittlesby bit first. Her sagging jowls bounced as she spoke. "But Guy, this is rather sudden. Don't you think it would be risky venturing into a foreign country so quickly? Who is to say that even if we were successful in obtaining and completing the work, that the company would get paid?"

Guy had the entire table exactly where he wanted it. "Point well taken, Eleanor. That is why Vito and I think it would be wise to set up an exploratory committee on the subject. We can have Vito's son, Vito Jr., head the committee, and travel to the countries to assess viability." Knowing that Jared Pym's lust for travel was deeper than his lint-filled professorial pockets, Guy turned to him as his first domino. "Professor, maybe you would also like to participate?"

The scholar's aging eyes limbered up. "I think it is a splendid idea, Guy. Northern Industries moves southward, spanning the Americas."

Though Whittlesby was shrewd, Guy knew that she had neither the will nor the capacity to challenge Pym's endorsement. "Does that satisfy your concerns, Eleanor?"

Whittlesby shifted her pearls around her neck. "I guess." She turned to Pym and started defining accountability on the issue. "So long as Jared is keeping a close eye on it."

Guy envied the way Pym cut his words, and often pawned them for himself. "Splendid. If no one has any objection, Jared will meet with Vito Junior, and set an agenda that will be presented at our next quarterly meeting."

Guy was anxious to wrap up the session. "The only item I have left is a personal one. My son Albert is going to run for the open seat in the United States Senate. My wife Marie and I will be hosting a kickoff fundraiser at our home in two weeks, where Albert will make the announcement. It is $500 a person, and we would be honored to have you and any of your friends attend."

There was silence, as the Board members busied themselves

to avoid eye contact with Guy. Whittlesby reached for her purse, while Covitt and Leach packed their briefcases. Pym folded his glasses into his shirt pocket.

Guy looked at David Rothstein, whose smirk confirmed that he knew what was happening, and then to Vito; Vito had to stare down to keep from laughing. Having just handed Jared Pym a travel voucher to South America, Guy again aimed at him as the weak link. "Albert is going to run as a Democrat. Jared, you served in a Democratic administration, didn't you?"

Pym stuttered. "Yes. Yes I did, Guy." When Guy's silence left Pym hanging, the professor knew he had to do something. "I will take one ticket, Guy."

David Rothstein curled his lip. "One ticket? What will you do, go by yourself?"

Pym raised his head and extended his hand toward Whittlesby. "Unless Eleanor will be my date."

Pleased that she could escape quickly with only one ticket, Whittlesby accepted. "I am charmed."

Nick Covitt extended his hand toward Bramford Leach. "Bram, shall we double date?"

Leach blew Covitt a kiss. "Perfect." He turned to Guy. "We'll see you in two weeks. Can we call your secretary for directions?"

Guy smiled. "You can pick them up on your way out."

Covitt pointed at Rothstein. "David, will we see you there?"

Rothstein snapped his briefcase shut. "Of course. I actually have a wife and friends who would also be honored to meet the next Senator. Put me down for six tickets, Guy."

After the others exited, Rothstein stayed behind. He laughed at Guy and Vito. "Can you believe this bunch of Beefeaters? A single ticket each?"

Guy collected his papers. "Probably no different than your graying partners at DeWitt & Case. Hey, I am happy that they even bought a ticket."

Vito Petrozzini shook his head. "The cheap bastards. They walk around like they have a potato chip up their asses that they don't want to break."

David Rothstein laughed; he always found Vito's crass sense of humor refreshing. "Well, Guy, I am in for six. Audrey and I have a bar mitzvah that afternoon, but we should be able to make it."

"Thanks, David, I appreciate it. You have always been there for us." Guy grabbed both Vito and David Rothstein by the shoulder. "Well, gentlemen, I have to hurry home, where Marie is cooking dinner for Albert's campaign manager, who I'm going to hire tonight."

Rothstein tilted an interested glance. "And who might that be?"

Guy looked back as he headed out the door. "Who else? My other son, Edward."

XXVII.

❦

Honoring Thy Father

Guy raced home, where he found Marie and Edward sitting at the kitchen table. Marie was already ladling her son his favorite dish of fetttucine carbonara. Were it one of her other children, Marie would have made them wait for their father before eating; inasmuch as Guy lived through Albert, Marie treated Edward as her favorite, for whom she always made an exception. Perhaps it was because of the life-threatening heart problem Edward had overcome as a child, or the sense of compassion it seemed to have engendered in him – whatever the reason, Marie always doted over Edward, and guarded him like she was his jealous girlfriend.

When Guy walked in with a bottle of wine, Marie smiled above the fragrant steam rising from the plate she was spooning Edward. "Guy, sit down. Your son has some news to tell you."

After sliding his car keys in the usual spot over the phone, Guy sat, and placed his bottle of wine in the middle of the table. "I am listening."

Edward blushed. "C'mon, Ma. It was really nothing."

Marie began serving her husband. "Edward won his first big case."

Guy slapped Edward on the shoulder, causing his son to drop his fork. "Congratulations, son. Tell me about it. What happened? In the meantime, I will break open this bottle of merlot. Cost me twenty-five bucks, but that's okay. This is a big night."

Edward retrieved his fork. "I am telling you, it was nothing. My client was a Colombian guy, with a pony tail. He gets pulled over by the cops, and when they see that his license is expired, they searched his car and found cocaine."

Guy scraped the plastic from around the neck of the bottle of merlot. "Maybe I shouldn't pour the wine just yet. You got some Colombian drug lord off?"

"Dad, if he were a drug lord, he wouldn't have come to me at the Public Defender's Office."

Guy smiled coyly. "Well, if he is not dealing drugs, how come he doesn't have a job to pay for his own lawyer?"

Marie banged her small fist on the table; she wanted to preserve Edward's moment. "Guy, would you let your son finish?'

"Thank you, Mom. Anyway, the guy tells me he has no idea how any drugs could have gotten into his car. He says he never touched the stuff. Too many friends had been hurt by it."

Guy poured Edward a glass of the five-year-old merlot. "Then why the pony tail?"

Marie pounded the table harder. "Guy!"

Guy poured his wife a glass. "Edward knows I am only kidding."

With the aid of his spoon, Edward rolled a fork full of the cream-painted fettuccine with chunks of bacon. "The D.A. offers my guy a final deal of seven years, with a possibility of parole in two. If we reject it, we go to trial. My guy says no, and we reject it. Two weeks later, I press the D.A. for his lab report on the cocaine. He keeps stalling me, stalling me, telling me I would have it before trial. I finally go before the court to get it, and it comes back negative. No cocaine – just a bunch of crumbs. All charges dropped."

Guy raised his glass for a toast. "Like I have always told you, son, everybody deserves a defense."

Mother, father, and son took a deep gulp together.

Guy licked his lips. "I just wish you were in a place where you got paid more for your talent. At Albert's firm, they get $5000 before they open a book."

Edward spoke through a mouth full of fettuccine. "I like the job, dad. It's exciting. If there were no public defender, the damn D.A. would have had my guy spending seven years in prison – just because he is Colombian and wears a pony tail."

Guy made the transition to the subject for which he had invited Edward to dinner. "Who was the D.A.? What's his name, Straid?"

"Dad, Tom Straid is *the* D.A. – the boss. I was against one of his lowly assistant D.A.'s. Rumor is that missing lab reports or bull-shitting about negative ones is the kind of stuff that happens all the time under Straid. The difference is that when he is handling the case himself, you never find out about it. I don't know how the guy sleeps at night."

Guy resisted another fork full of his wife's delicious carbonara. "How would you like to beat Straid?"

Edward laughed. "Dad, the guy has been prosecuting for ten years. I have been a lawyer for less than one. Besides, I thought he was busy running for the Senate."

"That's what I am talking about – beating him in front of a statewide jury, where you have more experience."

"What the hell are you talking about?"

"Your brother is going to run against Straid next year for that Senate seat. We want you to be his campaign manager."

Edward swallowed quickly. "Dad, I told you already. I am done with politics."

"Your brother said you told him in Italy that you would be there for him."

Edward snapped. "Then why isn't he asking me?" When Guy had no answer, Edward continued. "This is really your campaign, isn't it?"

Edward always knew how to hit the pressure points, especially when it came to his father. Guy spoke slowly to control himself. "You brother and his wife decided that this is what they want."

Edward shook his head in short strokes. "Sure, he pleases you, and Lady Victoria gets to go to more expensive parties, at taxpayer expense."

The veins on Guy's head thickened. "Will you or won't you serve as your brother's campaign manager?"

Edward looked at his mother. "Do I have a choice?"

Guy finished his glass of merlot. "Very well. Give your notice at the office, and call your brother yourself when you get home. He is very excited that the two of you will be working together. His treasurer is Michael Schwartz from his firm – a good Jewish lawyer."

Edward played with his food. "Why does it matter that he is Jewish?"

Guy made his way through a mouthful of macaroni. A drop of oil rolled from the side of his mouth. "Because Jews are good with finance. You two princes – your brother and you – can't manage your lunch money. Your heads are in the clouds. The Jew will make sure nothing gets wasted."

Edward rolled his eyes. "Oh, I see."

Guy continued his stride without pause. "Albert is going to announce in two weeks, right here in the backyard." Guy tried to arouse some excitement in Edward. "It's going to be $500 a ticket. Let's pack the place, huh?"

Edward sniped his revenge. "I'd better tell Nancy. We were supposed to go to Harvard that weekend for a reunion."

Guy wiped his mouth. "That's the Japanese girl, isn't it? I thought you weren't seeing her anymore."

Edward responded coolly. "Yeah, we started dating again. So, of course I am going to have to bring her."

Guy looked at Marie, who concentrated on her bowl. Guy wanted to say something, but could not, and Edward knew it. That is why he mentioned it to his father. Guy gripped the edge of the table in front of him. "That will be splendid. Your mother and I look forward to meeting your friend."

Edward took a sip of water. "Girlfriend, dad. She is my girlfriend. My Japanese geisha. Don't you remember? That's what the future Senator calls her. But don't worry. Once I tell her I am running Albert's campaign, she will probably leave me again."

Guy continued. "Your girlfriend, of course. That's what I meant."

XXVIII

Announcement Night

Highway America

The Bennetts scrambled for the next two weeks getting ready for the Announcement in Whitebridge. Edward did as his father told him, and gave notice of his leave at the Public Defender's Office; being that Albert's likely opponent was District Attorney Thomas Straid, whom the Defenders universally loathed, Edward's superiors and colleagues were supportive of his decision. Guy's wife worked with their daughter Lisa Marie on the catering and entertainment, while Lisa Marie's husband, VJ, was relegated to "gofer" errand boy, where he could not do any damage. Albert's wife Victoria helped him learn the names and matching faces that would attend the Announcement; Victoria was horrified at the prospect of Albert forgetting a name, particularly if it was one of her father's friends. And, of course, the speech. Guy and Edward spent days going over Albert's speech with him, arguing for hours over the right phrase or image. The Announcement became a total Bennett effort. Guy would accept nothing less for his family's coming out.

Limousines lined the street in front of Guy's house on Announcement Night. Guy and Marie, along with Albert and Victoria, greeted guests as they entered through the large wooden front doors. The foursome stood straight as a group of six approached, the men dressed in tuxedos, the women in gowns. Guy sucked in his stomach, and turned to his wife. "Look, here come the Ventillis. Carmine Ventilli has been telling everybody about this party. He has never been to a political fundraiser. Do you think they will notice I gained weight?"

Marie smiled ahead at the approaching guests. "Relax. You are the most handsome man in Whitebridge."

Albert muttered to his wife Victoria from the side of his mouth. "Who are these people, and why are they wearing tuxedos? We didn't write 'black tie' on the invitations."

Victoria shook her head, keeping the same steady smile as her mother-in-law. "How many times do we need to go over this, you idiot? They are the Ventilli brothers – Carmine, Joe, and Pat. They are wearing the tuxedos because that's their business – VB Formal Wear – you know, the chain of tuxedo stores! You rented your tuxedo from them for our wedding. You would probably like to forget that day, too."

"Oh," uttered Albert.

Victoria continued her forced smile. "When am I going to get through that thick goddamn skull of yours how important it is to remember names? Impressions are so important. I don't know why I even bother. They are your father's greasy Italian friends. It's probably the first fucking event they've been to where the main dish isn't sausage and peppers – with all that oil. Disgusting."

Albert whispered back. "Does your father know what kind of mouth he bought for you when he sent you to that all-girls finishing school in New England? You could make a sailor blush."

Albert stepped immediately ahead, and shook the hand of the first of the Ventilli men, an older gentleman with a gray mustache. "Signori and Signore Ventilli, *piacere*. So please tell me, what does the "VB" stand for in the famous VB Formal Wear?"

The Gray Mustache half smiled, and turned to his friend Guy. "*I Fratelli Ventilli.*"

Guy waited anxiously. He spoke to his wife through clenched teeth. "I hope Albert remembers some of his Italian from college. I endowed the Chair at that school to start the Italian department. Carmine's kids are fluent, and he didn't spend a dime."

Albert hesitated, then shot up his arms. "*Fratelli Ventilli* – Ventilli brothers – 'VB' – of course."

The Gray Mustache could not control himself. He kissed Albert on the cheek. "Bravo, Alberto." The Gray Mustache's brothers and their wives each gave Albert and his wife a warm southern Italian embrace, making Victoria visibly uncomfortable.

As Guy and his wife spoke with the Ventillis, Victoria brushed her bare arms with her hands. "Do all Italian men use such sweet cologne? I don't recall asking them if I could wear some of it."

Albert smiled as he watched his father, flush with pride, put his arm around the Gray Mustache. Guy took two glasses of wine from the white-gloved waiter serving them, and gave one to the Gray Mustache. "We have come a long way since our fathers made booze in the basement of your dad's store."

The Gray Mustache slapped Guy on the chest. "And from what I heard, your father could drink. But don't worry, I am not here to collect Dante's tab. The invitation makes us even."

Albert turned to Victoria with a sneer. "You should be flattered, Victoria. If you are lucky, maybe some of their emotion also rubbed off on you." Albert turned to the slam of another car door. "Well, you should be more comfortable with this one, the Great White Father of my law firm, Wade Billingsly. I am sure all that he uses is Ivory soap – the unscented kind."

Billingsly stepped up in his pinstriped suit and heavily starched white shirt, wearing his wife, Judy, at his side. "Albert, this looks like quite an event. I hope you are not spending too much of the campaign's money tonight. The firm is making a heavy investment in two of its valuable attorneys – you and Schwartz."

Albert stood tall, square with the imposing Billingsly. "You won't be disappointed, sir. I promise."

There was an awkward silence. Victoria looked at Albert with impatient eyes, and finally introduced herself. "I am Albert's wife, Victoria."

Billingsly's wife did the same, cracking her mouth ever so slightly. "And I am Wade's wife, Judy."

Instead of kissing or extending a hand, Wade Billingsly merely tilted his head forward. "Pleasure."

Victoria responded in kind. "The pleasure is ours." Once the

Billingslys moved on, Victoria held her chin high. "Now, that was an appropriate greeting."

Albert looked to the next guests. "If you're dead."

The Billingslys passed Guy and Marie without spending a word more than their names, and made their way into the party, their faces long with obligation.

Guy began to perspire beneath the setting autumn sun.

Albert's brother, Edward, and Michael Schwartz were busy maintaining order in the back, communicating by cellular phone across the yard's expanse. As much as it pained her, Edward's date Nancy stood faithfully by his side, smiling as her beau worked the crowd for his older brother. The experience was made palatable for Nancy by the way the bloated older men in attendance gawked over her; her sharp Far Eastern features, piercing brown-black eyes, and delicately carved figure gave her the allure of forbidden fruit.

Covitt and Leach stood in the distance inhaling jumbo shrimp. Out of the corner of his eye, Covitt noticed Nancy, the deep plunge in the back of her black dress reaching midway down her well-lined posterior. Covitt cleaned the cocktail sauce from his mouth. "Bram, who is that fine piece of half-wrapped sushi over there?"

Leach studied Nancy before answering, her head of straight black hair tossing as she turned toward them. "A fine piece, indeed. But I think she's Korean. Isn't that Guy's son Edward next to her?"

Covitt shook his head. "I have spent a lot of time in Asia trying to help them with their airlines. She is definitely Japanese." Covitt caressed his own cheeks and chin. "Her features are too sharp." He rubbed his hands together. "What do you say, old boy? I think it's time we get to know the Chairman's other son."

Leach reached for one last piece of shrimp from a passing wait- ress. "Excellent idea. And I bet you a dollar she is not Japanese."

"You're on."

Covitt and Leach approached Edward, Nick Covitt extending his hand first. "You must be Guy's younger son, Edward. I am Nick Covitt, and this is Bramford Leach. We both serve on the board of Northern Industries."

Edward knew that his father was not a big fan of either Covitt or Leach; he gave them only the obligatory welcome. "Of course, Father has told us so much about you. Welcome, and thank you for coming." Edward extended his hand toward Nancy to introduce her, when his cellular phone rang. "Excuse me."

Annoyed by the interruption and pomp of the entire affair, Nancy introduced herself. "I am Nancy Kane." Instead of describing herself as Edward's girlfriend, Nancy decided to taunt Covitt's middle-aged yet still mischievous smile. "I work with Edward at the Public Defender's Office."

Bram Leach tried to inject himself into the hunt. "You must meet a lot of interesting people in your business."

Knowing that neither Covitt nor Leach had any interest in her clients, but were instead piqued by her exotic beauty, Nancy replied, "Yeah, crackheads, prostitutes, murderers, it gets old after a while. But they all deserve a defense, don't you think?" Covitt and Leach smiled at each other. "Of course."

Nancy gave Edward a resentful glance as he continued on the cellular phone. Edward shrugged his shoulder that there was nothing he could do. A waiter approached the group with toasted corners, laid with cream cheese and a generous topping of Nova Scotia salmon. Nancy's eyes lit up. "Oh, salmon, my favorite."

Covitt grumbled to Leach. "The Japanese love raw fish. I win."

Nancy squinted inquisitively as she grabbed a corner. "Excuse me?"

Covitt extemporized, as he was wont do in acquisitions. "Oh, nothing." He grabbed a corner for himself. "It is just my way of telling Bram that I get the first piece."

Nancy removed the roll of salmon off its bread corner, unfurled it, and held it by one of its ends. "I hope you don't mind if I use my hands. It is the way my family ate it when I was growing up."

Covitt wrinkled his forehead and protruded his lips. "Of course, in Japan it is the only way..." His mouth stopped to join Leach in a lapdog stare, as Nancy threw her hair off her shoulder and forehead, and tilted her head backward. She held the long piece of pink salmon above her open mouth, and lowered it slowly. Mouths agape, the two men watched intently as Nancy's glowing white teeth pulled the chase over her thin purple lips, her curling tongue sounding wet with delight. They could hear her consumption, as the treat passed down her long thin throat.

Nancy closed her eyes and exclaimed. "That was delicious. So fresh."

Covitt hurried to shove his corner into his mouth. "Yes. Yes it is."

Leach tried to do the same, but could not because he had dropped his piece during the spectacle of the beauty swallowing her quarry. "Yes, so fresh. I think I will have another."

Edward caught only the tail end of the ruse before finishing his call and folding his cellular. He gave Nancy a disapproving glare before announcing, "Ladies and gentlemen, my brother is about to give his speech. Please gather around the eagle."

Guy stepped up to the microphone on the slightly raised podium. Marie stood off to his right, Albert and Victoria to his left. Behind Guy was an oversized ice carving of an American eagle that glistened in the dusk's glorious last light. Guy began to perspire heavily again; it was bad enough when he had to address the board of Northern Industries; an entire crowd made his tongue swell and legs shake. He took a folded piece of paper from his jacket pocket and laid it on the podium.

"Ladies and gentlemen, I want to thank you all for joining us on this wonderful evening. Welcome to the town of Whitebridge, and to our home."

The crowd lowered to a few whispers.

"My wife Marie and I were sitting in our kitchen last night over dinner, talking about Albert's big night. The thing that struck us most was that it was going to take place in our backyard, the place that we always encouraged our children to have their fun when they were young, playing football or baseball with the other kids. We would often peek through the kitchen window, always cautious not to let Albert see us."

The crowd gave a cocktail laugh.

"There were times that Albert came inside for dinner glowing with victory, and other times that he wore the bruises of defeat. Through it all, the thing that impressed us most was that he would always talk about the team, rather than dwelling on himself. He would be obsessed with what his team did or did not do during the game that day, and how they could do better in the next game. That is what always made us most proud."

Guy turned to Albert. "Son, you are about to begin the most competitive game of your life here tonight. The touchdowns and home runs may be many, but so too will be the bruises. Never forget the lesson you learned in the backyard – that the team – be it your family, your friends here tonight, or what will hopefully become your future constituency – is always greater than any one of its players. Your mother and I love you, son, and wish you and the team the best."

As the crowd gave a collective sigh and began to applaud, Guy and Albert embraced beneath the gaze of the ice-carved eagle.

Albert used his handkerchief to wipe a tear from his eye, and assumed the podium. "Thank you, Mom and Dad. I love you too."

As Albert's mother blew him a kiss, Victoria fidgeted next to her husband. "This is not a wedding anniversary. Get on with it."

"As you all know, I have asked you here tonight to announce my candidacy for the United States Senate."

The gathered crowd thundered in applause.

"In doing so, I could think of nothing more fitting than telling you about my father's father, Dante. His story is by now a familiar one shared by many American families. At the age of seventeen, Dante left a small town in Italy, and struck out for a place called America. I am not going to bore you with his struggles and achievements, which have become the clichés of political speeches. Trust me when I tell you there were many."

As the crowd smiled, the Gray Mustache jabbed one of his brothers in the rib.

Albert continued. "Instead, I want to share with you my grandfather's favorite pastime – taking a ride on Highway America. The thing that Grandpa cherished most about America was its vastness of possibilities. He wanted to enjoy them all. So he saved his money and bought a used Ford. He painted it his favorite color, which he called Liberty Green, the same as the beautiful lady in New York Harbor."

Albert looked at Edward in the crowd, who responded with a subtle thumbs-up to calm his brother. "And in his car he went, with the top down and wind blowing through his hair, across Highway America. He used to tell us about the excitement of finding something new at every stop – an endless field of wheat, a baseball game, a skyscraper being built, the ocean and the mountains – one breathtaking sight after another. He once even drove with Dad in his Liberty Green Ford to Florida, and bought a piece of land in the middle of the swamps, on Merritt Island. We now watch rockets launch into space from Grandpa's old land. It's called Kennedy Space Center." Albert injected a bit of humor. "If only ol' Dante could have held that land a little longer."

The crowd's faces lit, signifying to Albert that they belonged to him.

"But Highway America is in disrepair. It has become harder to travel, and inaccessible to many. Overregulation and its red tape have caused congestion and foreclosed expansion; bigotry, contentment, and neglect have become a roadblock to the poor, who can barely even afford a car. Even those who have the ability to travel the great Highway have decided against it because of the increasing danger it represents. We are regressing to the village mentality that my grandfather had the vision to leave behind. We are standing by idly, watching the determined crumble of the roads that connect us. I challenge you to join my pledge today to rebuild Highway America. It can and must be done." Albert turned to his father. "As a team."

The crowd only slowly accepted the varied message of Albert's challenge with graduated applause, until the Gray Mustache yelled out as if he were at an opera, "Bravo! Bra-vo!" The other Ventilli brothers joined in, and soon the clapping around them began crackling. A cheer emerged, "Ben-nett, Ben-nett, Ben-nett!"

Albert Bennett was on his way to the Democratic nomination to the United States Senate.

Victoria gave her husband the measured kiss of a candidate's wife. "C'mon, Daddy has some people he wants you to meet."

Lisa Marie and Vito Petrozzini, Jr., joined Guy and Marie on the podium. Lisa Marie hugged her father. "Daddy, you were great.

We are so proud of you. Both of you. I have a good feeling about this. We are going to win."

With his arm around his daughter, Guy looked to Vito, Jr. "What did you think, VJ?"

VJ offered a response through his dull gray eyes. "I know what Albert was talking about with the highways. They are terrible. Potholes, the lanes are not wide enough. Just yesterday, I spent two hours on the interstate in traffic."

While Marie Bennett received VJ's response, Guy whispered in his daughter's ear. "Does VJ realize that Highway America is only a metaphor?"

Lisa Marie patted her father on the chest. "Dad, leave him alone. You always said he may not be worldly, but he is a whiz with numbers. Would you have rather I married someone just like Albert or Edward?"

Guy watched Victoria pull Albert through the crowd like a puppy on a chain. "That woman is tough on your brother," he sighed. "Maybe D.C. will lighten her up." He then looked over at Edward, with Nancy in tow. "And that other one, I don't think I will ever figure him out. Don't you have any nice friends you can fix him up with?"

"Daddy!"

Guy smiled down at his daughter. "I know, I know. How about you? How are you and VJ, and when am I going to have a grandson?"

Lisa Marie perked up. "Not until we finish our trips to South America." Lisa Marie pulled VJ by the hand. "Right, honey?"

VJ responded with mouth drawn slightly. "What's that?"

"I was just telling Daddy how excited we are about the trips to Chile for the company."

VJ wiped a drop of red wine that was falling off his lip. "I always wanted to go to the place where chili was invented. It's one of my favorites, with some fajitas and a cold beer. I can't wait."

Guy raised his eyebrows and took a deep breath. "Yes. Chili, fajitas, and beer. We certainly look forward to hearing all about what you find. We'll talk tomorrow."

Guy excused himself for some privacy. He went over to the ice eagle and caressed its wing. Though still standing proud, it was beginning to melt as the sun set.

Down below, Victoria pushed Albert toward her father, Giles Kirby, who was busy holding court with some business colleagues. "Daddy?"

Kirby turned his tall frame that still fit well his veteran charcoal suit, cut conservatively with fine pinstripes – the kind that so survives the latest trends that it can barely be called a style. His graying hair was parted to the side, and combed straight back above his ears. "Victoria, Albert, I would like you to meet some of my friends." Kirby turned to his left, and extended a hand toward a rugged and husky figure of a man. "George Kelly, self-made dairy producer. He has revolutionized the industry nationwide. I am proud to say that we at Webb Investments took his company public five years ago."

Kelly reached out with his thick hand and forearm, his French-cuffed shirtsleeves held together by gold coin links. He wrapped his thumb tightly around Albert's forefinger to lay claim to the handshake. Kelly spoke rapidly and nonsequentially, the way he shouted orders to his subordinates in his dairy kingdom. "Yeah, yeah, pleasure to meet you, Al. Great speech. I agree with what you said – much too much government red tape. We need less regulation. I would have loved to have met your grandfather. Sounds like he was my kind of guy – an adventurer who pulled himself up by the bootstraps."

Albert smiled, and looked to the next suit, which was less flamboyant and more refined than Kelly. "Pleasure to meet you, Albert, my name is Cameron Krupp. I am the CEO of Bruckner-Phelps Pharmaceuticals." Krupp tilted his head slowly toward Giles Kirby. "Another creation of Webb Investments, except mine was a merger and acquisition." Krupp closed his eyes for effect before returning to Albert. He held his cocktail glass with both hands. "I too enjoyed your speech, and heard what you had to say about the poor and disenfranchised. The problem is that they have forgotten how to help themselves. There is little we can do for them until we get rid of welfare and the culture of dependency we have engendered in them."

Giles Kirby rejoined. "Based on our conversations during the merger, Cam, I would imagine that you would agree that two of the issues Albert addressed are interrelated – with less regulation, companies like yours can create more jobs for the poor."

Krupp raised his chin and eyebrows. "Exactly."

Kirby extended his hand toward the last of his trio, a short and thin darker man, dressed stylishly in a European three-piece suit, its vest cut smartly with lapels. Kirby attempted a Spanish accent that sounded odd coming from his lips. "And this is Felipe Cepeda, the head of Teléfonos Internacionales. His company has been busy rewiring much of South America. Felipe is living proof that anyone can make it when given the right incentive."

Albert felt the insult of his father-in-law's compliment to Cepeda. He sensed the little man's shyness in the trace of Incan origin that pinched his almond-shaped eyes. Though Cepeda's financial success probably dwarfed that of Kelly and Krupp, Albert knew that Cepeda was neither outspoken nor eloquent; like the Bennetts, he was a newcomer to events like Announcement Night, and therefore would speak only sparingly so as not to embarrass himself. Albert held out his hand. *"Buenas*, Don Felipe. It is our privilege to have you here."

Put at ease by Albert's salutation, Cepeda ventured with some modest English. "Thank you. The privilege is mine."

Edward broke into the crowd. "Excuse me, Mr. Kirby. Albert, may I speak to you for a second?"

Edward pulled Albert away nervously. He shook in the air a brick-like device that he had been speaking into.

"What the hell is that thing? It looks like a walkie-talkie. It's as big as your head."

"It's a handheld portable phone. Dad bought them for the campaign."

Albert raised his eyebrows. "Figures."

"Schwartz is on the other side of the yard. He says Gabrielle DeFiore, the writer from *The Daily*, is here and she wants a quick interview. I don't know how she got in. I told everybody no press, especially not that piranha."

Albert smiled. "I invited her. I admire her work. She has a poet's tongue."

Edward shot back. "And a pen like a knife. She can kill us at the starting line if she does not think the candidacy is credible. Are you crazy? Why the hell did you invite her? I thought I was the campaign manager."

Albert put his hand on Edward's shoulder. "Calm down, little brother. She is the most influential political writer in the state. We cannot win without her support. Besides, she is Italian. That has to bode well for us. Bring her over. I will gladly give her an interview."

Edward gave Schwartz the go-ahead, and Schwartz went to fetch DeFiore. Like Albert, Michael Schwartz was a bold young attorney who sought a law degree as the key to unlock the door of power. His parents were working class Jews from Brooklyn, and their parents refugees who had escaped Russian pogroms. The Schwartzes skipped the generation of wealth building that patriarchs like Guy believed was the proper foundation for real influence. Schwartz was impatient, and for much of his life dreamed of being a politician, but had grown politically jaded enough in recent years to realize that his place was behind a candidate, directing the moves. Schwartz's practicality and capacity to calculate coldly made him a natural complement to Albert's good looks and charismatic air. Perhaps more importantly, he too both loathed and longed for the Establishment; his open distrust of the privileged was betrayed by his tortoise-shell glasses, Brooks Brothers suit, and Alden shoes.

Schwartz's escort of Gabrielle DeFiore across the Bennett yard was a long one, made nervous by the reporter's great beauty and subtle wit. Just before reaching Albert, DeFiore reached for a flute of champagne from a passing white-gloved waiter. She smirked. "Schwartz, just so I am clear, Mr. Bennett is running as a Democrat, isn't he?"

Schwartz gave DeFiore only a quick side-glance as he continued to walk toward Albert. "Of course."

DeFiore smiled at the bubbly that she held with her long fingers. "I guess he is a new Democrat. The old ones wouldn't even pretend to be so patrician. They couldn't afford it." DeFiore raised her thick brow. "I must say, Schwartz, that is a fine tie you are wearing. What is it, a Hermès?"

Schwartz's eyes remained fixed ahead. "My mother gave it to me."

When Schwartz and DeFiore reached Albert, the reporter offered her own introduction. "Good evening, Mr. Bennett. My name is Gabrielle DeFiore. I am the political reporter from *The Daily* whom you invited to tonight's event."

Albert looked admiringly at DeFiore, who stood only a few inches shorter than he. Her pronounced forehead was a provocative warning above lashes that flittered like a matador's cape before dazzling green eyes. A long flow of black hair rested feline atop strong shoulders that narrowed into a generous hourglass figure. Even the plastic pen that DeFiore held seemed potent in her rich, olive-skinned hand. Albert responded to the reporter's luxuriant lips without thinking about the hard questions they might pose. "Your reputation precedes you, Ms. DeFiore. You need no introduction."

DeFiore smiled quickly and started scribbling in her reporter's notebook. "Thank you sir, but with all due respect, you do need an introduction. You have held no prior political position or office. The voters need to find out who you are."

Upon noticing the reporter, Albert's wife Victoria joined the group, pushing out a laugh. "When the voters find out who he is, maybe they can tell me." Victoria extended DeFiore a hand. "My name is Victoria Bennett, Albert's wife." Victoria cast her husband a jaundiced eye before assuming for DeFiore the smile of the candidate's wife. "It's just that my husband is a very complicated and thoughtful man."

"Judging from his speech, it sounds that way." DeFiore pressed her pen to her chin. "The repair of Highway America, as you put it, sir, was a striking image."

Albert tipped his head proudly. "Why thank you."

"But not one that I am sure we have the ability to finance. It sounded as though you want to address the problems of our cities and the poor, which we all know are costly. But without any mention of any tolls along the way, your notion of mending Highway America seems incomplete and perhaps misleading. Won't you need to raise taxes to get the job done? The government shuts down over tax increases of the magnitude you're talking about."

Edward tried to intercede on behalf of Albert, who he knew by nature was more versed in the big picture than the short strokes that compose it. "We will be issuing position papers in six weeks that set forth the details you are looking for. If you will leave me your card, I will have a set sent directly to you."

Albert placed a stern arm in front of Edward, as if to hold him back. "That will be fine, Edward, but Ms. DeFiore and her readers need some answers now. And the answer is this. Americans of every racial, ethnic, and religious denomination, of all political and social strata, need to know that it is in everyone's best interest to attack poverty and reconnect our cities. Otherwise, the poor will soon be pitted against the rich, Black against White, small against big. The fallout could be devastating. Unless Americans start developing an enlightened sense of self-interest, the United States will become an oxymoron."

DeFiore was moving her pen wildly, taking copious notes. "Are you suggesting some type of class or race war in America?"

Edward had skirted behind Gabrielle DeFiore where Albert could see him. He gestured a slit across his neck, signaling for his brother to stop.

Albert retreated. "All I am saying is that we will all be better off if we learn to work together. Government should not be a zero sum game among different players or groups. We all should play for the 'win-win.'"

DeFiore finished her notes. "Off the record, Mr. Bennett. That was some fiery rhetoric. Why didn't you use some of it in your speech?"

Albert took a sip of champagne. "Off the record, Ms. DeFiore." He tipped his glass. "I was saving it for you."

DeFiore handed Albert her card. "Keep in touch. I will be watching you in the coming weeks."

Victoria whispered in her husband's ear. "And so will I. If you have one more affair, you can call my lawyer and kiss your pretty little Senate seat goodbye." Victoria gave Albert a peck on the cheek, and smiled to the parting DeFiore. "Nice meeting you."

XXIX.

Front Page News

Eating Chili

The campaign crew gathered the next morning in its headquarters in the Northern Tower in New York City, the space created by Guy in the penthouse suite one floor above his own office. Guy assumed the empty desk, with Michael Schwartz sitting opposite, finishing the balance sheet for Announcement Night. Albert stood off to the side, with his back against the wall.

Guy held his cup of steaming black coffee. "How much did we net, Michael?"

Schwartz dropped the last check into the interoffice envelope, and punched some numbers into his miniature adding machine. He pulled the paper tabulation from the machine, cut it, and held it in the air to read. "After expenses, one hundred and thirty thousand dollars." Schwartz's teeth glimmered. "And nineteen cents."

Guy pounded on the desk. "Sonofabitch. That's what I love about you, Schwartz. Most guys would have forgotten about the nineteen cents."

Schwartz took off his glasses. "My grandfather was a tailor on the Lower East Side of New York. He used to say 'another cent means another stitch.' Every penny is going to count down the stretch."

Guy looked to his son Albert. "Do I know how to throw a party, or what?"

Albert smiled. "I would like to think it was my party."

Guy waved off his son. "You know what I mean."

Edward burst through the door with four editions of *The Daily*.

He started handing them to his father, Albert, and Schwartz. "*Daily* here, get it while it's hot."

Guy shouted excitedly. "What does it say? Are we the headline?"

Edward handed a copy to Schwartz. "I just got them downstairs. We are not the headline, but the piranha has us front page. We'll see if your little gamble paid off, bro."

Schwartz read the headline out loud. "Bennett announces for U.S. Senate in Whitebridge."

Reading from his copy, Guy rejoined with the subscript. "At Five Hundred Dollars a Plate, Democrat Challenges Crowd to Reach Out to Poor."

They all read their copies quickly, eager to get to the punch line. Edward chewed nervously on a bagel as he read the first paragraph. "Against a backdrop of chrysanthemums and an ice-carved American Eagle in his parents' backyard in affluent Whitebridge, Albert Bennett last night announced his candidacy in the Democratic primary for the United States Senate. Speaking to a crowd that paid five hundred dollars to enjoy champagne, salmon, and the company of fellow chief executive officers and captains of industry, Bennett challenged those in attendance to rebuild what he called 'Highway America' for all of its users, including the needy. Bennett's plan for Highway America appears to invite all comers."

"Sounds great so far," said Guy from his chair.

Edward continued reading DeFiore's review. "Unfortunately, the young lawyer provided little explanation of how the government will finance his grand public work; in the coming months, it will be incumbent upon him to do so if his candidacy will have viability with a jaded electorate. If ever his candidacy's machinery falters, however, Bennett seems to have the genuine conviction to refuel it, a commodity that is rare in these political times. This is a new voice worth listening to."

Schwartz looked up gleefully. "I consider that a win coming from her."

Leaning against the wall, Albert pinched his chin. "Geez, she really does have a lot of spunk."

Relieved, Edward rocked back in his folding chair. "Yeah, she is not your typical Italian daddy's girl."

Guy dropped his smile. "What do you mean by that, son? Is your sister Lisa Marie a typical Italian daddy's girl? She beats the market daily on Wall Street, and now she is going to start night classes in journalism. She'll show you real writing – after she starts a family. I bet this DeFiore girl isn't even married."

Edward raised his hands to stave off the charging bull. "Take it easy, Dad. All that I am saying is that DeFiore seems to have a little edge. That's all. A little more maverick than most of the Italian girls I know."

Michael Schwartz cut the cord of tension that was tightening between Edward and his father. "That's because she is half Puerto Rican."

The Bennett trio looked at Schwartz puzzled.

Schwartz continued. "Yeah, I thought you guys knew. She does a ton of work with the Hispanic community in the city. If I had known she was going to be at Announcement Night, I probably would have made a few suggestions for the speech along those lines."

Guy tapped the desk in front of him. "The speech was perfect the way it was." He stood up, rolled his copy of *The Daily*, and banged it on the desk's edge. "We are off to the races, fellas. Let's go get some votes."

Vito Petrozzini poked his head through the door. "Excuse me, Guy. VJ, Mohammad, and I are ready for the meeting downstairs."

Guy smiled at his sons and Schwartz. "In the meantime, I've got to go make some money."

As Vito and Guy walked to the elevator, Vito studied the freshly painted walls of the penthouse suite that had been renovated to become Albert's campaign headquarters. "The carpenters did a nice job up here." He knocked on a doorframe. "And fast."

Guy smiled. "They charged me double time to do it."

Vito gathered his courage. "But Guy, I thought we were going to use this floor for executive suites."

The elevator bell rang. Guy extended his arm to invite Vito to enter first. "We will, eventually. The election is less than a year away. And if Albert wins..." Guy folded his hands in prayer, and looked to the ceiling of the descending elevator. "If he wins, he should probably keep his home office there. That way, we get the state to reimburse us for the space, and at the same time get access to the players that will come calling on Albert. It's a win-win."

Vito flexed a limp smile. "I guess." The bell rang for Vito and Guy to exit. "That was a helluva party last night. Had to be the biggest bash in Whitebridge in a while."

Guy responded wryly. "Actually, my neighbor Chauncey Stoddard is a Senior V.P. at National Communications. He had a huge party for company executives just last month – string quartet, a speech by the Secretary of State, the whole nine yards." Guy was enjoying the dividends of his American journey. "They are almost a regular thing in Whitebridge. Don't they have parties like that at your place in Middletown?" Guy was referring to the upper-middle class town in which he, Vito, and their families had originally settled, where Vito had chosen to remain ever since. Though comfortable, it was modest relative to the sprawling mansions of Whitebridge. Guy had always urged Vito to make the move to Whitebridge, but Vito felt that his family did not have the pedigree to belong. Besides, in Whitebridge, Vito would always be second fiddle to Guy; in Middletown, he held first chair.

Vito opened the door to the meeting room where VJ and Mohammad were waiting. "No expensive parties. In Middletown, we have our fun with each other, in shorts and a T-shirt over a barbecue."

Guy ignored Vito's counter-jab, instead choosing to address the sitting Mohammad and VJ. "Well boys, what do you have for me in South America?"

Mohammad stepped up. "Chile, sir. We like Chile. The economy continues to grow. And there are huge public works projects under way. They have approved funding for a number of hydroelectric and telecommunications programs."

Guy smiled at Vito. "Maybe I should talk to my neighbor Chauncey Stoddard on the telecommunications end." Guy spoke with a fake English accent. "Actually, he told me to call him Chaz."

VJ interrupted. "Guy, the hydroelectric projects can be very lucrative. Mohammad and I have been running the numbers, and with the low cost of labor down there, we can have profit margins as high as twelve percent." VJ looked over at Mohammad. "The only thing I am unsure of is the political stuff."

Guy was taken aback by VJ's enthusiasm and sharpness on the subject. He raised his eyebrows and looked at Mohammad. "Well, what about the political stuff?" Guy looked back at VJ quickly after emphasizing the "f" in stuff, so as to mock VJ's parochialism. Despite the fact that he had encouraged his daughter to marry VJ, Guy had always harbored a lingering resentment of his partner's son. It was bad enough that partnership had been handed to Vito by Dante and Adamo through their bargain; VJ's inheritance of position in the company that Guy and his father had built galled Guy all the more.

Mohammad answered Guy's question with a studied response. "The government has been civilian quite some time now, with the military at a safe distance looking over its shoulder. The Mexicans and Japanese have already gotten in, and the rate of pay on government contracts is over 92%. That's better than Uncle Sam these days."

Vito grumbled. "I still like Uncle Sam better. At least I know him. And he speaks my language – English."

VJ spoke out again, a rare instance in which he questioned his father in front of others. "Dad, these are real numbers and real dollars. You are being thickheaded."

Vito bit his lower lip, annoyed by both the project and his son's defiance. "I guess I will go along for exploratory purposes." He looked at his son. "Are you sure you can handle this? You and Lisa Marie are going to have to take some trips down there. It's far. What the hell will you eat?"

VJ smiled from ear to ear. "Chili."

XXX.

Pots Boiling Over in a Mother's Kitchen

A flurry of activity energized the Northern Tower in New York City during the rainy primary campaign. Vito assumed more of the management responsibilities within the company, as Guy shuttled often to the penthouse to check the status of Albert's run. The majority of Guy's trips outside the office were for the solicitation of campaign contributions from colleagues. A driven father, tireless brother, and politically ambitious friend fended off the challenge of a host of other primary competitors, Albert's troubled marriage, and the critical writings of Gabrielle DeFiore. When the rain dried and the spring flowers began to bloom, Albert was the Democratic candidate for the United States Senate.

To celebrate the primary victory, Guy and Marie took Albert and Victoria for a much-needed vacation at Guy's second home in Glendale, Arizona. Set among orange-brown desert cliffs and the plush man-made greens of the New Horizons Country Club to which Guy belonged, "Bennett West" had become Guy's retreat, a place to contemplate and taste his achievements. Guy loved to simply sit on the porch of his desert oasis in the late afternoon and enjoy the sun splashing down on him from the boundless blue sky above. Ever confident, he bought the tickets for the trip before the first primary vote was cast.

Back in Whitebridge, the family home had been left to Edward for the weekend, who had some catching-up of his own to do. His on-again-off-again relationship with Nancy had suffered from his absence during the homestretch of the primary campaign, and he wanted to make it up to her. He invited her to Whitebridge for a dinner that he would attempt to prepare himself. Reared by a doting southern Italian mother, Edward and his brother never had to pick up a plate during their childhood, much less learn how to boil a pot of water for cooking. He bought an expensive bottle of Italian red wine to ease the pain of any fallout from his culinary debut, and tried to keep the menu simple: a mozzarella and tomato salad that he could not possibly burn; some of his mother's leftover homemade tortellini and spinach soup whose proportions were already set; and an intermezzo of store-bought raspberry sherbet. His real test would come with the main dish that he chose – his favorite, fettuccine carbonara, with bits of bacon. He called his sister Lisa Marie for the recipe, which he jotted down on a paper towel. With his devilish smile that no one seemed to trust, he told his date to bring the dessert.

At 8 p.m sharp, while Edward was struggling to read the recipe for fettuccine carbonara that was bleeding on the wet paper towel, the doorbell rang. He turned down the heat on his wheezing pots and pans, and ran to open the door. There Nancy stood, straight and slender, with her hair pinned up and blouse buttoned down. She was holding a carrot cake topped with whipped cream and freshly cut strawberries. Edward hesitated before saying anything, taking in the magnificence he had missed during the dog days of the primary.

Content with the effect she was having, Nancy smiled. "You did say eight o'clock, didn't you?"

Edward responded quickly, as if a cold pail of water had been thrown on his face. "Yes, yes. As usual, you're right on time. I guess that's your Asian punctuality." Edward fumbled to wipe his hands on the apron he was wearing, on which was written *Casa Italia*, the name of his parents' favorite restaurant when they were younger and less socially sensitive; it featured etched pictures of a gondolier in Venice, the Vatican in Rome, and the statue of David in Florence, all in green, white, and red. The Bennetts and Petrozzinis had frequented the restaurant before the Bennetts moved to Whitebridge. As Edward wiped his hands, he noticed Nancy studying the apron with a smirk, and felt he had to explain its tacky design. "My dad is friends with the owner." He reached for the cake. "Let me take that."

Nancy marveled at the vaulted ceilings of the foyer as she followed Edward to the kitchen. "When I came to the house for your brother's party, I realized that this place was big, but with no one in it, it feels like a cathedral." She peeked at a fresco that hung over the dining room table. "And decorated like one, too. This painting is stunning. What is it, and where did your family get it?"

Edward left Nancy behind to attend to his work in progress. He yelled. "It's an original, from the Vatican collection, Christ as a young man turning over the tables of the moneychangers in the temple. Dad loves it because it shows a son protecting his father's house."

Nancy drew closer to study the masterpiece. "Did you say that this was from the Vatican collection? I know that they don't sell originals in the Vatican gift shop. How did your dad get it?"

Edward placed two candelabras on the kitchen table, where he had already set his and Nancy's places. "Dad's from the old school. He gives the church a lot of money. He calls it tithing – you know, voluntarily giving the church a certain percentage of your income." As he struck a match for the candles on the table, Edward thought of the many that he had lit as an altar boy in his local church. "It reminds me more of indulgences – the kind of church-designed payment for your sins that Martin Luther got so pissed off about. Anyway, he is real tight with the Cardinal because of it. And when Mom and Dad were in Rome, the Cardinal arranged for them to have a private audience with the Pope. Two weeks after they got home, a huge wooden box came to the house with the painting in it. Dad said it was a gift from heaven."

Nancy wandered into the sitting room, where a large oil painting of Edward's grandfather was displayed. "And who is this other guy painted in oil? St. Peter?"

Edward struggled with his dishes. "No, not quite. That's my grandfather, Dante. Straight from the Old Country."

Nancy followed. "Edward talked about him in his announcement speech."

"Yeah. Dad said he had the heart of a lion. Legend has it that when he realized that a guy sold him imitation bootleg during the Depression, he went to the guy's house and broke his jaw. I don't know what happened though, because he kind of faded in his later years. Didn't seem to have that same spirit when I knew him."

Nancy entered the kitchen. "Well, didn't he become crippled? That'll do it, you know."

Edward pulled a couple of strands of fettuccine from his rattling pot to test how much longer they needed. "I don't know, it's as if he stopped living until we revisited his hometown in Italy a year and a half ago."

Nancy lowered the heat on Edward's overrunning pot.

Edward looked down. "Thanks." He wiped the hot spill. "Maybe you're right. All I know is that my father would do anything for his father."

Nancy looked back at him. "They both seem to be men with a strong will."

Edward poured Nancy a glass of sangiovese red wine. "A little too strong if you ask me." Edward held out his forearm. "May I show you to your seat, signorina?"

Nancy clasped Edward's elbow. "You may. And tell the chef that if he is not too busy, I would love to have him join me for dinner."

Edward threw one of his father's opera disks onto the stereo carousel to set the mood. He dimmed the lights and brought two plates of mozzarella and tomato to the table, with a flask of extra virgin oil. "A little starter to get the juices flowing."

Nancy rubbed her hands in delight. "*Turandot*, my favorite."

Edward looked down at his plate. "No, tomato and mozzarella."

Nancy giggled. "I am talking about the opera that's playing on the stereo, silly boy."

Edward smiled back. "How do you know opera? You are not even Italian."

Nancy took a delicate bite, and pointed her fork at Edward. "Does your family define everything in terms of ethnicity? I am Asian, so I am punctual. You are Italian, so only you can appreciate opera. Do the two ever mix in your family's world? I bet your Mom and Dad don't even know that your little half-Japanese girlfriend is here tonight, do they?"

Edward poured extra virgin oil on top of his tomato and mozzarella without answering.

Nancy kept her fork aimed at Edward. "They don't know, do they?"

Edward looked up. "Let's just say I am easing them into the idea. My dad actually asked about you the other day. I think he likes you. It's just that, the way he explains it, it's not racist. It's a cultural thing. Different groups of people have different ways of thinking."

"Yeah."

"You have to admit, the Jews are fiercely loyal to one another because of the Holocaust, and very pushy. Blacks seem to have an alien set of beliefs because they don't feel they have a stake in this society." Edward tore a piece of Italian bread for himself, and offered the balance of the loaf to Nancy. "If they weren't already, the Germans and Japanese became incredibly well ordered to rebuild their countries after World War II. That's why you are so damn meticulous and punctual – everybody at the Public Defender's Office says it. God knows what makes the French think they can be so arrogant. The only thing they ever won was their own revolution. The WASPs – they need to be reminded every once in a while that they are no longer in control, and that their way is not the only way."

Nancy smiled.

Edward took a sip of the sangiovese wine, and held up his glass to look at it. "And the Italians – we are the masters of wine, music, food, and love. The other stuff doesn't faze us." Edward got up to get the tortellini soup. He stopped short, snapped his fingers and pointed. "Oh, and don't forget about art. Like the painting in the other room."

Nancy listened patiently to her suitor, then crossed him directly and calmly, as was her trademark as a public defender. "If the 'other stuff' doesn't matter to your wine-drinking, opera-singing, pasta-eating, love- and art-making master race, why does your dad care that I am Japanese?"

Edward served the soup. He bought himself some time to think of a response. "*Tortellini in brodo, signorina*. Observe the steam rising from the dish, dancing to the serenade of Torandeau."

Nancy ended the stall. "It's *Turandot*. You pronounce the 't,' Johnny Opera. Now answer my question. Why doesn't your father want you with a Japanese woman?"

Edward sat, and placed one of his mother's linen napkins on his lap. He spooned himself some soup. "*Perfecto*. Try some."

"First, answer my question. If you can, that is."

Edward squinted. "I can, I can. It's just that I have to think of the right way to put it without doing my father a disservice. I don't think it's that you are Japanese, or not Italian, that bothers him. It's just that we are from different backgrounds."

Nancy swallowed her tortellini. "C'mon Edward, get real. At least I am Catholic. And I go to church every Sunday. When was the last time you went to church?"

Edward scowled. "My faith is more profound than that. It's just me and my creator, *mano a mano*." Edward again tried to change the subject. "How do you like the soup?"

Nancy folded her arms in objection. "More than I like you."

Edward collected the dishes. "C'mon, you don't mean that. You find my Italian charm and good looks irresistible. I will bring on the intermezzo – raspberry sherbet."

"Geez, Edward, I never thought you had this Old World side to you. I thought it was only your father and brother. I am beginning to think you believe some of this stuff. It's medieval."

Edward rejoined Nancy, and served her the plate of sherbet. "I believe some of it. Hey, God must have created the differences among races for a reason." Edward scooped some sherbet for himself. "Have some, it will cleanse your palate for my fettuccine carbonara." Edward's boiling pots grew louder on the stove. "Let me hear about your family. And what they think about your dating a guinea wop like me?"

Nancy wiped the sherbet from her mouth. "Not much. My mom's biggest concern is that with your looks and money, you are going to leave me behind for some good old-fashioned Italian girl who will make nice Italian babies for you." She sat back in her chair, and held her wine glass with two hands as she enjoyed a soprano-sung aria. "The same way Calaf left Liu for Turandot. I love this song. It's so beautiful." She took a sip. "And so sad."

Edward's eyebrows bore down hard. "What the hell are you talking about? Did I give you too much wine?"

"The opera, Edward, the opera. In *Turandot*, Calaf the prince seeks the love of the immovable Chinese princess, whose name is Turandot."

Edward ran his tongue over his lips. "Yeah, I remember my dad explaining this to me when we were making wine. And he has to solve three riddles to get her, right?"

Nancy took a deep breath. "Yes, but that's not the point. The woman who has loved him all along is his servant, named Liu. She loves him so much that she is willing to die so that Calaf's name can remain a mystery, and he can be with the princess, Turandot." Nancy took a deep breath, and threw her head back. "This aria is called *'Tanto Amore Segreto'* – my secret undeclared love, in which Liu explains to the princess her love for Calaf. She shows the meaning of love by dying for him so that he can have the princess. She probably knew in her heart that the prince could never marry a servant like her."

Edward wanted to lunge for Nancy's wine-red lips, but stayed the course. He picked up the empty plates. "Yes, now I remember that part, too. Silly, don't you think?"

Nancy took another sip of sangiovese. "I don't know, is it? Are you going to leave me behind while you and your family chase the ice-cold princess of power?"

Edward looked at his cauldron boiling on the stove. "I think the fettuccine is ready." He tried to distract himself by piling the flask of virgin oil on top of the plates, but in the process spilled some on Nancy's chest, left bare by her unbuttoned shirt. The olive green oil started streaming toward her breasts. Edward paused before touching her chest with his finger to stop the flow. He spoke slowly as his lips drew close to hers. "I'm sorry. It was an accident."

Nancy grabbed Edward's hand before he could remove it, and slid it across her chest to spread the oil. Edward clenched his lips to Nancy's, and with his free hand placed the dishes on a nearby counter. He lifted Nancy so that she too was standing, and handled her slim body in his strong grasp, unbuttoning her clothing as she raced her fingers through his hair to pull it. When Edward had Nancy completely naked, and she him, he lifted her and laid her bare torso on the kitchen table with her head toward his father's chair. He emptied the rest of the virgin oil in the flask over Nancy's neck, breasts, and stomach, and separated the lit candles so that they were on either side of her, illuminating the olive coat on her skin. He slid his body against hers to the point of fit, kissed her, and then looked up to his father's empty chair. "Are we sure we are ready for this?"

Nancy awoke slowly from her inner delirium, and opened her eyes, her pupils rolling back into her head. "I want you."

The steaming pots popped, and the boil spouted over.

XXXI.

❦⊙℃❦

Fighting Back

Guy and Albert returned from their break in Glendale, Arizona, and the general election against Republican District Attorney Thomas Straid was on. At 8 o'clock Monday morning, Guy, Albert, and Michael Schwartz were gathered over coffee at campaign headquarters in the Northern Tower, poring over Gabrielle DeFiore's coverage of Straid's attack of Albert immediately after Albert's primary victory.

Edward stumbled in late. He tossed his disheveled hair. "Sorry, guys, there was a delay in the subway."

Guy looked up from his newspaper. "Is that why your tie is undone and your socks don't match? You have to get your sleep at night, son. We can't miss a minute between now and the election. And why didn't you call us in Glendale about this press conference held by Straid over the weekend?"

Edward's eyes bulged as he knotted his tie and studied a spare paper. "What press conference? What are you talking about?"

Albert was pacing. "Straid held a press conference in Middletown this weekend. That bastard – right where we grew up. Do you think that was an accident?"

Edward was still shaking the dust from his eyes. "Yeah, and what did he say?"

Schwartz continued. "He did everything but call your brother Benedict Arnold. He attacked Albert for being an elitist liberal who is going to try to buy the election the same way he has with everything else in his life. He said that Albert is soft on crime. He even attacked the family personally for not having any empathy for middle-class values since moving to Whitebridge. The asshole actually asked the crowd how many of them remember the last time they saw Albert in Middletown. This guy knows no limit. He is an animal."

Edward was finally focused. "The same way he is in the courtroom. He is a class warrior, who will try to bully you off the starting line. That's why we have to take the high road. We have to rise above it, and stick to policy. He will get impatient and self-destruct."

Albert snapped back. "Bullshit, this guy attacked our family the minute the election began. We have to fight back. This is honor."

Guy raised his hand. "Edward has a point. We can't get emotional about this. That's exactly what he wants. We will counter with policy, but we are going to add a little 'zing' of our own to it. Michael, let's watch the ads that Roger Hollings put together for us."

Edward stood above his father. "You hired Hollings as a media consultant without speaking to me? He is one of the most racist, negative campaign strategists in the country. The guy is a creep."

Guy looked to Schwartz. "And he never loses. Play the video, Michael."

As the title of the first ad appeared in red writing against a white backdrop, Edward read it out loud. "Thomas Straid Is A Traitor On Trade." He turned to his father. "What the hell is this?"

Albert bit a nail as he watched the video. "If I am soft on crime, that sonofabitch is soft on trade. Watch."

As warplanes dive into naval carriers, the voice of an elderly narrator speaks.

On December 7, 1941, our navy was attacked, without warning, by air, causing a severe loss of American lives. It was the first time our great country was ever invaded by a foreign power, and we vowed to never let it happen again.

The battle scene fades into the background, as a Japanese assembly line manufacturing cars comes to the fore.

Today, we are again experiencing a second invasion. This time, they are trying to destroy our economy. They pump millions of cars and other products out of their factories for sale in the United States, with no restrictions.

With warplanes still ramming into American ships, a closed American factory with an empty parking lot, weeds growing in its cracks, becomes the main focus.

But when we try to do the same in their country, they impose exorbitant tariffs. The result – our goods aren't sold and Americans lose jobs.

A four-starred General Armstrong Fiske appears on the screen.

My name is General Armstrong Fiske. When Pearl Harbor was bombed in 1941, I was one of the young naval officers who survived. Many of our workers today have not been so lucky. In the upcoming election between Albert Bennett and Thomas Straid for United States Senate, you are going to have a choice – between someone like Mr. Bennett who wants to fight back with tariffs to protect American jobs, and someone like Mr. Straid who does not seem to care. Don't let history repeat itself. Vote for Albert Bennett.

General Fiske is replaced by the silent image of Tom Straid pulling up to work in his black Honda Accord, waving to the crowd. The last frame, written in red against blue, reads "Bennett for Senate."

Schwartz pressed the remote to stop the video. "That will knock Straid on his ass for a while. Hollings is a genius. In one fell swoop, we outflanked Straid on economics and look like super-patriots. Who is going to argue with General Armstrong Fiske? The man is an institution."

Albert smiled. "Dad, how did you ever get him to do the commercial?"

Guy smiled back. "Let's just say that he owed me a favor." Guy turned to Edward. "Well, son, what do you think?"

Edward spoke from behind his folded hands. "I hate it. I think it's xenophobic racism. Gabrielle DeFiore will be all over us if we air this commercial."

Albert came back. "I think it's his little Japanese geisha Nancy that he is worried about. The commercial doesn't say anything more than you would hear during a tour of Pearl Harbor. We don't even use the word 'Japanese.' That was my cut."

"You are such a corporate lawyer. By changing a word from an offensive commercial, you think it is somehow less obnoxious. You can rationalize anything."

"We are both lawyers, little brother. Words and rationalization are what we do." Albert paused. "Lisa Marie told me that he had her for dinner over at the house on Saturday."

Guy held his hand for Albert to stop. "Is that true, Edward?"

Edward breathed in deeply, and sneered at his brother before looking straight back at his father. "Yeah, I did. Do you want me to stop dating her just so you can get your little Senate seat?"

Guy sat back and gripped the ends of his chair. "Edward, this election is not about you or me. It's not even just about Albert. It's bigger than that. We have to fight back against Straid if we are going to win. And I can think of no better endorsement than General Armstrong Fiske. He said he is only doing one commercial, and this is it."

As Edward began storming out of the room, Albert tried to stop him. "C'mon, Edward. It's not as if we are exploiting the Blacks, in which case I would agree with you. The Japanese are not vulnerable. They have done well."

Edward looked down at Albert's hand on his arm. "Aren't we all vulnerable?" Edward glared at Schwartz, and addressed him with the Yiddish derogatory word for black that resembled his last name. "Isn't that why we are all here, Schvartze?" Then to his father, "Why did you even ask me to become campaign manager if you are running the show, anyway? Face it, Albert's life is more important than mine. It always has been." He slammed the door behind him.

Guy looked sheepishly at Albert and Schwartz. "Don't worry, he will calm down. He is my son."

XXXII.

Campaign Fallout

The campaign was white hot from the start, with Albert and Straid taking swipes at one another daily. Even though poll after poll told the campaign that the voters were tired of negative campaigning, the electorate was gobbling it up like fast food. In the opening weeks, the people of New York became consumed with the private lives of the candidates, and the images that their highly paid media consultants were projecting: the silver-spooned and golden-tongued Bennett versus the middle-class and under-styled Straid; the political neophyte invading the world of the life-long public servant; the elitist defense lawyer heralding the rights of the accused that his opponent prosecuted. When voters discussed their preference, barely an issue was mentioned: it was either the handsome Bennett or the trustworthy Straid.

On the way out of the penthouse headquarters one busy Monday afternoon, Guy stopped by Edward's desk and read from an article written by Gabrielle DeFiore. "Gabrielle DeFiore says that the election is virtually guaranteed to be a dead heat, with Albert taking the large cities and its minority voters, and Straid shoring up support among the working class suburbs and upstate. The key, she says, will be who is more effective in crossing over to the other candidate's camp and stealing away votes."

Without looking up from the typing he was doing at his computer, Edward answered in a low monotone. "I couldn't agree with her more. That's why I want to challenge Straid on issues. He has no patience. He will wear down."

Guy looked down at his son. "Edward, look at me. We are going with the General Fiske commercial. It is starting tomorrow night.

We need blue collar votes." Guy spoke through Edward's interruption. "Tell your girlfriend it was my idea, and that you had nothing to do with it. You can also tell her that your mother and I would love to have her over for dinner." Guy smiled sarcastically. "Maybe this time she will get a meal."

As Edward wondered to himself what exactly his father knew about his dinner with Nancy at the house, and how he could have possibly known it, Guy exited.

The day before the General Fiske commercial flooded the airwaves, Edward told Nancy to meet him the next evening at "The Bar," the aptly named watering hole across the street from the county courthouse where prosecutors and public defenders gathered after work. Edward approached Nancy gingerly from behind. He could see her crying eyes staring into the bar's mirror as she sat alone on an elevated stool.

Edward placed his hand on her shoulder. "Nancy."

When Nancy turned, her eyes were red with anger in the swell of tears; her slight makeup had run. "That commercial was disgusting. How could you? Maybe you should have included a scene from the concentration camps in this country? Do you know the pain that you caused last night?"

Edward stuttered. "It was not my idea…"

Nancy clenched her teeth. "You are the campaign manager, and you let it happen." Nancy threw her cocktail in his face before storming out. "You, your father, and your brother. I hate all of you."

XXXIII

A Surprise Visit

Back at campaign headquarters in the penthouse at the Northern Tower, Albert burst into the reception area, where a woman in a black dress and sunglasses was waiting. Albert queried the receptionist as he went through the handwritten messages left for him. "Jane, who is the woman with the sunglasses?"

"She has been here since two o'clock, sir. She won't leave until she sees you. She says that she represents a large political action committee that is thinking of supporting you."

Albert stuffed his messages into his shirt pocket. "Well, what are you waiting for? Ask her if she wants some coffee, and bring her to my office."

As Albert rummaged through position papers left on his desk, the woman closed the door behind her. She took off her sunglasses and hat, setting free her blue eyes and blond hair, igniting a spark of recognition on Albert's part.

"My name is Ellen Straid, Tom Straid's wife," she said by way of unnecessary introduction.

Albert stared in shock as he lowered himself into his seat. "Perhaps you and your husband don't talk about your professional lives, and that's fine. But if he didn't tell you, I am running against him for the United States Senate."

The two laughed nervously.

Ellen Straid looked down at her lap to gather her composure, then to the waiting Albert. "I know who you are. Unfortunately, I know all too well. My husband is obsessed with you and this race."

Albert smiled. "I hope you don't take this personally, but I am pretty consumed with him these days, and I am none too happy with the relationship. You can have him."

Straid crossed her legs, and pulled her skirt over her knees. "He can be a bit aggressive, I know. But if it's any comfort, he always tells me that it's only a game, and that we shouldn't take any of the attacks personally. Like that commercial you aired last night. It was quite clever. Irresponsible, but clever."

Albert squinted. "Well, obviously you didn't come here to discuss the trials and tribulations of Senate campaigns. What can I do for you?"

Straid bit her lip. "I know that this campaign is going to get dirty before it's over, and that's to be expected. As much as I would like to stop it, I know there is nothing I can do." She stroked her index finger across her eyebrow. "But I would like to make one personal plea to you."

Albert reached into his side desk drawer, and turned on the micro cassette tape recorder that he used for dictation. "I'll listen."

Straid held her hat in her lap. "My husband and I have been married fifteen years. High school sweethearts, three kids, and a white picket fence – the whole thing. He coaches the kids in little league baseball, and they absolutely adore him."

Her eyes started welling, and Albert offered her a tissue.

Straid held up her hand. "No thanks, I will be fine." She continued. "I don't know whether it's me, or some male thing he is going through. But he has been having an affair for quite some time. It has gotten so bad, there are some nights he doesn't even bother to come home. I have to tell the kids that he is away for work." She took a deep breath. "Let me cut to the chase. I am asking you not to make an issue of it in your campaign."

Albert tapped a pen against his chin, wallowing in his newly found leverage. "Why shouldn't I?"

Straid reached and turned around a picture of Albert with his wife and kids, with his mother and father. "Is this your family?"

Albert placed the pen on his desk, and moved forward. "Yeah, that's a picture of my wife, Victoria, our kids, and my parents when we moved into our new house."

Straid tilted her head to one side. "How do you think they would feel if they found out that you were having an affair?"

Albert wrested the picture away from her, and returned it to its place. "Not good."

Straid sat back in her chair. "You are a handsome man, Mr. Bennett, and rumors do fly, you know. I can assure you that nothing of the sort will come from my husband's camp, unless, of course, I suspect that something is coming from yours." Straid studied Albert's silence while he rubbed his fingers across his bottom teeth. "Do we have a deal?"

Albert turned off the micro cassette recorder. "Deal." With that, he shook Straid's hand.

Straid stood up, and dusted her skirt. "Now as a sign of good faith, why don't you hand over that recording of this conversation you just made."

Albert reached into his drawer, ejected the tape, and flipped it on his desk with a smile. "You are a ballsy lady, Ellen Straid."

Straid reached over and fixed Albert's ill-knotted tie. "And you really are a charming man. You just need someone to take care of you."

With that, Straid reassumed her sunglasses and hat, and left Albert's office.

XXXIV.

Getting More Votes

A Tribute to the Past

abrielle DeFiore was right. The race was dead even until Albert found an issue he could use to cross over into Straid's working-class constituency. Although the General Fiske commercial drew sharp criticism from civil rights groups, DeFiore, and even ordinary citizens when asked, Albert had found his wedge theme and slowly gained a lead. With the Russian Cold War over and the American Pie shrinking, Bennett had served New Yorkers their much-needed culprit. As Election Day neared, the polls had Albert ahead of Straid by four percentage points. Still, the campaigners wanted more.

Two weeks before the election, Albert was looking over Edward's shoulder as Edward typed a response to Straid's latest attack on Albert for being soft on crime. "C'mon, bro. Move those magic fingers. We only have forty-five minutes to respond to that cop in a lawyer's suit if we want to hit tomorrow's papers."

Schwartz broke in, swimming in sweat, eyes bugging with glee. "Albert, we've got it. The atom bomb. One of our opposition research guys got a tip today from a reliable source that Straid has been fucking his secretary for the past two years, and she is supposedly willing to tell all so long as we take care of her after the election."

Albert continued to look over Edward's shoulder at the press release, ignoring Schwartz. "Add the word outrageous before allegation, Edward. The voters have to feel my passion."

Schwartz grabbed Albert by the shirt. "Albert, forget about your goddamn press release. Don't you understand? The election is over if this goes public. The timing could not be better. Straid will never have enough time to explain."

Albert removed Schwartz's hand from his shoulder. "He won't have to. We are not going to use it."

A baffled Schwartz pleaded his case. "But Albert, we are ahead by only four points. With a margin of error of three points, we could be tied or even losing for all we know. This is a gift. Let's release it through one of our surrogates, or give it to the papers anonymously so they can't trace it back to us."

Albert stroked his chin and traced a hard line down his neck. "Let me make myself perfectly clear, Michael. I don't want to use it, and I don't want anyone else to use it on our behalf. If this goes public, I am holding you personally responsible, and it won't be pretty. You can forget about a job if we win. End of discussion. Now if you will excuse Edward and me, we have a press release to finish."

Schwartz slammed his fist against the desk, and walked away.

Without saying a word to his brother, Edward smiled at his screen as he pecked at the keyboard.

On Election Day, Albert walked into campaign headquarters early in the morning with a champion's smile. He was greeted by phones ringing off the hook, campaign volunteers running into each other, and a blue sky that lent a clear view for miles across Central Park.

Guy discontinued the orders he was giving, and walked toward Albert with a rolled newspaper in hand. "Well, son, she gave it to us. Your friend Gabrielle DeFiore finally endorsed you, even though she thinks you had a weak moment in your campaign when your advisors got the best of you with that commercial." Guy smirked. "I guess that means me. She says you have energy and vision. Even though it only came on Election Day, her word should be good for a few votes."

Schwartz joined the duo, his eyes bloodshot from an all-night meeting with union officials and other friends of the campaign. "Well, you sure as hell look like a winner, Albert."

Guy turned to Schwartz. "Michael, you delivered that $50,000 in street money I gave you, right?"

Albert pretended to be surprised. "What street money, Dad?"

Guy rubbed his son on the head. "You know, the money that puts gas and lunches in the buses that pick up our voters and bring them to the polls. Let's just say it's an early birthday present from your mother and me, delivered by the National Committee. You know, soft money. I don't know who ever came up with that term. Any money I ever earned was hard." Guy lowered his voice. "Quiet, here comes Edward. He'll go nuts if he finds out. The accountants will take care of it after the election."

Albert straightened his brother's tie. "How do we look, chief?"

Edward read off his tally sheets. "We won't know for sure until New York City's numbers begin coming in late tonight. But the weather is a good sign. Our voters need sunny skies to come out. Republicans vote rain or shine. They're a well-trained army. If we stay close upstate and in the 'burbs, it's a lock. Gabrielle DeFiore's endorsement is big. I think it's going to put us over the edge."

Guy hit Edward over the shoulder with his rolled newspaper. "I told you that commercial was nothing to get upset about. DeFiore got over it. Why can't you?"

Edward shook his head in disgust. "You just don't get it, do you?" Before his father could muster an answer, Edward retreated to his computer.

The champagne corks popped early and often in penthouse headquarters that evening, as Albert Bennett was declared the winner, a United States Senator. Campaign workers partied through the night, intoxicating themselves with fantasies of their newly found power.

The long journey started by Dante and continued by Guy was finally over. Guy felt a lonely peace amidst the frenzy.

Before leaving the Northern Tower just before daybreak, Guy stopped in his boardroom to look at the old black and white photo of him, his father, Guido Scarpetto, Fernando, and Giuseppe in the pick-up truck. He smiled as a tear crawled down his cheek. "We won, Pop. Somehow, you always knew we would."

Guy walked to the window to watch the sun rise over Central Park. A gentle breeze was blowing through the trees, and the radiant foliage of an extended autumn was beginning to fall.

XXXV.

A Trader With a Steel Briefcase

Guy and Vito were in the Northern Industries boardroom for their pre-meeting pow-wow. Even though it had been months since the election, Guy's eyes were still lit with triumph.

Vito sipped his coffee. "So how does it feel to know that you raised a United States Senator?"

Guy replied tongue-in-cheek, "Probably no different than it feels to know that you raised a son who married my daughter."

Unable to garner a counter-barb, Vito looked down to rotate his Styrofoam coffee cup on the mahogany table. "What can I say, Guy? I can't keep up with you. When you're hot, you're hot. I was just curious."

Guy slapped Vito on the hand. "C'mon, Vito. You know I'm only kidding. If you want to know the truth, I am still pinching myself, waiting to wake up from a dream. My son, a United States Senator. It boggles the mind. This is going to be a big year for us, my friend."

Vito inhaled some of Guy's enthusiasm. "I have to say, VJ is very excited about the possibilities in Chile. He has been talking to a lot of business people and government leaders down there. They are very refined, he says. A lot of class. He says the people who run the place are Castilians from Spain – pure breeds for centuries. I don't think I have ever seen VJ this confident. He has even started taking Spanish classes. He almost has me believing."

Guy smiled in kind, but made sure to keep Vito as a sidebar to Albert. "That's great. I told you this project would be good for him. Hey, if the Spanish lessons go well, maybe Albert can arrange for VJ to become ambassador to Spain. Wouldn't that be a kick?"

Vito pushed a "hmm" through his nose, and continued his coffee. "Well, if there's nothing else, I guess we are ready for the Board." Vito looked at his watch. "They are not due for another five minutes. Just enough time for me to return a call."

"Yeah, let's hope the morticians are in a good mood today." As Vito rose from his seat, Guy raised a finger. "Wait a minute. I knew there was something else. Mohammad stopped me in the hall on the way in to tell me that he has been tracking a weird pattern in the trading of our stock. I told him we would call him before the Board meeting." Guy waved his hand to signal Vito to return to his seat. "Sit, we will call him right now." Guy buzzed the intercom. "Barbara, please send Mohammad in immediately."

Vito shook his head. "I don't know what it could be. Our stock has been trading at a consistent price. Probably another guy trying to justify the high salary we pay him."

Guy raised his eyebrows. "Let's hear what he has to say."

Three raps shot through the door. Guy got up to answer. "Mohammad, come in. I was telling Vito what you started to explain to me before. What was it that you found?"

Mohammad took a sheet of paper from his folder, and handed it to Guy. "As I told you in the hall, sir, I have noticed something strange in the trading of our stock."

Guy smiled and showed the report to Vito. "This guy is the best. Look, pie charts and everything."

Vito wasn't interested in the graphics. "What is it, Mohammad?"

"It's the trading volume report that I keep for our stock. It highlights single purchases and sales that represent more than four percent of our outstanding stock." Mohammad used his pencil to point to the various highlighted trading days. "If you will notice, on a fairly regular basis there have been large block movements of our stock, in excess of four percent but less than five percent. As you may know, if it is one person or entity doing the trading, and the acquired ownership remains below five percent, he or it does not have to file a Form 13D with the Securities and Exchange Commission that would identify him."

Guy nodded without question.

Vito placed his right forefinger on his chin, and tilted his head backwards. "What makes you think it is one person doing the trading? It could just be a coincidence."

Mohammad was ready for Vito's question. "I think not, sir. Ever since I first told you about this some time ago, I have been watching the pattern closely. Once I noticed that these large trades were usually being made on the last Friday of the month, I asked some of our friends on the floor of the exchange to tell me which broker was doing the executing."

Guy looked at Vito before posing the next query. "And what did you find out?"

"I found that, without exception, the trades have been executed by Leo Wong. He is a young economist from Beijing, China, who fled the country when he was on a sabbatical program here. They say he is brilliant, and very private. He was being groomed to become one of the chief economists to oversee Hong Kong interests when it reverts to Chinese control. He trades for only a handful of institutional clients, usually Asians, and does not normally even bother to go to the stock exchange on Fridays. Our sources tell us that on the Fridays these trades were made, Leo Wong walked into the ring in the afternoon, opened his steel briefcase to take out his trading card and pen, and bought or sold only Northern Industries stock. When he was done, he put his card away, and left without saying a word."

Vito raised both hands. "What the hell are you saying, Mohammad? Speak English!" Detecting a wince from Mohammad, Vito tried to amend his words. "You know what I mean. Make it understandable for me and Guy."

Mohammad spoke quickly to make his point. "What I am saying, sir, is that Leo Wong is making these trades on behalf of one client, who deliberately keeps his holdings below five percent to avoid disclosure – to stay unknown – and in the process has made some nice profits for his client. It's as if he has inside information as to when to buy or sell the stock at a low profit margin per share but in large volume, or he is sending us a warning – or both."

Guy spoke slowly. "Sending us a warning of what, Mohammad?"

"A hostile takeover, sir."

Vito waved Mohammad off. "You're crazy, Mohammad. You have been watching too many movies." Vito grabbed one of Nardeen's trading volume reports. "If Wang is making all these trades below the breaking point, what the hell are you worried about today that you haven't been charting in your fancy little reports all this time?"

Mohammad grew stern. "It's Wong, sir. Leo Wong. And this morning, he bought approximately ten percent of our stock, giving his interest a net holding of fifteen percent. If my theory is correct, in ten days the purchaser will have to file a 13D with the SEC, and send a copy to us. If in fact it is the beginning of a hostile takeover, we will then know our enemy. I hope I am wrong."

Guy took the rest of the reports from Mohammad. "Thank you. That will be all for now."

After Mohammad left, Guy scanned the reports. "When did Mohammad first tell you about this, Vito?"

Vito got up to throw away his empty Styrofoam cup. "When you were in Aquino. Don't you remember? I told you when you called. You were so excited with what was happening over there – the torches, the singing in the piazza – you probably didn't even hear me. I think our little Indian friend is paranoid. The profit margins on those trades had to be small. Our stock has been consistently low the last two years, moving back and forth in a range of about fifteen dollars. The purchases that the Chinese mystery man made today were probably for a bunch of clients, or somebody who has no intention of stepping into this nightmare. In the condition we are in, who the hell would want to buy us?"

Guy stroked his upper lip with his index finger, staring Vito back into his seat. "Somebody who knows that our stock is undervalued and due to rise."

The intercom buzzed. "Mr. Bennett, the Board members are here."

Guy sat motionless, in a trance-like state. "Send them in."

David Rothstein was the first through the door, and made it a point to commend Guy in front of the others. "Congratulations on the big win, Guy. Or should I now call you the Senior Senator?"

Guy smiled modestly. "Thank you, David. And thanks for the case of champagne you sent us. I don't think Marie and I have ever drunk such expensive bubbles. We have been so busy, I haven't had time to call anybody. Please give Audrey our best."

Jared Pym waited behind Rothstein to pay Guy his respects. "Good show, sport. My wife and I were also going to send you over something, but decided instead to invite you and the Senator to our home for dinner. It's become sort of a tradition for Phoebe and me when new Democrats from New York are elected to the state-house or Congress."

Guy scrambled for the right response, which he had waited years to give. "That sounds splendid, Jared. We would be honored. I just have to check with the Senator's busy schedule. He was at the White House yesterday to speak with the President. These days, I am lucky if he even calls me back."

Eleanor Whittlesby piped in. "Tell Albert that the next time he is at the White House, he should make some suggestions to the President about the White House menu. I was there last month, and the food was dreadful – woefully bland." Caressing her dulled pearl necklace, Whittlesby smiled at Nick Covitt and Bramford Leach as they assumed their seats. "Being that Albert is Italian, maybe the President will listen. He could slip the President some of his mother's Neapolitan recipes. Now there's a goal worth pursuing for young Albert."

David Rothstein cut through the group giggle being shared by Whittlesby, Covitt, and Leach. "I think the President is probably more interested in Albert's ideas about cutting the military budget and getting more jobs at home. If the President doesn't watch it, Albert may have his job in a few years." Rothstein turned quickly to Whittlesby. "And Eleanor, then maybe he would consider hiring you to do the cooking."

Whittlesby shot back a horrified look, as Guy covered his mouth to conceal his laughter.

Nick Covitt intervened, extending his arms toward Rothstein and Whittlesby as if he were a referee. "Ladies, ladies. That will be enough." He turned to Rothstein. "Before you go cutting the military, my friend, let me remind you that the defense industry provides the jobs at home." Covitt grinned proudly. "I should know, I once took over and ran an arms company before selling it at a nice profit. If you really want to trim the budget, maybe Albert should suggest that we cut back on aid to Israel. There would be a savings."

Bramford Leach joined in. "And there would go the President's campaign contributions. I like it, a sure way to get a Republican back in the White House."

Professor Pym disciplined his pupils. "Enough with pasta and politics. We are here to talk about Northern Industries. Let me begin by saying that I believe the South American project is going quite well, Guy. You are to be commended for the idea. We have made some nice relationships in Santiago, Chile. If we continue to develop inroads, I believe we can penetrate the Chilean infrastructure market within a year to eighteen months." His belly bloated with Chilean beef and wine courtesy of Northern Industries, Pym relieved one of the buttons on his vest. "Of course, it will take several more trips. A visit by me with New York's newest Senator might help."

Vito Petrozzini inserted himself. "I hate to say it, but I am beginning to agree. My son VJ is very excited about Chile, and has enjoyed working with you on the project, Professor Pym. How is he doing?"

Pym paused, before serving Vito a lukewarm smile over his folded hands. "He is doing fine. He has some learning to do, but is performing as well can be expected."

Dejected, Vito laid back in his seat.

Guy pressed his thumb against the end of his fountain pen. "Very well, then unless anyone objects, I say we forge ahead."

Staring with his eyes glazed over, Guy continued. "The next order of business concerns the trading of our stock."

Bramford Leach busied himself in his briefcase. "I noticed some heavy trading this morning, and an uptick in the price. That's got to be good news."

Guy bit his pen, and responded to Leach. "Perhaps, unless it is the beginning of a hostile takeover."

Pym lowered his bushy eyebrows. "Whatever do you mean, Guy?"

Guy spoke slowly to Leach. "Bram, what do you know about a fella named Leo Wong?"

Leach stuttered. "Well, what is there to know? He is a broker who defected from China. He has about as much personality as the metal briefcase he carries. He talks to no one, and works for no one but himself. He is a hired gun, a mercenary in acquisitional trading. If somebody big wants to take over a company smoothly and efficiently, Wong is usually on the short list of people to get it done. Companies will go so far as to use Wong alone instead of trying to disguise their purchases through multiple brokers; it is a condition Wong supposedly insists upon. Rumor has it he is really a Communist spy buying American companies for the Beijing government."

Vito Petrozzini snapped. "What the fuck are you talking about?"

Guy scolded his partner. "Vito! This is a Board meeting."

Leach scratched the back of his head. "The theory is not off the wall. Most of his clients are relatively new companies in Hong Kong."

Covitt placed his pen down on his pad, and looked up. "That might explain why these obscure companies use only him as their broker. If Beijing has a master plan, loose lips can sink ships. Be that as it may, why in the world are we speculating about Leo Wong?"

Guy poured himself a glass of water from the pitcher on the table. "He bought about ten percent of our stock this morning, which, if our analysts are correct, would give a client for whom he would be purchasing the stock approximately fifteen percent ownership of our company, requiring them to identify themselves within ten days in a 13D. If what Bram is saying and our analysts have already told us is true, someone is about to launch a hostile takeover of Northern Industries." Guy took a long and measured sip from his glass. "Based on Wong's trading patterns over the past year and a half – buying or selling large volume just before and after significant company developments – we suspect that his client may have inside information." Guy took another sip. "Which may mean we have a leak on this Board."

Without moving his position, Guy looked sideways at Nick Covitt, catching him in a brief stare with Eleanor Whittlesby.

Vito Petrozzini looked up at the ceiling in disgust. "Let me guess. The theory is that someone on the Board is in cahoots with the Chinese government to take over the U.S. economy. And Northern Industries is one of Beijing's targets – the first big domino." Vito started to get up from his chair. "If there's nothing else, I think I have heard it all. If China wants the company, they can have it. It'll give them all the rice they can eat for about a day."

Guy suppressed his rage. "Sit, Vito. You are the only one who has us in the middle of a Communist plot."

Pym studied Guy. "So what do we do, Guy?"

Guy crossed his legs, and folded his hands atop his knee. "I don't know. Why don't we ask the specialists, Masters Covitt and Leach?"

Leach spoke first. "There's nothing to do but sit and wait."

Covitt echoed the sentiment. "Bram's right. The worst thing we can do is lose our cool. As someone who has been on the other side, I can tell you that there is nothing that animates an acquirer more than a whiff of panic. For all we know, it's no takeover at all – just a fake designed to make someone a quick buck."

Guy leaned forward. "Come again."

Covitt admired one of his buffed fingernails as he rubbed it. "It's called greenmail. Someone buys a bunch of stock at a low price to make the target think a takeover is under way. When the company panics and buys back its stock at a higher price, the would-be acquirer dumps his holdings at a profit and walks off into the sunset. The lawmakers have tried to stop it, but it still goes on." Covitt smiled. "Of course, I have never done it. I've only heard about it."

David Rothstein took off his glasses and rubbed his eyes. "Bram and Nick are right, Guy. We have to stay cool. Why don't we have a special meeting of the Board twelve days from now – a week from Wednesday? If the 13D is here, we will look at it together. If not, we can finish that champagne Audrey and I sent you."

Guy shook his head. "That's fine. But I thought the 13D has to be sent to us within ten days. Why are we waiting twelve?"

Rothstein laid his horn-rimmed glasses on the bridge of his nose.

"They only have to drop it in the mail within ten days. Believe me, I've done it for clients a thousand times. It will go in the mail at 4:30 on the tenth day."

Eleanor Whittlesby rose from her seat. "Will that be all, Guy?"

Guy finished his glass of water. "Yes."

While the others packed their briefcases in silence, Guy stopped the hastily departing Vito outside of the boardroom door, and held him by the shoulder with one hand, pointing in his face with the other. "Don't ever cross me in front of the Board again. Do you hear me? You work for me. You always have, and you always will."

Vito removed Guy's hand. "You are a fucking nut. Now you know what it feels like to be down here instead of spending all of your time in the penthouse playing Senator. Welcome home, partner."

Guy re-entered the Boardroom, where only David Rothstein remained. Rothstein was holding his briefcase over Vito Petrozzini's seat at the table. "Guy, do you really think that someone is trying to take over the company with the help of someone on the Board?"

Guy rested his face in his hand as he stood. "I don't know, David." He opened up the folder Mohammad gave him before the meeting. "Look at these trading volume reports. They reek of inside information." Guy pointed to an example. "Look at this purchase, just before we got the huge Ohio and Pennsylvania projects last year. Then, a sale in roughly the same quantity just before we went public with the losses due to the flooding."

Rothstein analyzed the reports. "This is pretty sophisticated stuff, Guy. Who has been tracking it?"

"A young financial analyst named Mohammad Nardeen. The guy is brilliant – an Indian guy, very meticulous. He is the one who noticed it. I am just glad we had him to warn us."

Rothstein handed Guy back the reports. "I hate to burst your bubble. But are you sure that he is not your mole trying to cover himself by bringing it to your attention?"

Guy shook his head. "I didn't even think about that. But it could be anybody. The Professor for the first time is pretending to be dumb, Whittlesby doesn't say a word, Covitt seems to be playing some kind of Machiavellian mind game with me, and my partner the hothead doesn't want to even hear about it. To tell you the truth, I never thought I would say this, but the only one in here who I trusted was Leach and his crazy theory about Leo Wong being a Communist spy. He seemed genuinely interested in figuring out the puzzle."

When Rothstein offered no response, Guy continued. "And you, of course. You and Leach are the only ones I trust on this one. I don't know, David. Marie and I are supposed to go to Arizona tomorrow morning for a long weekend of business and golf. But with this going on, maybe we should stay."

"Don't be silly. Go to Arizona, get some rest, and look forward to drinking champagne with these assholes when there is no 13D."

As Rothstein departed, Guy called out. "Hey, you said you have been involved in a thousand of these things. Maybe this will be one thousand and one."

Rothstein turned and laughed. "At least you still have your sense of humor. See you next week. With a tan."

Guy pushed down on the button to the intercom. "Barbara, any messages for me?"

"Just one, Mr. Bennett. Your wife called during the meeting to say that your son Edward is coming to your house for dinner tonight. She said to be home early."

Guy smiled. "Now there's a table I think I can still handle."

XXXVI.

❦

A Special Plate Broken

uy sped home, and burst through the door from his garage with forced gusto, anxious to leave behind the troubling board meeting. "Honey, I'm home. Where is my youngest son?"

When silence answered, Guy stepped quickly toward the kitchen. "Marie?"

Guy entered the kitchen, and found Marie and Edward sitting together at the table, pale and glum. "There you are." Guy looked at Edward. "When you were a little squirt, you and your mother would run when I called out like that." He threw his eyes back toward his wife. "What's for dinner, Marie? I'm starving."

Marie spoke slowly from the table. "Guy, Edward needs to talk to us about something."

Sensing more bad news, Guy scrambled to avoid it. He went to the bread drawer, and tore the end off a fresh loaf. He spoke through his chewing, spitting crumbs with his words. "Hey Edward, you remember that foundation you made me set up last summer for inner city kids? A Black kid was given the first scholarship today. He starts next fall at City University." Guy clung to the bread drawer, and took another bite from the heel of the torn loaf. "I can't remember the damn kid's name. But I kept my promise. I told you I would."

Edward could barely look at his father. "That's great, Dad. But we have to talk. I have a problem."

Guy shuffled to the table. "You're not in trouble, are you? I'll call David Rothstein."

"No, Dad, I am not in trouble. It's about Nancy."

Guy sat and folded his hands on the table. He looked intensely at Edward, and drew a deep breath. His voice thinned, and cracked with apprehension. "What is it, son?"

Edward's arms were laid flat on the table. He fixed on the empty plate set in front of him. "She's pregnant, and I am the father."

Guy receded slowly in his chair. He stared silently away from his wife and son.

Edward looked at his father, and tripped through his thoughts as he hurried to speak. "Don't worry, Dad, she is not due for five months, and we're going to get...We're not going to have an abortion, if that's what you're worried about. We're having the baby. And we're going to get married beforehand. A nice simple wedding."

Guy laughed giddily as he continued to stare away. "That sounds great. Call Monsignor McNabb. I am sure he will have no problem doing the ceremony. And I'll tell you what, we'll invite the neighbors, the members of my board, the Petrozzinis – they'll love this. Especially Vito. Maybe Albert can get the President to come. And let's not forget about the ambassador from Japan. We have to give Nancy equal billing."

As everyone sat in an eerie silence, Guy leapt from his seat like a tiger, causing the statuettes of saints on the windowsill to come crashing down. He pulled Edward by the collar out of his chair. In the same swift motion, Guy hurled his son against the wall.

Marie grabbed her husband from behind and screamed. "Guy, stop!"

Guy's eyes were ablaze as he lifted his son off the floor against the wall. "And while we're at it, we'll have the reception right here in our backyard. Because after all, you created the kid in my house while we were away. Didn't you, you sonofabitch?"

Marie pulled harder. "Guy, leave him alone. He's your son."

Guy would not relent. "If he is my son, he will tell me the truth. You had sex with that little Japanese whore in my house, didn't you?"

Edward looked away.

Guy pulled tighter on Edward's collar, and lifted him higher on the wall. He shouted. "Answer me, goddamnit, like a man." Guy lowered his voice, and brought his face against Edward's. He clenched his teeth. "You don't even have to tell me if it was in my bed, because then I would probably kill you. Did you screw her in my house?"

Edward looked back at his father, and spoke slowly to lend himself poise. "No, I did not."

Father and son seethed face to face, breathing each other's anger.

Edward continued. "I didn't have sex in your house. It was in a hotel late one night during the campaign."

Guy let go of his son, and retreated to the cooking island on the other side of the upset kitchen table. Marie scooped up the saintly statuettes, and placed them back on the windowsill. Then she began crying, as she crouched on the floor beside the family's shattered special day plate. She had served her children countless meals on the plate, as a reward for their achievements: the winning hit in a baseball game, a straight "A" report card, a good deed. As her husband and son sucked heavily the waning wind of rampancy between them, Marie scrambled to piece together the family's broken dish.

Edward spoke first. "That's really what this is all about, isn't it?" When Guy did not respond, Edward continued his counterattack. "It's about what kind of party you can throw in your backyard – the kind of champagne you can serve – the compliments you'll get."

Marie tried to stop Edward; she knew that her son's tongue sharpened on those rare occasions when he was moved to fury. She held him by the shoulders. "Edward, don't. We'll pull through this the way we always have – like a family."

Edward grabbed his mother's hand. "No, Mom, let me finish, because I have something that he needs to hear. He said it himself – his life is about who he can invite to his mansion – Monsignor McNabb, those idiots on his Board of Directors. It's one big show and tell. Nancy and I ruin the picture – we always have. What can I say?" He threw his head upward in the direction of Guy, as blood trickled from his lip. "Sorry about that, Dad. We'll move far way so you don't have to deal with it. You can make something up if you want."

Marie pulled one of the chairs from the floor. "C'mon, boys. You got it all out of your system. Now, let's talk like human beings."

Guy lifted his eyes from the floor, as he continued to lean against the cooking island. "Get out of my house, and don't come back unless you are asked."

Marie tried to lighten the situation. "Guy, c'mon and sit down. I'll make some pasta."

Guy rejected his wife's extended arms, and resumed his evicting glare. "Get out before I throw you out."

Edward obeyed, and made his way through the kitchen to the front door.

His mother ran to stop him in the foyer. "Edward, this will pass. Your father is under a lot of pressure at work." She paused to whisper. "He will always be your father."

Edward looked over his mother, at the painting of Christ chasing the moneychangers from the temple. "The problem is, I don't think he still considers me his son."

As Edward exited the front door, his mother called out, "I'll talk to him."

Marie returned to the kitchen, and began putting her table back in order, picking up the pieces of the family's shattered special day plate.

Guy tried to regain equilibrium. "What are you doing?"

Marie spoke softly. "I am trying to fix the special day plate." Marie smiled. "I remember the first time Edward ate off it after hitting a home run in little league. It seemed like we would never be unhappy again." Marie looked up at her husband. "Guy, this is not the time to drive our children away. We have to pull together."

Guy was still on the island. "What are you talking about? Our other children are fine. Except for this bohemian, we have a great family. What the hell? My other son is a United States Senator."

Marie tried to arrange the plate's fragments, as she sat solemnly at the kitchen table. "Albert called today. He and Victoria are separated. They are going to get divorced. For political reasons, she agreed to do it slowly."

With a hard grimace, Guy spoke in a monotone, "Why are they getting divorced?"

Marie continued to study the plate. "You know why. That girl has no love in her. We knew it from day one. She always acted like she was above Albert, doing him a favor. We should have never let him marry her."

Guy walked to the other side of the cooking island, and started twisting the stove's knobs nervously. "I'll talk to him and straighten it out. They're acting like children." One of the flames from the stove lit. "And I thought this was the worst day of my life before I got home."

Marie left the plate's shards alone, and scampered to her husband's side. "Guy, what is it? Your secretary told me you went to the doctor this morning. Are you okay?"

Guy put his arm around his wife's shoulder. "I'm fine." He kissed Marie on the head. "But I think someone is trying to take over the company with the help of one of my board members."

Marie laid her head on her husband's shoulder. "Who do you think it is?"

Guy looked to the kitchen counter, at a picture of the Bennetts and Petrozzinis away together on summer vacation. "I don't know." Guy tried to reverse the somber situation. "But what I do know is that you and I have a 7 a.m. flight to Glendale, and we haven't even packed yet."

"Are you sure you still want to go?"

Guy turned off the stove's flame decisively. "I'm positive. We couldn't cancel even if we wanted to. I am supposed to play golf on Monday with the Governor of Arizona. I think his name is Lloyd Kwid." Guy jested to his wife, "Do you think he is northern Italian or southern Italian?"

XXXVII.

❦

A Secret Club

Sinking the Putt

D ue to the unseasonably driving rains in Glendale, Guy and Marie spent most of the weekend inside their condominium alone, vacillating between disciplined quiet and conversation about how to improve the interior design of their vacation home. Thoughts of Albert and Edward filled the gaps.

Early Monday morning they were greeted by the blazing Arizona sun. Guy stretched in front of the opened Madeira wood French doors that he had shipped to the condominium from New York.

Marie turned over in bed and woke slowly. "Are you going to play golf?"

"Yeah, I was hoping it would rain again so I wouldn't have to. I hate these tournaments." Guy caressed the Madeira frame of one of his doors. "I tell you, these doors were worth every penny we spent to get them out here from Brooklyn." Guy looked at the simple wooden doors of his neighbors, all the same. "These cowboys in Arizona have no style."

Marie got up and put on her bathrobe. She kissed her husband on the cheek. "Try and have a good time. And get back early so we can spend some of the day together."

Guy looked out on the course. "Believe me, I will. If this guy didn't owe us so much money for the aqueduct projects, I wouldn't even bother going."

Guy threw his golf bag over his shoulders, and made his way to the New Horizons clubhouse. As he drew near, he saw the large banner draped in front: "Welcome to the New Horizons Tournament of Champions." As the tournament's participants huddled around the grandstand with their Styrofoam cups of coffee, a giant knot tightened in Guy's stomach.

A tall gray-haired man stepped to the microphone, his face wrinkled with the lines of deal and compromise. "Okay, boys, if I can have your attention." The fluorescent-panted congregation abided, and the master of ceremonies continued. "My name is Governor Lloyd Kwid. I want to welcome you to the great state of Arizona, and the tenth annual Tournament of Champions."

The members of the herd clapped for one another energetically yet deliberately, sure to disseminate glimpses of their polished white teeth.

"For those of you who are first timers, we have invited you today as achievers and leaders in your various communities." The Governor looked up at the deep blue sky. "And as usual, the sun has found a way to shine down on you."

Similarly styled heads of hair bobbed in affirmation.

Governor Kwid pointed to Guy. "I want to personally welcome my partner and first-time tournament participant, Guy Bennett from New York, the CEO of Northern Industries."

An ovation of watch-strapped wrists and evenly tanned faces turned and bombarded Guy like a kaleidoscope. A well-groomed gentleman standing next to him extended a hand. "Welcome, friend."

Governor Kwid concluded his remarks. "So go out today, make new acquaintances, catch up on old ones and enjoy yourselves." He looked at Guy. "I know I will." The Governor put on his New Horizons golf cap. "And remember – no matter what happens on the course, you are all champions. Otherwise, you wouldn't be here. For lunch, we have beef, or my favorite – mahi-mahi. Had it flown in from Hawaii. The Senator from the Aloha State owed me a favor."

Guy joined in the laughter and applause, never having heard of mahi-mahi.

Guy and Governor Kwid loaded their golf cart and made their way through the New Horizon holes. Guy both played and spoke conservatively, careful not to embarrass himself in front of the

Governor. Golf was one of the few endeavors in Guy's life that he had come to realize could not be conquered by sheer force and desire; the making of a great cabernet wine was another. They were the games of the second generation – contests of finesse, whose spoils were more often garnered by the methodical and patient rather than the strong. Guy shot respectably down the first seventeen holes, as the Governor engaged him in conversation that was restricted to family and sports.

As they walked the carefully cropped green fairway of the eighteenth hole, however, Governor Kwid shifted the discussion to business. "So how are the aqueduct projects coming along, Guy?"

"So far, we are ahead of schedule, Governor." Guy's back was soaked with sweat as he stepped up to his ball to shoot. He swung hastily and sliced it right, into the taller, more difficult grass.

Governor Kwid held his hand above his brow to shield the sun. "I saw it, Guy, it's in the rough next to mine."

The Governor drove the two to their balls. "Yeah, my Secretary of Transportation told me on Friday that you submitted a bill last week for $3 million."

Guy stared straight ahead, pretending to look for the balls. "Yes, sir. Those are extra items that your Department of Transportation had us do that were not part of the original contract."

Kwid took a sip from his bottled water. "Problem is, Guy, we are in the middle of budget negotiations, and the state is in a bit of a recession. There is no telling when we are going to be able to pay that kind of money, when we're talking about shutting down schools."

Guy cracked a nervous smile. "With all due respect, sir, it's part of our deal."

The Governor pushed the brake on the cart, and the two went to the rear to select their clubs. "Did I hear that your son the Senator was assigned to the Water and Power subcommittee of Energy and Natural Resources?"

Thinking that the issue of the $3 million owed Northern Industries was behind him, Guy joked. "Yeah, they told him that was part of his rite of initiation. A good time to catch up on sleep."

The two walked toward Guy's ball. "It would seem to me, Guy, that if your son were to push some federal funding for public works in our state, it might expedite your projects here, and maybe even lead to new ones. Just speculation on my part."

Guy looked down at his ball to address it. "I don't know. I'd have to think about that. He is only a freshman. He doesn't have his sea legs yet."

Governor Kwid interrupted by extending his club to Guy. "Here Guy, try this. It works wonders in tall grass. It's called a 'Gopher.'"

Guy studied the club's wedged bottom and carved notches. "Geez, I have never seen a club like this." He laughed. "Is it tournament legal?"

The Governor's smile bunched the wrinkles on his face. "Probably not. But I won't tell if you don't."

Guy swung the Gopher, stroking his ball onto the green.

The Governor reached to retrieve the club from Guy. "We'll just consider it our little secret."

A golf cart with a young caddy approached. He handed Guy a cellular telephone. "Mr. Bennett, phone call for you. It's a Mr. Nardeen from your office in New York. He says it's important."

Governor Kwid tried to clean a piece of mud out of the bottom of his Gopher. "The only problem with this club is that it collects so much damn dirt." He turned to Guy. "You take your call, Guy. I'll meet you on the green."

Guy took the cellular and walked a few steps away for privacy. "What is it, Mohammad? You know I'm playing golf with the Governor of Arizona."

"I know sir, and I apologize. I would not have called if I did not think it was urgent."

Guy raised his voice. "Out with it, damnit. I've got an important game to finish."

Mohammad's voice split. "We just received tender offer documents, sir."

"What?"

Mohammad hurried to furnish his boss the critical information. "A company from Buenos Aires called 'La Compañía del Sur' is offering our shareholders twenty eight dollars a share for all of their outstanding stock. That is ten dollars higher than what the stock is trading at today."

Guy began pacing in the rough. "What do we know about the company? Who is in charge?"

Mohammad took a deep breath. "A man named Bruno Petrozzini."

Guy stopped pacing. "Bruno Petrozzini? That's Vito's older brother. Vito hasn't seen him in years. Have you told Vito?"

"No, sir. You are my boss. I thought you should know first."

Guy resumed walking through the rough, and barking into the phone. "La Compañía del Sur – the fucking Company of the South. Sonofabitch! Where the hell is Bruno Petrozzini getting that kind of money to offer our shareholders twenty-eight bucks a share?"

"I am sorry to say, but it's your daughter-in-law's father, Giles Kirby. His investment banking firm – Webb Investments – is underwriting the deal."

Guy put his hand over his eyes. "I can't believe this. Tell Barbara to call the Board of Directors for a meeting tomorrow morning at 9 a.m."

"What about Mr. Petrozzini, sir?"

"You've got to tell him about this. Hell, it's public information by now. Just do me a favor. When you give him the documents, tell him what you told me. Everything. And watch his reaction very closely. We'll talk when I get back."

Guy handed the cellular back to the caddy, tipped him, and went to the green where Governor Kwid was waiting. The Governor pulled the pin from the hole. "Your shot, Guy. You're out." He laid the flag on the grass. "I hope the phone call was nothing serious."

Guy crouched over his ball. He had learned from his father years earlier never to show emotion in business; the golf game with Governor Kwid was business. "Nothing important enough to take me away from a good game of golf with new friends."

Guy aimed and sank his putt.

"Great read, Guy."

"Thank you, Governor," replied Guy, feeling a pit in his stomach. "Time for some," Guy rubbed his belly as he tried to recall the exotic lunchtime entrée the Governor mentioned as the beef alternative.

The Governor picked Guy's ball out of the hole, and placed it in Guy's hand. "Time for some what, Guy?"

Guy looked the Governor straight in the eye and smiled. "Time for some Hawaiian."

XXXVIII.

❦

Bidding From Another Hemisphere

Guy ate lunch cordially, and he and Marie caught the first plane back to New York. Guy didn't bother to set up a pre-board meeting with Vito. He went straight to Mohammad's office at five minutes before nine. "Is everybody here, Mohammad?"

Mohammad looked up from his computer. "They're in the boardroom waiting for you."

Guy rifled through Mohammad's shelves. "Do you have a pad?"

Mohammad offered his own. "Take mine, sir."

"Thanks." Before exiting Mohammad's office, Guy turned. "What was Vito's reaction when you told him the news yesterday?"

"Difficult to tell whether he was stunned or indifferent. He didn't so much as ask a question. It was almost as if he already knew."

Guy entered the boardroom, and closed the door behind him. "Well hello, gang. Thank you for coming. Seems we've been seeing a lot of each other lately."

Professor Pym studied his photocopied set of the tender offer papers. "Guy, what do we know about..." Pym struggled with the accent, "...'La Compañía del Sur'? And why would they want to take over Northern Industries?"

David Rothstein responded first. "I had my associates do some digging on the computers last night. It is a huge livestock and leather conglomerate in Argentina. One of the biggest privately held companies in the region. The funny thing is, it used to be called 'Italargo' until a couple of years ago, when it was changed to 'La Compañía del Sur.'" He turned to Eleanor Whittlesby. "That means 'The Company of the South' in Spanish." He reported back to the group. "If my dates are right, the name was changed just after we went public and changed our name from 'Aquino Construction' to 'Northern Industries.'" Rothstein looked at Vito. "The company was founded and headed by a fella named Bruno Petrozzini, who appears to be quite a player in Argentine circles. His name pops up in all kinds of newspaper stories. A huge philanthropist with a lot of money and influence. He has an opera house named after his mother, and there are stories of private meetings between him and the King of Spain. But most reports say he is a reclusive guy, who rarely talks to the press. He hates publicity. Nobody even knows exactly where he lives, but they suspect he moves from ranch to ranch in the Pampas region of Argentina."

Nick Covitt interrupted. "Las Pampas is beautiful countryside. My wife and I took a trip out there a couple of years ago when I did a deal in Buenos Aires."

Bram Leach cut to the chase. "Vito, is this guy related to you?"

Vito sat still in his seat, with his hands folded on his lap. He bit his lower lip, paused, then spoke slowly. "Bruno Petrozzini is my older brother. He left home when I was very young. Apparently, he has done well since then."

Professor Pym stroked his hand through his thinning hair. "Do you speak to him?"

Vito responded coolly. "I haven't seen or heard from my brother Bruno in years."

Leach followed. "Why would he want to take over Northern Industries? Did the two of you have a falling-out of some sort? And what is his connection to Leo Wong, the broker? Does Bruno have any business in Asia?"

Vito grew stern. "I thought I said that I have not heard from my brother in years. Who knows why he wants to take us over? Maybe he is doing us all a favor."

Guy slammed his fist on the marble table, and yelled. "God-damnit, Vito!" The echo from the table halted Guy, as he realized that for the first time, he had both lost his composure and split ranks with his partner in front of his Board.

Guy looked around the table at his Board members, and folded his hands on the table in front of him like a schoolboy. He spoke in a monotone. "The Board is curious about the person who is seeking to take over our company. That person happens to be your brother, who, coincidentally, appears to have been trading our stock for the last year or two on inside information. It should not surprise you that they have a few questions." Guy extended himself toward Vito. "Now why don't you give us some answers?"

Vito squinted back at Guy, pushing poison from his pupils. "I refuse to be treated like a jailhouse suspect. I have told you everything. I know as much about Bruno as all of you do." He rose from his seat. "If you don't mind, I would rather not take part in a witch hunt where I am the witch."

As Vito got up from his chair, Guy grabbed him by the forearm and gritted his teeth. "This is not the way to make a power play, you jealous bastard. I'll crush you."

Vito looked down at Guy's trembling grip.

Eleanor Whittlesby spoke for the first time. "Guy, let Vito go. He is an officer of the company."

Guy let go, and Vito left.

Guy tried to restore order. "David, what are our options?"

Rothstein straightened his glasses. "We can launch a massive public relations campaign with the shareholders, telling them that they should hold onto their stock for the long haul with the prospect of making more money as the company's earnings grow. But it's going to be awfully hard to convince them why they shouldn't take ten dollars on their shares today. The stock has been flat. They are going to want to cash out. I think our only hope of defeating Bruno Petrozzini is to try and outbid him."

Covitt commented. "But then the company would be private again." Covitt turned to Guy. "Is that what you want? And at what expense? Do you have the resources to wage a fight like that? I know you don't want to hear this, Guy, but you could sell your stock at twenty-eight dollars a share and leave quite a legacy." Covitt smirked. "I would use the time and money to brush up on my golf."

Miffed at Covitt and his suggestion, Guy responded without hesitation. "David, arrange a meeting with the investment bankers immediately."

Rothstein leafed through his pocket diary. "We will have to be ready to move fast, Guy. These things take on a life of their own."

Guy continued with more orders. "Fine, today is Tuesday. Let's have another board meeting on Thursday. We'll make a decision then."

Professor Pym raised his hand. "I can't, Guy. VJ and I are going down to Chile tomorrow to put the finishing touches on a couple of major deals. We'll be back late Friday." He rubbed his hands across his belly. "So long as we are still the Directors of Northern Industries, it is our fiduciary duty to close those matters."

Guy extended his hand to David Rothstein. "Can we wait?"

Rothstein tilted his head. "We would have to meet over the weekend, before the market opens on Monday."

Guy brought his folded hands up against his chin. "I will see everybody on Saturday morning. I'll bring the bagels."

Only David Rothstein smiled in reply.

After the others left, Rothstein lingered. "Guy, you have to stay cool. I've never seen you lose control like that with Vito."

Guy sat exasperated. "I know."

Rothstein continued. "And we didn't even discuss the fact that the deal is being underwritten by Webb Investments. Isn't that the place run by your daughter-in-law's father, Giles Kirby?"

Guy got up from his seat, and turned to the black and white photo of him, his father, and the laborers in the Aquino Construction's first pick-up truck. "You got it. buddy. I didn't want to get into it because I think Albert and Victoria are getting divorced. Believe it or not, Kirby being involved in this thing is about the only piece of the puzzle that makes sense." Guy turned from the photo back to Rothstein. "WASPs are such vindictive bastards. And now I've got to figure out if my partner has become one of them."

Rothstein put his hand on Guy's shoulder. "I'll set up a meeting with the investment bankers immediately. We'll go to Sharpstone. We used them for the initial public offering. We have a good relationship with them. Are you available?"

Guy snickered. "Can I afford not to be?"

XXXIX.

❧❦

Daddy's Girl

Guy and David Rothstein spent the next two days crunching numbers, and meeting with the investment bankers at Sharpstone. No matter how they spun it, the task of outbidding Bruno Petrozzini to save Northern Industries was daunting, and could potentially squeeze Guy down to his last penny. In the meantime, Vito Petrozzini did not even bother to show up at work.

When Guy came home Thursday night, he grabbed a bottle of his homemade wine from the garage where he stored it. He paused to admire the bottle's label, which he had embossed with the family's original name – "Vino Di Benedetto" – and recalled the days as a young boy when he helped his father crush the grapes for fermentation. It took young Guy years to understand the process, which he was still trying to conquer in pursuit of a great cabernet.

Guy entered the kitchen, where Marie was preparing one of his favorite dishes – rigatoni with broccoli *rabe* and large chunks of sausage. Guy loved contrasts; the clash of the bitter green with the sweetness of sausage and pecorino cheese tingled his tastebuds. Guy kissed his wife on the cheek as she stirred her pot, and went to the drawer for a corkscrew.

Marie kept stirring. "How did it go with the bankers?"

Guy twisted the corkscrew. "So long as I am willing to offer them everything down to my shirt buttons as collateral, they'll give me anything I want. When we did the public offering with these guys and they had nothing to lose, they were more than happy to sit with me for hours on end racking up huge fees. They told me, 'Guy, this is the beginning of a winning partnership between Sharpstone and Northern Industries.' They made me feel like one of them." Guy popped the cork and poured himself a full glass as Marie took her pot of rigatoni to the sink for straining. "Today, they barely gave me forty-five minutes to explain how little they could do. They acted as if they didn't even know me. One of the sons of bitches called me Gaetano at one point, as if he had just seen my name on a loan application for the first time." He tossed down a healthy dose of the red. "Bastards. I'm tired of trying to win over guys who have first names that sound like last names – Duncan, Macallister, Hunter." He took another gulp, and laughed in disbelief. "Gaetano."

Marie absorbed the steam rising from the colander to her face, as she shook the water from the rigatoni. "Guy, do you think you should be drinking so much? You've practically had a bottle every night."

Guy held up his glass and studied its bulb, which was still half-filled. "Look at that clarity." He took another sip. "Wine's good for you. It relieves the tension. By the time this nightmare is over, my wine may be the only thing I created that's still mine."

The doorbell rang. Guy quickly poured himself another glass of wine, and made his way to the foyer. "I'll get it. Maybe it's Bruno Petrozzini to tell me that the whole thing is a joke."

Guy opened the door to find his daughter Lisa Marie. He smiled and gave her a bear hug. "Even better."

Lisa Marie caught her breath. "Even better than what, Daddy?"

Guy put his arm around his daughter's shoulder as he escorted her inside to the kitchen. "Seeing you is even better than the magnificent rigatoni that your mother is making."

Guy brought her to the table, where Marie had her husband's plate of pasta waiting for him. "So what brings you here? Do you want a glass of wine? It's some of our best stuff. Not quite a cabernet, but almost. That'll be ready for drinking in a few years." Guy raised the bottle. "But in the meantime, you'll have to settle for this."

Lisa Marie held up her hand to stop her father. "I can't, Daddy. Doctor's orders."

Guy and Marie volleyed smiles to one another, sensing good news on the way. Guy asked the question. "What do you mean, sweetheart? You never had a problem with my wine before."

Lisa Marie blushed. "VJ and I are going to have a baby."

Guy swallowed the air around him. "My little girl is going to have a baby. Now that's a cause for celebration." Guy looked fondly into his daughter's eyes. "You have the same beautiful look your mother did when she told me she was pregnant with you." He kissed Lisa Marie on the cheek. "Marie, bring your daughter some pasta."

Marie scurried to the table with a heaping serving in hand. "I'm coming, I'm coming." She presented the dish to Lisa Marie. "Here, on the special day plate. Remember how much fun we used to have when you kids ate from the plate?"

Lisa Marie received the meal with a wide smile. "The only problem was Albert and Edward always seemed to eat from it more than I did."

Guy plunged a fork into his rigatoni and a piece of sausage, wrapping it with a strand of broccoli *rabe*. "That's not true. You were always the most special to me." He pinched her cheek with one hand, as he fed himself with the other. "You're Daddy's little girl. Those other two idiots just needed more massaging for their egos."

Lisa Marie studied the perimeter of her plate that was not covered with pasta. "Ma, what happened? The special day plate is cracked."

Guy's and Marie's enthusiasm halted, as they looked at each other wondering if Edward had told her about his argument with Guy; Guy surmised that he had not. "I knocked the plate over by accident the other day. But your mother did a great job putting it back together, didn't she?"

Lisa Marie pointed to a gap on the edge of the dish. "Yeah, except there is still a piece missing."

Marie joined her husband and daughter at the table, and smiled sternly at Guy. "Your father is going to fix that."

Guy tore a piece of bread. "Don't worry about the plate. Eat." He reached over and soaked the bread with virgin olive oil from Lisa Marie's plate, and held it in front of her mouth. "Here, the dunking is the best part."

Instead of letting him feed her, Lisa Marie took the bread from her father. Before biting into the oil-drenched bread, she looked at the plateless space in front of her mother. "Ma, aren't you going to eat?"

Marie puckered her lips, and shook her head. "I picked while I was cooking. Don't worry about me. How's VJ? He must be very excited."

Lisa Marie hurried to swallow. "He is. I told him in the airport, just before he and Professor Pym left for Chile. I told him I was going to take off from work for a few days while he was gone, to begin to get everything ready. You know, the room, crib."

"What did VJ say?" asked Guy.

Lisa Marie giggled. "He said that while I was home, I should go to the spa. He's like you, Daddy. Very generous, but not big on the mushy stuff. Anyway, I hope you don't mind that Professor Pym knew before you did."

"My board members seem to know a lot of things before I do these days." Guy sat back in his chair to catch his breath. "So are you ready to become a full-time mommy? You're going to have learn to cook like your mother, you know." He pointed to his near empty dish. "Little elves don't come and make this stuff at night when you sleep. Your dinner table is very important. It keeps your family together. Your kids are not going to sit around very long if it's only pizza or cheeseburgers every night."

"I'll be fine, Daddy. I'll tell you what. I'll take cooking lessons from Mom after I finish my journalism classes." Lisa Marie spoke coyly as she eyed her plate. "I know how much you love my journalism classes."

Guy reassumed the eating position, elbows on the table and spear in hand. "I think it's a great hobby, honey, but don't you think you should take some time to be a mother first?"

Lisa Marie wiped her mouth with a napkin. "Are we going to go through this again? I can do both, Daddy. Albert set me up an internship with Gabrielle DeFiore, who has been letting me do some small pieces for *The Daily*. That woman is amazing. She's beautiful, eloquent, graceful, and has incredible energy. I don't know how she does it."

Guy spoke through a mouthful. "She's single with no children."

Lisa Marie looked to her mother for help. When none was forthcoming, she continued with her father. "She's only twenty-eight and can have any man she wants. She just hasn't found anyone as special as VJ." Lisa Marie grabbed her father's free hand. "Which is the other reason I came over tonight. VJ told me about your argument with Mr. Petrozzini."

Guy slammed down his fork, and looked at his wife. "Vito never learned that you can't mix family with business. He tells his son everything."

Marie nodded in agreement.

Guy turned back to Lisa Marie. "You don't worry about a thing, sweetheart. I will take care of Northern Industries; you take care of my grandson."

"First of all, we don't know whether it's a boy or a girl, and frankly don't care so long as it's healthy." Lisa Marie moved up in her seat. "And if you are fighting with Mr. Petrozzini, I have to care. Because he is also going to be my child's grandfather."

Guy held out his arms. "You're so smart, my little journalist. What do you suggest that I do with a partner who is trying to take my company from me?"

"He's not trying to take your company from you. He told me and VJ that he has no idea how his brother got involved, and I believe him. I think he's hurt that you are not giving him the same benefit of the doubt." Lisa Marie looked down at her plate. "If you ask me, Daddy, Mr. Petrozzini idolizes you." She then looked up at her father. "You're like the brother this guy Bruno never was for him. That's the part that hurts him most."

Guy stroked his teeth with a toothpick. "You may be right. Bruno left home when Vito was so young. And his father, Adamo, he was a nice man. But he was weak. Vito never had a strong figure in his family – other than his mother Lucia." Guy grabbed his wife's hand. "That woman was a rock. And sharp as a knife."

Marie's eyes opened wider. "And very sad. I don't think she ever got over Bruno leaving home."

Guy threw away his toothpick. "What do you want me to do?"

Lisa Marie jumped. "Have dinner with Mr. Petrozzini, tomorrow at 6:30 at his house. It would mean so much to him if you went over there. He's always complaining that you never go visit him in

Middletown anymore. And I'm not asking you to apologize. Just go over and talk to him around his table."

Guy smiled. "I assume you have already spoken to Vito about this."

"I'm just trying to be the guy with the ball that everyone's chasing," Lisa Marie squinted as she suppressed a smirk. "Isn't that what you always told Albert and Edward?"

Guy waved his white napkin. "All right, all right. I give. You win. Sometimes I think maybe you should have become the Senator." Still in search of even a tiny concession, Guy followed. "But why 6:30? That's so early."

"Daddy, you know that's the time the Petrozzinis have eaten ever since we have known them. Church at 8 on Sunday morning, and dinner at 6:30. They're very regular people." Lisa Marie paused and grew wistful. "The way we used to be."

"Okay, okay. I'll do it. But I'm not promising anything. I'm doing this for you." Guy pointed to his daughter's plate of pasta. "Now finish your macaroni before it gets cold."

Lisa Marie kissed her father on the cheek, and ate her meal with ardor.

XL.

Steak Pizzaiola

An Anonymous Caller

Guy made his way to Vito Petrozzini's house the next evening, filled with suspicion and angst. In Guy's mind, Vito had always been jealous of him and his family, and over time convinced himself that he could have been as successful as Guy as head of the company, if not more, if he had only been given the opportunity. Whenever Vito tried to negotiate power from Guy, Guy reminded his partner that the company was started by him and his father Dante. With that, the decision was final, but the conversation would not end without Vito reminding Guy that were it not for the loan from Vito's father Adamo, there would have been no company to start. Guy never responded, but always wondered about the debt, and why his father never let him simply pay it back without having to make Vito a partner. It was the Old World, Guy suspected, and its fierce loyalty and passion – the same intensity that was pushing Guy's foot hard against his car's accelerator. The same surge of emotions that was driving Guy to the precipice of hatred.

When Guy exited the highway in his Mercedes and entered Middletown, however, his press eased. As he rolled through the town's cozy streets, his thoughts were warmed with the images of the Bennetts and Petrozzinis enjoying them together: Marie and Lena shopping with credit their parents never had; their children playing stickball instead of working to support their families; and Guy and Vito treating them all to sweet vanilla ice cream from the

Good Humor truck. Guy desperately wanted to believe his long-time friend and partner, but would not allow himself to be betrayed.

To get to the Petrozzinis' front door from their cracking driveway, Guy had to walk the slate slabs that he had helped Vito lay across his grass. For the first time in a long while, he studied the Petrozzini home. When it was first built, Vito and Guy thought it was large enough to fit three families; it now seemed small and simple to Guy, its roof in need of an upgrade, its lawn begging for fertilizer.

Guy rapped three times on the thin wooden front door.

Vito's wife Lena answered. She looked back over her shoulder to see if Vito was behind her, then sneaked Guy a kiss on the cheek. She whispered so as not to be heard. "Congratulations, Grandpa."

"*Grazie,* Pasqualina," answered Guy in their childhood tongue, calling Lena by her full Italian name.

Lena blushed. She turned and yelled. "Vito, Guy's here."

Vito did not answer, as Lena led Guy to the living room. Vito was standing at the head of his table. He extended his hand toward the place setting next to him, inviting Guy to sit.

Lena pushed Guy's chair behind him, then did the same for her husband. "Well, I know you men are hungry. So I'll go get the spaghetti. But don't fill up, because then we have steak *pizzaiola*, which I know both of you love."

Guy decided to speak first. He looked at the bottle of pinkish wine in the middle of the table. "Is it homemade?"

Vito pulled the cork from the bottle. He knew that Guy was an elitist when it came to homemade wine, always bragging about the full and oaken taste of his regal reds. "Yeah, it's nice and sweet, the way I like it. I used to make the big reds, until I admitted to myself that I liked rosé better." He poured Guy a glass, and spoke through a mouthful of bread. "I got nothing to prove to anybody."

Guy ignored Vito's jab, and lifted his glass for a toast. "To our grandchild."

Without touching Guy's, Vito extended his glass forward. "*Salute.*"

As Guy downed Vito's wine, he fought its brackish taste. He commented with a subtlety that he despised in others, such as his Board members. "Interesting. Tastes can be so different."

Vito grabbed the bowl of spaghetti with thick red sauce that his wife brought from the kitchen. "Whatever that means."

Pressing his fork against his spoon, Guy twirled his spaghetti neatly. "It's funny. Even though you don't care for red wine, you always liked the thick red stuff on your spaghetti. You were never one for white sauces or pesto with your pasta."

Vito grumbled. "I don't eat pasta. I eat macaroni. Macaroni is served with gravy, not sauce. Gravy, my friend, is always red."

Guy did not protest, careful to measure his responses. "We missed you at the office the last couple of days."

Vito smiled as his wife entered with the main dish. "I didn't think you would notice."

Lena laid the steak *pizzaiola* in the center of the table. Fresh tomatoes were heaped on a pile of steaks four high, the dish's vapor full with a bouquet of garlic and oregano. "That should be enough. If not, I have more in the kitchen."

Guy rubbed his hands slowly. "Lena, if we eat more than this, we'll be having dessert in the emergency room through a tube." He leaned closer to the dish and inhaled. "I always knew that if I had a cold, the garlic in your *pizzaiola* would do the trick."

Lena smiled shyly. "It's the same recipe your fathers brought from Aquino."

Vito took two steaks for himself, then passed the dish to Guy. "Lena, the knives. We need the steak knives."

Lena returned with thick, wooden handled steak knives, their blades wide with sharply serrated edges. She laid one next to each of the men.

Guy lifted his knife in front of him, and studied it. "These knives look familiar. Where have I seen them before?"

Lena turned and pressed her hands tightly together, as if she was praying. "They're the same ones they use at *Casa Italia*. The owner, Tony, he gave them to us at Christmas." Lena paused and looked at both Guy and her husband. "Do you remember when we used to bring the kids there? It was so much fun."

Vito stared back at his wife, his mouth dripping with tomato and garlic, signaling for her to leave.

As the kitchen door swung closed behind Lena, Vito cut into

his meat. "Yeah, Tony gave them to us. You know he had a heart attack two months ago."

Guy was about to take his glass of wine, but reached for his water instead. "No, I hadn't heard."

"That's because you don't go to *Casa Italia* anymore. Tony keeps asking, 'how come I haven't seen Gaetano since he moved to White-bridge?'" Vito imitated the restaurant owner as he cut into his meat again. "He says, 'wass a-matta, they only eat-a filet mignon now?'"

Guy swallowed his water. "You know, with the campaign and all, we just haven't had the time."

Vito continued to feed himself. "We had some nice times at that damn restaurant."

Guy's eyes crinkled softly. "Do you remember the time VJ kept asking you for more salt on his pasta?"

Vito nodded as he chewed his red meat. The beginnings of laughter slipped from his nostrils.

Feeling a rhythm, Guy continued. "And you got so mad, that you loosened the top on the salt shaker and gave it to him." The two men started laughing together. "When he shook it and the top came off, there was that huge pile of salt on his pasta." Guy corrected himself. "I mean macaroni. You made him eat the whole damn thing. He must have drunk three pitchers of water that night."

Vito held his hand up as he laughed, begging Guy to stop before he lost complete control and spit the food from his mouth. The two men enjoyed the happy frenzy.

When Vito swallowed, he sat back in his chair, and grabbed his glass of wine. "And Lisa Marie is the only one who didn't laugh. Do you remember how she kept giving VJ her water?" Vito raised his glass. "To our families."

Guy joined the toast. "*Cin – cin. Cien d'ann'*. One hundred years of prosperity."

As Guy put his glass down, Vito queried him. "Guy, why do you think I have had something to do with this takeover? And why did you embarrass me in front of the Board like that?"

Guy straightened his back, and opened his hands. "Vito, put yourself in my shoes. This Chinese guy, Leo Wong, has been doing large buying and selling of our stock just before some big develop-ments in the company are made public. Nobody can figure out the connection. Then, the proxy statement comes, and we find out that your brother in Argentina is trying to take over the company."

Vito spoke without blinking. "Guy, I'm telling you, I don't even know him. I have been partners with you longer than I lived with him. He left the house when I was thirteen. Think about it. To treat me that way in front of the Board..." He leaned forward. "You are more of a brother to me than he ever was."

Guy took another sip of Vito's wine. "I'm sorry I yelled at you in front of those assholes. I just don't know what to do." Guy made his first cut into the *pizzaiola* and began eating.

The phone rang, and Lena answered. She came into the dining room and summoned Guy. "Guy, it's for you."

Guy cleaned his mouth. "This is delicious, Lena." He stood up. "Who is it?"

"I don't know, he wouldn't say."

The conversation was very short, relegated to a series of "yes" and "uh-huh" responses from Guy.

Guy clicked the phone shut and gave it to Lena. "This thing keeps getting weirder and weirder."

Vito looked up. "Who was it?"

Guy rubbed his brow, and looked Vito straight in the eye. "I don't know, he wouldn't tell me either. Whoever it was said that if I wanted to keep Northern Industries, I had to meet him at 7:15 at the old rail yards, with full authority to negotiate."

Vito stood up immediately. "How the hell did he know you were here?"

"He probably has somebody following me."

Vito put down his napkin. "Let's go, I'm coming with you. I'm gonna end this thing right now. I don't know what the hell Bruno is trying to prove, but I'm not amused."

Guy put his hand on Vito's shoulder. "No, you can't come. He said I have to come alone. He said this would be my only chance. I'll be fine." Guy looked down at his watch. "It's seven o'clock. If I leave right now, I'll be there by seven fifteen." He kissed Lena on the cheek. "I'll be back to finish my steak."

XLI.

Yellow Tape

An Interrogation

When Guy returned one hour later, the Petrozzini home was surrounded by police cars' lights swirling fiery red in the night. An officer stretched yellow masking tape across the front door that read in bold black "Crime Scene – Do Not Cross This Line."

Guy asked the officer. "What's going on here?" When the short, brittle-haired officer refused to answer, Guy followed. "I'm Vito Petrozzini's business partner, Guy Bennett."

The officer smirked as he continued to draw his line.

Guy snapped. "Guy Bennett, officer. The father of Senator Albert Bennett."

Without breaking his step or looking at Guy, the young officer cut his tape and planted it. "You'll have to speak to the sergeant in the driveway, sir. No one allowed in the house except detectives."

Guy peeled his way through the gathered crowd, until he reached the center, where his daughter Lisa Marie was standing crying, with an apple pie in hand. "Daddy, Daddy. Tell them you didn't do it. Tell them you didn't kill the Petrozzinis."

Guy looked at the officers surrounding Lisa Marie, and questioned Sergeant Dailey, whom he long knew from his days in Middletown. "Charlie, what the hell is going on here?"

Dailey stepped forward. "Mr. Bennett, Mr. and Mrs. Petrozzini were stabbed to death in their home. Your daughter came with an apple pie that she said she was bringing for you and Mr. Petrozzini for dessert. She says that you and Mr. Petrozzini were supposed to be having dinner at the house tonight. Is that true, Mr. Bennett?"

Guy swiped his hand repeatedly through his hair. "Oh my God. Stabbed to death? That can't be. I was just with them." Guy reached for his daughter and embraced her. "Don't worry, honey. The police will find out who did it."

Dailey interrupted the embrace. "Excuse me, Mr. Bennett. But did you have dinner with Mr. Petrozzini tonight?"

Guy looked up puzzled. "What's this 'Mr. Bennett' stuff, Charlie? You've known me for twenty years."

Dailey looked to the pavement. "Just answer the question, sir."

Guy let go of Lisa Marie, feeling the hot and coffee-scented breath of the officers around him. "Yes, yes. I had dinner with Vito tonight. What about it?"

Dailey nodded at a plain-clothed detective, whose tie knot was pulled down below his opened top two shirt buttons. "Mr. Bennett, would you mind going with Detective Kauftman to police headquarters? He just has a few questions for you."

Guy's heart pumped. "Sure. But do I need a lawyer?"

Dailey squinted his crow-footed eyes. "That's up to you."

Kauftman joined in. "You know how lawyers are, Mr. Bennett. They're always getting in the way, making things complicated. C'mon, we'll just be a few minutes. Then you'll be done with us. Just routine stuff – to help figure out who killed your partner and his wife."

Guy looked at his old friend Charlie Dailey for a sign, but saw none in his granite face. "Okay, I guess so." He turned to his daughter. "Lisa Marie, call David Rothstein right away and tell him what's going on."

Guy went toward the police car. "Should I come with you, detective?"

Kauftman moved to the passenger's side door of Guy's Mercedes-Benz. "No, we're kind of short on cars, with so many guys here. Why don't we take your car, Mr. Bennett? The only time I've been near one of these is watching *Lifestyles of the Rich and Famous* on television." As Kauftman entered Guy's car, he nodded at Sergeant Dailey before slamming the door shut.

When Kauftman reached under his seat to adjust it for his

heavy frame, Guy directed him to the buttons on the door panel. "The buttons on the side adjust the seat. They're arranged in the shape of the seat so that you can move what you want – seat or back. The little button on top is for the head rest."

Kauftman pushed the little button, and turned to watch his headrest elevate. "Would you look at that. My wife won't believe this when I tell her."

Guy threw the car into reverse. He bumped into the curb.

"You seem a little nervous," said Kauftman as he fastened his seatbelt.

"I'll be okay," answered Guy. He straightened his wheel, and started driving to the Middletown police station.

Kauftman made small talk. "So Char..." He stopped himself. "Sergeant Dailey told me you used to live in Middletown before you moved to Whitebridge. Says he hasn't seen you around in a while."

Guy remained fixed on the road. He was uneasy with Kauftman's forced friendliness. "Yes, my family and I moved to Whitebridge a few years ago. Tell me, are there any clues regarding Vito and Lena?"

Kauftman looked down to adjust his gold-plated tie clip that cradled a fake gemstone. "Whitebridge. That's where all the rich people live, isn't it?" When Guy didn't answer, Kauftman continued. "I just moved here from upstate. I'm still learning the area. So in the meantime, I just repeat what I hear. I didn't mean anything by it, of course. Rich people can be nice, too – I guess."

Guy turned toward Kauftman's beady eyes. "Whitebridge is a nice town with plenty of nice people, just like Middletown. Detective, do you have any information on what happened to Vito and Lena?"

"Much too early to tell, sir." Kauftman caressed the dashboard. "Is this real leather?"

"Yes."

Kauftman looked at his fingers to check if the material left any residue. "Yeah, well they say that the wrong element is creeping into Middletown from the city. People are getting scared. More crime, real estate going down. The schools are supposedly getting worse."

Guy turned the conversation back to Kauftman. "So then why did you come here?"

"My mother-in-law had a stroke. She's bedridden. My wife and I can't really afford to put her in a nursing home, and she refuses to leave her house. So we decided to move here to be close. We're lucky that my Navy pension came just in time."

Guy tightened his lips. "I'm sorry to hear about your mother-in-law."

Kauftman reached beneath his sagging belly to tuck in his shirt. "That's okay. Hey, in my book, family and friends are everything. All the money in the world can't take the place of family and friends. Wouldn't you say so, sir?"

Guy turned into the Middletown police department driveway. "Yes, I would."

Kauftman pointed. "Just pull around to the garage, sir."

Guy's car was met by three policemen in front of the lighted and opened garage. "Where should I go?"

"Would you mind authorizing us to search the car?" When Guy pulled his Mercedes to a stop inside the garage, Kauftman lowered his window. "Great windows. This is one helluva car." He reached outside the open window to grab a paper form and pen from one of the waiting police officers. "The search is standard for anyone who has been with a victim within the past six hours." Kauftman handed Guy the form. "You don't have to consent. But that means we'll have to get a judge involved, and then things get complicated. So if you consent, just sign on the bottom line. It'll speed up the process. Routine stuff."

Without saying a word, Guy signed the form and gave it back to Kauftman.

Kauftman folded it. "Thank you, sir." As he exited from his door, Kauftman handed the folded consent form to the officer who gave it to him, and whispered in his ear. "Turn the bastard's car inside out. There's got to be something in there."

Kauftman took Guy to a small windowless room where another detective was already waiting with a Styrofoam cup of coffee in hand. "Mr. Bennett, this is Detective Brower. He works with me. He is going to sit in on the interview." Kauftman began pouring himself a cup of coffee. "Would you like a cup of coffee, Mr. Bennett?"

Guy nodded "yes" as he slowly took a seat. "Black with sugar, please."

As Kauftman handed Guy the cup, he smiled at Brower. "I bet I'm not as pretty as the woman at Mr. Bennett's office in New York City who serves him his coffee."

The two detectives shared a laugh.

Guy grew uncomfortable with how much Kauftman seemed to know about him. "How did you know that I work in New York City?"

Kauftman stirred his coffee with a thin red plastic straw. "Oh, I don't know." Kauftman finished stirring, then bit the red straw. "I figure an important guy like you with a big fancy car must work in the city. Just a hunch."

As Guy took a sip from his cup, he noticed a huddle of cockroaches beneath the coffee table. He put the cup down immediately, and folded his hands like a schoolboy. "What can I do for you, gentlemen?"

Brower put a mini-cassette tape recorder on the table, and activated it.

Kauftman spoke. "Well, as you know, Mr. Bennett, you do not have to speak to us. You have the right to remain silent, you have the right to have a lawyer..."

Guy broke in. "Am I a suspect?"

Kauftman looked at Brower before responding. "Sir, it's just something the courts make us do every time we bring someone in here." He showed Guy the card he was holding. "We have to read off this little card. I'm sure you know all this already. It's for the lawyers – they always need to complicate things. Just relax and we'll be done in a few minutes."

Kauftman looked at Brower again with eyes widened. Before Kauftman could resume speaking, Brower stopped him. "Wait a minute, Hank. The tape got caught. We'll have to start again."

Kauftman clicked repeatedly the plastic pen he was holding, spacing his intervals. "Are we ready now, Brower? I am sure Mr. Bennett would rather be somewhere else."

Brower shook his head and spoke in quick rounds. "Ready, chief."

Kauftman sat up in his chair, and rested his plastic pen on the table. "Okay, we are back on the tape after a mechanical malfunction with our recorder. It's 8:20 p.m. on March 31, and Detective Brower and I are here with Mr. Guy Bennett investigating the murder of Vito and Lena Petrozzini. Before beginning, sir, it's just a formality, but your name is Guy Bennett, isn't it?"

Guy cleared his throat. "Actually, it's Gaetano. Guy is just a nickname."

Kauftman smiled at Brower. "I don't think I have ever heard that name before. But it makes sense. Guytano – Guy. It must be Italian." He turned back toward Guy. "Just like Vito and Lena."

Guy nodded.

"Another formality, sir, but we can't record your gestures." Kauftman pointed to his lower lip. "You'll have to speak up so we can hear you. Obviously, that last question and answer about your name doesn't matter much."

Guy kept his hands folded, and felt the sweat welling up inside of them. "I understand."

Kauftman got up from his seat, and walked casually toward the coffee maker and a box of sugar donuts. He spoke as he walked. "Now, Mr. Bennett, you understand that you don't have to speak to us, that you have the right to remain silent, and the right to a lawyer?" Before Guy could answer, Kauftman broke a donut, and extended half toward Guy.

Guy looked to the floor, where the cockroaches were feeding on the crumbs that fell from the donut. He nodded in the negative.

Kauftman followed. "You understand those rights, don't you sir?" When Guy simply nodded affirmatively, Kauftman pointed to his lower lip. "I realize that this is probably the first time that you have done this, Mr. Bennett, but you have to speak up for the recording."

As Kauftman took a bite from his donut, Guy pulled closer to the wooden table by dragging his chair across the concrete floor. "Yes, detective. I understand my rights."

Kauftman cleaned his hands of the donut's sugar, and returned to his seat. "And you wish to waive them? That is, you are willing to speak to us without a lawyer?"

"Yes, sir. I am."

Kauftman grabbed his plastic pen from the table and clicked it. "Mr. Bennett, when was the last time that you saw the Petrozzinis?"

"Earlier this evening."

"Were you with both of them?"

"Yes."

Kauftman smiled. "In your own words, describe for us your time with the Petrozzinis tonight."

"Well, I went to their house around 6:30 for dinner, and..."

Kauftman extended his hand that was not clicking the plastic pen. "Was it a special occasion? Were you just going over to say hello?"

"Vito and..." Guy stuttered. "Yes, it was a friendly visit."

Kauftman looked over at Brower, and clicked his pen twice. "That's funny, because there were only two sets of plates at the scene. If it were a friendly visit, I would have thought there would be at least three, including one for Mrs. Petrozzini. Maybe even four if Mrs. Bennett came along. Are you sure this was strictly a social call? Your daughter Lisa Marie seemed to have a different impression."

Guy realized that Kauftman had set him up with information the detective obtained from Guy's daughter. Guy studied the sense of control that Kauftman exercised over his pen as he continued to push it.

Click, click.

Guy wanted to speak, but did not want to offer the detective a motive, nor did he want to make another mistake.

Click, click, click.

The question that Guy pondered was just how much information Lisa Marie had given him.

Click-click, click-click.

Finally, he spoke. "Yes, I guess you could say that I was there to discuss the future of our company, Northern Industries."

"What about it? Was there a problem?"

Guy could see the suspicion that lay heavy on Kauftman's and Brower's eyelids. Had Lisa Marie told them about the argument? Guy decided to say only what he had to without lying. "Vito and I had different plans as to where the company should be headed."

"How long were you there?"

"About a half an hour, then I left."

Kauftman looked over at Brower again. "I don't know, with big juicy steaks like the ones on that table, I don't think I would have left so soon, huh, Brower?" Kauftman glared back at Guy. "Unless something caused you to lose your appetite. I know that the smell of flesh always makes me a little queasy." Kauftman kicked back his chair and stood up over Guy. "Now are you going to start telling us the truth? Because otherwise, this is going to be a long night." He clenched his teeth in contempt. "Guy-tano."

Kauftman's continued clicking of his pen thundered inside Guy's head. Click...click...click, click, click...click, click, click, click. It was interrupted by a knock on the door.

Kauftman looked at Brower, and twitched his head toward the rap. "Go see who it is."

Brower opened the door. It was David Rothstein and another lawyer that Guy did not recognize, accompanied by the same officer who had given Kauftman the search consent form. The tall dark lawyer with Rothstein spoke immediately with a smile. "Good evening, Detective Kauftman." He looked at the recorder still running on the table. "You can turn that off now. Your interview with Mr. Bennett is over."

After Kauftman turned off the recorder, the lawyer went over to Guy's seat, and pulled out his chair for him. "What's the matter, Kauftman? You finally became too much of an embarrassment for even the New York City Police Department? I am surprised I didn't find Mr. Bennett bound and gagged in here, and you with a rubber hose in your hand. That's your usual M.O., isn't it?"

"Very funny, Mr. Gonzalez. I'm still trying to figure out how much blood you need on your hands before you stop representing murderers."

Gonzalez began leading Guy out the room. "If you're done now, Detective Kauftman, my client and I will be leaving."

The officer who escorted Gonzalez and Rothstein went over to Kauftman and whispered in his ear. A smile spread across Kauftman's face. "Just one more thing, counselor. Before we came in here,

Mr. Bennett signed a form of consent to search his car. I'm sure you want to cut that off too. I'll save you the breath." Kauftman held a sheet of paper in front of Gonzalez's face. "But first, Mr. Bennett will have to sign this inventory of the shovel, plastic bags, and dirt that we found under the floorboard in his trunk." Kauftman looked at the officer. "It probably explains why Mr. Bennett left dinner so early, and why he looks so spiffy now." Kauftman raised both eyebrows at Gonzalez. "So if he could just sign the inventory and pick up his homicide game board on the way out..."

Guy signed the form, and as he and his lawyers were exiting, tried to speak to them.

Gonzalez put his index finger over his lips to keep Guy quiet.

When the trio reached the parking lot, Guy couldn't restrain himself any longer. He spoke directly to David Rothstein. "Will someone please tell me what the hell just happened to me? One minute, this guy Kauftman is telling me how he moved from upstate to be with his sick mother-in-law, then before I know it, he is accusing me of a double murder. I had to endure his coffee breath and his constant clicking of his damn pen. And the cockroaches!" Guy turned to Gonzalez. "Who the hell are you?"

Gonzalez stood with his head raised and chin stern above Guy. "My name is Elwin Gonzalez. I work with David." Gonzalez looked at Rothstein impatiently. "He asked me to come down. Said he needed a hand with a friend who was trying to be his own lawyer." He forced a smile at Guy, his white teeth gleaming in contrast to his dark skin. "My clients and friends – both of which I hope you will become – call me Win for short."

Guy was embarrassed by his outburst. "I'm sorry, Mr. Gonzalez. It's just a lot happening."

Gonzalez held the handle of his briefcase in front of him with both hands, and tilted his head to speak to Guy. "Please, call me Win. We are probably going to be spending a lot of time together."

Guy perked up. "What do you mean?"

"I mean that the detective you just spoke to did not come to Middletown to be with his sick mother-in-law. He is Harry Kauftman, a no-holds-barred detective from New York City whose wife left him so long ago he probably doesn't even remember his former mother-in-law's name. He got thrown out of the New York Police Department for beating a Hispanic kid to death. They banished him here for punishment. I guess now he wants to pick on big kids like you." Gonzalez raised his eyebrows. "That whole charade was orchestrated to search your car and get you talking. You probably haven't heard this very often, Mr. Bennett, but you've been had."

Guy tried to follow. "But, Win, all I told him was…"

Gonzalez put his hands on Guy's shoulder. "You can explain it tomorrow morning at my office at 9 a.m., after you get a good night's sleep. In the meantime, don't be surprised if you read about this in the paper tomorrow morning. Kauftman loves to leak information, even though he is not supposed to. And don't talk to anybody about this except David and me."

"But I have a meeting tomorrow morning at nine with an investment banker."

Gonzalez smiled. "From now on, Guy, this takes priority until it's over. This is everything. We're talking about your liberty." He started walking away. "I'll see you at 9 am." Gonzalez looked at his watch, then to Rothstein. "You'll go over the rest, David? I have to go."

Rothstein shook his head. "Go ahead, Win. I'll take care of it. And thanks."

As Gonzalez got into his BMW convertible to drive away, Guy questioned his friend. "David, what's the rest that we have to go over?"

"Nothing, Guy. You just have to realize that you are going to be a prime suspect, if you're not already. Win wants you to think about that before you go see him tomorrow morning and tell him what happened. It makes his job a lot harder if you talk without thinking."

Guy shook his head as Gonzalez sped away. "What the hell kind of name is Elwin Gonzalez?"

"I don't know, but we don't call him Win for nothing. The guy never loses. He is a sorcerer with juries." Rothstein broke his admiring stare. "Oh, and that's another thing, Guy. He charges five hundred dollars an hour, and will need a retainer tomorrow morning for sixty thousand dollars. I told him it would not be a problem."

Guy smiled. "You always were generous with my money."

XLII.

Takeover

Guy showed up late for his Board meeting that Saturday, where the others were waiting for him. His eyes bloodshot from lack of sleep, Guy apologized, huffing as he spoke. "I'm sorry I'm late. I'm sure you have all already heard the news."

Eleanor Whittlesby folded the newspaper she was reading. "Just dreadful." She squinted. "It must be particularly hard on you and your family, Guy. It said in the paper that the police spoke to you. They came to see me late last night, and I didn't think I had much to offer them. But that didn't stop them from questioning me for over an hour. What did you tell them, Guy? The paper said you had dinner with Vito last night."

David Rothstein stood up. "The police came to see me as well, as I am sure they did the rest of you." Rothstein glared at Whittlesby. "It's really not proper for any of us to talk about those conversations. We're all shocked about what happened. Let's let the police do their job, and we'll do ours. I believe the reason we came here was to discuss a hostile takeover. Now, Guy and I met with the investment bankers…"

Guy's secretary Barbara buzzed over the speaker. "Mr. Bennett, it's a Detective Kauftman. He says he forgot to give you something when you left the police station last night." Guy looked at Rothstein for approval, who nodded "yes." Guy cleared his throat. "Send him in."

As Kauftman entered the door with two other officers, Rothstein got up from his seat. "What is it, Detective Kauftman; what do you have for Mr. Bennett?"

Kauftman handed Rothstein a piece of paper. "A warrant for his arrest." He looked at Guy as the officers cuffed him. "Gaetano Bennett, you are under arrest for the murders of Vito and Lena Petrozzini. You have the right to remain silent. Anything you say can and will be used against you. You also have the right to an attorney." A smirk curled from one side of Kauftman's mouth. "If you are indigent and can't afford an attorney, one will be provided for you."

Rothstein called out. "Guy, don't say anything. I'll call Win."

Kauftman turned to Rothstein and smiled. "Arraignment will be on Monday, counselor." He looked to the rest of the Board. "Sorry for interrupting your meeting."

The cold steel of the handcuffs pinched Guy's wrists, as he was escorted from his office in the sky.

XLIII.

A Conflict of Interest

Following arraignment, Elwin Gonzalez tried to maintain his legendary poise, while Joe the bailiff processed Guy's belongings in the anteroom outside the court. His voice still jolting from Judge Masterson's decision not to let Guy free on his own recognizance pending trial, Gonzalez put his hand on Guy's cuffed forearm. "Li...listen to me, Guy. It's going to be all right. I'll make sure they keep you in a safe place. In the meantime, don't talk to anybody about the case." Gonzalez glanced at Joe the bailiff, and back to Guy. "Nobody."

Gonzalez felt a heavy paw on his shoulder, from behind him. It was the County Prosecutor, Thomas Straid. "Elwin, what a shame. I was so looking forward to a rematch with you. It's always a treat to watch you cry in front of the jury during your closing. Well, maybe next time."

Gonzalez curled his lip. "What are you talking about, Straid? Are you backing out of another one with me?"

Straid slapped a rolled set of papers he was holding in his right hand against the palm of his left. "No, no, my friend. I will be on this case from gavel to gavel." He raised his eyebrows at Guy before handing Gonzalez the papers, which were covered with a blue sheet. "Which is more than I can say for you."

Immediately recognizing the light blue paper as the standard cover for a motion, Gonzalez began leafing through it. "What kind of garbage have you thrown together this time?"

"Oh, nothing much. Just a motion to disqualify you and your firm from representing Mr. Bennett."

Gonzalez shook his head. "Do you mind telling me on what

grounds you are moving to disqualify? It's not exactly jumping off the pages of your brief. All I see is a lot of long block quotes, which is usually a sign that you have nothing to say."

Straid stood with his hands crossed in front of him. "Sure, Elwin. I'll explain." Straid delighted in addressing Gonzalez by his first name, which he knew infuriated the celebrity defense attorney. "It's very simple – the attorney-witness rule. Whether he likes it or not, The People plan to call to the stand David Rothstein from your firm, as well as the entire Northern Industries Board of Directors, to testify as to what transpired at the Board meetings leading up to the murders. We can't have one attorney from your firm testifying on behalf of The People, and another representing Mr. Bennett. It will confuse the jury." He smiled at Guy. "It might even hurt your client."

Gonzalez was caught off guard, but wielded a quick response. "First of all, Mr. Prosecutor, any communications between David Rothstein and the Northern Industries Board of Directors are protected by the attorney-client privilege, which neither you nor anyone else can waive. Second, you know that the attorney-witness rule does not apply to an attorney who is not the witness. But I do appreciate your concern for Mr. Bennett."

Straid simpered. "Elwin, I am surprised at you. You are getting rusty. I hope you are giving Mr. Bennett a discount off your hefty rate for that kind of advice. The attorney-client privilege is obviously of no relevance to board meetings of a publicly owned company, for which transcribed minutes are available." He turned to Guy. "Perhaps you should have kept your business private, sir." He continued his legal sparring with Gonzalez. "As for your second point, counselor, I am sure you are aware of the recent line of cases that supports the argument that the attorney-witness rule applies to attorneys in the same firm." Straid planted his index finger in the middle of one of the pages of his motion that Gonzalez was still holding in front of him. "It's in the long block quotes."

Gonzalez shot his head back. "You know as well as I do that those are cases in which an attorney is a witness to settlement negotiations or some tort which makes him an indispensable witness.

It's a little different in a murder trial. In case you've forgotten, the court gives great deference to a criminal defendant's choice of attorney. It's in the Constitution – you know, that piece of paper you and your colleagues prefer to use as a door mat."

Straid pursed his lips. "You may be right, Elwin. But before you throw ten of your associates into researching the issue, I've also just found out that your firm has a contract as special counsel with the Whitebridge County Improvement Authority. If I am not mistaken, you grossed $400,000 in fees last year, and the contract is up for renewal next month. That sounds like a conflict of interest to me." He shrugged. "I would have included it in this motion, but you know, with our limited resources and all. Consider it a favor to your firm, letting them bow out gracefully before they are forced to give up one or the other – the County contract or the defense of a double murderer."

Gonzalez slid the motion into his briefcase. "And may I ask why you didn't mention either of these so-called motions to the judge?"

Straid lifted his belt and pants up his husky torso. "I just got it from my assistant D.A. Had to make sure I had the grounds. Like I said, we don't have quite the resources you do. Otherwise, I would have been glad to hand deliver it to you yesterday." Straid cracked his knuckles. "Think of it this way. I've given your firm the opportunity to make it a moot point before it becomes an embarrassing public issue."

Gonzalez buttoned his jacket. "I'm overwhelmed by your generosity today, Mr. Prosecutor, but don't count on us backing out. I've already done a conflict check. The firm will stand behind me. And now I want this one, because it's clear that you guys aren't ready for a real fight." The attorney addressed his client. "I'll be back to see you in a few days to talk about this bullshit motion." He looked at Joe the bailiff, then back to Guy. "Until then, don't forget." He held his forefinger against his locked lips.

XLIV.

Cool Lemonade on a Hot Summer Day

With everyone gone, it was now only Guy and Joe the bailiff in the anteroom. Joe could see the shock and confusion in Guy's fixed eyes, the anger in his taut chin. He broke Guy's transient stare. "Time to go to the cell." Suddenly, Joe could see the daze in Guy's eyes freeze into fear. "Look, I don't know what you did. That's for the judge and jury to decide. But you can be sure that while you're on my watch, ain't no harm gonna be done to you."

Joe the bailiff took Guy to his cell. Sitting on a stool, next to the lower of two bunks, was a muscular African American man whose shaved young head bore gray roots. Joe turned the key. "Freedman, you got yourself a new roommate. His name is Guy Bennett. He's good people." Joe turned to Guy. "There are no single cells left. Don't worry."

Guy whispered to Joe while his cellmate scribbled on a pad. "What's he in for?"

Joe locked the door behind Guy, and whispered back. "Murder, just like you."

Guy took only half a step into the cell, not wanting to violate his cellmate's space. His heart raced at the sight of the Black man's brawny left arm, thick with veins, and the intensity with which he was pressing his pen to his tablet. Guy interpreted his refusal to even acknowledge Guy's presence as a warning to keep distance, lest the inmate's pen would turn on Guy. Guy walked gingerly around the stool.

Freedman popped up from the stool, nearly pinning Guy to the wall. "What?" Guy jumped excitedly.

Freedman placed his large left hand on Guy's shoulder, and pressed down on it.

Guy's trembled in the Black man's grip.

"How you doin', Mr. Guy? My name is Amos Freedman." He put his pen in his mouth so that he could grasp Guy's other shoulder. "Welcome to our digs. Ain't much, but it sure as hell beats the state big house. Bottom bunk is yours."

Still quaking, Guy looked at the pen in Freedman's mouth. "The pen. What are you gonna do with that pen?"

Freedman retreated to sit on the stool. He flicked at the pen's tip. "You ain't got nothing to worry about, Mr. Guy. This ain't nothing but rubber."

Now in full frontal view of his cellmate, Guy studied Freedman's bulging right bicep, tattooed with a clarinet surrounded by musical notes.

"Thas right." He pointed to his tattoo. "I's writing music for my clarinet. My grandmama who raised me made me play it as a kid. Told me music liberates the soul, and in the soul is where beauty lives." Freedman extended his muscle-laden arms. "My problem was working since I was thirteen, I didn't liberate nothin' but the bricks I was hauling. Made me look like this." He smiled. "These arms and hands ain't much good on that skinny little horn. But grandmama always told me to find the time to try, never give up on your soul."

Still trying to process the situation, and now finding his cellmate uncomfortably chatty, Guy pointed behind Freedman to his bunk. "That bed is mine?" he asked.

"Yeah, yeah, I get out of yo way, Mr. Guy, so that you can settle in." He pulled a box out from underneath Guy's bunk. "But first let me show you my clarinet." He opened the box like a little kid at show-and-tell. A perfectly preserved clarinet lay neatly inside. "It's all I got left."

Guy found a smile, and extended his hand in return. "Nice to meet you, Amos."

Amos shifted Guy's traditional handshake upright, into the wrapped thumb-forefinger grip customary in the African American community. He could see that it made Guy feel awkward. "Don't worry about it, you'll get it. We gonna have plenty of time together. What you in for?"

Guy rubbed the palm of his right hand. "Murder."

"Same with me, 'cept I heard yours was a double murder." Freeman closed the box with the clarinet, and slid it back under Guy's bunk. "You don't mind if I use the space for my clarinet, do you?"

"No, of course not."

Freedman climbed into his bunk and lay on his back, with his hands clasped behind his head.

Guy chose to sit on his bunk. He turned to touch the concrete wall. It was cold.

Freedman continued to talk. "My job was drivin' trucks outa Alabama, my home state. On our way to Maine after drivin' twenty-eight hours straight, me and my other driver stopped in one of your local bars to eat and play us some pool. There were no brothers in the place, but we figure we all right because we in New York, in the North you know. While we playin' pool, some fat ass white trash come lookin' for trouble. He and his boys di'n't like havin' two niggers where they drink. Told us to move on. My boy Cornelius had a temper, and di'n't care much to be pushed aroun', especially by white trash. Cornelius started beatin' that white boy silly. Lotta anger Cornelius had inside a him. His daddy was hung by the Klan in the '60s. I tried to get in the middle of it to stop Cornelius, but the rest of the white boys in the place saw it differently. When Cornelius ran and I stayed behind, I took the rap. They say Cornelius and I were both beatin' that white boy. That dead white boy and me the only ones know the troof."

Guy listened attentively. "Have you gone to trial? If you're innocent, I'm sure your attorney will be able to prove it."

Freedman laughed. "Oh yeah, I had me a trial. Judge said all those nice things about how I'm innocent until proven guilty, and the Court even gave me a public defender because I had no money. God bless America." Freedman's voice straightened to a far less playful tone. "Gave me some sorry-ass public defender who won't let me testify for myself. He sat there the whole time like the cat got his tongue. He done proven my innocence all right. Straid ran all over him like a treadmill, and kindly ol' Judge Masterson done give me life." Freedman pulled back. "But I guess Straid gone too far. Didn't give me some evidence that he should have. Appellate Court done give me a new trial." His tone lightened again. "Prosecutor-al misconduct. I'll be damned if I get that same sorry-ass public defender again. I told them they gots to get me a new one. Not some P.D. that pisses his pants every time the judge say something cross to him."

When Guy went silent, Freedman filled the void. "Don't worry none, Guy. I know your son is a public defender. It wa-n't him. I hear only good things about yo boy. They say he a real comer. The boys inside startin' to aks for him."

Guy looked up in surprise. "How do you know my son?"

Freedman laughed out loud. "You find out all kinds of shit inside. Ain't not much else to do. With a double murder case, won't be long before you start hittin' the law books."

Guy drew a breath of superiority. "No, I don't think so. I have a private lawyer."

"Who he be?"

"A gentleman named Elwin Gonzalez."

Freedman jumped down from his bunk, startling Guy. He touched Guy's shoulder with his forefinger, and pulled back as if he was burnt. "OOOO-e. You must be very important, Mr. Guy, because Gonzalez the best in town. That boy's a hero around here for the way he beat up on Straid. And the Lord know he ain't cheap. Yeah, yeah." Freedman waved the same forefinger. "But let me give you a piece of advice. Don't be coppin' an attitude in here, tryin' to impress people who you is or how much you worf." He rubbed between his fingers the light brown shirt that all of the prisoners were required to wear. "You may wear fancy suits on the outside, but we all dress the same in here. If anything, you in the back of the line on the inside." Freedman ascended to his bunk, and reassumed his position with his hands clasped behind his head. "I just tellin' you that for your own good. Besides, I hear Straid gonna get rid of Gonzalez as you attorney."

Dumbfounded, Guy did not even bother to ask Freedman how he found about Straid's intentions.

"Well, time to hit the rack," yawned Freedman.

"But it can't even be 6:00," offered Guy, as he looked down at the wrist that used to sport his watch.

"Long days and ain't much to do at night," quipped Freedman. "Don't let the bed bugs bite."

While Amos Freedman slept above him that night, Guy stared long at the single wired mattress that was his roommate's raised throne.

The next morning, Guy woke to Freedman's intermittent playings of his clarinet and rubbing of his pen on paper. He cleared his eyes, and looked at Freedman sitting on the stool next to the bunks, scribbling on a pad with one hand as he held his instrument in the other.

Freedman noticed that Guy had woken. "I'm sorry, Guy. I tried to keep it quiet, doin' more writin' than playin.' I find that early in the mornin' is the best time for it. Everythin' is quiet. No distractions, if you know what I mean."

Guy sat up, and winced as he put his bare feet on the cold cement floor. "No, no. No problem at all. I'm usually up pretty early myself, but didn't sleep much last night." Guy pointed. "What is it that you're writing?"

Freedman held the pad up for Guy to see. "My music. Like I told you last night, been workin' on it for years. Bein' inside has given me a lot more time to do it. I'm almost finished. Gonna call it 'Cool Lemonade on a Hot Summer Day.'" He puckered his lips. "There wasn't nothin' better than grandmama's ice-cold lemonade when the sweat come pouring down – brought you from wishin' you was dead to bein' grateful you was alive. Was nothin' more than a li'l drink mixed with a lotta love."

Guy shook his head in disbelief. "That's great. How did you learn how to read music?"

"What's a-matter, Guy, you ain't never known a po' black boy that know how to read music?" Feeling bad that he embarrassed Guy, Freedman continued. "Don't worry, I ain't never known one either. Grandmama taught me. She done sung in the church choir every Sunday. But like she always say, readin' is the easy part. Writin' is the struggle."

Guy smiled.

Amos grinned back. "What you laughing at, Guy?"

"Ah, nothing. I was just thinking. My father told me the same things about opera that your grandmother taught you about the clarinet. It sounds like they were both ordinary people with a whole lot of depth."

Guy wanted to continue, but felt his body calling. He asked Freedman, "Hey Amos, I have to go the bathroom. Do I call the guard?"

Freedman laughed. "Why, you want him to watch?" He turned and pointed to the small steel toilet in the corner. "Go right ahead. I won't look."

Guy walked sheepishly to the toilet, and dropped his pants.

Freedman kept his back to Guy, and continued writing. "C'mon, Guy. Do whatever it is nature need you to do. I done smelled it all."

As Guy crouched on the small toilet, Freedman started playing his clarinet. Guy cringed before looking ahead with eyes glazed, relieving himself to the serenade of Freedman's choppy music.

XLV.

Speaking Through Glass

Lockdown

That afternoon, a prison guard came to Guy's cell with welcome news. "Bennett, your wife is here to see you. She's in the visitors' room." The guard unlocked the door, and freed Guy for his first visit. "Down the hall and to the right."

With the guard trailing him, Guy stumbled his way down the corridor, as other inmates jeered him. One pressed his face between the bars. "Hey rich boy, seein' that you won't be usin' your money no mo', how about sharin' some wif us? We yo' new family. You be my sugar daddy, I be yo' boy."

Another shouted "Look who it is, Guy the Sly. Can't be too smart if you inside with us."

The air in Guy's head thinned. He became disoriented, and turned left down the hall instead of right. The guard grabbed him from behind. "Bennett, where are you going? The visitors' room is the other way. Turn around."

Guy stumbled in the right direction. He saw an inmate doing laundry in one room, and a guard berating another inmate in the next. When Guy stopped to watch the verbal assault, he felt a nightstick in his back. "Move on, Bennett, or you'll be next."

Guy kept stepping until he found his wife sitting, waiting with others in the visitors' room, on the other side of the thick glass divide. The sight of her tired eyes and drawn face made him speechless. Guy hurried toward Marie and threw his hand up against the glass as if it were not there. When Marie put her hand on the other side of the glass to meet his, a tear fell from her eyes. Her body was still, wanting the life that had been taken.

Marie sat in her chair, and Guy in his. They both picked up their phones. Marie tried to speak before her tears drowned her voice. "Guy, when is this going to end? Tell me it's not happening."

Guy held his phone with both hands, safeguarding the sound of his wife's voice. "I'm going to be fine. I have the best lawyer money can buy. The prosecutor is terrified of Elwin Gonzalez."

Marie wiped her tears with a handkerchief. "Everybody says he is the best."

Guy's spirits started rising. He removed one of his hands from the phone. "A lot of people have called you, huh?"

Marie paused and looked down. "The phones have been quiet."

Guy swallowed hard.

Marie looked up. "I just think people are giving us our space." She picked up her pace. "Anyway, I've read about Gonzalez in all of the newspaper stories. They said that winning your case will be the jewel in his crown." Marie closed her eyes to regain some composure. "The press has already convicted you, Guy. They say that your case is a long-shot. Every time I turn on the television, someone different is giving their opinion why you did it. Attorneys, psychologists, jury consultants. They don't even know you! How could they say that?"

"It's just talk."

"Straid was on last night saying the death penalty should be brought back for people like you." Marie slammed her small fist on the table top. "That bastard, I hate him. I wish Albert had never beaten him." She wiped a tear from her eye. "I wish Albert had never run."

The pain in Marie's voice rattled Guy's bones. So did the increasingly violent sounds coming from the guard and inmate down the hall. Guy steered his thoughts elsewhere. "Don't be silly, Marie. Albert's running for Senate was the best thing he ever did."

"I don't know. I am not so sure."

Guy pushed forward in the conversation. "How is Albert? Have you spoken to him?"

Marie's tears started pulling her breath, causing her to huff. She fought through it. "He flew in last night. He feels frustrated. He says that he has tried to contact everyone – the Governor, the State Attorney General. They won't take his calls. I think he feels responsible for the way Straid is rushing to judgment."

"That's silly. Straid's problem is that he doesn't like us because we have money and influence, two things he'll never have. When Gonzalez is done with him, he'll wish he never became a lawyer. You should have seen the way Win handled Straid yesterday when Strai...."

Guy was halted by the sound of a club pounding against the back of the inmate in the room down the hall. "How's Lisa Marie? What does she say?"

"Her and VJ have been busy with the funeral and taking care of the estate."

Guy knew that his wife was hiding something. "She doesn't believe me, does she? My daughter thinks I murdered her in-laws!"

It was now Marie who played consoler. "It's too early, Guy. They're not thinking clearly yet. She feels her own guilt about setting up the dinner." Marie tried to change the subject. "Edward also came over last night. He said you are in good hands with Gonzalez."

Guy raised his eyebrows, and spoke in a subdued tone. "How's he doing?"

"He's confused – about this and everything. He doesn't know what to think. He says Nancy is getting bigger." Marie wiped her tears with a handkerchief and smiled briefly. "She's due in only a few months, you know. I think he wants to see you, but you have to ask him to come, Guy. You said it yourself that night at the house..."

With the sound of a chair breaking angrily over an inmate's head down the hall, the prison's obedient din was ruptured by a fight between jailer and jailed. Several guards appeared on both sides of the glass-divided visitors' room. One of the guards grabbed Guy, the other Marie. Sirens sounded and the intercom boomed. "Lockdown. All prisoners return to your cells immediately. Lockdown. All prisoners return to your cells immediately. All visitors must be evacuated." When Guy reached to touch the thick glass that framed Marie's image, the guard holding him pulled away. "This is a lockdown, damnit. He'll take care of your wife. Let's go."

Guy grasped, only to gain himself a handful of nothing.

That evening back in the cell, Freedman began giving Guy his daily prison tutorial. He spoke from his top bunk, where he was lying on his back with his hands folded, while Guy paced the floor. "So what you think of yo' first lockdown, Mr. Guy?"

Guy kept pacing. "I don't even know what the hell a lockdown is. All I know is that I didn't get to see my wife." When Freedman didn't respond, Guy looked up at him. "All right, Amos, I don't want to interrupt your fun. Tell me, what the hell is a lockdown?"

"If you don't want to know, fine by me."

"Tell me, Amos."

Freedman remained lying on his back, with his hands folded. "Lockdown be when there some kind of threat to prison security, like a breakout or fight. Somethin' like dat. They lock the whole damn place down so that nobody can move or get involved. Nothin' scares these boys more than losin' order. It's like there's a fire in the house. Just about the only time you see fear in their eyes. Next time we in a lockdown, look in their eyes. Make you feel good, like you got some kind a power."

Guy held out his hands. "So who caused it?"

Freedman locked his hands behind his head on his pillow. "Young Earl Strickland. He was in the room down the hall from where you and your wife was talkin'. He was washing the floors. He always talkin' about fightin' back against the guards, young Earl."

Guy smirked. "That's what I heard when I was talking to Marie. So he had it coming to him?"

Freedman pulled out one of his hands from behind his head to raise his forefinger. "Now, I didn't say that. When Earl done finish cleaning that floor, the guard called in another guard to come walk all over it with his dirty boots and make Earl clean it again. I guess Earl wasn't much in the mood to clean the same floor twice. He started beatin' the guard with the mop."

Guy stopped pacing, and looked at the wall above where Freedman was lying. An ant was trying to squeeze his way through a small crack in the concrete, his tiny legs flailing in the air.

Freedman continued. "I keep tellin' that boy not to waste his energy on the inside. These guards be judge, prosecutor, and jury, and they know it. Save your energy for the outside, I say to Earl, where the real judge and jury be at. Because yo' goin' to need it wif them."

Guy watched the ant on the wall, continuing to struggle against the crack, trying to wiggle through.

"The justice and yo' so-called jury of peers, they ain't there to help you. They there to punish you. You just got to survive on the inside, and hope you get lucky when yo' day of reckonin' come."

The ant pulled itself out of the crack, and began scurrying along the wall again.

XLVI

The Ghost of Christmas Past

The next morning began with the sound of the iron-barred cell door sliding open. A prison guard barked at Guy. "Bennett, your lawyers are here. They're in the conference room next to the visitors' room. This time, try not to get lost."

Guy threw on his clothing as he walked anxiously to the conference room, which was a table surrounded by wooden chairs. Elwin Gonzalez and David Rothstein sat together on one side of the small table, with their leather briefcases at their side snapped shut.

Guy's unshaven face perked up. "Finally, my team is here. How do we look on Straid's motion to get rid of you, Win? Do you have something for me to look at?" When neither of the lawyers was able to make direct eye contact with him, Guy tried to draw out David Rothstein. "Hey, David, I'm not getting charged for your time too, am I?" He chuckled. "Straid said you're testifying against me, and I'm sure as hell not paying for his witnesses."

Rothstein looked up sheepishly and whispered, "Guy, sit down. We need to speak to you."

Guy pulled the remaining wooden seat beneath him, and leaned to one side only to find that the chair's right arm was missing. He snapped himself back, and rubbed the chair at the point at which the arm had been broken off. "I guess we can't call the front desk to complain about the furniture."

David Rothstein moved his briefcase nervously from one side of his chair to the other. "Guy, this is serious."

Guy sat back in his one-armed chair. "Oh really, David? And I thought I was in here for a traffic ticket. I've just been having the best damn time of my life. Don't tell me I have to leave so soon."

Guy grabbed the tabletop by its side and squeezed it, sending blood rushing through his veins to his head. "Fellas, what the hell is going on? I feel like I'm at a goddamn funeral! Talk to me!"

Gonzalez interceded for his partner. "Guy, I can't represent you."

Guy kept his focus on Rothstein while addressing Gonzalez. "Why? You said it yourself. The motion to disqualify you is bullshit."

Gonzalez removed a sleek silver pen from his shirt pocket and started stroking it with his forefinger, staring at it as he spoke. "The motion is bullshit, Guy. But the firm had a long meeting last night about the case. Our partners don't want to make trouble with the Prosecutor's Office."

Guy pounded his fist against the table. "Why don't you say what you really mean? You don't want to lose those fat White-bridge County contracts that Straid threatened to take away." Guy stood up, and toppled his chair. It fell to the side with the missing arm. "What about me? My legal fees aren't high enough?" He stood over Rothstein. "Did you remind your partners how much I paid you for taking my company public? Or am I the goddamn ghost of Christmas past?"

As Rothstein continued to look down, Gonzalez remained seated and spoke with his silver pen in hand. "Guy, we tried. But Straid is making the heat unbearable. There is a leak about the case on almost a daily basis. Yesterday, the press reported the results of blood samples taken from the plastic bag and shovel they found in the trunk of your car. They match the Petrozzinis' blood." Gonzalez reached into his briefcase, pulled out a newspaper, and gave it to Guy.

Guy started reading, then closed his eyes. "Jesus."

Gonzalez turned his head inquisitively. "What?"

Guy tossed the newspaper on the table. "The story. It's written by Gabrielle DeFiore. I guess she's going to start following the trial. She never really trusted me and Albert during the campaign. That General Fiske commercial really bothered her."

Gonzalez redirected Guy. "Look, I don't know anything about any political campaign and don't care whether this Gabrielle DeFiore does or doesn't trust you. What I am telling you is that that motherfucker Straid knows he can't hold press conferences about this shit, so he has someone leak the information for him – anonymously of course. He will stop at nothing." Gonzalez squeezed his temples with his left hand.

Guy shot back. "You're cowards. You're afraid of Straid. Your goddamn county contracts and all the silver pens and marble floors they buy are more important than my life!"

Gonzalez dropped his silver pen, and stood up behind the table that separated him and Rothstein from Guy. "Damnit, Guy, I want to beat the sonofabitch as much as you. I want to help you. But what can I do? They won't let me. I don't blame you for being mad." Gonzalez looked at Rothstein. "I can convince a jury, but I can't convince our partners."

It was now Rothstein's turn to defend Gonzalez. "Win damn near resigned last night, Guy, and he barely knows you. There's really nothing we can do. The firm is bigger than us." Rothstein could sense Guy cooling. "Now let's sit down and sort everything out. We're not running away on you."

Guy and Gonzalez sat back in their seats. His voice still excited, Guy spoke first. "All right, which of your big shot friends do we get to replace you?"

Rothstein looked at Gonzalez, who in turn interrupted Guy. "I don't think you should go with any big names. Straid will play the same tricks with them if he's afraid of losing, and you'll be worse off. I think you should get someone young and unknown, but capable. Someone that'll ease Straid into leaving his guard down. Someone who can make it as a much a trial between him and Straid as between you and The People. To win, you almost have to be a sideshow. The evidence that is stacking up against you is overwhelming."

Guy tapped the side of the table with his forefingers, and spoke slowly yet methodically. "What unknown boy-wonder do you have in mind?"

Gonzalez sat back, cueing Rothstein to come forward. Rothstein rubbed his palms against one another. "Your son, Edward."

"You're kidding, right?" Guy buckled his eyebrows. "Edward just started doing trials. He wouldn't know the first thing about a murder case." Guy pleaded. "Fellas, I know my son's limitations. I'm not going to test them when my life is on the line."

Gonzalez picked up his pen, and held it tightly. "Guy, I've seen your son in action. He's a little nervous yet, but he knows what the hell he's doing. That'll be a great contrast to Straid's bravado. Plus the fact that he'll be defending his father – the jury will love him." Gonzalez put his free hand over Guy's. "I'll stay involved behind the scenes. If you hire another big name with a big ego, he won't listen to me. I'll be out of the case completely." He tapped Guy's hand. "Trust me, Guy. David and I have been up all night talking about it. This is your best chance."

Guy looked at Gonzalez's hand on top of his, then to Gonzalez's other hand holding the silver pen. He looked back and forth again, before staring forward. "I had a huge argument with Edward before I got arrested. I haven't spoken to him since. I don't even know if he'll do it."

Rothstein pulled off his glasses. "He has to, Guy. He's family."

Guy smiled, and spoke gently. "That's what I thought about you, David."

Rothstein started stuttering. "Come...well. Guy, c'mon...you... that's different."

Guy held up his hand. "David, you don't need to explain. I understand." He drew a deep breath. "If you guys are saying Edward's the man, I'll have Marie talk to him. I don't think he has ever said no to her."

Gonzalez handed Guy his business card. "Give her my card to give to him. I'll talk to him."

Guy got up, and stood behind his seat. "Well, gentlemen, if that's all you have for me, I think I could use some time alone."

Rothstein grew nervous again. "Guy, there is one more thing."

In response, Guy's body went limp, as if he had just been beaten.

Rothstein continued. "The Board of the company voted that in light of the current situation, they are not going to resist Bruno Petrozzini's takeover bid."

"What does that mean, David?"

Rothstein put his glasses back on. "It means that they are going to recommend to the shareholders that they take the money that

Bruno is offering for their shares. I tried to convince them otherwise, Guy. I really did."

Guy cut through with an eerie monotone. "Your firm is bigger than you, and now my company is bigger than me. Who would have thought?" Guy shook his head and looked to the cement floor. "Am I to assume that for the company's sake, your firm will be handling the transaction?"

"I have told them I won't be involved, and refuse to accept a penny for it. It may be a while before it happens, Guy. But I don't think it will pay for you to try to fight it on your own. You have more important things to deal with."

Guy continued to shake his head in disbelief. "Maybe I should have Edward try his hand at corporate acquisitions." He looked at Gonzalez. "Who knows, maybe he can catch Bruno with his guard down, the same way he is going to with Straid." Guy extended his hand to Gonzalez to end the conference. "Well, gentlemen, I used to think I knew everything. I now realize that I knew very little other than what I wanted to see." He paused. "But believe me, I understand."

Guy shook his former lawyers' hands, pushed his seat beneath the table, and exited the conference room alone.

XLVII.

❧❧❧

Taking a Plea

Days later, Edward was finishing his work at the Whitebridge County Public Defender's Office when his supervisor, Pilar Merced, planted herself in front of his desk. Merced was tall and thin, her hair brown, and her plain but pleasant face conspicuously fair and void of cosmetics. A great trial attorney in her own right, she had rejected the corporate firms, with their lavish corridors and large salaries, to remain in the dusty and underfunded offices of the Public Defender. Edward considered her a mentor, and watched closely her every move in the hope of emulation. With her long fingers, she pushed down gently on the folder that Edward was reading. "What do you have, Bennett? Anything interesting?"

Edward straightened. "Nah. Just a plea agreement from the Prosecutor's Office."

Merced rubbed her chin, and looked up, feigning curiosity. "Which young P.D. was it that once told me that plea agreements are a defense attorney's concession speech to the Prosecutor's Office?" She looked down at Edward, who was blushing, then looked up again still rubbing her chin. "I know, it's the same guy who was bugging me every week to sit second chair with me at trial." She looked down again, and shook her forefinger at Edward. "That's it. That's the guy. Do you know who I'm talking about? Because I forget. I haven't seen him in a while."

Edward responded defensively. "C'mon, Pilar. You've told me yourself. When a good deal comes, take it. Never put your own interests in front of your client's."

Merced dropped her arms. Her unpainted short fingernails grazed his desk. "Yes, I said that. But Edward, I just checked your docket. You've pled out your last twenty cases. I wonder if you are actually putting your own interests in front of your client's.

Prosecutors are licking their chops to get paired up with you. I know it's getting bad when Judge Masterson starts telling me what a fine job you're doing – how you're finally starting to settle down."

Edward sat silently, staring at the plea agreement.

Merced pulled up a chair. "It's your father, isn't it? I know the looks and sounds, Edward. The signs of a defense attorney who doesn't believe anymore, who has lost his will to fight. Believing in what we do is all we have in this business. Because we sure as hell aren't getting anything in our paycheck."

Mentor and student smiled.

Merced continued. "Defending is not a nine-to-five job. You have to live and breathe it every day of your life, here and outside – when a little kid is being picked on, when a crippled woman stumbles, or when an old man is lost." Merced paused. She looked straight into Edward's eyes without blinking. "Or when a father is accused of murder, and a District Attorney wants to make sure he never sits at the table with his family again."

Edward took a deep breath. "It's just so complicated."

"It's no different than any other case. We say it everyday. Innocent until proven guilty." Merced got up from her seat. "It's not some fiction. It's real. It's the only rope most defendants have to pull themselves out of the snake pit we call justice, and a thin one at that." She grabbed his desk with her long hands and leaned forward. "You've argued it for strangers. Don't you think you owe at least as much to your dad, the same benefit of the doubt?"

"I'm sure that Win Gonzalez will take care of that."

Merced grabbed the folder that held the plea agreement Edward was reviewing when she first came to his desk.

Edward reached for the folder. "What are you doing?"

"You're not signing anything until you start believing again. You're due for a vacation, and I'm ordering you to take one immediately." She looked down at the folder. "Jamaal Watkins. Possession with intent to distribute. This is my case now."

As Merced walked away, Edward called out. "Thanks, Pilar."

Merced turned around. "For what? I'm going to have fun defending Mr. Watkins." She smiled. "If you hurry back, I might even let you sit second chair during the trial."

XLVIII

To Save the Lifesaver

As Edward walked through the front entrance of his apartment building that night, the tabletop lamp that lit the small foyer was flickering. He pulled open the table's drawer, and rummaged for a new light bulb.

With the hefty endowment Edward's father had already made to him and his siblings through irrevocable trusts, Edward had the means to own ten such apartment buildings, stocked with smartly dressed security guards who would have already changed the light bulb for him, and had his mail and dry cleaning waiting. But ever since his visit to his great-uncle Father Francesco in Italy, Edward had vowed not to use any of Guy's money to subsidize his public pursuits; instead, he would live as best he could on a Public Defender's salary, and save his inheritance as a gift for his children. So it was that he came to live in a tiny rent-controlled apartment in an undesirable corner of Whitebridge County.

Edward found a new light bulb to replace the old. The bulb's glow was dimmed by the dirt that had accumulated on the bell lampshade.

With the building's elevator out of order, Edward climbed the stairs to his second story abode, still thinking about what Pilar Merced had told him. Maybe his father did deserve the benefit of the doubt in his trial, but the way he threw Edward out of his house cut even deeper. Insofar as Guy had disowned Edward in a time of need, Merced was asking Edward to do for his father what his father had refused to do for him – stand firm as one. A tall order indeed for a young man who himself was about to become a father.

As Edward neared his studio, he could hear two voices inside, one that was distinctly Nancy's, the other sounding like his mother's.

He opened the door, and found his mother and the pregnant Nancy sitting on the sofa together. Marie was displaying a knit blanket to Nancy, and Nancy was smiling back with eyes wide in appreciation. When the door opened, they both shifted their smiles to Edward.

Nancy pushed her enlarged body off the sofa, and presented the small blanket to Edward. "Look at what your mother made for the baby. Isn't it beautiful?"

Marie responded to her son's silence. "I have a lot of spare time on my hands these days."

The despair in his mother's voice sent a chill through Edward's body. He held the blanket in full view, and gasped. "It is beautiful." Edward sat by his mother's side, hugged her with the blanket in hand, and kissed her on the cheek. "Thanks, Mom. It will keep the baby nice and warm."

Nancy stood in front of them with her hands on her hips. "Your mother needs your help, Edward."

Edward hurried. "What is it, Mom? Anything."

Marie looked down at her crossed legs. "Elwin Gonzalez can't be your father's attorney anymore. Some kind of legal conflict. I don't really understand it."

Edward shook his head as he processed the news. "I had a feeling his firm would back out. Greed. Okay. Do you want me to get you a list of possible replacements? I'll talk to Pilar Merced. She probably knows ten guys who would jump at this case with all the publicity it's getting."

Marie looked up and drew a deep breath. "Your father wants you to represent him."

Edward shot up from the sofa, still clutching the blanket his mother had knit for his baby. "He wants me to represent him? After what happened at the house? He told me never to come back until I'm asked to."

Marie followed. "He's asking."

Edward paced back and forth in the limited space of his studio, squeezing the blanket in one hand, disheveling his hair with the other. "I don't know, Mom."

Marie folded her hands on her crossed legs. "Do you remember when you used to go ice skating with your father as a little boy?"

Edward grinned. "On Willow Pond."

"Every time you fell, your father was right there to pick you up."

Edward pursed his lips.

"You called him your 'lifesaver.'"

Edward dropped his head.

Marie stood up, and placed a finger beneath her son's chin, to raise his head. "Your 'lifesaver' needs you."

Edward whispered, his throat dry. "What about Lisa Marie and VJ? What will they think?"

Marie spoke with a mother's confidence, as she dusted her skirt. "You don't worry about that. That's my problem. I'll deal with your sister."

Edward resumed his pacing, rubbing the blanket against his face. "Dad's going to go from Elwin Gonzalez to me?"

Marie chased her son with her large expressive eyes. "It was Gonzalez's idea. He thinks you are your father's best chance." Marie knew that her words were taking hold of Edward, but also knew she couldn't push her son too hard. It had to be Edward's decision. She handed him Gonzalez's business card. "At least go talk to Gonzalez about it. That's all I ask."

Edward stopped pacing. He bit his lower lip, and looked at Nancy, who was still standing, rubbing her enlarged stomach with both hands. She spoke softly. "He is your father."

Edward took the card from his mother, and looked at it. "Elwin Gonzalez is recommending me. He must be good if he convinced Dad that I should be his attorney."

Marie enjoyed a momentary elation. "So you'll do it?"

"Mom, I'll talk to Gonzalez. But does he know that I've never done a murder case?"

Marie got up from the sofa. "He knows." She kissed her son. "He also knows what I already knew – that you are the best attorney out there." Marie walked toward the door. "Well, I have to go now. Have to get to the supermarket before it closes."

Edward trailed her. "Why don't you stay for dinner, Mom?"

"My dear son, you should know by now that when we eat together, it's in my kitchen." She stopped and looked up at the low ceiling that was dripping water. "Edward, why don't use some of your trust money and buy you and your family a nice apartment?"

Edward opened the door. "Isn't that supermarket about to close, Mom?"

Marie kissed her son again, holding his face between her hands. "My son, the saint."

"I'll call Gonzalez first thing in the morning."

Marie pulled her keys from her purse. "Why don't you try now? I bet Gonzalez works late." She waved to Nancy. "Goodbye, Nancy. Take care of the little one."

Edward closed the door behind his mother, and looked at Elwin Gonzalez's business card. He stared at Nancy as he pressed his brow, and Nancy looked back, massaging their child in wait. Without a word between them, they knew what each other was thinking. Edward went to the phone and dialed Gonzalez's number. Edward's mother was right. Gonzalez was not only still in the office; he picked up his own phone.

"Hello, Mr. Gonzalez. This is Edward Bennett; my mother asked me to call you about my father..."

Edward stopped speaking to listen to the fast voice that cut him off. He resumed quickly. "Sure. Ten o'clock tomorrow morning is fine." Edward hung up the phone slowly.

He did not utter another word that night.

Nancy was careful not to interrupt his silence.

XLIX.

❧⟨✿⟩❧

Transferring the File

Edward's subway ride to Elwin Gonzalez's office the next morning was a menagerie of images: two women dressed stylishly discussing their shopping plans, shifting their mascara-brushed eyes nervously to monitor the unkempt man standing in front of them clinging to a pole, ranting out loud as he appeared to be falling asleep; a Chinese woman struggling to keep her children and bags of produce from getting away from her; an African American boy bobbing his head to the booming march of music through his headphones.

As Edward got off the train and exited the station with the horde, he watched a man in his thirties, in a European cut suit, bark out orders from his pocket-sized cellular phone. Edward's study of the young executive was broken when he almost tripped over an older man with no legs, leaning against the wall begging for money. He reached deep into his pocket for a single dollar, and dropped it into the cardboard box top that the severed man was holding.

Once Edward entered the building where Gonzalez worked and boarded the elevator to his office, the picture became more uniform, less fragmented – men and women alike dressed in dark striped suits, holding their briefcases, their eyes glued to the flashing number of the floor that they were approaching. The only wrinkle was a mentally impaired looking man in the corner, standing behind a handcart loaded with boxes.

Edward got off at the thirtieth floor, and walked the marble floors to the firm's large mahogany reception desk. As he waited for the gray-haired female receptionist to finish answering the phone, he wandered to the wall to look at an oil painting of a man in a three-piece suit, sitting in a high-backed leather chair, with his spectacles and a law book laid atop a table beside him. The small golden plaque screwed firmly to the bottom of the frame read "P. Randall DeWitt, Governor of New York, Republican Presidential Candidate, Founder of DeWitt & Case." Edward felt a tickle inside of him as he thought about the prospect of a future engraver someday etching "President of the United States" below an oil of his brother Albert, a distinction that evaded ol' P. Randall and his Pilgrim lineage.

The slow English accent of the receptionist called from behind. "May I help you, sir?"

Edward turned quickly. "Ah-h-h. Edward Bennett to see Elwin Gonzalez."

The stately receptionist looked to the tall grandfather clock in the corner that read 10:15 a.m. She paused long enough to make Edward realize he was fifteen minutes late. She turned back slowly and before speaking, checked out Edward from unsewn pant cuff to unpressed cotton shirt. "Oh yes, Mr. Bennett. Mr. Gonzalez has been waiting for you." She smiled politely. "Would you like any tea or coffee?"

Edward lifted his knee to pull up his socks as he remained standing. "No thanks."

The receptionist raised her eyebrows in disbelief and picked up the phone. "I'll tell him you're here."

Edward was greeted at the doorway by an average height woman in her early thirties, dressed in a glowing white jacket and skirt that contrasted well with her light brown skin. Her hazel green eyes and strong curves whispered mischief, while her trained posture articulated self-help and advancement. A trace of a Spanish accent was apparent, despite the woman's best efforts to suppress it. "Mr. Bennett. Yolanda Thomas. I work wit' Win Gonzalez."

The woman's tamed bustling beauty and extraordinary eyes threw Edward. "Hel…Hi. Yes, I'm Edward Bennett. Please…I mean, I'm pleased to meet you."

Yolanda Thomas smiled. "Win is-s ready to see you."

As they started down the barren hallway, Edward apologized for his tardiness. "I'm sorry I'm late. I'm terrible with time."

Yolanda smiled reassuringly. "Don't worry. Win wasn't ready at ten anyway."

Edward squinted as he tried to keep up with Yolanda. "Really? The woman up front made it sound as though Mr. Gonzalez was waiting."

Yolanda pressed her sumptuous lips together, and waved her hand toward the reception area with disgust. "Who? Beatrice? Don't pay attention to her. She has nothin' better to do." With the same hand, Yolanda pointed a painted fingernail at Edward to scold him. "And it's not Mr. Gonzalez. It's Win. Tha's his nickname. Because he always wins."

The pair made a sharp right down another hallway, this one lined with small holes on either side, from which young lawyers darted wrapped in their dark jackets, their faces mute and tired. Edward whispered. "Does everyone here always wear a jacket?"

Continuing down the hallway, Yolanda peered over her shoulders. Under the cover of ringing phones, she responded. "It's a firm tradition. Win's a little different." She spilled a proud smile, and her large green eyes seemed to grow even wider. "If he doesn't have a court appearance or meeting, he'll wear a short-sleeve shirt." She giggled. "Sometime', he'll even wear the kind wit' the crazy designs on them." She finished. "Win doesn't care much for the older par'ners' traditions."

Edward admired Yolanda's long smooth forehead, made prominent by her tightly pulled back hair. "And what do the old partners say?"

Yolanda snapped. "What can they say? Win brings in too much money." She lightened her tone. "They need each other. He need' someone to take care of his telephones, typing, and Ivy League research, and they need his billings. They learn to live together."

Yolanda and Edward reached the end of the hall, where Gonzalez was standing behind his crescent-shaped desk talking on the telephone, high above the backdrop of New York's East River and its row of confident bridges. When he noticed Yolanda and Edward, he waved them in.

While Gonzalez continued on the phone, Yolanda gave Edward the tour of the defense attorney's decorated walls. She pointed to a blown-up framed newspaper article featuring a picture of a young

Gonzalez and a former New York City mayor raising their hands in victory. "Thas after Win get the Mayor off on bribery. The government even had tapes of conversation – where they talked about the payoff."

Edward spoke as he read the article. "How did Win get him off?"

Yolanda replied matter-of-factly. "He get the jury to think less about the tapes, and more about how the government disguise a detective as a janitor to plant the bug."

"Really." Edward divided his attention between Yolanda and Gonzalez, who was negotiating with a client over the phone.

Looking out his window over the East River and not realizing that Edward was listening, Gonzalez sounded impatient with the faceless client. "Gordon, I understand. Of course I'm your lawyer. The deal is, send me the thirty-five-thousand-dollar retainer, and then I make the calls. The prosecutor isn't going to do anything between now and the time I receive the check. C'mon, thirty-five thousand dollars is about two hours of work for you."

Yolanda directed Edward to the next frame on the wall. "This one was a black kid named Chris Wilkes. He was-s in a gang, and they was..." Yolanda corrected herself by speaking more slowly. "They were accused of shooting a white kid because he was dating one of their girls." Yolanda paused for dramatic effect. "It was Wilkes' gun."

Edward asked the question. "How did Win do it?"

Yolanda looked back at Gonzalez admiringly. "He convinced the jury that another gang member, Tracy Vaughn, took the gun from Wilkes and did the killing. Win told them if they wanted to punish Wilkes for what he did wrong, they should convict him of illegal possession of a handgun." Yolanda crossed her arms. "That's what they did. Because he was-s a firs' offender, Wilkes never served a day in jail."

As Gonzalez was closing out his phone call, Edward whispered. "How could the kid afford to pay for Win?"

"He couldn't. Win got the firm to do it pro-bono. Win says the reason for criminal defense attorneys is for the Chris Wilkes of the world. Win got him out of the gang and into a county college.

Two more years, and Chris Wilkes will be a college graduate. All because of Win."

Gonzalez hung up the phone, and Yolanda introduced Edward. "Win, this is Edward Bennett, your ten o'clock."

Gonzalez extended his hand over his desk. "Of course, thanks for coming." Gonzalez pointed to one of the sleek black leather seats in front of his desk. "Please, sit." He looked at Yolanda. "Yo, did you ask Mr. Bennett if he wanted coffee?"

Edward held up his hand to cover for his new friend Yolanda. "No, thanks." He smiled at Yolanda. "The kind woman up front already took care of it."

Gonzalez looked back at Yolanda. "Thank you, Yo." As Yolanda left the room and both men admired her, Gonzalez called out again. "Hey, Yo. When are we going to go over that Wilshire Academy application for that son of yours?"

Yolanda turned and meekly replied, "Next week?"

Gonzalez reprimanded her. "The deadline is in a month and I'm having dinner with the headmaster in a week. I want to be able to talk to him about Victor."

Yolanda fluttered her lashes over her green eyes and smiled. "Yes, sir."

Gonzalez continued the smile with Edward after Yolanda left. "Yo is a great girl. Still a little rough around the edges. Brought herself up from a broken family and a dirt bag that left her alone with her son, Victor. I'm trying to get him into my son's prep school on a scholarship. He's a great football player – he's already six-four and runs like a gazelle. The school can really make a difference for him."

Edward looked over Gonzalez's shoulder out his scenic window. "That's great."

Gonzalez swiveled in his seat, and admired the East River along with Edward. "Fantastic, isn't it? Best view in the office. I made it a condition of my coming to the firm."

Edward spoke wistfully. "With a clear shot of the Brooklyn Bridge. Dad's company restored it for its hundredth birthday."

Gonzalez rubbed his chin, and inhaled through his teeth. "Yeah, I should have done like your dad and gone into business. More money when the sky is the limit. There are only so many hours a lawyer can bill in a day."

Edward smiled politely but pointedly. "I wouldn't know. I work on a salary."

A tinge of red spread across Gonzalez's face. "Well anyway, now we need to help your father."

Edward continued his offensive. "From what my mother told me, it sounds like 'we' is a lot of people, and you're not one of them."

Gonzalez leaned forward. "Listen, Edward. I'd love to represent your father, but I can't." He looked out his door into the hallway with disdain. "Firm bullshit, you know."

Edward challenged the legal giant again. "No, explain it to me. I'm a little confused, because when we get a case at the Public Defender's Office, we see it through to the end. There are no conflicts." Edward pulled back. "I guess private firms are different."

Without touching it, Gonzalez stared down at his silver pen in the middle of his desk. He spoke somberly. "I'll be the first to tell you not to race to join a firm. I'd switch places with you in a minute." Gonzalez looked up and addressed Edward without blinking. "But you see, my dad wasn't really interested in making money to buy me the choices you have had. I have to work so that my son has those choices." He cut himself off, and stepped it up. "Whether you like me or my firm or not, your dad is about to get a prison cell for his lifetime and then another one, and you are the only person who can stop it."

A brief silence mediated peace between the marvelous and the missionary.

Edward leaned back in his black leather chair. "Mr. Gonzalez, I have never done a murder case."

Gonzalez smiled. "Please, call me Win." Gonzalez dropped the silver pen he had begun playing with, and came around his desk to sit next to Edward. "No one ever does a murder case before they do their first."

"I would think they at least second-chair one before taking the lead."

Gonzalez shifted his weight in his seat. "You will be second chair." He tempered his statement. "Well, kind of. I will be there all the way for you. I'll help you prepare behind the scenes, sit in on trial some days, and you'll get me daily transcripts for the others." Gonzalez put his hand on Edward's shoulder and looked the young lawyer in the eye. "But, you're right. Whatever we prepare, you are going to have to sell it to the jury. The tricky part is that there are some murder cases where you go for it all, and others where you hedge your bet by admitting that your client did the deed and you try to get him convicted of a lesser offense like manslaughter."

"You mean like simple possession of marijuana instead of possession with the intent to distribute."

"Sort of," Win said slowly. "My personal feeling is that in your dad's case, he can't afford to admit anything, because the jury will automatically assume that he killed for greed and they'll give him life in prison. Besides, with your dad's age, even a lenient sentence will be a death certificate. So you're going to have to be ready to go for it. All or nothing. He either goes home with your mother or he dies in prison. That's the way the system works."

Edward slumped in his seat, beneath the weight of Gonzalez's words. He squinted and struggled to speak. "Do you think my father killed the Petrozzinis?"

Gonzalez craned his neck away and spoke to the East River outside his window, whose current crept slowly to the ocean. "It's not my job to say. " He looked back at Edward. "But I think your father has a strong defense that he deserves to have presented – that he deserves to have presented by you. What do you say, Edward?"

Edward's voice stumbled. "What can I say?"

Gonzalez retreated behind his desk, to a stack of papers and photos. "That you'll start by taking a look at the discovery provided by The People. The witness statements, the reports, the photos. There's something weird, some inconsistencies that I can't put my finger on yet." He unloaded the file on Edward's lap and followed with a business card. "And here's the name of the forensic pathologist you need to call to take a look at the crime scene photos and The People's autopsy report. His name is S. Jackson Cudder. He is in a small town in Alabama called Tuscumbia. It's near the

Mississippi border. He's the best there is. Tell him Win Gonzalez referred you, send him what he wants, and go down to see him. He's the best."

Edward took the card from Gonzalez. "Why are you doing this?"

Gonzalez smiled. "After you try the case, you'll know why." He looked down at his watch. "I'm sorry I've got to run. But I've got another appointment coming up."

Edward struggled to lift and manage the file Gonzalez had left on his lap. "Sure. And thanks."

L.

Mother Daughter Wife

Back at the Bennett home later that week, Lisa Marie sat pregnant at the kitchen table while her mother prepared her toast. The house was quiet and cold, the frenzied energy that once heated it sucked from its cavernous lungs. Rain was driving down on the Bennett backyard making the ungroomed grass muddy. Conversation between the two was not coming easily. Lisa Marie shivered and rubbed her arms. "Mom, can you turn on the heat?"

Marie approached the table with a plate of buttered toast. "It's already on. Here, eat. You need your strength." She put the plate in front of her daughter and sat. "So are you and VJ going to find out the baby's sex?"

Lisa Marie crunched into one of the carefully cut slices. "Mom, you've already asked me that a dozen times. Are you okay? Is there something you want to tell me?" She wiped her mouth. "If it's about Dad, save it. I don't want to talk about it."

"It's Edward."

Lisa Marie slowly took another bite. "What's the matter? He wants to marry Nancy? Mom, you can't stop him even if you want to. He loves her."

Marie poured her daughter a large glass of juice. "They say orange juice is good for you when you're pregnant. But not too much, you know the sugar…"

"Mom, what about Edward?"

"Well, you're right. He is going to marry Nancy, and I can't stop it. And really, I like her. It's just that they are so different." She paused. "They are going to have a baby, too."

Lisa Marie put her hand over her mother's. "And you're upset that it's out of wedlock?"

Marie started crying.

Lisa Marie consoled her mother. "Mom, it happens all the time. I'm proud of him, that he and Nancy didn't abort. That takes guts."

Marie took a napkin from the special day plate that she had repaired after the fight between Edward and Guy, and wiped her tears. "Yes, your brother is brave." She crossed her hands on her lap beneath the table, and fought back the tears. "He is going to defend your father at trial."

Lisa Marie looked down at her plate, grabbed another piece of toast, and continued eating.

Her mother waited for a response, but received none. "Lisa Marie, talk to me. I asked your brother to do it. So if you're going to be mad at anyone, be mad at me. He didn't want to do it. I had to practically beg him."

Lisa Marie smiled subtly. "You remember when we were little and we used to go visit Daddy's parents? Grandma always had little toys waiting for us when we came to see her. She was so happy when we were there, and I never really understood why. I always figured – who could possibly be happy to see Albert and Edward?"

Mother and daughter enjoyed a warm chuckle.

Lisa Marie continued. "I was just happy that she was happy. She was a great lady. She loved to tell that old Italian story about the house that was being flooded, with the child, mother, father, and father's mother inside. You remember?"

Marie nodded her head affirmatively. "Of course I do. My mother used to tell me the same story as a little girl."

Lisa Marie gestured with her hands. "As the water started to rise inside the house, she said, the father picks up his wife and puts her on his shoulders to keep her safe. And as the water kept rising, he lifted his child on his wife's shoulders so that his whole family was safe." Lisa Marie brushed some of the toast's crumbs off the table into her hands. "This was always the tough part. When the father's mother asks, 'what about me, I'm your mother?' he explains that he can only take care of her after he takes care of his family. I never understood that either, it sounded so cruel, until I married VJ and became pregnant." She dropped the crumbs back into her plate. "I can't be mad at you or Edward, Mom, because you are protecting your family, the way Grandma told us to. But you have to understand, I have to protect my family, too. Right now, my husband is hurting badly, and I have to be there for him."

Marie reached over and hugged her daughter. Her tears gushed uncontrollably. "My little girl has grown up and become a wife and mother."

Lisa Marie extended her arms, drawing her own tears from within. "I learned from you."

Mother and daughter embraced, their bodies pressed against one another. They wept until their sorrows ran dry.

LI.

❧❧❧

A Sharp Instrument

Faith

Guy lay in his bottom bunk in the County Jail, his head resting on a pillow that separated it from the cold steel of the cell's cross bars. He was reading the libretto to his favorite opera, Giacomo Puccini's *Turandot*.

His cellmate, Amos Freedman, was uncharacteristically jumpy, pacing hard in the small space of the windowless box. He slapped the palm of his large hand against the cubicle's concrete wall and muttered. "Fuckin' Judge Masterson, goddamn sonofabitch." He came away from the wall and kicked his stool. His mumblings continued to flow like a volcano bubbling over.

Although he wanted to ask Amos what was bothering him – what Judge Masterson had done to him – Guy refrained. Though friendly to him, Amos and this tiny cell were still too new to Guy, and there was nowhere to hide.

Amos cooled gradually. He picked up his overturned stool, sat on it, and pulled his clarinet case from beneath Guy's bed. His assembly of the instrument seemed to soothe him, and his setting up of his sheet music and pen on the floor in front of him lent an air of self-control. Once Amos began his discourse, the notes from his clarinet were off-key. He scribbled revisions to his composition with urgency, but at least he was back in his sanctuary. Peace appeared to be returning.

Sensing the calm, Guy ventured to the precipice while he

continued to read Puccini's *Turandot*. "What a story this is!" he exclaimed out loud.

Amos tried to continue with his clarinet and paper, but was distracted by Guy's contentment. "What you reading?"

Guy kept his eyes on the libretto. "Nothing much. Just an old opera my dad and I used to listen to together. It's called *Turandot*."

Amos resumed his starts and skids with his horn.

Guy continued. "It really is an amazing story. It's about a prince who wants to win the love of a Chinese princess, and he has to solve three riddles to do it. A lot of guys tried before him, but none of them could do it. They were either beheaded or thrown into the fire. But not this fella. He was determined. He was going to solve the riddles and get the princess. Nothing was going to stop him from winning."

The clarinet flared, its blowings more fierce.

Guy ignored the warning. "It's kind of like this whole process. To get through it, you gotta believe in yourself."

Freedman's eyes bulged, their veins red, as he blew harder into his clarinet.

"Live as if everything depends on you. Pray as if everything depends on God. You have to believe that God will make it right."

Amos shot up and exploded. He slammed his clarinet against the cell crossbar just beside Guy's head, sending the horn's end flying into the hallway. He brandished like a spear the jagged edges of what remained of his instrument, and shouted intensely. "What the fuck you talking about? All you got to do is believe!" His forearms' thick veins coarse with hatred and resentment, Amos thrust the sharp wood inches away from Guy's eyes and held it there. "This ain't no fairy tale, motherfucker! I'm a nigger on trial for the murder of a white boy! I'm gonna spend the rest of my life in the big house and there ain't nothin' I or yo God gonna do about it!"

Guy tried to lie still beneath the sharp blades of Amos's broken clarinet. The jagged edges were so close, Guy could see the different shades of the wood's cut grains. He trembled as he spoke. "There is...there is something you can do about it." He swallowed. "You can stop acting like niggers own injustice, and that no one else can understand it." Guy's voice strengthened as the rancor in Amos's eyes lessened. "In case you forgot, I'm on trial for the death of two white people. But I still have faith. You gotta have faith, Amos. Without it, all you have is fear, and fear will eat you alive."

Amos backed away, draped his arms over the cell's crossbars next to Guy's bed, and dropped his clarinet's stump into the hallway in despair.

Guy asked the question. "What happened today, Amos? I thought The People were going to make you a new offer."

Amos spoke slowly as he looked sadly into the hallway. "They did. Second degree murder wit' a thirteen-year parole disqualification. A promise to stay inside thirteen mo' years for something I di'n't do. I told the Prosecutor he could keep his deal. I ain't interested."

"So why are you upset with Judge Masterson?"

Amos's lips marched steadily. "Because the motherfucker looked down at me from on high in his black robe and he say, 'Mis-sa Freedman, this a generous offer by The People. You' rejection of it can have serious consequences.'" Amos laughed. "The motherfucker called me Mis-sa when what he really think is that he lookin' at an animal." He erased his smile. "For the first time, Guy, I feel I ain't never gettin' out."

A guard appeared at the cell's door. "Stand back, Freedman." He looked at Guy. "Visitor for you, Bennett. It's your son Edward. He is in the attorney conference room."

Guy started to say something to Amos as he left the cell, but stopped himself. As a father, Guy could sense when a simple touch will help steady anxiety more readily than a bushel of words. He put his hand on his friend's shoulder, squeezed it, and headed for the conference room to meet his new lawyer.

LII.

Client Interview

Edward waited at the conference room table with a blank pad and pen. When his father entered, he stood to greet him, but could not speak. Currents of love and betrayal, sympathy and confusion crossed at the sight of his father in a prison jumpsuit, an inmate of the inescapable box. Edward had seen hundreds of prisoners as a Public Defender, but never before had the air been so dank and cold, the walls so close to one another. Edward could not remember ever sharing with his father a room so small.

Guy sat in the one-armed chair, his eyes opening wide before returning to normal. "Hello, son." When Edward did not respond, Guy followed. "Thank you for coming. It means a lot to me."

Edward folded back a leaf of his pad to make busy. "When Mom asks, it's hard to say no." He started to write something down. "We have a lot to go over. I'm scheduled to go visit the pathologist in Alabama, and we need..."

Guy pushed out a smile, which by now was only a shadow of its former self. "How's Nancy?"

Edward squinted. "Come again?"

Guy's smile flowed with more ease. "Nancy. Your wife. My daughter-in-law. The mother of my grandchild."

Edward laughed nervously. "Whoa, whoa. We're not married yet. Next month."

"Whatever. How is she?"

Edward bit his lower lip. "Why do you ask? After what happened at your house, I thought you didn't want to know."

Guy pinched the bridge of his nose and closed his eyes. "Son, I was a foolish man racing through life at a dangerous speed." He opened his eyes, and lowered his thumb and forefinger to his bottom lip. "Being thrown into this hellhole and forced to sit still for hours on end has made me realize that choices and their consequences are not that simple. When you peel away the images of the houses, the schools, and the titles, most of our options are gray, and even the best of them can hurt someone else without us even knowing it. Which isn't to say life is bad and doesn't have its triumphs. It's just a helluva lot more complicated than I ever imagined."

"You can say that again."

Guy took a deep breath, and dropped his hands into a prayer fold. "I'm sorry for what I said to you at the house. I was wrong. Nancy and your child will be part of our family just like everybody else – no different." He pointed with his index finger. "After you make it right by getting married. That hasn't changed. I haven't been here that long yet."

Edward smiled. "Thanks, Dad." He rolled his eyes like an embarrassed son. "And I promise we'll be married by this time next month." Edward sobered and looked at his pad. "But now we've got to talk about this thing."

Guy exhaled a nervous air. "Yeah, this thing."

Edward burrowed ahead by venting on the prosecutor. "Straid's evidence is being reported by Gabrielle DeFiore on almost a daily basis. The fucking guy has no scruples. It's obvious that he is going to hammer away on this takeover bid for your company, and the argument that he says you had with Mr. Petrozzini in front of the board the week of the murders. So let's start with that. Is it true that there was some kind of takeover bid going on for your company?"

Guy responded curtly. "There still is. By Vito's brother in Argentina, Bruno. We need to talk about that too, you know. How can we stop it? I am not letting anyone take away my company."

Edward took copious notes. "We'll deal with that later, Dad. I think this other thing is a little more important." When his father assented with a nod, Edward continued. "I didn't even know that Mr. Petrozzini had a brother."

"He hadn't seen him in years. They weren't very close."

Edward processed the information as he was trained to do as a defense attorney, and made a series of statements that he wanted to believe. "So when the prosecution leaks that during your argument with Mr. Petrozzini in front of the board, you accused him of being in cahoots with his brother, that's bullshit. Isn't it? You knew he wasn't close with his brother."

Guy rubbed his chin. "Yes, I knew Vito wasn't close with his brother Bruno." He paused. "But I still accused him."

Edward nodded his head. "So the board meeting and the takeover announcement were on a Tuesday and the Petrozzinis were murdered three days later, that Friday."

"Yep."

"And did you tell the police you went to the Petrozzinis that night for dinner?"

Guy stepped up without hesitation. "I did. I wanted to nip the takeover situation in the bud. Your sister actually asked me to do it. I was there at 6:30 on the button, the time the Petrozzinis always eat. Lena made Vito's favorite, steak pizzaiola."

"How long did you stay?"

"About a half an hour, until 7:00."

Edward looked up to see that his father had begun walking the room's narrow floors. "Why did you leave so fast?"

Guy spoke in choppy phrases. "I got a call while we were eating. It was some guy who wouldn't say who he was. He spoke very fast, as if he was out of breath. He said that if I wanted to keep my company, I had to meet him at the rail yards in fifteen minutes, alone. To leave my car by the front and meet him inside at the station."

Edward did not know which way to spin his questioning. "And you went?"

"Yeah, yeah. I went, and nobody showed up."

"Did somebody see you?"

Guy scratched his head. "Nope, it was deserted. Not even a security guard."

Edward studied his notes. "And you got back to the Petrozzinis at around 8:00?"

"Yeah, yeah."

Edward flipped his written notes back on top of his pad, and put his pen into his shirt pocket.

Guy stopped in his tracks. "Wait a minute. You're not done, are you? You haven't asked me about the shovel and plastic bag in the trunk. You haven't asked me if I did it."

Edward stood up. "What do you know about the blood stains on the shovel and bag?"

Guy lowered his brows, and shook his head. "Nothing."

Edward walked to his father and looked him in the eyes. "Did you kill Mr. and Mrs. Petrozzini?"

Guy stared back and swallowed. "No."

Edward put a hand on his father's shoulder. "We'll talk after I visit the pathologist."

As Edward walked away, Guy called out with a rare expression of emotion. "Thank you, son."

Edward turned. "You're welcome, Dad." He rang the buzzer for the guard, and turned again before leaving. "Take care of yourself."

"You know I always do."

LIII

Interpreting Wounds

A Sickening Note

Edward made his apartment into his working office, where he felt he could work without distraction, without anyone asking him how it was going – or telling him how difficult it must be to represent a father in a double murder trial. But the file of *The People of the State of New York v. Gaetano Bennett* lay untouched on Edward's kitchen table for three weeks. He did everything he could to avoid the many folders bulging with evidence of the crime. He paced the floors, went for jogs, wrote out tasks for himself, but refused to peer into the Redweld, much less dig into it. Midday on a Tuesday, Edward was napping in his chair, the newspaper in his lap.

He was awakened by the rattle of keys in his door lock. The door swung open. "Surprise. I brought you lunch," exclaimed Nancy.

Edward shot up in his chair, flapping out the newspaper as if to straighten it for a better view.

"I have two sandwiches of prosciutto and mozzarella." She rubbed her tummy. "Baby is getting an appetite."

"I don't know if I'm hungry yet," Edward replied. "But thanks."

Nancy set the table with the sandwiches. "C'mon. I have to get back to the office and you have to eat." She moved aside the Redweld, noticing that its folders were undisturbed. "How is it going on the case, honey?"

"I was just reading the coverage of it in the newspaper. There is a story every day. Everybody feels Dad is guilty." He sat at the kitchen table, his body limp. The problem is, it is almost as if they want him to be guilty."

Nancy took a big bite into her sandwich. She chewed before speaking. "Win Gonzalez called me."

"Yeah, he and I have been trading phone calls. What did he want from you?"

"He said you have not been calling him back at all. And that you have not contacted the pathologist in Alabama. That stuff takes time, Edward, something you have precious little of. The trial is two months away."

"I left Win messages. He must not have gotten them."

Nancy looked at Edward's sandwich, which he he had not yet unwrapped from its white paper. "What's the matter? You usually inhale prosciutto and mozzarella."

"Not hungry."

"You're scared."

Edward twitched, as if a nerve had been struck. "What are you talking about?"

"You heard me. You're scared. You are not working the file, not calling Win or the pathologist." She pointed to the chair in which she found Edward. "It has been three weeks and you have done nothing. You are just sitting in that damn chair reading about how The People are winning. They are right. You are losing."

Edward was not ready for the attack. "What's up with you?"

"I am pregnant out of wedlock, my future father-in-law, who doesn't even respect me, is an inch away from life in prison, and the father of my child is intimidated in the biggest case of his life. No exactly what I had in mind when I started Harvard Law School."

Edward put his hand on Nancy's to try to calm her. "C'mon, Nancy. At the PD's office, we usually don't get ready until two months beforehand."

"That's bullshit, Edward." She reached into her handbag, pulled out an envelope, and threw it on the table. "Your father's life is on the line, and so is ours."

Edward opened the envelope. "Airplane ticket to Birmingham, Alabama."

Nancy got up from the table to leave. "I made the appointment with the pathologist, Dr. Cudder, for you to see him tomorrow. I bought you the ticket. You can pay me later." As she exited the door, she called out, "You better take a look at that file before you get down there."

With Nancy gone, Edward knew that there was truth in what Nancy had said to him, that he had been overwhelmed by the task ahead of him. He had to begin working in earnest. He proceeded to unroll the sandwich she brought him and took a bite.

Edward boarded a plane the next day to Birmingham, Alabama, to visit Jackson Cudder, to whom he had already sent The People's discovery and coroner's reports. En route, Edward perused the doctor's impressive résumé: Chief Medical Examiner in three different states in the South; involved in over five hundred homicide investigations; member of international human rights teams; and the author of numerous papers on stab and gunshot wounds. Edward had never imagined a person whose life was so devoted to death and its causes, and wondered to himself about the dark world he was about to enter.

The middle-aged man sitting next to Edward on the plane piped in with a Southern twang. "This yo' first time to Alabama, young man?"

"Yes, it is."

The fast-speaking man, with large nose and beady eyes, fell in with a handshake. "Pleased to meet you. My name is Avery Himple. And welcome."

"Edward Bennett. Thank you."

Himple rubbed his chin and pointed. "Now, you be sure to get down to the Gulf Shores. It's downright gorgeous this time of year. Right there near Florida. Alabama has some of the nicest beaches in the country, and nobody knows about it."

Edward responded politely. "Thanks, but I don't think I'll have the time. I'll barely be able to visit the historical sights in Birmingham."

"Which historical sights you talkin' about?"

Edward could sense the agitation in Himple's voice, but did not retract. "You know, the civil rights demonstrations of the 1960s."

"Now, how do you know about that, young man?"

"I studied it in high school and college. I wrote my senior thesis about it."

Himple flipped open the magazine he was reading, and spoke as he retreated into it. "That's all you people ever talk about, what you read in those books of yours. Little do you know they run the place now." Himple forced a smile. "I hope you enjoy your stay."

The exchange made clear to Edward that he was already in the heart of the Deep South, the birthplace of the American Civil War of the 1860s and the Civil Rights Movement of the 1960s, both of which he had studied voraciously at prep school and in college. After landing at the Birmingham Airport, Edward had to rent a car to travel the ninety-minute balance to Dr. Cudder's office in the small town of Tuscumbia, which was pinched in the northwest corner of Alabama between the Mississippi and Tennessee borders. As he walked to the rental car counter, Edward for the first time felt like a visitor in his own country.

When he pulled out of the airport, Edward took a detour to visit Birmingham, a city he thought he already knew, where difference was identity, and racial animosity a political currency – a place where it had long been acceptable to harbor hatred without knowing its object. But gone were the stark television images of Negro Protest being repelled by White Only Security with its fire hoses and attack dogs. Amidst the near empty streets and beaten pace of Birmingham, Black men boarded the aged public buses alongside White women and children. Perhaps the fighting had stopped, or maybe nothing remained worth fighting for. Businesses were boarded shut, and there was nary a sign of activity in the public parks. A sentence of silence was being served without protest, but beneath it an eerie menace seemed to lurk still.

Back on Interstate 65 on the road north to Tuscumbia, Edward turned on the car's radio. As he rotated the dial, evangelical ministers, one after another, broadcast their gospel, each of them promising salvation, all of them purporting to be the voice of God. Fear and obedience were the lyrics of the airwaves, underscored with appeals for money.

Edward exited Interstate 65 to journey westward toward Tuscumbia. The scenery beside the road was like an old-fashioned movie background whose frames repeated themselves: a church, a series of houses, a gas station, and a windowless restaurant. Edward thought about stopping for a bite, but when he saw a neon stand-alone sign lit with a menu that featured fried quail, he kept going.

As he neared Tuscumbia, Edward yielded for a car entering the roadway. His mood elated when he noticed a sign marking the birthplace of the famous Black runner, Jesse Owens, whose four–gold medal prowess in the 1936 Olympics in Munich, Germany, so angered Nazi Führer Adolf Hitler. Edward might have missed the small sign had he not slowed to give way. Shame, he thought to himself, that such a great competitor was later reduced to a penniless circus act, racing against horses.

Then came the more prominently advertised birthplace of Helen Keller, the deaf and blind educator whose fixed eyes and strong profile were an icon for persistence and courage in the face of overwhelming handicaps. Amazing, Edward pondered, that a woman could have such vision traveling mutely through the night.

And a sign for Muscle Shoals, that small town made famous by Baby Boomer rock-n-roll artists of the 1960s, who selected it as their recording studio and hangout. Though he had enmity for the self-aggrandizing generation that defined the 1960s and each decade since, Edward could not ignore the slow rhythmic sounds that pulsated in his head as he passed through the otherwise obscure spot.

When Edward parked his car in front of the Colbert County Courthouse in Tuscumbia, he was shocked to be greeted by a concrete statue dedicated to the "Confederate States of America and its Misunderstood Soldiers."

A portly police officer, with crewcut and brown-shaded sunglasses, strutted his way from the County Courthouse toward Edward and the soldier statue. Just as he was about to pass, Edward called out. "Excuse me, Officer. I'm looking for the office of Dr. Jackson Cudder. I was told it's near the Courthouse."

The officer stopped, and with both hands gripped his thick leather belt that was saddled with a gun and handcuffs. He smiled, and spoke with a thick Southern drawl. "You a far way from home, ain't ya, Yankee?"

Edward looked back at the officer beneath the blazing sun. "How do you know I'm from the North..." he hesitated, "sir?"

"Only people find themselves lost in this town is Yankee do-gooders tryin' to tell us how to run the place." When Edward looked down, the officer cocked his head forward. "You a lawya, ain't ya? Down here on one of them death penalty cases. Which one you here for, Jimmy Ray Hunter?" When Edward failed to respond, the officer came again. "Now I know that everybody deserves a defense, but how does a smart fella like you sleep at night representing someone who raped and murdered three innocent girls in the woods?"

Edward looked up into the sweltering heat. "I don't represent Jimmy Ray Hunter. I don't represent anyone down here. Can you please tell me how to find Dr. Cudder's office?"

The officer pointed across the street. "Right there."

"Thank you, sir."

As Edward walked away, the officer called out with a smile. "You enjoy yo' self down here in Tuscumbia, ya' hear? You need any mo' help, you give us a holler." He shook his head and returned to the Courthouse.

When Edward reached Dr. Cudder's office, there was a message taped to the door. "Mr. Bennett – Gone to lunch. Be back at 12:30 p.m. Go in and make yourself at home – S. Jackson Cudder."

Edward stepped inside. It was anything but home – papers everywhere, the walls covered with bookshelves spilling from ceiling to floor. The only light came from a small window behind the doctor's antique wooden desk. The air was filled with the haunting allegretto of Beethoven's Symphony No. 7, Opus No. 92; it came from a barely visible portable stereo in the corner. Edward walked gingerly, careful not to tip the room's balance.

To the left was a pine table, with pictures of death's victims organized on top of it.

As Edward studied a frontal photo of a man's punctured face and mouth open in terror, a cello gave procession to the low steady strokes of Symphony No. 7 in three trios of five – the second and third beats in each tied together – followed by a single four. The inscription beneath the photo read: "Billy Joe Wheeler. Age 43. Suspected cause of death – ice pick. Closed."

Edward moved to the next photo of a woman whose neck was severed, exposing her trachea. The cello became intermittent background to a violin, its thinner and higher pitch now played the same trio of three fives – the second and third tied – followed by a four. The explanation on the picture: "Tammy Jean Hackett. Age 19. Suspected cause of death – machete. Closed."

A shriller violin assumed the fore with the others behind, and Edward looked in horror at an infant's black pocked face and forever shut eyes. The epilogue: "Becky White. Age 5 months. Suspected cause of death – cobra attack. Closed."

Edward then reached the photos of a blood-soaked couple, lying on their backs. The violin broke out screaming longer, its strings sounding as if they were being cut; a horn picked up the trio of three fives – the second and third tied – then the four. The orchestral sounds rattled inside Edward's head, and his heart sank as he read the newly written script: "Vito and Pasqualina Petrozzini. Age 61. Suspected cause of death – repeated stabbings with steak knife. Preliminary."

A creaking door cut the music, and a rangy Dr. Cudder stepped inside, standing imposingly in his snakeskin cowboy boots. "Mr. Bennett. Jackson Cudder. Sorry for the wait." Cudder walked around his desk, and sat behind the wooden carved nameplate that read "Dr. S. Jackson Cudder IV." He rustled through his papers. "I hope you had a good trip."

Edward smirked, "Interesting." His head momentarily cleared of his short but wide travels from the airport, Edward concentrated on Cudder's blue-gray eyes. "Thank you for meeting with me."

Cudder leaned back in his chair, and stroked his thick mustache gently with his forefinger. He spoke with a suppressed Southern drawl, which sounded manipulable depending on the audience. "Another man's liberty is a very serious matter..."

Edward interrupted. "I'm glad to hear that you believe in presenting a zealous defense."

Cudder finished his thought. "Actually, what I was going to say was that because the taking of another man's life is a serious matter, I usually testify for the prosecution in murder cases."

Edward dropped his jaw. "Well then, my father. Why are you..."

Cudder did the interrupting. "Because Win Gonzalez is a friend of mine." Cudder looked toward the pine table where the Petrozzini photos lay. "And The People have said some things they shouldn't have, neglected to say some things they should have, to support their theory that your father is the killer."

Edward perked up. "So you think there is some real doubt?"

Cudder leaned forward. "Now I didn't say that. What I said is that there is some serious sloppiness in the coroner's report that looks like an attempt to race to justice. I'm surprised. Frankie should know better."

"Frankie?"

Cudder smiled. "Dr. Francine Scarborough, the New York Medical Examiner. We trained together. She still blames me for losing her position in Florida. As colleagues, I pointed out how she restitched a body incorrectly, leading to a false conclusion about the width of a knife used to stab a young woman. Haven't spoken since. But I heard she has been doing well in New York, which is why I'm surprised."

Edward shook his head. "Small world, I guess. Who would have thought?"

Cudder spoke slowly. "Let's just say that there is never a real glut in the market for forensic pathologists. There are not too many of us."

Edward took a pad out of his knapsack and began to take notes in the dark room. "So what is it about the report that you think is sloppy?"

Cudder sat tall in his chair, the light through the small window behind him illuminating only half his face. "For example, Dr. Scarborough concluded that because the depth of the deepest wounds in the Petrozzinis' bodies was five inches long, the knife that inflicted them was probably that long. Five inches happens to be the length of the steak knife that had your father's fingerprints on it."

Edward shook his head. "Yeah, I read that. It actually sounded pretty damaging to me. What's wrong with it?"

Cudder reached over and pulled a stack of tissues out of a box and placed them on his desk. "I'll show you." He pulled a pocketknife from his pants, and flipped open the blade. "This here is my pocket knife that I use for fishin'. I do no more harm with it than cut my lines. Blade can't be more than two inches." He raised it, and thrust it violently into the stack of tissues. He left it upright, stuck into the top of his wooden desk, piercing the stack of tissues. "Because body tissue contracts or bunches together as you push through it with a knife, a two-inch blade can go five inches deep, dependin' on how much tissue there is. Same thing when a knife is cutting through a body's fat."

Edward offered an image to see if he understood. "Almost like an accordion."

"Exactly."

Edward grew excited. "So the knife wasn't five inches. That excludes the knife with my dad's prints."

Cudder pointed. "No. You lawyers are always jumpin' to conclusions and tryin' to put words in our mouths. All I'm saying is that the knife was not necessarily five inches the way Frankie's report suggests. Could have been two inches. If the killer didn't go all the way could have been eight inches. Or it might have been the five-inch knife with your daddy's prints on it. There's no way of tellin', and Frankie Scarborough knows that. The only thing I can say for sure is that you have a strong-willed prosecutor up there who is leaning real hard on Frankie. I noticed that according to the police report, he personally called in the dimensions of the knife to Frankie before she was done with the autopsy."

Edward scribbled another fact that he had missed in his review. "Anything else?"

"Yeah." Cudder went over to the pine table, and picked up Dr. Scarborough's report. "Something I have to look at again, because it doesn't make much sense." He began reading. "It says here that there was stuff broken on the floor, vases and what not. There is also a small trail of blood behind Ms. Petrozzini where she was found under the phone on the wall in the kitchen, with the receiver off the hook." He spoke slowly as he continued to read. "Frankie says that this suggests some kind of struggle between the killer and the victims, ending with Ms. Petrozzini's attempt to call the police. Fits well with what I understand is The People's theory that your daddy and Mr. Petrozzini had been fightin' over business earlier that week. That your daddy threatened to kill him. "

Edward wrote hurriedly, trying to keep up with Cudder. "And?"

Cudder looked up. "Well, there were no defensive wounds on any of the bodies, you know, bruises from stuff being broken on their forearms or other parts of the body. And there was no real blood splattering, which usually happens during a violent struggle. The wounds were real neat and close together, which suggests to me that most of them were inflicted after the fact, when the victims couldn't defend themselves. Passion, rage. Again, no struggle. Surprise and done quickly, down and dirty."

Edward tried to play pathologist on the only terms he knew. "What about the broken stuff? Were Dad's fingerprints on it?"

"Good question. They weren't able to lift any prints, which indicates that bare human hands hadn't touched the items in a long while. And that really puts a knot in The People's theory. Why would your dad be dumb enough to leave prints on the knife, but think to have gloves on when throwing a vase? I'm just thinking out loud, but it doesn't make much sense."

Edward put down his pen. "What are you saying?"

Cudder returned to his seat. "What I'm saying is that I don't think there was a struggle, and that either your father or somebody else staged it to look like there was one. The positioning of Ms. Petrozzini's body was part of it. The photo of the blood trail behind her was not a splatter or drip. It was a drag. The body was dragged under the phone."

Edward chose his words carefully. "Are you saying that there is a possibility that someone framed my father?"

"It's a possibility. But based on the lack of evidence indicating a struggle, it would have had to be done by somebody watching him, or someone close to him." Cudder laid his hands flat on the desk, leaned forward as far as he could, and stared at Edward with his blue-gray eyes, his face half shaded by the darkness. "Edward, I gotta ask you somethin' personal."

"Go ahead."

"Have you looked your daddy straight in the eye and asked him if he done it?"

"Yes. He said he didn't do it."

Cudder was so intense that he appeared more interested in the message in Edward's eyes than he was in Edward's response about his father. "Do you believe him?"

Edward spoke with cotton-mouth. "Yes, I do."

Cudder remained, before throwing himself back against his chair. "Okay, 'cause I ain't workin' to free no guilty man. You'll need to fly me up there to take a look at the crime scene." He leafed through his calendar. "Two weeks from now looks good. And I'll need a $10,000 check made payable to the University of Alabama."

Edward reached into his knapsack for his checkbook. "Sure, but how about you? How will you be paid?"

"University has me on salary. They let me do this on the side so long as they get paid for my services."

"So why do you do it?"

"It's the kind of thing that once you start, you can't get out." Cudder changed the subject while Edward wrote the check. "What kind of name is Bennett, Irish?"

Edward tore off the check and handed it to Cudder. "No, Italian. It used to be Di Benedetto. My grandfather changed it when he came from Italy."

Cudder folded the check and put it in his shirt pocket. "I didn't think you were Irish." He paused. "*Vi dove proviene la tua famiglia in Italia?*"

Edward looked up shocked. "What?"

Cudder smiled. "What's the matter Mr. Di Benedetto, don't you know Italian when you hear it? I just asked you where in Italy your family is from."

"A small town called Aquino. How do you know Italian? Is your real name Cudderino?"

"I studied it in college so that I could read Dante Alighieri's *Inferno* in the original text. Fascinating stuff. And no, my name is not Cudderino. It's Stonewall Jackson Cudder the Fourth."

Edward packed his bag. "Why don't you use your full name? I would imagine that a guy down here named Stonewall Jackson, after the great Confederate general, would be pretty popular."

Cudder explained. "My daddy was Stonewall Jackson Cudder the pathologist. My granddaddy was Stonewall Jackson Cudder the pathologist, and my great-granddaddy, who was named after *the* Stonewall Jackson, was Stonewall Jackson Cudder the pathologist. It's time for a little change."

Edward stood up. "Well, my grandfather grew up a grape farmer in Italy, working alongside my great-grandfather, and if I had to guess, my great-great-grandfather did the same." He extended a hand. "And my dad is in prison. It's too bad that's what it took for us to meet, but thanks. I appreciate your help."

Edward spent the car ride back to the Birmingham Airport thinking about who could have possibly murdered the Petrozzinis to make it look like it was his father. Or was it his father?

Before boarding the plane back to New York, Edward called Nancy. "Nance, how are you feeling?"

Nancy's voice was somber. "Edward, I'm on my way to your mother's. Go there when you get home."

Edward snapped, "Why? What's happening?"

"Just go there when you get home."

"Is my mother okay?"

Nancy started bawling, her words barely audible. "It's Albert. He's dead. Your brother killed himself in a hotel room with a glass of wine laced with rat poison. He left a note."

"What? What are you saying? There was a note?"

Nancy tried to put Edward off. "You'll read it when you get here. Just hurry up to your mother's."

Edward became excited. "Nancy, tell me what the fucking note said."

Nancy took a deep breath. "He asked for forgiveness for killing the Petrozzinis."

Edward put his hand over his face. "Oh my God."

Nancy finished. "He told your father to confess and ask for the same forgiveness."

Edward hung up the phone without saying a word. He began to lose his breath, feeling like someone was trying to suffocate him with a pillow over his face. He became disoriented, confused as to where he was.

A loudspeaker sounded. "Last call for flight 241 from Birmingham to New York. We are about to close the doors at Gate 89. Birmingham to New York."

Disorientation gave way to the fear that his brother and father were murderers, and the realization that his brother was dead. Vomit heaving from his throat into his mouth with an acidic taste, Edward walked toward Gate 89 in a cold sweat. He hoped the plane he was about to board would never touch down.

LIV.

❧

Wooden Words

A Thin Black Line

Albert's funeral was a carnival of carnivores, its barkers the press with its lens ever-focused on the Senator's suicide and the murder of the Petrozzinis as far as possible. At the cemetery, a host of other curiosities were in full view under the summer sun. The armed policemen flanked Guy closely, as if there were any room for escape. The Very Reverend Monsignor McNabb, whose haste and hard brow betrayed his embarrassment at being in such a place. The pregnant Lisa Marie, unaccompanied by her husband VJ, standing separate from her family next to her mentor, the famous reporter Gabrielle DeFiore, who had the discretion to leave her pen and pad behind. Albert's wife Victoria, with their children Albert Junior and Alexandra, presenting the crowd a proper mourning for her husband, without spending a tear on her black sheer veil. Bracing Victoria, her father, Giles Kirby, whose firm Webb Investments was in the process of underwriting Bruno Petrozzini's hostile takeover of Northern Industries. And at David Rothstein's urging under the auspices of business etiquette, the Northern Industries Board of Directors – Bramford Leach, Nick Covitt, Eleanor Whittlesby, and Jared Pym – all of them giving good form.

Only the pregnant Nancy and Edward, whom Guy had previously disowned, stood by Guy's side with his wife Marie. Even Albert's coffin seemed anxious to distance itself from Guy as it was lowered into the grave.

And on the horizon, behind the view of the crowd, stood a Thin Black Line.

When Monsignor McNabb's wooden words finished, Edward held his ashen-faced mother in a deep embrace. When he moved on to his father, he was relieved by Nancy. Reporters' pens moved violently, their cameras shuttering with fervor.

Edward could not think of anything to say to his father, other than what was spinning relentlessly inside his head. He whispered in Guy's ear. "Dad, we have to talk about Albert's note."

Guy responded sternly. "Not today, Edward. I just buried my son."

Edward knew when to back off from his father, and did just that.

With his arm around Nancy, he stood guard over his brother's grave until the appetite of the onlookers was sated, and they dispersed to give their review. All except the Thin Black Line on the horizon.

As Edward and Nancy approached their weather-worn used car, they could see that the Thin Black Line standing dutifully next to it was a tall woman in sunglasses, shoes, stockings, dress and hat – all dipped in the color black. Nancy whispered. "Edward, who is that woman?"

Edward directed Nancy to the car. "Probably another reporter. Get inside. I'll take care of her."

Edward held his chin high. "May I help you?"

The Thin Black Line spoke as if she was in trance. "I would actually like to help you."

Edward became irritated. "Who are you, and what do you want?"

The Thin Black Line spoke softly. "My name is Ellen Straid, the Prosecutor's wife."

Edward smiled incredulity. "I doubt there is anything you can do for me. I have no idea why you are here, and don't want to know. So if you don't mind, I'll be leaving."

As Edward returned to his car, the Thin Black Line called without moving. "There was someone else at the rail yards the night of the murders."

Edward turned on a dime. "What?"

The Thin Black Line repeated herself with more detail. "The night your father went to the rail yards – the night of the murders . He did go to the rail yards. There was someone else there. Someone who put the shovel and plastic bags in your father's trunk."

Nancy opened the door to the car, holding her swollen abdomen to protect it. "Edward, is everything okay?"

Edward waved her off. "Fine, we're just talking. I'll be right there." He kept his eyes on the Thin Black Line. "How do you know this?"

The Thin Black Line took a deep breath. "Detective Kauftman came over to our house one night to tell Tommy about it. He said he and Detective Meeker went to the rail yards to check out your father's story, to see if they could find anything to discredit it. They got more than they bargained for. They found a homeless guy who saw the whole thing. Your father leaving the car. Then this other person sneaking behind and putting the shovel and bags in the trunk. Then he left. Tom told Kauftman that if that statement ever made its way into a report, the case against your father was shot, even if it was coming from a homeless guy. They couldn't afford to take a chance, he said."

Edward spoke slowly. "So, where's Detective Meeker?"

The Thin Black Line looked into the blinding sun, shielded by her glasses. "Special reassignment until further notice to some little town near the Massachusetts border. I think it's called Grafton." She laughed. "A real crime belt. Kauftman was supposed to take care of the report, and he did." She looked down. "In other words, if Meeker stays quiet in the middle of the woods where no one can hear him, he can come back after the case is over, when they all have to keep the secret unless they want to be indicted for obstruction and perjury."

Edward looked straight. "Why should I trust you?"

"Because I don't think my husband is telling the whole story. He doesn't want it to get out." A tear rolled from beneath the Thin Black Line's sunglasses. "And I loved your brother."

"Were you and Albert having an affair?"

The Thin Black Line stopped herself from saying more. "It's probably best we leave it at that, because as far as you know, you never met me. Let's keep it that way out of respect for your brother, his children, and my children."

The Thin Black Line turned and walked away, into obscurity; her slow steps left a printless trail of despair, never to be traced.

LV.

Working Up the Food Chain

In part to keep his mind busy, in part because he was fast running out of time before his father's trial, Edward dropped Nancy off at home after Albert's funeral and went immediately to Win Gonzalez's office. He needed advice on how to handle the information given to him by the Thin Black Line without disclosing its source.

When Win's assistant Yolanda knocked on her boss's door and opened it, the litigator jumped from the rapt concentration he had been paying to the large binders that surrounded him. "Yo, I told you not to interrupt me unless it was an emergency. I've got to get ready for the Bank of Commerce suppression hearing tomorrow morning."

Yolanda whispered, shifting her eyes in the direction behind the door where Edward was standing. "It's Edward Bennett; he says he needs only a few minutes."

Win bit his lip and paused. "Sure, send him in."

Edward apologized as Win cleared a chair of the binders he was studying. "I'm sorry, Win, but I just came from my brother's funeral because I got some new information."

Win continued to remove the binders. "Yeah, hey, I'm sorry about your brother's death. I meant to go to the funeral but this Bank of Commerce thing, you've probably been reading about it in the paper. Big suppression hearing tomorrow. The media people have been calling all day." Win sat in his chair, and got right to the point. "What's the new information? Is it Albert's suicide note? I read about it in the paper."

"Well, kind of. A confidential source told me that Kauftman and a Detective Meeker checked out Dad's story at the rail yards, and they found some homeless guy who said that on the night of the murders he saw Dad. But he also saw another person, who Dad didn't see, sneak in behind Dad and put a shovel and bags in the trunk. Supposedly, Kauftman and Straid reassigned Meeker to some podunk town called Grafton and buried the information."

Win displayed the irresistible smile that had won over countless jurors. "This is serious shit. But what's this confidential stuff? Who's your source?"

Edward did not return the smile. "I can't say. I promised."

Win used a few more seconds of silence to ask again. When he saw that Edward was not breaking, Win respected the secret and moved on. "Let's see. Obviously you can't accuse Straid and Kauftman right away, because that will give them time to get their stories together. The trick is to get Meeker to come clean, because once he does, Kauftman and Straid will have no choice but to do the same, or throw Meeker under the bus. Either way, you'll get what you want. You've got to get the facts first."

"Okay, but how?"

"Work your way up the food chain, starting with the homeless guy. Lock him in, then go to Meeker. After you lock Meeker in, you can hit Straid and Kauftman with it. But you gotta stay cool going up the chain, otherwise you'll break it. React as the stuff comes at you." Win scratched his forehead with his index finger. "Timing will be key. You got to throw this stuff out there fast and just before trial to put them on their heels. Prosecutors hate surprises, and don't handle them very well. They think the whole damn thing is their show."

Edward nodded his head. "Okay, okay. Do you think I should bring a witness with me when I go talk to the homeless guy?"

"No, definitely not. You know who the homeless guy probably is, don't you?"

Edward twitched negatively.

Win continued. "Harold Thistledown. He has been living in a deserted rail car for years. Don't you remember? When the police threw him out, he got the American Civil Liberties Union to sue the county and the state to establish his right to live in the rail car by adverse possession. The state put all kinds of money into the fight, and Thistledown won. It was all over the papers and radio. Conservatives wanted him in jail. It must have been when you were away at law school."

"I do remember Dad and Albert talking about it. They had mixed feelings."

Win looked at his watch. "Well, anyway. I wouldn't bring a witness with you to see Thistledown because he is a savvy guy. And the motherfucker is paranoid and delusional. He came from a decent family, but when he was a kid, his dad, who was a train conductor on the old New York City Line that came in and out of that station, died in a terrible crash. The kid had a breakdown and started drifting. When they closed the station, he started living in a deserted train car there."

"It's a helluva way to live, when there are plenty of homeless shelters."

"They say he's still waiting for his dad to pull into the station. I almost represented him in his civil suit, but I just didn't have the time." Win grabbed his silver pen, and stood up to end the session. "Well, anyway. Go to Thistledown first, and see what you can get. We can talk about Albert's note and whatever Dr. Cudder thinks about all this later." Win looked down at his thick binders, and back at Edward. "Good luck, my friend."

LVI

Waiting for a Train

Edward drove to the rail yards, where he found a boarded-up station house and tracks overrun with weeds. As he stepped to the lone deserted car that he suspected was Harold Thistledown's home, the dirt that kicked up hung heavy, amidst the smell of urine in the air. He banged on the sliding doors that were closed at the center of the car. "Mr. Thistledown. Mr. Harold Thistledown."

The door cracked open, and all that peeked through was a shaggy head and face wearing a conductor's cap with "H. Thistledown" inscribed on its front. "The four fifteen is not due for another eleven minutes, sir. So if you will please stand away from the tracks and have your ticket ready. All the seats on this car are already taken." Thistledown withdrew from the cloud of vodka he emitted as he spoke, and slid the doors shut. He shouted inside the closed cabin. "Let's get ready to pull her in, boys. Tickets please."

Edward banged on the door again. "Mr. Thistledown. Mr. Thistledown. I need to talk to you about what you saw on the night of March thirty-first. About what you already told the detectives."

Thistledown split the doors quickly again, displaying only his hatted hair and liquored breath. "You're with the police, aren't ya?"

Edward decided that no reply was the best reply, and would see where Thistledown would go with it.

Thistledown smiled. "You are with the police, ain't ya? You wanted to chase me out of here during my lawsuit. Now you can't get enough of me." Thistledown stood proud, with his thumbs under his armpits. "Ol' Harold Thistledown has become an important person all of a sudden to the men in blue. Yeah, sure. I'll help you fellas get it right." Thistledown threw the doors wide open, buttoned up his fecal-stained conductor's pants and shirt, and jumped to the ground in his untied ankle-high sneakers. "What do you want to know, Mr. Officer? But let's make it quick, because daddy is due to pull in the four forty five."

Edward winced as he tolerated Thistledown's ripe and aged odors. "I want you to go over with me what you already told the other detectives."

Thistledown tweaked his beard. "Sure, as soon as you show me your badge."

"My badge?"

Thistledown thrust his head forward. "I got to know what I'm dealing with, don't I?"

Edward thought and spoke fast. "Sure." He patted down his pants. "Oh, geez. I just ran over from headquarters. I must have left it behind. But the detectives you spoke to – Kauftman and Meeker – they work for me. We feel that a person like you deserves attention from the top."

Thistledown enjoyed the deference and respect that was being paid to him. "Very well then, if you'll just give me your name. The railroad requires that we keep a log of everyone we talk to on official matters."

Edward didn't want to give Thistledown his real name in the event that the vagrant may have somehow heard about his father's case. "Di Benedetto."

"Well, Officer Di Benetto, like I told your underlings, on March 31, I saw this man drive to the front gate in a big black car. I know it was night because I was getting the train ready for its runs the next day." Thistledown rubbed his long beard. "Let's see, it had to be past seven, because the 6:45 had already come in."

Edward wondered to himself about how he could possibly put Thistledown in front of a jury with such a story.

But then Thistledown's account crystallized with crisp detail. "The black car was a Mercedes-Benz, a large sedan type, with a gray racing stripe down the side with license plate LB-488J."

Edward went through each of the items in his own mind, and realized that Thistledown had described his father's car exactly.

Thistledown then stated an observation that he could have only made first hand. "And it had a little dent on the back passenger side. A shame. Because otherwise, it was a beautiful machine." He pointed to the rail car and began wandering. "Just like the one my daddy and me drive." He looked down at his watch. "We better hurry, Daddy'll be here in a few minutes."

Because he was also anxious, Edward complied. "So what did the man in the Mercedes do?"

Thistledown straightened the cap atop his bushy head. "The fella, who was a big guy about six foot in a suit, walked over to the station house and just waited there. He waited there for a while. Seemed nervous. Walking back and forth. I was going to tell him that the last train had already pulled in after I finished cleaning. But then this other guy – or was it a gal? It was hard to tell because he, or it, was all in black, and like I said, it was dark. Well anyway, this other person comes running up behind the Benz, pops the trunk, and drops a shovel and some bags inside. Then ran away before the big guy saw him. The big guy must have realized that he missed the train, came back to his car, and pulled off." Thistledown paused. "This is about that double murder in Middletown, isn't it Officer Di Benetto?"

Edward answered officially. "Yes, it is."

Thistledown smiled. "That case is getting almost as much press as mine did when I sued the state for the right to keep working on the railroad. My lawyers used some fancy theory – called me an adversity possessor. But what it came down to is that you can't deny a man his rightful job on the rails with his daddy. The judge agreed. People seem as excited about this case." He grimaced. "Which is why I was surprised when your junior officers didn't seem too happy with what I told them. Almost as if they didn't appreciate it. Obviously you do. Otherwise, you wouldn't be here."

Edward put his hand on Thistledown's shoulder. "We do appreciate it. And we may need to speak to you again. But in the meantime, you can't say a word to anyone."

Thistledown gave a military salute. "Anything I can do to help, Officer Di Benetto." He jumped back into his deserted rail car. He faced Edward, gripping the sliding doors on each side, and looked to his left down the long expanse of grass-covered tracks. "But I gotta get back to work now. I can see Daddy's train coming in for the hookup." He cupped his hands around his mouth and yelled in the direction where a train came no more. "We're ready for you, Daddy." He closed the sliding doors and yelled again. "Everyone take your seats. Tickets please."

LVII.

A Dispirited Client

Edward waited a few days before visiting Guy. While sitting in the jail's conference room before his father's arrival, he read an article by Gabrielle DeFiore paying tribute to his deceased brother. The piece was titled "Flawed Conviction." When Guy walked in, dragging and despondent, Edward shared some of the story with his father. "Gabrielle DeFiore is the only one of those maggots who call themselves reporters who can write a story about Albert without trying to play detective."

Guy sat diffidently in the one-armed chair.

Edward tried to rally his father's spirits. "She said that Albert was a rare politician who was poising himself so that in time, he could make some choices based on what is right instead of what plays in the polls. She said he had real conviction. She pointed to his First Step initiative for kids in the city as a good example."

Guy stared without blinking.

Edward folded the newspaper and laid it on the table. "She said that until there is judgment on who killed the Petrozzinis, that is how Albert should be remembered – for what he did rather than the crimes he might have committed – no matter how overwhelming the evidence might be." He raised his eyebrows. "The woman has a lot of class, despite what we said about her during the campaign."

"Whatever."

Edward crossed his arms on top of the conference table that separated him from Guy. "Dad, I got some new information that could be a big help to our case. Do you remember Harold Thistledown?"

Guy kept his eyes on the floor. "Sure, the homeless guy."

Edward picked up the pace. "Well, he was in the rail yards on the night of the murders, and he says he saw you pull in and wait at the old station house, just like you said. But he also saw someone sneak behind your car, pop the trunk, and drop a shovel and plastic bags inside. He explained all of this to Detectives Kauftman and Meeker, but they never put it in their report. Meeker got shipped off to some small town called Grafton so he wouldn't say anything."

Unmoved, Guy queried, "How did you find this out?"

Edward knew that Guy was the last person whom he would tell about Ellen Straid and her affair with Albert. "It just kinda hit me how you and Albert used to talk about Thistledown's case while I was in law school. Knowing he was living there, I went and talked to him."

"No one is going to listen to a homeless guy."

Frustrated that his father was not more excited about the break, Edward blurted out, "Dad, there was a shovel and bags with the Petrozzinis' blood in your trunk, and a suicide note from my brother that says you did it. Right now, Harold Thistledown is your best friend."

Guy took a deep breath. "Even with what Thistledown saw, we still can't prove who did it."

Edward shuffled around the table and put his hand on Guy's knee. He leaned under to intercept Guy's gaze to the floor. "We don't have to, Dad. All we have to do is create reasonable doubt. The pathologist, Dr. Cudder, says the autopsy report is off, and there's evidence you were framed. If I could flip Detective Meeker, it'd blow a hole right in the middle of their case. I talked to Win about it, and he said it was best to wait until just before trial to do that. Then bang."

"What about Albert's note?"

It was now Edward who chose to look at the hard floor. "I don't know. I am not even sure it's admissible. Straid will argue that it's some sort of dying declaration, but I'll argue that it's too unreliable because no one saw him write it. And Albert's – he's not here to explain."

Guy continued to speak slowly, with a tired voice. "How about the company? The takeover."

Edward rubbed his eyes. He couldn't understand how his father, mere inches from being locked away forever, had remained so concerned about Northern Industries. Guy talked about the company as if he were asking about the well-being of another of his children. "I actually did speak to David Rothstein about it the other day. He said the Board of Directors is still going to recommend to the shareholders that they take Bruno Petrozzini's offer, and Nick Covitt in particular wants to push ahead quickly while the offer is out there. Apparently, Leach and Whittlesby are behind him on it, and Jared Pym has kind of remained neutral. Luckily, the whole thing has been held up on Bruno's end. They think he might be in the process of liquidating some assets so that he doesn't have to borrow so much of the money from Webb Investments." Edward snickered. "Maybe Mr. Kirby will lend him a few bucks out of his own pocket, that bastard."

"Another great move by me," said a despondent Guy, "encouraging my son to marry Victoria Kirby."

Edward put his hand back on his father's knee. "But getting back to the case, Dad. For the first time, I'm beginning to think we have a shot."

Guy pushed a single laugh through his unclipped nose hairs.

Edward turned his head. "What?"

Guy smiled. "Nothing. It's just that all these years, I thought that money could solve any problem. Now with my life on the line, my best hope is with a homeless guy who has none." Guy put his hand on Edward's knee. "I appreciate everything you're doing for me, son. But go spend some time with your mother. She needs you now more than I do. And give Nancy and that little baby of yours a kiss for me."

Guy patted Edward twice on the shoulder, and buzzed for the guards. As he stood waiting solemnly at the door, he didn't have the heart or energy to turn around and look at his son.

LVIII.

❧❧❧

Trial Calling

The intial paralysis that Edward had suffered in getting started on the defense had left him with precious little time. After taking off only a couple of hours for a brief civil wedding ceremony, the honeymoon deferred until circumstances would permit, he prepared all of the other elements of his case, leaving his visit to Detective Meeker for the eve of trial. He went over each detail of the police reports repeatedly, highlighting every inconsistency and potential shortcoming that could be used to impeach The People's witnesses. Dr. Cudder visited the Petrozzini home and reiterated his earlier findings: it was highly implausible that there was any kind of struggle with the vase and overturned furniture given the lack of defensive wounds or bruising on either of the Petrozzinis or Guy; equally suspect was the absence of any fingerprints on the broken items when Guy had left such a clear signature on the alleged murder weapon, the steak knife; and the trail of Mrs. Petrozzini's blood from the dining room to the kitchen was more consistent with her being dragged by someone else than her struggling to the kitchen to call the police. All of this suggested that the scene might have been staged after the killings rather than, as The People would have it, being the debris of a violent argument between Guy and the Petrozzinis over the control of Northern Industries.

But still, Edward knew that S. Jackson Cudder's forensics alone would not carry the day given the melodrama of Guy's relationship with Vito, the optical impact of the bloodstained shovel and plastic bags in Guy's trunk that would be introduced as means for Guy to bury his clothing, the testimony that would come from the Northern Industries Board of Directors, and Albert's suicide note. Even if the note and some of the other details never made their way into evidence, there would hardly be a juror in the County who wasn't already familiar with them. Straid made sure of that through his leaks to the press. The prosecutor was not taking any chances.

Because of the prejudicial die cast by Straid into the potential juror pool, Edward made a motion for change of venue. Judge Masterson listened politely to the defense and prosecution arguments on the issue, and long considered how to craft a decision that would serve his own interests, but be safe from overturn on appeal. His order, buttoned impenetrably with the buzzwords of judicial discretion, was for him and his entire courtroom staff, right down to stenographers and Joe the bailiff, to continue to preside over the case, but in a different, neighboring county. This way, the Honorable would at once maintain control of Guy's fate in a year that he was up for re-election to the bench, and appear to give Edward what he requested for his father, even though the neighboring county in which the Judge chose to sit was just as likely to have been poisoned by the highly publicized details of the case. Displaying an expression of fairness and concern for the defendant, the Judge spent more time on the minutia of moving everything to the new venue than he did on any other aspect of the trial.

Guy's day in court was to begin immediately after Judge Masterson concluded the retrial of Amos Freedman. The two accused men learned more about each other in their short time together as cellmates than acquaintances, partners, or even brothers acquire in a lifetime. That is why, while Amos paced the short expanse of cold gray floor, waiting to be taken to the Court for the opening statements of his case, Guy tried to calm his friend, despite the agony that had been tearing him since Albert's death. Amos's efforts to soften for his mate the hard walls of the box taught Guy the idea of giving when all had been taken – a charity that must be drawn from within and not plucked from a wad in one's pocket.

Guy smiled. "You and your lawyer better give 'em hell, Amos. I'm counting on your trial taking a long while. Because as soon as you're acquitted, Edward and I have to mix it up with Straid and Masterson."

Amos was sweating. He forced denial through his own pessimism. "Yeah, yeah. Everybody talk about how bad it be at the state prison. I ain't goin'. This time gonna be different. My new boy work real hard." He started pacing faster. "Come up with some new stuff that the jury and Masterson didn't see the last time. This a new day, Guy. Yes sir, a new day. This trial gonna take at least a week, maybe two. My boy is got a lot to say. We gonna win, just like that prince you and your daddy used to talk about. Whas his name – Turn-dot?"

Guy smiled. "You remembered." He extended his arms to stretch. "They might even decide to set you free today, and I won't see you. So you gotta do me one favor after you walk out of this place." Guy reached under his bunk, pulled out Amos's clarinet case, and opened it. Inside lay Amos's clarinet, which he had not seen since he had shattered it on the bars over Guy's head and brandished the remains. "You have to finish writing that damn song about your grandmother's lemonade."

Amos stopped pacing the cold gray. He stood gawking at the instrument, as if his feet were glued to the floor. His whisper trembled. "How the...?"

Guy eyes wrinkled with compassion. "It wasn't easy. Part of it flew into another cell. Another part down the hall. And I'm not too good with my hands. I haven't had to be in a long time. Joe the bailiff helped me track down the pieces and put it back together."

Amos's smile lit the cell.

Guy handed Amos the clarinet, and stood to extend the handshake his friend taught him on his first day in, the kind with the thumb up. "You're a good man, Amos Freedman. Don't let anyone ever take your soul."

Amos wrapped his big hand around Guy's. His brow dipped as he fought a tear. "Ain't nobody since Granny ever been this good to me." He raised the clarinet like a staff in the air. "And when I'm done writin' about her lemonade, I'm gonna play a tune for you, Mr. Bennett, one of yo' operas, and play it in that big ol' house of yours until it break those expensive windows."

The two laughed giddily, tightening their hold on one another.

Joe the bailiff interrupted with the turn of his key. He spoke in low tones, as if he regretted what he had to say. "C'mon, Amos. The judge is ready."

Amos packed his clarinet excitedly, and gave Guy a wide smile before leaving. "Don't you worry, Guy. I gonna be all right."

Guy looked briefly at the deep sense of foreboding in Joe the bailiff's eyes, then returned Amos the smile. "I know you will, Amos."

Later that afternoon, while Guy was napping, the same turn of the key woke him. He popped upright, as if escaping a dream. It was Joe the bailiff. "C'mon, Guy. We gotta get you transported. Judge Masterson is ready for jury selection. Doesn't want to waste any time. He already called your son."

Guy looked in horror. "But Amos. What about his case?"

Joe rubbed his keys. "Jury convicted him of everything. They were only out forty-five minutes. He's on the bus back to state prison. Judge is going to sentence him in two months. He said to say goodbye to you." His voice cracked. "Said you should listen for him playing that opera he promised."

Guy gripped Freedman's top bunk with both hands, and peered into the empty space above it. He felt a cold sweat. After a still moment, he gathered his documents, including his libretto of Puccini's *Turandot*, and went with Joe the bailiff.

Guy Bennett had just lost a dear friend, whose skin color was no longer relevant nor a prefix to who and what he was – a good man who, on his way to a ghastly place, took the time to say goodbye.

LIX.

❧❀❧

Country Kitchen Talk

On Win's advice, Edward chose to wait until after jury selection to visit Detective Meeker in Grafton. Win knew that Masterson always gave a full day break between jury selection and opening statements in order to gird the credibility of the process. The move was definitely a gamble, but as Win told Edward, even if he got a clean story from Meeker behind the backs of Straid and Kauftman, they would erase it if given enough time before testimony was taken. Edward had to strike quickly.

The jury selection process took longer than anyone had antici-pated. Juror after juror had either already formed an opinion about the case, had a relative in law enforcement, or a friend who was supposedly the victim of a crime. Judge Masterson dismissed many of them for cause, diligent to protect his record. Edward struggled to keep the few racial minorities in the pool, as it was his belief that only they would be willing to believe any evidence of prosecutorial mischief he presented. And he knew he needed only one vote of not guilty to hang the jury, at which point Straid might be more amenable to a guilty plea with a reduced sentence, which would allow his father to come home.

In the game of chess that ensued – he on one side and Straid and Masterson on the other – Edward was able to keep only one minority, a retired African American woman who used to work for the Internal Revenue Service. Straid did not use one of his discre-tionary peremptory challenges to remove her because he believed she was a law-and-order civil servant who would provide cover for the other minorities he dismissed for the very reason Edward wanted them; Edward kept her because he suspected her job was nothing more than a means of providing, and thought he saw in her eyes the pain that comes from being forced to grin and bear.

No sooner had the jury been chosen than the press that Judge Masterson banned from the courtroom started theorizing about the jurors' backgrounds and perspectives, referring to them by their court-assigned numbers indicating where they sat behind the wooden rail. Everyone on the outside worked feverishly to appear as though they were in the know.

Edward used Judge Masterson's customary break in the action to seek out Detective Meeker in Grafton. As he traveled the thruway north, the bustling city and its suburbs decompressed into the rest of America: small towns with odd names, farms, and closed factories. When he reached Albany, with its behemoth masonry struggling to draw attention, he crossed the spine of the state, the Hudson River, and continued east on Route 2.

After passing through the erstwhile industrial city of Troy, where only shadows were on the streets, the humanscape spread even thinner amidst the hills that separated New York from Massachusetts. It was becoming clear to Edward why Straid and Kauftman sent Meeker to this corner of New York. Though it was mere hours from where the trial was taking place, it was worlds away. Edward might as well have been back in Alabama, brushed with a coat of white New England paint. Shuttered one-story cottages on either side of the highway, which served as each town's main street. An occasional glimpse of a gurgling brook or nineteenth-century farmhouse. The only trace of community where news might percolate was in places like Brunswick's Elks Club, but the sign outside suggested that its congregation was more interested in its upcoming "Las Vegas Night" than it was in Guy's trial. Cropseyville was next, and then Grafton. Edward negotiated each turn with his head peering intently over the wheel, anxious to find the town's center.

After passing the abandoned Grafton Volunteer Fire Department, Edward eventually happened upon the town's small white wooden police department. An elderly woman sat at the front desk beside a rotary dial telephone; behind her was a police officer reclining, reading a newspaper. The woman squinted, and turned her ear toward Edward. "May I help you?"

Edward walked the creaking floors leading to the desk. "I'm looking for Detective Meeker. I understand he has been temporarily assigned here."

The woman looked back at the police officer, who continued his reading. She turned slowly to Edward, again positioning her ear for better reception. "What is it you need with Detective Meeker?"

Edward hurried for a lie. "I'm a relative of his in the area. So I thought I'd drop by to see him."

The old woman shuffled her feet to face the police officer in his chair. She waited for an answer.

He spoke as he read his paper. "He's down at The Country Kitchen." He turned the page. "He seems to have set up shop there."

The elderly woman spoke loudly as she pointed. "He's at The Country Kitchen. It's down the road a way. You can't miss it."

Edward gave a quick smile. "Thank you."

Edward found The Country Kitchen, a cozy red luncheonette with a wood-burning stove. Huddled around the counter were two elderly men, one with bright royal blue polyester pants, the other wearing a scratchy voice that sounded as if it was being amplified with an electronic aid. Royal Blue was in the middle of explaining to Scratchy Voice how the upcoming baseball game was going to turn out. "If Biggs is healthy, we're gonna whoop 'em."

Scratchy Voice mustered a response. "I don't know. He looked out of sorts last week. He might be still hurtin'."

Royal Blue yelled across to the corner table of the restaurant, where a younger man sat around his donut and coffee. "What about you, city boy? What do you think?"

The younger man, who Edward figured must be Detective Meeker, shrugged his shoulders. "Don't know. Tough to tell."

Royal Blue waved him off, his voice echoing in the small empty luncheonette. "City boys don't know nothin' about baseball. How's your special assignment goin' anyway? You gonna find those boys who been stealin' those tractors? I heard Jack Milloy lost his last night."

A middle-aged woman came limping out of the back with a pot

of coffee and a smile for the waiting Edward, but would not interrupt Royal Blue, who continued. "We ain't used to this kind of crime out here." He looked at Scratchy Voice. "The deal is you're supposed to keep it down there in the big city."

Scratchy Voice nodded his head. "That's right."

Pot of Coffee opened her smile to Edward. "What can I get for you, young man?"

Edward looked at the chalkboard menu, and spoke softly, so as not to provoke Royal Blue or draw his attention. "I'll have the turkey soup, and a Coke please."

As Edward walked to Meeker's table, Royal Blue stage whispered to Scratchy Voice. "He must be with city boy."

Scratchy Voice assented. "Yeah."

Edward offered his hand. "Detective Meeker. I'm Edward Bennett."

Meeker stopped chewing his donut. His mouth opened in confusion, spilling a few crumbs.

Edward smiled. "Yes, the same Bennett. I'm Guy's son. I'm representing him in the trial. I was wondering if I could speak to you for a few minutes."

Meeker didn't return the handshake. "Does the prosecutor know you're here?"

Edward danced around the question. "He told me I could talk to any of his people."

Meeker was not quick enough to pick up Edward's wordsmithing. He continued chewing, and offered Edward a seat. "So long as the prosecutor knows. Go ahead, shoot."

As was his style, Edward tried to loosen Meeker up a little with some personal questions that might also help his father's case. He looked out the window, and whispered, "So, how the hell did you wind up out here?"

Meeker chased his donut with a shot of coffee. In the background, Royal Blue and Scratchy Voice were still talking baseball. Meeker swallowed before he replied with official tone. "There's been a string of tractors disappearing up here. They called Detective Kauftman for help, and Kauftman sent me. It ain't so bad. It's quiet."

Edward thought of taking out his notepad, but thought again.

He didn't want to get Meeker's guard up. "Well, I'm sorry to bother you. But I really have to talk to everybody. You probably don't have much to add, but I just gotta check. I wouldn't have even come if I didn't have to meet one of my experts out here."

Taking Edward at his word, Meeker started to open up a little bit. "Sure, I understand. You have a job to do. And hey, it's your father."

Edward pulled out the thick police report, and started leafing through it. He corroborated some innocent facts with Meeker, to keep him relaxed. "Let's see, you went with Kauftman to the Petrozzinis' house, and took detail there. You delivered the steak knife in the bag to the forensic lab for printing."

"Yes, sir."

Edward kept reading. "And you were the only person who had custody of the knife from the time it left the premises until it arrived at the crime lab?"

"Absolutely."

The limping woman brought Edward his Coke and turkey soup. He looked up. "Thank you, ma'am." He scrolled the report with his finger as he continued to read. "And you were with Detective Kauftman when he interviewed the Northern Industries Board of Directors?"

Meeker clarified. "Yeah. We talked to each of them separately. That's the customary practice. What they said is right there in the report."

Edward shook his head. "Okay. And you also spoke to the neighbors and my sister, Lisa Marie?"

Meeker took another bite of his donut. "Yep. Nice girl, your sister. Considering all that happened."

Edward leafed further into the report. "Let's see. Who else?" I'm just making sure I spoke to everyone, then I can leave you alone. Like I said, I've got to get over to see my expert. He lives in Williamstown, Mass. Fancy place from what I hear." Edward stayed silent, hoping that Meeker would fill the gap.

"Well there was Thistledown, the homeless guy at the rail yards."

Edward was careful to remain nonchalant. "Yeah, where was that?"

Meeker pointed over the top of the police report that Edward was reading. "It should be right there, after the interview of your sister. Kauftman let me write it up myself. Here, you want me to show you?"

Edward shook his head. He knew there was absolutely no mention of Thistledown or an interview of him in the entire report. "You know, I've torn this thing apart and rearranged it so many times it's not worth it. I know I read it, but I don't even know if it's here." He shuffled through his papers, and pretended to search his knapsack. "Just remind me what you wrote."

Meeker sat up straight. "Sure." He tried to downplay the interview. "It wasn't much. He said he saw someone come in the rail yards that night. Then I think he said something about putting some stuff in the trunk."

Edward knew that Meeker was purposely not recalling the interview in detail. "That's right. He said he saw the guy put a shovel and some bags in the trunk, didn't he? And the car was a Mercedes."

"Yeah."

"The guy who put the shovel and bags in the trunk. Did Thistledown say it was it the same person as the guy waiting or someone else?"

"At first he said it was someone different, but then he started ranting about his dead daddy's train and I didn't know what to make of it." Meeker tensed up. "That's what he said, and that's what I wrote. You read it yourself."

Having snatched what he wanted, Edward tried to disarm the detective. He shook his head. "But that was in the newspapers. And Thistledown's been homeless for about twenty years, hasn't he?"

"Yeah, he's a little..." Meeker spun his finger next to his head to indicate that he thought Thistledown was mentally ill. "And he drinks a lot. I couldn't wait to finish the interview just so I didn't have to smell it anymore."

Edward eased his way out of the Thistledown issue. "And you wrote the report...?"

Meeker interrupted. "The day we took the statement. Detective Kauftman commented on how good a job I did."

"And the same with the forensic evidence deliveries and photos you took. Same day?"

Meeker nodded. "Yes, sir."

Edward looked at his watch. "Well, I better get going if I'm going to catch that expert." He took a folded piece of paper out of his pocket. "Oh, one more thing. You've probably seen one of these before. A subpoena. It's a formality. But, I have to do it. As you can tell, your testimony will be short. But I have to put everybody up there. I'll call you the night before to give you enough time to get down."

Meeker took the subpoena tentatively. "Sure, but if you don't mind me asking, what's your defense?"

Edward concluded the ruse. "Crime of passion. I just want to give my father his day in court. To give him the best defense he is entitled to. That's why I'm going to Williamstown, to talk to a psychologist."

Meeker took the subpoena and the lie. "I can understand that. Crime of passion is probably your best bet. Sorry I couldn't tell you more."

LX

Opening Statements

The People's Case

Opening statements went off as scheduled. The courtroom was packed with press and onlookers. There was actually a lottery each morning to determine who would be allowed inside, and trailers outside for reporters to transmit their stories. Win Gonzalez and Gabrielle DeFiore were among those in the courtroom.

Judge Masterson slammed his gavel. "Order, order." The buzz subsided for the main event. "Mr. Prosecutor, are you ready to proceed?"

Straid looked appropriately grim, buttoned his jacket, and walked to the jury box. "When is enough enough? How much does it take to fill one man's appetite? That is what you are going to ask yourself when you hear how Guy Bennett viciously murdered Vito and Lena Petrozzini. In all of my years as a prosecutor, I have never seen a crime so heinous."

Straid started walking the wooden railing of the jury box to address each juror individually. "You will hear how the defendant already had more than most of us could imagine. A big house in Whitebridge, a fancy car. He was the head of a giant publicly owned company. His son Albert, who confessed to helping him in the murder, was a United States Senator. But there was one problem. The business was suffering, and someone launched a bid to take over his company. And that someone was Bruno Petrozzini, Vito Petrozzini's estranged brother in Argentina, whom Vito Petrozzini had not seen in years. The defendant was in the middle of his worst nightmare. He was losing control."

He walked back along the railing. "Most of us probably would have retired at that point, to spend time with loved ones. The defendant's partner, Vito Petrozzini, suggested just that when the takeover bid was made. But the defendant wouldn't go for it. His greed and ego wouldn't allow it. Somehow, he hadn't had enough." Straid bulged his eyes. "He couldn't lose control."

Straid took a few steps back. "Unfortunately, the defendant found that even he did not have enough money to solve this problem. The asking price was too high. So he decided to eliminate the threat at its source. In his own sordid mind, he was convinced that Vito Petrozzini was the cause of the takeover bid, working with a brother whom he barely even knew on the other side of the world. Instead of believing Vito Petrozzini at his word when there was no indication otherwise, Guy Bennett assumed the role of judge, jury, and executioner. On the night of March 31, during an argument with Mr. Petrozzini at Mr. Petrozzini's home, he carried out his sentence. In the fight that ensued, he brutally stabbed Mr. Petrozzini twenty times, and his wife fifteen times more. All of this in the middle of eating a meal that Mrs. Petrozzini had cooked for him. What kind of animal, I ask you, behaves in such a wanton and savage way? One so calculating to know that he had to leave his fingerprints on the steak knife in order to corroborate his alibi that he was called away from dinner, but who also knew he needed to bury his blood-stained clothing. The problem is that he never thought the Petrozzinis' blood would leave traces on the shovel and bags that were the accessories for the attempted concealment of this heinous crime. That is why he did not bother to remove them from his trunk, where The People found them on the night of the murders."

He then turned and pointed to Edward. "Mr. Bennett will be represented by his son Edward, who is sitting next to him." He squinted for effect. "Because of the defendant's violent course of destruction, Mr. and Mrs. Petrozzini can no longer sit next to their son, or play with their grandchildren. The defense will try to poke holes in the facts. But he will provide no theory, no inkling, of the person who killed the Petrozzinis if Guy Bennett did not. It will make no sense. I ask you to use your common sense." He stepped up to the rail and gripped it with force. He looked at the lone Black juror, the former IRS agent. "Ladies and gentlemen, show all of the Guy Bennetts of the world that no matter how powerful they think they might be, the only real jury sits here, in this courtroom. Respect your oath, and right this bloody wrong. Show everyone that murder is still a crime that is punished in America." He pursed his lips. "Do it for Vito and Lena Petrozzini."

An awed silence filled the room.

Judge Masterson turned to Edward, who was scribbling notes on a pad. "Mr. Bennett." Edward continued to write. "Mr. Bennett, are you going to address the jury?"

Edward finished, then stood up. "Yes, sir." He corrected himself. "I mean Your Honor. You'll have to excuse me. I'm not quite as seasoned at this as Mr. Straid."

Edward turned to Win Gonzalez in the crowd, who gave the young lawyer a wink and a smile. Instead of going to the jury box, Edward stood by his father's side. "Ladies and gentlemen of the jury. In the course of this trial, you will be presented with truth and better truth. Your job is to seek the better truth." Edward banged his index finger on his notes. "For example, the Prosecutor talked about my father's house in Whitebridge. Yes, it is a large house, one that he worked hard for many years to earn. But it is more than that. It's a home. Where our family lived and breathed for one another. We had our disagreements, but Dad wouldn't let us leave until we patched things up. Because Dad always taught us that without family, a house is just that – a building made of concrete and wood. And the Petrozzinis were part of our family. My sister married their son. They were my godparents, and I miss them dearly. I hope that if any good comes out of this misdirected prosecution, it is that we get closer to finding out who the real killer is."

Edward stepped back to see, out of the corner of his eye, how the judge was studying the jury.

Edward pointed to his pad again. "Yes, my father did not want to give up his company to a takeover bid by Mr. Petrozzini's brother. Dad and Grandpa dreamed about the company. They worked day and night to make it a reality. They had employees who helped them and depended upon them. Many of them are still with the company. His desire to keep his company wasn't about money or greed. It was about maintaining a sense of purpose, and the relationships with those around him, including his partner, Vito Petrozzini. It was about a way of life for him and his employees that had nothing to do with money or power."

Edward looked back at Gonzalez, who nodded affirmatively. "Nor was it about losing control. But the prosecutor did have a point when he talked about that. You should keep in mind what lengths a man will go to in order to avoid losing control. Think about it every time you hear that the prosecution has disqualified a defendant's choice of counsel, overlooked an obvious lead, or shaded a fact to make it look incriminating when it's not." He paused. "Or kept a fact from your consideration because it hurts his case."

Judge Masterson gripped his gavel, and looked to Straid, expecting him to make an objection. Straid chose to remain silent, so as not to dignify Edward's suggestion.

Edward continued. "And yes, my brother was a United States Senator." He pointed to Straid. "He beat that man to get there, and that man has been bent on revenge ever since."

Straid had no choice but to object. He shot to his feet. "Objection, Your Honor."

Edward spoke through the objection still pointing at Straid. "So every time you have a question about the prosecution's case, consider the source."

Straid yelled louder. "Your Honor. May we approach the bench?"

"You may."

Straid tried to contain his rage. "Your Honor, I am not on trial in this case. Mr. Bennett is. Counsel's statements are irrelevant and prejudicial. They're grounds for a mistrial."

Edward cut in. "He made an issue of me at the end of his closing. Why can't I do the same?"

Masterson locked his jaw and addressed Edward. "Listen, young man. I don't know what you have in mind. But he's right. I'm surprised he didn't object earlier. Your father is the one on trial.

I am not going to grant a mistrial, but I am going to be watching you very closely. This is a court of law." He crossed his hands, and spoke slowly. "Stand back."

As Edward and Straid returned to their places, Judge Masterson extinguished the chatter of the crowd with his gavel, and gave the jury exactly what Edward wanted. "Ladies and gentlemen of the jury, you will disregard Mr. Bennett's last remarks about the Senate race between his brother and the prosecutor."

Edward smiled to himself. He knew that the instruction was tantamount to telling the jury not to think about pink elephants. The lost Senate race was now written all over Straid's face. Edward concluded, "The prosecutor is right. You are the only jury. Not him, not me." He glanced at Masterson to show that he would not be intimidated, and reinforce for the jury his underdog status. "Or anyone else." He moved his pad aside with one hand, and placed the other on his father's shoulder. "Show the world that in America, everyone is still entitled to a fair trial, by a jury of their peers. Do it for the Petrozzinis." He paused. "Do it for yourselves and for your children."

Joe the bailiff, who was standing between the prosecution and defense, glanced at Edward's pad at the edge of his table. He realized that Edward had not made any notes during Straid's opening, just wild movings of the pen. Joe pushed the pad back as if to keep it from falling, and when Edward looked up, smiled his knowledge of the ruse.

Straid shuttled his witnesses in one after another. They were well prepared, answering only what they were asked. He started with his pathologist, Dr. Francine Scarborough, who testified that based on the depth of the wounds, the knife used to inflict them was probably five inches long, consistent with the dimensions of the steak knife that bore Guy's fingerprints. She also opined how the broken vase and other scattered articles suggested a struggle between the assailant and victims that did not concern the taking of any household items, as none were missing. She had juror heads shaking swiftly in agreement when she described how the DNA lifted from the shovel and bags found in Guy's trunk matched the Petrozzinis'. With every breath and without ever accusing Guy directly, the attractive pathologist was saying that Guy Bennett was the perpetrator. The jury was getting its first impression, and Straid's stride knew it. Guy Bennett's fingerprints were all over the crime.

With S. Jackson Cudder at his side, Edward did his best to discredit Dr. Scarborough's story. Chewing tobacco while he sat, Cudder's presence alone unnerved his former colleague. Edward got the state's pathologist to admit that the five-inch wounds could have also been inflicted by a knife that was shorter or longer than the five-inch steak knife, and elicited her agreement that it was strange that the alleged murder instrument had such clear fingerprints while the broken items did not. She also made concessions about how the blood leading to Mrs. Petrozzini's body was more likely the result of her being dragged than a trail left behind during a desperate attempt to contact the police. But Edward knew that he and Cudder had nothing to contradict the DNA on the shovel and bags, and therefore did not question her on it. That issue would have to wait for Detective Meeker and Harold Thistledown. Edward had slowed the momentum of Straid's case, but by no means halted or misdirected it.

Straid then went to the Northern Industries Board of Directors. Covitt and Leach explained the corporate structure of Northern Industries, and the meaning and dynamics of the takeover bid launched by Bruno Petrozzini. He had both of them conclude by recounting the meeting at which Guy accused Vito of plotting with his brother Bruno, and threatened him. Guy's motive to kill filled the air.

But Straid wasn't satisfied. He wanted to suck the breath from any hint of competition in this contest. So he next brought Eleanor Whittlesby to the stand, to do little more than repeat the testimony of Covitt and Leach regarding the argument between Guy and Vito. It wasn't so much her content he was interested in, but her pedigree and grandmotherly reassurance that she lent being on his side. Straid treated her gingerly, walking her through her business achievements and legion of charitable activities.

The Prosecutor got what he wanted when Edward objected to the admissibility of Whittlesby's foundations and volunteer work. "Objection, Your Honor. Ms. Whittlesby's extracurriculars are irrelevant."

Masterson glared at Edward. "Objection sustained." He then looked at Whittlesby with an apologetic grin. "Technically, counsel is right. I might take objection to his characterization of your philanthropy as 'extracurriculars.' But, as an evidentiary matter, he is correct. Your charity, which I must say runs deeper than any I know, is not relevant to the murder charges against Mr. Bennett's father."

The exchange created the impression that only the son of a murderer would be so brazen as to object to the good works of an elderly woman. Win Gonzalez put his face in his hands in frustration. He saw the trap that Straid set, and there was nothing he could do to stop young Edward from walking into it.

Straid moved to the boardroom argument. "Ms. Whittlesby, were you at the Northern Industries Board of Directors meeting when it was revealed that the person who was sponsoring the takeover bid for the company was Bruno Petrozzini, the victim's brother?"

Whittlesby lifted her chin, the way she was taught at the all-girls boarding school of her youth. "Yes, I was."

He leaned against the wooden box in which she was sitting. "If you would, tell us in your own words, what happened. If you remember."

Whittlesby responded with the polite umbrage she and Straid had rehearsed. "Of course I remember, young man. I may be old, but I'm not senile."

During the laugh that Whittlesby got from the audience and jury, Straid followed on cue with a humble blush and a smile. "I never intended to suggest that you are, ma'am. Particularly, given your many successes. In your own words, please."

Whittlesby tilted her head. "Part of the reason I won't forget it is because of the intensity in Guy's eyes during the entire episode. When poor Vito tried to leave the room, Guy grabbed him by the wrist, and said…" She cleared her throat. "He said…well, I don't know if I can repeat in court what he said."

"You may, Ms. Whittlesby."

"Very well. Mr. Bennett said, 'if this is some sort of power play, you jealous bastard, I'll crush you.'"

Straid knew that if he asked Whittlesby what she thought Guy meant when he said "I'll crush you," Edward would make a sustainable objection because he was asking her to opine about Guy's state of mind. Instead, he elicited his desired response more subtly, so that any objection could be made only after the damage was done. The prosecutor raised his furry eyebrows quizzically. "He said 'I'll crush you?'"

Whittlesby looked at Straid, who had moved over to the jury box so that she would be responding to the jurors. "Yes, you know, as if he was threatening to kill Mr. Petrozzini."

Edward sprang to his feet. "Objection."

Masterson clamped his lips. "Sustained." The judge again looked warmly to Whittlesby, and did the prosecutor's work for him while purporting to protect the defendant. "Ms. Whittlesby, I would ask you to refrain from giving your opinion of what was going through Mr. Bennett's mind at the time." He looked to the jury. "The jury will disregard Ms. Whittlesby's last statement regarding what she thought Mr. Bennett meant when he said to Mr. Petrozzini, 'I will crush you.'"

Straid reapproached Whittlesby. "And what happened next, ma'am?"

Whittlesby looked disapprovingly at Guy. "I told Guy to let go of Mr. Petrozzini. That Mr. Petrozzini was an officer of the company, and should be treated accordingly." She paused, and when Straid nodded his head, she continued. "It was as if Guy wanted to eliminate him right there and then, and get rid of his problem."

Edward elected not to object to the last statement, when he clearly could have. Instead, he began his cross-examination by seizing upon it. "You said that it was as if my father wanted to, in your words, 'eliminate him right there and then, and get rid of the problem'?"

Whittlesby's jowls dropped as she spoke. "Yes, that is how it appeared to me."

"And the problem, according to you, was what my dad suspected was Mr. Petrozzini's role in the takeover bid for Northern Industries."

Whittlesby laughed nervously, trying to anticipate what was coming. "Yes."

Edward read from the police report. "And you told investigators that you had heard Mr. Petrozzini say that the board should not bother fighting the takeover. That they should just take the money and be happy?"

Whittlesby responded more quickly. "Yes."

"And Dad was also present when Mr. Petrozzini said this?"

Whittlesby puckered her lips like a schoolmarm. "Yes, counselor."

Edward scratched his head. "Well if my dad wanted to eliminate Mr. Petrozzini from this plot and all Mr. Petrozzini wanted to do was cash in on his shares, and Dad knew it, Dad could have simply bought the shares from Mr. Petrozzini, couldn't he?"

Whittlesby stuttered. "Yes, but..."

Edward smiled as he approached the jury. "A simple yes or no will do, Ms. Whittlesby." With his back to Whittlesby, Edward looked straight at the jury. "You don't like my father, do you, Ms. Whittlesby?"

Masterson gripped his gavel.

Whittlesby kept her composure. "What do you mean? We were professional colleagues. I served on his Board of Directors."

Edward looked at the African American former IRS agent. "Isn't it true that you once told the company's attorney, David Rothstein, who is Jewish, that you had no problem with *his* people? That they are some of the best accountants and lawyers you knew."

Whispers rose from the crowd.

Edward continued. "But that Italians like my father, who were barely off the boat, should not be running a publicly owned company. That they should stick to *La Cosa Nostra* and their pasta?"

Straid slammed his open palm against his table. "Objection, Your Honor. Any communication between Ms. Whittlesby and the company's attorney about the company is protected by the attorney-client privilege. Besides, it's completely irrelevant. It's just more mud slinging by Mr. Bennett."

Edward turned. "In order for the statement to be protected by the attorney-client privilege, it has to be made for the purpose of soliciting legal advice. Is the prosecutor suggesting that Ms. Whittlesby was looking for legal advice on how to be a bigot? If he is willing to stipulate that, I will move on."

Whittlesby looked at Edward in social horror as a buzz circled the courtroom, and Gabrielle DeFiore jotted her story.

Edward continued. "As for Mr. Straid's relevance argument, isn't it strange that the prosecution insisted that Win Gonzalez, the famous defense lawyer who was my father's original attorney, could not represent him because he and Mr. Rothstein, the nice Jewish lawyer to whom Ms. Whittlesby was conveying her bigotry, were from the same firm, and the prosecution was going to have Mr. Rothstein testify. Here we are at trial, and the prosecution has decided not to have Mr. Rothstein take the stand. Sounds like they know what he's going to say about this conversation with Ms. Whittlesby, they know that it's relevant, and they know that they don't want the jury to hear it."

The crowd's buzz graduated into chatter that Judge Masterson swatted dead with his gavel. "Order. Or-der." He signaled to both lawyers. "In my chambers." As soon as he left the bench, the crowd broke out again, feeding on what was clearly the sharpest moment of the trial thus far.

When Straid and Edward filtered into chambers, Masterson was standing by his bookshelves. Straid tried to start arguing, but Masterson held up his hand to stop him. He was infuriated. "We're off the record, so I'll be short. Mr. Bennett, if you plan to make this trial into a string of character assassinations, including my own, tell me now. Because I will assure you that the remainder of this case will be very short."

Edward tried to interrupt. "But Your Honor..."

Masterson yelled back. "But nothing. Don't speak unless I ask you to, young man." He pointed to a commission on his wall. "You see this. It's a letter asking me to serve on the select committee for revision of the state constitution. It's from Eleanor Whittlesby. She is also Chairperson of the Liberty and Conservation Foundations. You would have found that out if you didn't make an ass of yourself by objecting to the prosecutor's questioning of her. This woman is a pillar of our community. She is a personal friend of the last three Presidents of the United States." The judge's finger trembled as he pointed. "I will not allow you to try to drag her through the mud. Do you understand?"

Edward bit his lip. "Yes, Your Honor."

Judge Masterson looked at the Prosecutor, then back at Edward. "If you have any more questions for Ms. Whittlesby, proffer them now so that I can save us another trip back here."

Edward thought for a moment, and decided that strategically it was best to leave the jury as it was with Whittlesby, rather than allow her to rehabilitate herself with questions that Masterson would sanitize. If Straid wanted to address the issue on re-direct, all the better. "No, Your Honor, I have nothing more."

Judge Masterson looked at his watch. "Very well. It's time for a break. Mr. Bennett, I am not going to amplify your outbreak with an instruction. Ms. Whittlesby never responded, and never will. She is done." He looked at Straid. "Who do you have after the break?"

Straid shrugged. "I'm just going to wrap up with Detective Kauftman, then some miscellaneous matters. Shouldn't take an hour." He looked disgustedly at Edward. "Then the ball is in his court. Unless he would prefer to go directly to sentencing."

Masterson dusted his robe. "That will be enough. Fifteen minutes. Mr. Bennett, have your witnesses ready to go."

Edward tried to grab a coffee with Jackson Cudder and Win Gonzalez at the hallway kiosk. A reporter approached Edward with a tape recorder in hand. She widened her small eyes as much as possible. "Mr. Bennett, I'm Cynthia Rhoden from *The Herald*. Vito Petrozzini, Jr., was just quoted as saying that no matter what happens to your father, both of his parents are gone forever. What do you have to say about that?"

Edward looked to Gonzalez, who tilted his head to indicate that Edward should answer. Edward cleared his throat. "I share VJ's..." He stopped himself. "We all mourn the loss of Mr. and Mrs. Petrozzini."

Reporter Rhoden looked over her shoulder to see a pack of her cohorts approaching. She again stretched her eyes, as she thrust the recorder before Edward hurriedly. "Would you consider a plea of manslaughter for your father?"

The other reporters came clamoring with questions of their own.

A young man in bifocals called out. "Is it true you haven't spoken to your sister since the trial began?"

A redheaded woman waved to her cameraman as she competed for Edward's attention. "Mr. Bennett, are you willing to state for the record that Eleanor Whittlesby is a bigot?"

An older man with sharp eyebrows and a toupee yelled. "Mr. Bennett, your mother was seen yesterday with New York divorce attorney Samuel Silver. Is she considering divorcing your father after the trial is over?"

Edward held up both hands. "I told you all before. I'm not giving any statements to the press until the case is over. If you want a statement, go to the prosecutor. I'm sure he would love to talk to you, or at least direct you to where to pick up one of his leaks."

Edward, Win, and Dr. Cudder slipped into their attorney conference room off the hallway, the press shouting questions as they followed. Even after Edward closed the door of the conference room, reporters continued to pound on it from the other side, as if they were trying to escape a fire.

Edward shook his head. "I thought their job was to report news. Not to try to make it."

Win smiled as he put his hand on Edward's shoulder. "You're getting a crash course in the art of staving off the kill. You're doing a good job. As for the trial itself, I was a little worried about you after you objected to Whittlesby's charity. But you sure as hell bounced back with a vengeance." He jerked his head toward the door, which was still being scratched and gnawed by the white knuckles and hot breath of the press. "You've got them moving. They've already got your dad down to manslaughter. That's what you want. What they write will get back to the jury. It always does."

Edward ran his hand through his hair. "Win, all I've proven is that Straid wouldn't let you defend my dad and Eleanor Whittlesby is a crusty old WASP who thinks everyone else is visiting her country on a visa." He looked at Cudder, who was drinking a cup of black coffee. "I still haven't gotten the bloody shovel and bags out of my dad's trunk." Edward scratched his head. "And he still hasn't mentioned Albert's suicide note. I am not sure why. I would be all over it if I were him."

Win pointed his finger. "You can't think too much. You're right where you want to be – inside Straid's head. He never expected this kind of fight from you. Hit him with Detective Meeker first thing in the morning, and he won't know what to do. Call the guy now, and tell him to head down so that you minimize his chances of hooking up with Straid and Kauftman." Win looked at his watch. "I'll see you then. I gotta go."

Edward pleaded. "But, Win. Straid only has Kauftman left. Then I'm up." He looked again at Cudder, who was already spitting tobacco juice into his empty coffee cup. "He's the only witness I've got ready, but I have to save him for last. He brings it all together."

Win started to turn the knob on the door, which was now rattling from the push and pull of the press. "Keep Kauftman talking. He's just like Straid. He loves the sound of his own voice. Just keep bullshitting with him. Build him up if you have to. It will set him up for a bigger fall if Meeker comes clean." Win opened the door, and pushed his way through the crowd of reporters outside.

As Edward re-entered the courtroom, Gabrielle DeFiore greeted him with her seductive smile. "Somebody's nervous."

Edward grew defensive. "Who? What are you talking about?"

DeFiore went coy. "Relax. I didn't say it was you."

Edward shook his head, and marched into the courtroom.

When the trial resumed, Straid was crisp with Kauftman. While in chambers arguing over Whittlesby, Straid had seen in Edward's eyes that he was not ready to begin his case. The prosecutor barely waited for Kauftman to finish his responses before teeing him the next. The entire direct was forty-five minutes. When it was over, Edward looked at his watch. It was only 3:30. He had an hour and a half to kill with Kauftman if he was going to keep his plan in synch.

Edward went through the police report page by page with Kauftman, checking every fact and detail, including who was actually responsible for typing each report. With each question, the hefty and balding Kauftman addressed Edward as "sir," even though he despised him, regarding him as a silver-spooned brat.

Every time he grew anxious, he rubbed the fake gem that was glued to the center of his gold-plated tie clip. The only real intrigue came when Edward asked Kauftman how he discovered his brother's body and the note at his side.

Edward put on his glasses as he studied the report. "How did you come to discover...?" He did not realize how difficult it was going to be to utter the next words. He paused to regain his composure. "How did you come to discover my brother's body, detective?"

Kauftman rubbed his faux ruby. "Like I said. We received a phone call from a guy at the motel who said he heard some sounds, like a TV was left on for hours in room 17. So we went and checked it out, and found your brother and the note."

Edward took off his glasses. "But the caller never identified himself, did he?"

"No he did not, sir."

Edward rejoined. "And you never ascertained the caller's identity, did you?"

Kauftman cracked his knuckles. "No, because after we found the note and verified the handwriting, the case of your brother's suicide was closed."

Edward went back to his table, pulled two sheets of paper, and presented them to Kauftman. "Did you even bother to check who was staying in the adjacent rooms the day of the phone call? In rooms 16 or 18?"

Kauftman handed the papers back. "Says here they were vacant. But that doesn't negate the fact that..."

Edward took the invoices and brought them back to his table and smiled. "There's no question pending, detective." He took his glasses off, and held up the police report. "But your investigation did determine that the phone call came from a pay phone on one of the motel landings down the hall from where my brother was found, didn't it?"

The heavy detective took a deep breath, and pressed the fake gem on his tie clip. "Yes, sir."

Edward put the report down. "Kind of odd that someone who said he was staying in the room next to my brother would call you from a pay phone in the hallway. Don't you think?" Edward grabbed the motel invoices, and followed with another comment before Kauftman could answer. "But then again, we know that no one was in either of the rooms next to my brother's, don't we?"

The courtroom buzzed.

Edward continued, "Sounds to me like someone is lying."

Beet red, Kauftman looked at Straid, who stood and raised his hand. "Objection, Your Honor."

"Withdrawn." Edward looked at his watch, elated that it was about to sweep five. He held up another piece of paper. "One last question, Detective Kauftman. The People's witness list, S-5. This is a list of everyone you and your men spoke to during your investigation?"

Kauftman clenched his teeth. "Yes, sir. It is. What would you like to know about it?"

Edward was already collecting his belongings. "Nothing, sir. I just wanted to make sure it was complete. Thank you."

Masterson invoked his gavel. "Mr. Prosecutor, I believe that you said that Detective Kauftman was going to be your last witness."

Straid held his finger in the air. "I said there might be some miscellaneous matters. If you will just give us a minute." He placed his hand over the microphone at his table to confer with his co-counsel in whispers. Co-counsel was holding a single piece of paper.

"Mr. Prosecutor," called the judge. "We are all waiting, anxious to get home."

Straid yanked the piece of paper from co-counsel's hand, and stood up holding it. "Your Honor, we would like to introduce the suicide note of Albert Bennett."

Edward's stomach sank. He was hoping that he had avoided the note's deadly content implicating his father, which Straid had appeared to studiously avoid for reasons unbeknownst to Edward. "Objection, Your Honor. May we approach the bench."

"You may."

Edward spoke first. "Your Honor, the alleged suicide note of Mr. Bennett, insofar as it implicates my father, is rank hearsay. The witness is not here to be cross-examined. Extremely prejudicial."

Straid cocked his head back. "It is a dying declaration of a co-conspirator, made against his self-interest. Besides, Detective Kauftman already testified to the authenticity of the handwriting to show that Mr. Bennett killed himself. There was no objection from counsel. He has waived. All I want to do is complete the picture of this dying declaration, which is rife with indicia of authenticity and reliability."

Judge Masterson nodded to the prosecutor. "I personally was surprised that you were going to finish The People's case without it." He looked to Edward. "I will allow it."

Straid had Detective Kauftman read the suicide note in its entirety. The jury was riveted. There was not so much as a cough during his recitation.

When Kauftman was done, Judge Masterson reached for his gavel, then pulled back, folding his hands. "Very well. Nine o'clock tomorrow morning. Mr. Bennett, be ready to proceed."

LXI.

❦

Up in Flames

Edward called Meeker that evening, and as inconspicuously as possible told the detective he needed him to testify the next day. Edward explained to Meeker that if he put him on the stand first, the examination would probably be finished in fifteen minutes. Just routine questions, Edward assured the detective, to help him establish that there was no premeditation. The detective raised no questions.

Edward arrived at the courthouse early the next morning. He ordered a coffee as he grabbed a newspaper from the kiosk, anxious to see how the previous day's court proceedings had been reported. He never got to the story, which was the headline, because of another article that ran in the far left corner of the front page. "Harold Thistledown, Homeless Man Who Beat City Hall, Found Burnt to Death in Train Car."

The old man behind the counter handed Edward his coffee. "Would you like any milk or sugar, sir?"

Edward didn't even hear the question as he continued to read the story's opening paragraph: "Harold Thistledown, the homeless man who sued county authorities to establish his right to live in a deserted train car, was found burnt to death inside the car late last night. Police report that they found an empty bottle of vodka and cigarette ashes next to his body, leading them to believe that he fell asleep while still smoking the cigarette that later caused the fire."

The man behind the counter asked Edward again, "Hey, do you want any milk or sugar? If you don't, it'll be a buck twenty-five."

Edward spotted Straid and Kauftman coming down the hallway, with Detective Meeker between them. He walked quickly toward them, and stood in front of the trio so they could not pass. He stared Straid in the eye. "You killed him, you sonofabitch."

Straid laughed. "Perhaps you are mistaking me for your father. Because otherwise, I don't know what the hell you are talking about."

Edward slammed his rolled newspaper against Straid's chest. "You know exactly what I'm talking about, you bastard." He looked over at Meeker, who shied from making eye contact, and back at Straid. "You found out that I was going to have Meeker testify, and you and your sidekick, Detective Henchman, killed Thistledown." Edward squinted, and spoke in measured tones. "You really will do anything to pin this murder on my father, even if it means committing one yourself."

Straid took the newspaper out of Edward's hand that was still pressed against his chest. He read the first paragraph, and frowned. "Says here Detective Kauftman said that Thistledown burnt himself to death while drinking." He offered the paper back to Edward. "What can I say? We always told him to lay off the booze, that someday it would kill him. He should have listened." Straid turned to Meeker and Kauftman next to him. "What do you say, fellas? We still have five minutes. I'll buy you a cup of coffee." He grinned at Edward. "I'll see you inside, Counselor."

Edward tried again to make eye contact with Detective Meeker, but none was to be had. He was certain that Meeker had already spoken to Straid and Kauftman, and his story would never be the same.

As the crowd and judge filed into the courtroom, Edward sat dazed in his chair next to his father. Meeker had been flipped, and with Thistledown dead, there was no way to contradict him. Edward either had to forgo what he planned as his last best chance to save his father's life, or put Meeker on the stand at the risk of offending the judge and jury with a line of questioning that would fall on its face. Edward could not even consult with Win Gonzalez, because the famous defense attorney had not shown as promised. Edward had to make the biggest decision of his and his father's life. He had to make it alone.

Judge Masterson slammed his gavel. "Mr. Bennett, we are ready to proceed. You may call your first witness."

When Edward remained distant, the Judge called again. "Mr. Bennett, are your ready to call your first witness or do you rest?"

Edward stood without blinking.

Guy elbowed him from the side. "Edward."

Edward twitched from his trance. "Your Honor, the defense calls Detective Meeker to the stand."

Judge Masterson looked at a piece of paper in front of him. "You did not have Detective Meeker on your witness list." He looked to Straid for an objection. "The Prosecutor has had no time to prepare for this witness." He held up the paper and shook it. "That is why we require witness lists."

Straid stood up only halfway in his seat, keeping his hands on the chair's arms. "That's quite all right, Your Honor. The State has no objection." He smiled at the jury, "Our only interest is in the truth."

Meeker took the stand, and Edward approached him slowly. "Detective Meeker, I'll be as brief with you as possible. You were originally assigned to work on this case with Detective Kauftman, were you not?"

Meeker kept his hands folded on his lap. "Yes, sir."

Edward looked into Meeker's sleepless eyes. "And in that capacity, you studied the crime scene, and followed up on all leads, correct?"

Meeker stuttered. "Well..."

Edward picked up the tempo. "Well, if you didn't follow all leads, you wouldn't be doing your job, would you?"

Meeker's folded hands perspired as he looked over at Straid, and Straid nodded. "Well, yes."

For dramatic effect, Edward strode back to his table, and picked up his copy of the police report. "And one of those leads, as explained by my father to the police, was that he was at the county rail yards at the time of the murders, wasn't it?"

Meeker answered slowly. "I don't know if it's a lead. When you catch a guy, he says a lotta things because he is usually pretty nervous. They're not all leads." Meeker looked over again at Straid, who smiled approval. Jurors whispered to one another, and there was a light hum in the courtroom.

Angry at the effect of what he knew was a response scripted

by Straid for Meeker, Edward snapped a question. "Before coming here today, did you discuss your testimony with either the Prosecutor or Detective Kauftman?"

Meeker responded politely. "Yes, sir."

Edward hoped he might have hit an opening. "What did you discuss?"

"The Prosecutor told me to get up on the stand and tell the truth."

Disappointed and realizing he was losing ground quickly with this witness, Edward tried another tack. "Detective Meeker, do you have any children?"

"Yes, sir. I have three."

Edward got as close as he could to the detective, and stared into his sagging eyes. "And you realize of course, that lying in this courtroom is a crime for which you can be prosecuted?"

Meeker swallowed deeply, and pushed the words from his parched throat. "Yes, sir, I do."

Edward stayed to his fix. "Isn't it true, Detective Meeker, that you and Detective Kauftman checked out my dad's story at the rail yards by going there, and spoke to a Harold Thistledown, who burnt to death last night in his sleep?"

Masterson shot a glance over at the silent Straid, whose stare was busy with Meeker. The Detective unfolded his sweaty hands, and squeezed each of his knees before speaking. "I don't know what you're talking about." His voice split. "Sir."

Edward's words were heated. "I'm talking about what you told me at that little restaurant in Grafton, New York, the other day, the place where you were shipped before your investigation was completed."

This time, Meeker looked at Detective Kauftman, who was sitting beside Straid. He crossed his arms. "Yes, we spoke. There were other people in the restaurant who could tell you that. But we never said anything about no rail yards. I really don't know what you're talking about, sir." He paused. "I do remember you saying that your best defense was to prove your father committed a crime of passion."

Edward was stymied. He never thought his statement to Meeker, made to disarm the detective, would ever come back at him. It had, and it was devastating.

As Edward walked back to his table defeated, Meeker volunteered inexplicably. "And about Mr. Thistledown." The young detective's brow went heavy, and his chin tight, as all eyes were glued upon him. He shot a cool glance at Straid and Kauftman, and meted a pregnant pause. "I'm sorry to hear that he's dead."

Edward stood behind his table, with his fingertips grazing its top. He looked at Meeker, and saw genuine remorse in his beaten frame. "So am I."

When Edward sat down, the courtroom air weighed heavy with conviction. Everyone, including Edward and Guy, saw Meeker as credible and Edward as desperate. Edward had given back any points he had scored thus far, and then some. He had few if any opportunities remaining.

Joe the bailiff approached Edward's and Guy's table with a pitcher of water. Edward appreciated the small gesture in his time of despair. But as Joe laid the pitcher down, he toppled it over, causing water to spill on Edward's papers and lap. Joe immediately helped Edward salvage his work. "I'm sorry, Mr. Bennett, I didn't mean to..." As Joe helped Edward gather his papers, he stuck a leaf to the attorney's chest and muttered under his breath. "I don't know what the hell it means, but the guy in the back with the hat asked me to give it to you." Joe resumed his normal tone. "I'm sorry, Counselor, I'll go get some more towels."

Edward grabbed the paper, and looked to the back of the courtroom. A swarthy man dressed in a three-piece suit and mustache stood with a hat upon his head. The man touched the hat's front bent brim with his forefinger and thumb, and smiled at Edward to acknowledge the delivery. As Joe the bailiff continued to clean the spilled water, and the Judge allowed the crowd to engage in idle chatter, Edward read the piece of paper.

To Guy:

Words of solace to a man of The Book. The scripture according to Matthew chapter 21, verses 33–44.

Hear another parable. There was a landowner who planted a vineyard, put a hedge around it, dug a wine press in it, and built a tower. Then he leased it to tenants and went on a journey. When a vintage time drew near, he sent his servants to the tenants to obtain his produce. But the tenants seized the servants and one they beat, another they killed, and a third they stoned. Again he sent other servants, more numerous than the first ones, but they treated them in the same way.

The message spooked Edward, ushering a chill through his body. He looked to the back of the room for the sender, but he was already gone. Edward continued reading:

Finally, he sent his son to them, thinking, "They will respect my son." But when the tenants saw the son, they said to one another, "This is the heir. Come let us kill him and acquire his inheritance." They seized him, threw him out of the vineyard, and killed him.

His mind swirling with speculation, Edward finished:

"What will the owner of the vineyard do to those tenants when he comes?" They answered him, "He will put those wretched men to a wretched death and lease his vineyard to other tenants who will give him the produce at the proper times." Jesus said to them, 'Did you never read in the scriptures: The stone that the builders rejected has become the cornerstone; by the Lord this has been done, and it is wonderful in our eyes.'...The one who falls on this stone will be dashed to pieces; and it will crush anyone on whom it falls."

The note's farewell read, "You are the landlord whose tenants have betrayed you. Make not the same mistake in the house that you inhabit, and you will be saved."

Edward sat in shock, as Joe the bailiff finished his cleaning. Edward needed an adjournment to talk to his father about the message, and pursue any leads its cryptic words might provide. Given that it was Friday before a long weekend, with a judicial conference scheduled for Monday, Edward hoped the three days ahead would be enough time. But he had to get there. It was only 9:30 a.m. and Jackson Cudder had to be his last witness. He could risk putting his father on the stand when he didn't want to, but wanted to wait until he decoded the missive.

As Edward contemplated an excuse for an adjournment, an officer stormed through the courtroom doors. He approached the bench immediately to whisper something into Judge Masterson's ear. The judge thanked the officer, and administered his gavel. "Ladies and gentlemen. I ask you to remain calm. An officer just received an anonymous phone call that there is a bomb in the courthouse. Exit orderly from the rear." He looked to the attorneys. "Gentlemen, we are adjourned until Tuesday." He addressed the jury. "Thank you for your service, and enjoy your long weekend. In the meantime, remember, no discussion of the case."

As the crowd gathered in front of the courthouse, and the talking heads with their news cameras rolled the story of the bomb threat, Edward and his father stowed behind one of the court's tall concrete columns. The officers guarding Guy gave him privacy with his lawyer. Guy shook the piece of paper and whispered so as not to be overheard, "I have no idea what it means, Edward. Either someone is screwing with me, or wants to help. If the guy with the hat who sent this to you wants to help, he chose a weird way to do it." He gave the piece of paper back to Edward. "Go see Monsignor McNabb. Maybe he can help you figure it out."

Edward looked at Guy in disbelief. His patience had run out indulging his father's delusions. "Wake up, Dad. Monsignor McNabb acted as if he didn't even know us at Albert's funeral. He can't take any more of your money, so he won't give you any more time. I'll go up to the monastery and talk to Brother Anthony about it."

Guy exhaled a hard breath, responding to Edward's harsh but true words about Monsignor McNabb. "Whatever. Do whatever you have to, son. I trust you." Guy walked over to the officers to be escorted back to the jail. He smiled back at Edward. "Keep me posted."

LXII.

A Visit to the Monastery

Later on Friday, after reviewing his file exhaustively one more time to see if any of its details shed light on the biblical message, Edward went to find Brother Anthony at the monastery of the Benedictine Academy, where he had attended prep school. As he drove up its long driveway lined with deep crystal ponds and large green fields, Edward enjoyed a brief flashback to his days at the all-boys high school where he and then Novice Anthony had forged their friendship. When he walked up the hill into the cinder block church, its ceiling criss-crossed at wild angles with blue wooden beams, darkness and incense presided as the brothers sang their evening vespers:

> But I, when they were ill, put on sackcloth;
> and afflicted myself with fasting
> and poured forth prayers within my bosom.
> As though it were a friend of mine, or a brother,
> I went about;
> like one bewailing a mother, I was bowed
> down in mourning.

Edward sat in a back pew and continued to listen to the monks' slow tones:

> Yet when I stumbled they were glad and
> gathered together;
> they gathered together striking me unawares.
> They tore at me without ceasing;
> they put me to the test; they mocked me,
> gnashing their teeth at me.

The choir reached its strongest pitch at the end:

> Let all be put to shame and confounded
> who are glad at my misfortune.
> Let those be clothed with shame and disgrace
> who glory over me.
> But let those who shout for joy and be glad
> who favor my just cause;
> And may they ever say, "The Lord be glorified;
> he wills the prosperity of his servant!"
> Then my tongue shall recount your justice,
> your praise, all the day.

With these words, the monks dispersed and exited silently for their dinner.

Brother Anthony noticed Edward, and walked to him to break the pall. "Hey, buddy. How are you holding up?"

Edward put his hands on his knees and leaned back. "Geez, Anthony, those were some pretty vengeful thoughts. Maybe my dad and I feel like that, but you guys..."

Anthony looked at Edward straight. "Are just as human as you are. They are part of the cursing psalms. We sing them all the time. It's therapeutic." The friar put his hand on Edward's shoulder. "You surely didn't come here to talk about vespers. How's the trial going?"

Edward exhaled. "Not very well." He took the message out of his pocket, unfolded it, and handed it to Brother Anthony. "But we got this biblical message from somebody who seems like they want to help us. I can't figure it out. That's why I'm here."

Brother Anthony began reading. "Ah, The Parable of the Tenants." He spoke as he continued reading. "I've got to warn you, Edward. People who quote the bible to convey messages tend to be extreme, even megalomaniacal. They'll take things out of context, and make parallels that oftentimes only they can see." As he read deeper into the message, his speech slowed. It was obvious that the message struck a chord. "But if they're well read in the scripture and its meaning, there's usually some hint of what they're saying."

Edward quickened. "Give me the hint. What it is it?"

Anthony looked to the ceiling. "Well, scholars disagree on whether the allegory or images in this parable come from Jesus or church theology. Be that as it may, there are some definite messages on its face. The owner of the vineyard and tower is obviously the Lord, and the tenants who work it are his people, whose job it is to cultivate his produce, or his good works."

Nothing was yet registering in Edward's mind. "Yeah."

Anthony thrust his finger in the air. "But when the Lord leaves them to go on a journey, instead of yielding his fruit, they hoard it for themselves, denying God's prophets, or the servants, his produce when he sends them for it." He tapped the paper. "In your case, and this is only an educated guess, the kicker is the part about the owner's son. They killed him. If a Jewish proselyte died without an heir, the tenants would have final claim on it. In other words, if they kill the son while they're in the tower in the vineyard and there is no one to compete with, they get the whole thing. To me, that jumps out as a parallel to something your father has, that Albert stood to inherit unless he was killed. Now I don't know what the tower in the vineyard represents to your father."

Edward snapped his finger with revelation. "It's the business. The tower in the vineyard. That's the Northern Industries tower in New York. This is somehow linked to the takeover bid by Bruno Petrozzini to get the business and the tower. And killing Albert was part of the plan. I knew my brother wouldn't commit suicide." Edward looked quizzical. "But I am also an heir. So is Lisa Marie. That part wouldn't make sense unless we were killed."

"Like I said, you can't always take this stuff literally when people pretend to be God. Maybe the sender of the message, or the perpetrator, if you will, didn't see you as the real threat." Brother Anthony looked down at the note. "But the weird part is at the end where it says, 'You are the landlord whose tenants have betrayed you. Make not the same mistake in the house that you inhabit, and you will be saved.'" He pasted the note to his leg. "What he's obviously saying is that the parable applies to your father, and his tower in the vineyard. But by the same token, he seems to be making the same parallel to himself with respect to your father. That your father is in the writer's tower in the writer's vineyard. And that your father would be wise not to deny him what is rightfully his." Brother Anthony raised his eyebrows. "At least that is the writer's view."

Edward shook his head. "It's Bruno Petrozzini. He wants the business. I bet he was the guy who was wearing the hat."

"Who?"

Edward answered. "The guy who sent the message was in the courtroom wearing a hat. He had a mustache. He was there and then he wasn't. That must have been Bruno."

"Whatever he looks like, it also sounds like Bruno wants to talk to you. I would find this guy pronto."

Edward grabbed the note from Brother Anthony. "Thank you, Anthony. I can't tell you how much I appreciate this."

"Be careful, Edward. Those who see themselves as God can be dangerous."

Edward could not help but notice how Brother Anthony's arms were crossed comfortably beneath the scapular that was draped, front and back, over his shoulders and habit. The safe space that the monk appeared to be in agitated Edward. "I don't have time to be careful."

LXIII.

❦

Blind Pursuit

A Father's Son

Edward raced to the jail and retrieved from his father some of the corporate takeover papers that Guy had with him, looking for a number at La Compañía del Sur at which he could contact Bruno Petrozzini. Once he found it, he went and called it immediately so as not to miss the close of business.

The operator who answered the phone at La Compañía del Sur transferred the call to a silky female voice whose grammar was choppy. "Yes, I may help you?"

Edward's heart pounded. "This is Edward Bennett. I'm looking for Mr. Petrozzini."

Silky Voice responded slowly. "Mr. Petrozzini is no here now."

Edward spoke loudly, as if he were shouting across the ocean. "I know that he is not there, but I need to speak…"

Silky Voice continued as if she wasn't even listening to Edward. "Mr. Petrozzini was expecting you to call. He says if you like to speak to him, be in the lounge of the Alvear Palace in Buenos Aires, tomorrow morning at ten o'clock."

Edward tried to interrupt. "But…"

Silky Voice flowed on, making it apparent that she was to give Edward only a message, and not to respond to anything he might say. "Alvear Palace is at Avenida Alvear, número 1891, in Buenos Aires." The voice repeated itself. "Alvear Palace is at Avenida Alvear, número 1891, in Buenos Aires."

Edward fumbled for a pen and piece of paper on his night table, and noted the information. He tried to be heard one more time. "But ten tomorrow morning, I can't..."

Silky Voice proceeded undeterred. "There is ticket waiting for you at the counter of World Airlines, for nine o'clock this night. You must bring legal document. Power of Attorney for your father, so that you can sign papers for him." Silky Voice repeated, "You must bring legal document. Power of Attorney for your father, so that you can sign papers for him. Mr. Petrozzini look forward to seeing you."

Edward drafted a Power of Attorney, brought it to the jail for Guy to sign, and sped to the World Airlines counter at the airport to pick up his ticket. Though the flight was long, Bruno Petrozzini had eased Edward's burden by booking him first class. When Edward landed, he carried his knapsack over his shoulder into the brisk early morning Argentine air, and hailed himself a cab. "Alvear Palace in Buenos Aires." Edward hesitated. "*Por favor.*"

Edward's Spanish tongue disappeared when the cab driver started speaking to him in English. "What part of America you from?"

Edward took his bag off his shoulder. "How did you know I was American?"

The cabbie spoke as Argentine tango music pulsated from his radio. "You wear no jacket. Americans only ones who thinka when eet ees summa in America, ees summa everywhere. When you haf summa, we haf weenta. When you haf weenta, we haf summa. Ees weenta now in Argentina my frien'."

Edward defended himself. "I knew that. It's just that I was in a hurry when I was leaving. To answer your question, I'm from New York."

The cab driver smiled, and looked into his mirror to see Edward. "What kind of American you are in New York? Inglese, Irish, Germania?"

"I'm Italian."

The cab driver spoke in Italian. "Ah, *bene.* Me too. My grandfather come-a from Italia."

Edward was trying to concentrate on Bruno Petrozzini, but could not resist the allure of the driver's conversation. "My grandfather also came from Italy."

The cab driver lowered the volume on the tango music. "I guess da difference ees, you grandfatha go to Ameriga to stay foreva, and ee make a nice family. My grandfatha come to this place, Buenos Aires, to make some-a money and go back, but for somma reason, he never leave. We never leave. We never make-a rich like in Ameriga. We joost-a stay in da port. That's-a why we are da people of da port – *los porteños*." He turned the volume up again. "Maybe ees because of da tango music we never leave." He shot back his head. "Well, anyway. You Italiano rich guy in Ameriga, me Italiano *porteño* in Buenos Aires. 'ow you say? We are so close, yet so far."

The driver's words turned over in Edward's mind as he remained silent the rest of the trip. Chasing riches in America had already cost the Bennetts one life, Edward thought to himself. What price remained to be paid?

When the cab entered Buenos Aires proper, Edward admired the city's wide avenues, hemmed in by jacaranda trees and palace-like buildings from a bygone era. The driver made a sharp turn into what appeared to be a fashionable, more affluent section or suburb of the city, and then pulled to a stop in front of the Alvear Palace. Edward paid the driver the fare with a generous tip, and the porteno thanked him with a smile. "Gracias, Ameriga. I 'ope you find-a what-a you look for."

Edward was met by a bellhop with top hat and regal uniform, who welcomed him and offered to carry his knapsack for him. Edward chose to carry his bag himself, and walked through the large golden doors of the converted luxury apartment building, which were held open by two other men. As soon as Edward set foot in the hotel's magnificent corridor, he saw the man who had been in the courtroom with the hat. Edward went to him immediately. "Mr. Petrozzini."

The man's mustached upper lip replied stoically, with an English accent. "Did you bring the Power of Attorney for your father?"

The unshaven Edward reached into his knapsack and produced the Power of Attorney.

The man, dressed as smartly as he had been the day before in the courtroom, with the same hat, examined the document.

Edward was anxious. "Mr. Petrozzini, what is it that you want to tell me about my father's case?"

The man folded the document and put it in his jacket pocket. He signaled to another man, who exited immediately through the front doors of the Alvear Palace. He put on his leather gloves. "I am not Mr. Petrozzini, Mr. Bennett. My name is Gaspar Dos Santos. I work for Mr. Petrozzini. If you will come with me, he is waiting for us."

Gaspar Dos Santos brought Edward to a waiting limousine, inside of which the two sat across from one another. When the limousine started moving, Dos Santos gave Edward a blindfold. "We will need to take a bit of a ride to see Mr. Petrozzini. If you will just wear this." Dos Santos could see the fear in Edward's eyes. "Not to worry, Mr. Bennett. You're not being kidnapped. It's just that Mr. Petrozzini is a private man. And he likes to keep it that way. If you need anything during the trip – tea, a sandwich, a beer – just call it out. I will always be at your side and service. I was told to have you well rested and fresh by the time we arrive. Mr. Petrozzini will have lunch waiting for us."

Edward chose to ask for a beer, and to his surprise, received an amber brew in a frosted mug, just the way he liked to treat himself at home after a hard day in the office. He wondered whether it was just a coincidence, or a subtle warning from Bruno Petrozzini that he knew the young lawyer's every move. When the music of Edward's favorite rock artist, Elton John, filtered into the back chamber, Edward decided that he was best off staying quiet during the dark car ride.

After two hours' time, the car came to a stop, and Edward's door was opened for him. Gaspar Dos Santos got out of his seat, and called from above, outside the car door. "Come, Mr. Bennett, Mr. Petrozzini awaits us."

As he stepped out with the aid of a leather-gloved hand that he assumed was that of Dos Santos, Edward asked, "Can I take this blindfold off yet?"

Dos Santos responded dryly. "I will tell you when to do so. Be patient."

As Edward continued to be led by Dos Santos, all he could sense was the leather wrapped around his hand, the dry grass beneath his feet, and the sound of wind and crows whirling overhead. For the first time, Edward started fearing that he was in danger, in the middle of a sick intrigue that had him as its target and prize. Cutting through the brush, Edward could hear another pair of feet rustling toward him and Dos Santos with urgency.

Dos Santos gave the order to the new set of faceless feet that had now arrived. "Shoot him!"

Edward's body filled with shock. "No! No!"

As Edward screamed his last "no," the Faceless Feet shuffled, cocked, and blasted a high-powered rifle.

Edward stood pale, his blood stopped in his veins.

Dos Santos pulled him by the hand. "Come, Mr. Bennett. It was only a bear." He paused. "On second look, it was only a Spectacle Bear at that. You don't have them in North America. They have white rings around their eyes when you can get close enough to see them. It's a sign that they're friendly. It's too bad. The ol' chap wouldn't really have been dangerous at all. He eats mostly fruit. Not much interested in human flesh. But we can't afford to take any chances. Mr. Petrozzini is waiting."

The trembling Edward was led onto an asphalt area, and up a short flight of steps. When he heard a plane's propeller sound, he realized that his trip was not over, but instead had entered its second phase. When he sat with his heart thumping, he asked for another beer, which was served again in a frosted mug.

Once the plane landed, and Edward exited by Dos Santos' leather hand, the air was colder and thinner, pelting his face with small chunks of ice as it whistled by. Edward surmised that he must be somewhere in the Andes Mountains. Dos Santos put a lush fur parka around Edward's shoulders, and led him up a winding hill into a lair. The cavernous foyer echoed with the barking of large-bellied dogs. Dos Santos brought Edward down a long hall, and into a room. He closed the thick wooden doors behind him. "You may remove the blindfold. Mr. Petrozzini will be with you momentarily."

While he waited, Edward studied the large windowless room, which abounded with masculine force. Its chestnut walls joined with thick timber beams cutting across a white stucco ceiling; at the center hung a Castilian-style wrought iron chandelier. Beneath the steel light lay a centuries-old hand-carved wooden table that could seat twelve comfortably, all of whom would be warmed by the flames from the oversized fireplace behind them. Above the fire's mantle appeared the only chink in the hunting room's armor – a large oil painting of a beautiful young woman, her dark-as-night curly locks flowing voluminously upon her shoulders.

Edward snooped further, desperately seeking any clue of who Bruno Petrozzini was, and what he wanted from the Bennett family. There was a cigar box on top of the mantle, which Edward opened to find filled with Churchill-sized Romeo y Julieta cigars from Havana, Cuba, with a handwritten note – *"Amigos para siempre –* Fidel." Edward's basic Spanish told him that this gift was personally delivered from the longtime dictator of Cuba, Fidel Castro, who seemed to consider himself a friend of Bruno Petrozzini.

Next to the cigar box rested a stack of newspapers. Edward grabbed the issue at the top. Instead of finding an international gazette or business journal that he expected, he read the headline indicating that it was the current day's edition of *The Daily*, the newspaper subscribed to by Edward and his family. His hands trembled. He opened it to find underlined in red pen excerpts from Gabrielle DeFiore's daily coverage of his father's trial. Edward checked the others in the pile to find the same, dating back to the day the trial began.

"According to Gabrielle DeFiore, your father's trial is not going so well," uttered a baritone voice from the doorway to the room.

Edward threw down the newspaper hurriedly and turned. There in the frame stood an aged man whose sharp peasant features had been groomed regal: he was of average height made taller by a muscularity pared down to negotiating proportions; his surging eyes and high cheek bones were restrained by their intimacy with money and power; and his thick black hair and eyebrows were softened by the grays of time, pain, and wisdom. His left hand, barren of wedding band or mark where it may have once been worn, was wrapped around a glass of scotch, his right busy with the Romeo y Julieta missing from the box sent by his friend Fidel. He was cloaked in a silk smoking jacket and ascot, with Gaspar Dos Santos and his St. Bernard dogs obediently at his side. He entered with his troop; soon after them followed a maid with silver servings of fettuccine carbonara and goblets of wine.

Rather than going to the head of the table, Bruno Petrozzini assumed the place directly in front of where Edward was standing, leaving Edward no choice but to sit with his back to the roaring fire. "You must be hungry, young man. A long trial, and an even longer trip."

As Edward gawked at the maid serving him his favorite dish of fettuccine carbonara, Petrozzini snapped his fingers. "Oh, yes. How could I forget? You like yours with extra pecorino cheese." He turned to the maid in fluent Spanish. "*Más queso pecorino, por favor.*"

Edward looked up, his eyes charging at Petrozzini. "What the hell is going on? First the beer in the frosted mugs, then the Elton John music." He pointed to his bowl. "Now this. I don't know you from the abominable snowman, but you somehow read my newspaper halfway across the world when I do, keep track of my trial, and know that I like extra pecorino cheese on my fettuccine carbonara. Maybe it's the jet lag, or the goddamn bullet that whistled by my ear while I was blindfolded, but I think I deserve some answers."

Petrozzini drew from his chocolate-color wrapped Romeo y Julieta. "I'm already seeing the passion that makes you a great American trial attorney." He exhaled his smoke. "Gaspar, whom you have had the pleasure of meeting, is well trained. He is graduated from the London School of Economics and Oxford. His job is information, and I pay him well for it."

Edward began to feel the heat build from behind. "I don't care if he is Sherlock Holmes. He is getting his information from someone, and that someone has told him when to buy and sell Northern Industries stocks, and I have a feeling that you, Gaspar, and that someone know who murdered the Petrozzinis."

Petrozzini looked up at Gaspar, who was standing behind him. Dos Santos unzipped his black leather folder, and pulled out ten sets of papers that he laid in front of Edward, offering Edward a pen for signing.

Petrozzini put down his cigar. "I will give you the answers that you wish. But first, you must sign these papers transferring your father's stock in Northern Industries."

Edward stared steely. "I am not about to reward you for framing my father." He raised his voice. "I am not signing until I have my answers."

Petrozzini stood up and squinted, and spoke just above a whisper. "That's a shame. I thought we could trust one another." He bit his lower lip. "I was hoping your father would trust me." Petrozzini turned to exit the room. "Well, enjoy your meal. Gaspar will get you back to the airport for the next flight to New York."

Edward stood and shouted at Petrozzini's back. "My father is sitting in a prison cell, waiting to rot away because of you. Why the hell should he trust you?"

Petrozzini turned, while the polar winds outside surged against the room's walls. A flame crackled loudly from the fireplace, beneath the oil painting of the woman with the black locks. "Because I am Guy's brother." Without moving an inch of his body, he continued. "I am your father's father's son." He looked at the oil above Edward's head. "I would never do anything to hurt my brother."

Edward remained tall, while his body trembled within. "What are you talking about?"

Petrozzini kept his distance, pointing to the painting above the fire. "That woman is my mother, Lucia. She and your grandfather Dante were young lovers in America when Dante first arrived. From what I can tell, I was conceived at a prize fight in Jersey City in July of 1921, right around the time of American Independence Day."

Edward shook his head incredulously. "That cannot be. My grandfather would not have left her and you to fend for yourselves."

Petrozzini returned to his seat at the table. "I am not saying that he did." He gripped the backing of his chair, and gazed admiringly at the portrait. "My mother never told him. After the prize fight, your grandfather learned that his little sister in Italy had died. He hid from everyone, including my mother, who kept writing to him. He did not answer her letters." Petrozzini paused, biting his upper lip. "She made a personal plea to Dante to marry her without letting on about me. When he refused, she and her family returned to

Italy to hide their embarrassment." He remained staring; revisiting his dark beginning shrank him.

Petrozzini was snapped out of the stupor by the second crackling of the flames from the hearth beneath his mother's bust. "Fortunately, your grandfather's friend Adamo also loved Mother, and followed her back to Italy to marry her. He was not a strong man like Dante." He looked down into the seat of the chair he was holding. "Then again, maybe he was stronger than us all. "I loved..." He stopped speaking. He released the chair with one hand, and clenched his fist tightly. "He was special to me. I would never have done anything to end his other son's life." He pounded the chair. "The life of my other brother, Vito."

Edward suppressed his own emotions to test the veracity of what Petrozzini was saying. "Are you saying that my grandfather never knew that you were his son?"

"My mother eventually told him, but swore him to secrecy. She told him that what was done was done, and your grandfather, my real father, owed his friend Adamo a debt. That is why Dante insisted to your father that Vito be his partner in business. Dante was paying back his debt to Adamo. Adamo took care of me, and it was Dante's responsibility to take care of Vito."

Satisfied that he was hearing truth being spoken, and feeling its tremendous weight, Edward sat down. "But what about you, how were you to be taken care of?"

Bruno sat back in his seat, and drew from the cigar he had left behind. "I would accept nothing from no one, particularly your grandfather. I struck out on my own, the way he did. My mother wanted me to go to America to be part of what Dante and your father were doing. I didn't want anything from Dante, and your father meant nothing to me – at least not then. I wanted to be greater than Dante – larger in every respect. The acquisition of money and influence became my therapy. That is why I bought your grandfather's family vineyard in Aquino from his brother, Father Francesco." Bruno dug deeply into his cleft chin with his forefinger, and grew wistful. "An incredibly spiritual man." He smiled tenderly. "Truly a man of The Book, your great-uncle and my uncle, Francesco."

Edward paused to capture the thought that was triggered, then reached into his pocket for Bruno Petrozzini's scriptural message. He laid it flat on the table. "You bought the family vineyard in Aquino. I guess that's the vineyard in the Parable of the Tenants."

"Yes it is. I am the first son of the landlord – your grandfather." He closed his eyes in anguish. "I will not be denied my legacy."

"But Dad is the one..." Edward started to offer respectfully.

Bruno interrupted immediately. "If you had read the documents that I offered for your signing, you would have seen that I am not seeking to take your father's vineyard and tower away from him, but merely to share them. In exchange for half of his shares, I will pay him cash and fifty percent interest in the vineyard in Aquino."

While his mind swirled, Edward pretended to read the documents, so that he might gather his thoughts.

Bruno quoted the parable. "'He will put those wretched men to a wretched death and lease his vineyard to other tenants who will give him the produce at the proper times.'" He studied his cigar's golden ring. "I was the first-born son. Northern Industries would have been mine. I didn't want it while Dante was alive, but now I do – alongside my brother." He looked back at Edward. "All that I am now asking is that my brother agree to become a partner in what belongs to me, which I will otherwise acquire if he does not consent." Bruno blew another cloud of smoke. "I could have had it already. Those people your father calls his Board of Directors folded like a chair, and served up control on the company's finest silver."

"So why didn't you take it already?"

"I wanted to work the vineyard and the tower together with my brothers. I wanted them to understand. But then it went wrong." He halted. His eyes glazed. "I am willing to pay more than a fair market price."

Feeling that Bruno's thinking was not altogether linear, but anxious to do what he could to save his father, Edward began signing the papers. "Well that's fine, but in order for you to be Dad's partner, we have to get him out of jail. So why don't you now tell me who the wretched tenant in the tower is?" He collected the signed papers and handed them to Bruno. "Who has been giving you information?" He folded his hands on the table, and spoke slowly. "Who killed the Petrozzinis?" With Bruno sitting attentively, Edward finished. "Who framed my father?"

The fire from Lucia's hearth crackled a third time. "Vito Petrozzini, Junior." He squeezed his hands together in anguish. "The Petrozzinis' son. Your sister's husband." The fire reflected off Bruno's eyes. "I am sorry to say, I believe VJ is also the one who killed your brother Albert." He slammed his fist against the table, closing his eyes as he did so.

Edward's voice shook. "How?"

Petrozzini covered his face with his green-veined right hand, and spoke into it in grief. "Vito, my brother, sealed his fate the day he told his son about me."

Edward's heart beat into his throat. "Tell me, how did he kill my brother?"

Petrozzini now spoke into both his hands, which covered his face. "Explain, Gaspar."

Gaspar Dos Santos stood with perfect posture, his hands behind his back. "Very well, sir." He began lecturing Edward. "Mr. Vito Petrozzini, Junior, first made contact with La Compañía del Sur over a year ago, stating that he had information that could be very valuable to Master Bruno. I put him in direct contact with Master Bruno, which is something I rarely do." Dos Santos looked down at Bruno. "Master Bruno selects the people with whom he would like to speak, and not vice versa."

Edward rubbed his hands. "What did he say? What did he want?"

Dos Santos nodded his head and continued. "He said that Mr. Bennett, your father, had been holding him back. That he had big dreams for Northern Industries that his own father did not have the courage to pursue with your father. His chief complaint was that your father was standing in his way. It is fair to say in retrospect that he at once envied and loathed your father, because he had a boldness and keenness that VJ admired, but never accepted VJ as a colleague. As for your brother Albert, VJ downright despised him. He thought he was an arrogant chap. VJ always felt that your father and Albert did not hold him in high enough regard to marry your sister, that he was not worthy. For that matter, he felt that his own parents did not have much confidence in him. In retrospect, it appears to have built a rage inside of him."

He looked at his boss Bruno, who remained sitting with his head in his hands, and back at Edward. "Returning to the sequence of events, VJ told Master Bruno that by working together, they could teach your family a profound lesson, and at the same time, he and Master Bruno would get what was theirs. The Petrozzini brothers would run Northern Industries, and when they retired in the near future, VJ would be the sole heir."

Edward extended an open hand toward Bruno Petrozzini. "How the hell did you trust him?"

Bruno slid his hands up his face and over the top of his head, and looked up at his white stucco ceiling. Edward had asked him a question that he had obviously asked himself a thousand times, and had not yet answered. The frigid winds from outside continued to beat against the room.

Dos Santos filled in for his struggling *patrón*. "He didn't trust VJ at first. Master Bruno is much too wise for that. He first asked young VJ to show that he had access to real corporate information about Northern Industries. VJ conveyed the information to me, such as projected earnings and losses that were not yet publicly known, and I forwarded the information to Leo Wong, our stockbroker. Leo Wong did quite well for us based on VJ's information."

Edward interrupted with a snicker, "You mean inside information."

Dos Santos tilted his head politely. "Depending on your market school of thought. You Americans consider it inside information and criminal. We prefer to think of it as complete or full information that makes for a pure or perfect market."

Edward blew a hard breath. "Whatever. You stole information and you know it. We're not here to argue economics."

"Very well." Dos Santos continued. "Once Master Bruno was satisfied with VJ's position, he asked him his plan. VJ suggested a simple hostile takeover by La Compañía del Sur, the deal being that once the guard changed, Master Bruno would invite VJ and his father back into the company, without any sort of buy-in. He even went so far as to line up the financial backing of your brother Albert's father-in-law, Giles Kirby. He apparently knew of the problems your brother was having with his wife Victoria, and worked with Victoria to have Giles Kirby's investment bank, Webb Investments, offer Master Bruno favorable terms." Dos Santos tweaked his moustache and held up the share transfer papers that Edward had signed. "Master Bruno never let VJ know that he was going to give back shares to your father, making the three brothers truly equal partners. Master Bruno always drives the final details of all of his deals, and does so at the last moment."

Bruno looked down from the ceiling, and spoke for the first time since Gaspar Dos Santos began his discourse. The fire from the hearth beneath the portrait of Lucia filled his eyes. "VJ tapped the rejection in all of us – me, him, and Albert's wife. He outsmarted me. It was as if he knew that I would ultimately want to work with my brothers rather than him, so he eliminated them. For the first time in my life, I underestimated another man's avarice, and because of my mistake, I cost myself and your family dearly. You and I lost a brother." His eyes dropped. "My only desire was to work with my brothers in the family vineyard, Northern Industries, before I left this life, but had not the courage or confidence to ask them myself. Instead, I tried to speak to them with the force of the only language I know – money."

Edward bit his lip, speechless.

Bruno rolled one set of the share transfer papers, and clenched them in his right hand. He got up from his seat and walked toward the wall that separated him from the gusting winds. He stared at the wall.

Edward continued to search for the answers he needed for trial Monday morning. "I need to know. How can you be certain that VJ killed his parents and my brother?"

Bruno stayed trained on the wall, as far as he could be from his mother's picture and still be in the same room, with his back to her. He struck the wall with his deal-filled fist. "Gaspar will go fetch the evidence, and accompany you back to the trial to testify."

Gaspar went to the doorway, signaling to Edward that it was time to leave. Edward collected his papers and walked to the exit without saying a word.

As Edward and Gaspar departed, Bruno called out from his isolated spot against the wall. "Tell my brother that I am sorry."

LXIV.

❧

A Hostile Witness

B ack in the courtroom Tuesday morning, the usual horde gathered. At Edward's request, Joe the bailiff secured a seat for Gaspar Dos Santos, directly behind Edward's table.

Judge Masterson slammed his heirloom gavel. "Mr. Bennett. Will you be calling any witnesses?"

Edward stood and looked back at Win Gonzalez, who gave him a wink. He addressed the Court. "Your Honor, the defense calls to the stand Mr. Vito Petrozzini, Junior."

The spectators buzzed, prompting Judge Masterson to slam his gavel again. "Mr. Bennett. Mr. Petrozzini was not on your witness list, was he? Haven't we been down this road before?"

Edward swallowed. "No, Your Honor. Because Mr. Petrozzini is on The People's list, this cannot represent an unfair surprise. I would just like to question Mr. Petrozzini on the statement he gave to the police." Edward looked at Straid. "As The People themselves stated, with respect to Detective Meeker, our only interest is in the truth."

Masterson glared at Win Gonzalez, whom he had by now surmised was Edward's private co-counsel. "Very well, if the prosecutor does not object."

Straid stood tentatively. "He is on our list, Your Honor. I'll reserve objection until I hear the questioning."

Judge Masterson pointed to VJ. "Mr. Petrozzini, if you will take the stand to answer Mr. Bennett's questions. I promise you it will be brief."

As VJ got up from beside his wife, Edward and his sister exchanged a cold look. Once the witness took the stand and was sworn in, Edward recessed from his table to lean against the railing behind it. Gaspar Dos Santos was sitting to Edward's rear left, on the other side of the rail, in full view for VJ. "Mr. Petrozzini, you told the police that on the day of the murders you were on business in Chile for Northern Industries. Is that true?"

VJ's body warmed as he stared at Gaspar Dos Santos.

Edward waved. "Over here, Mr. Petrozzini."

VJ responded slowly. "Yes."

Edward grabbed a partially burnt passport off his table, handed copies to Straid and the Judge, and approached VJ. He flashed the passport in VJ's face. "But this is your passport, isn't it?"

"I guess," VJ responded slowly, touching its blackened edges.

"According to this passport, you flew out of Chile on the afternoon of March 30, arrived in New York on the morning of March 31 and went back to Argentina that night. Your arrival in Argentina on April 1 is the last entry in this passport. According to the police report, you flew home from Argentina on April 2."

"You are correct," Petrozzini shot back.

"Do you mind explaining to me your travels from March 30 through April 2?"

The witness looked up at the ceiling while drawing a breath, then back at Edward. He exhaled slowly. "Sure. Professor Pym and I had taken a business trip to Chile on March 29. I decided on March 30 that I wanted to get home as soon as possible. I got a direct flight. But on the way back, because it was last minute, the only flight I could get to Chile was with a stop in Argentina."

Edward was surprised at how relaxed and fluent VJ was in explaining that he was in New York on the day of his parents' murders. It appeared as though he was ready to confess. "And why did you want to get home on March 31, as 'soon as possible' as you put it?"

"I am embarrassed to say," VJ raised his eyebrows.

"You must give an answer," Edward's adrenaline pumped.

"I was suspicious that my wife – your sister – was having an affair."

The gallery murmured.

"When she saw me off at the airport on March 29, she told me she was pregnant and she was going to take a few days off while I was away, to get ready. She never takes off for anything, and she had only just learned that she was pregnant. She had months to get ready. That had my head spinning. I came home to follow her at a time when she thought I would be away."

Edward stepped back, his voice cracking. "But she had just told you she was pregnant!"

"I didn't think the child was mine."

"Dear God," a female voice from the gallery cried out.

"You didn't think the child was yours?" Edward stammered.

VJ looked away. "Like I said. This is embarrassing. I had problems."

"What kind of problems?"

"Performing at night with my wife." He looked at Lisa Marie, whose mouth was in her hands, above her pregnant womb. "You can ask her yourself. I thought it was not likely that I was the father."

Edward raced back to his courtroom table, picked up a document, and studied it as he asked the next question. He flapped the document in the air to straighten it before his eyes. "Where did you follow her on March 31?"

"I believe it was the grocery store, then her friend Jenny's, to the post office, and back to the house."

Edward laid the statement down. "Hmm." He tapped his table repeatedly with his fingertips. "I can see you read your wife's witness statement carefully, perhaps memorized it, because that is exactly what she said."

"Where is this going, Your Honor?" piped Straid. "Mr. Bennett is badgering the witness over clearly personal matters."

Frustrated, Edward looked at Win Gonzalez in the crowd.

Gonzalez nodded, and pointed to the judge.

Edward proceeded to exploit Straid's objection. "Your Honor, at the very least Mr. Petrozzini lied to the police when he told them he was not in New York on the day the Petrozzinis were murdered. And I will be seeking a "False in One False in All" instruction to the jury, allowing them to conclude that if Mr. Petrozzini..."

"Objection!"

Edward raced to finish his sentence. "...if he lied to the police about this, he is lying about everything."

"Objection! Request for a mistrial," Straid threw his pen to the table.

Judge Masterson drew a deep breath. "Mr. Bennett, you know that you should not have made a comment about the jury instructions prior to the close of the case."

Straid sat, easing back into his chair.

"But it is not grounds for a mistrial." Judge Masterson turned to the jury. "You will disregard Mr. Bennett's statement about a potential jury instruction." He pivoted back to Edward. "You may continue, Mr. Bennett. But one more slip like that, and I will declare a mistrial."

Edward made a request. "Permission to treat the witness as hostile, Your Honor."

The judge stared expressionless at Straid. "Granted." He turned to Edward with the same stoic look. "But I am watching you."

Edward returned to VJ. "Why did you lie to the police?"

The skin on VJ's nose bunched. "I did not want to embarrass your sister. My suspicions about her were wrong."

"You don't seem surprised that I have your passport," said Edward, leafing through it.

"I have no idea how you found it."

He turned to face Gaspar Dos Santos, and pointed at him, "Would it surprise you if I told you that a man named Mr. Gaspar Dos Santos gave it to me?"

VJ looked directly at the jury. "Nothing would surprise me after your father murdered my parents."

Edward leaned on the box in which VJ sat, extending his jaw at the witness, while the witness looked intently away. "You know Gaspar Dos Santos, don't you?"

"He works for my Uncle Bruno in Argentina. As you know, Bruno Petrozzini is my father's brother." The left side of his upper lip rose. "What you don't know is that my Uncle Bruno is also your Uncle Bruno. Your grandfather had him out of wedlock with my grandmother."

While the crowd moaned and the judge slammed his gavel,

Edward looked at Win Gonzalez, who mouthed to Edward, "Move to strike as non-responsive."

Edward shook off Gonzalez's advice. He turned to VJ. "I did know about my grandfather and our Uncle Bruno. Uncle Bruno told me himself. He appears to have been very hurt by the whole affair. Very emotional. Some might say vulnerable to being manipulated. Wouldn't you agree?"

"If you say so," replied VJ, his upper lip straightened and stiff.

"You are the one who brought up the issue."

VJ stayed silent.

Straid rose. "An interesting conversation between Mr. Bennett and Mr. Petrozzini on shared lineage, Your Honor, but can we move on?"

"Move on, Mr. Bennett."

"So getting back to Mr. Dos Santos, when did you last see him?"

"I met him while visiting my uncle. I was with him and Uncle Bruno on April 1 in Argentina. When I landed there, I learned that my parents were dead. I told Uncle Bruno about the murders and that I had lost my passport. Uncle Bruno helped get me a new one."

"More facts that you left out of your statement to the police."

"He and my father had been estranged for years. I wanted to let him decide how and when he wanted to reenter our family's life."

"'Estranged' is a pretty big word for you, VJ. I didn't think you had it in you. Then again, you are probably just repeating something that you heard someone else say in this case."

VJ snapped his head back at Edward. "You and your brother Albert always thought you were better than me. Smarter than me. Arrogant spoiled brats."

"Let's leave our personal relationship aside," responded Edward coolly, sensing that VJ was starting to break. "You talked to Bruno Petrozzini about Northern Industries, didn't you?"

"You say that you knew Bruno Petrozzini is our uncle, counselor, yet you can't seem to bring yourself to call him 'Uncle Bruno.'"

Edward thought about making a motion to strike the witness's testimony as non-responsive, but decided against it. He knew that VJ was right, and did not want to go down a path that might cause him to lose his cool. VJ had become much more formidable an opponent than he had anticipated. "Answer my question. You talked to Bruno Petrozzini about Northern Industries, didn't you?"

"Yes. General business matters."

"You plotted with him on the hostile takeover, didn't you?"

"I had no idea what he was doing."

"What if Mr. Dos Santos testifies that you were part of the hostile takeover?"

VJ looked at the jury. "I guess it will be my word against his."

"And getting back to the passport. What if Mr. Dos Santos testifies that he got the passport from Mr. Bruno Petrozzini's fireplace in Argentina when you tried to burn it the day after the murders?"

"Wouldn't surprise me. Because I did try to burn it so that no one would know that I was spying on your sister."

"I see. That's very sensitive of you." Edward walked to the far side of the room, away from the jury and witness. "That's what you told Bruno Petrozzini – that you lost your passport?"

"Yes. As I just testified. I called him from the airport and told him I had just found out that my parents were dead, and that during the layover, in the confusion, I lost my passport."

"What layover? Where did you tell him you were coming from?"

"Santiago. He didn't need to know I had been in New York. I didn't want anyone to know. I didn't want anyone to know that I had come home to follow my wife, so I had to get rid of my passport. I did not want to take any chances. It was a crazy time. My parents had just been killed. So I told him I lost the passport. He brought me back to his place in the Andes while he made some calls to get me a new passport."

Looking for an opening, Edward interrupted. "Why didn't you go back to Chile before making up your story about losing your passport?"

"Because my parents had just died. God knows how long it would have taken to get a new passport in Chile. In Argentina, I knew Uncle Bruno could get it done quickly."

Edward came again. "If you were so distraught after hearing your parents were murdered, why did you make up the ruse about the passport at all? Why didn't you just go home?"

"As I said, Mr. Bennett, I had just lost my parents. I did not want to lose my wife as well." He paused. "Besides, I was not ready to accept that my parents were dead."

VJ continued to speak unprompted. "While I was in Uncle Bruno's place that night, I threw my passport in the fireplace in my room so that I would never have to explain my trip home to follow my wife. I guess it didn't burn and Mr. Dos Santos found it. In any event, Uncle Bruno pulled some strings to get me the passport and fly me home the next day. I told everyone, including the police, that I lost my passport. I just didn't tell them about the trip to New York. That's it. If I am guilty of lying to the police to protect my marriage, after I lost my parents, I am willing to bear the consequences."

Edward changed the subject quickly, to stop the sympathy he felt was flowing from the jury to VJ. He had to trip VJ up, to get some momentum back. "And what about Professor Pym? You never told him that you were going to New York?"

"No. Once we landed in Chile, we had a lot of ground to cover, so we separated. We had to visit both Santiago and Valparaíso. I gave him Santiago because he wanted to take an excursion to Easter Island to see those giant statues, I think he called them Moai. They're real ugly." VJ made a long face to mimic the statues.

The crowd chuckled.

Professor Pym, who was in the gallery, looked quickly from side to side before joining in the laughter.

VJ continued. "So I was supposed to go to Valparaíso as soon as we got there, which gave me the cover to turn around and come home to track your sister. Pym had just landed on the island of his Moai when he heard the news about my parents, so there was never a real possibility of the two of us traveling home together. It was all a bit chaotic."

Edward was astonished at VJ's performance, but wanted everyone to know he was still in control, even though he feared he might be losing it. "Bravo, Mr. Petrozzini. An incredible display of wit and charm."

VJ winced. "I don't understand."

Straid stood up. "Is there a question pending?"

Judge Masterson spoke evenly. "Move on, Mr. Bennett. I have given you a lot of latitude with this witness, who was not even on your witness list. Let's do what we can to finish up."

Edward went back to the table and picked up a phone bill. He walked over to stand in front of Straid, cutting off the witness's line of vision with the prosecutor.

"You have a portable handheld phone, don't you?"

"Yes."

"Can you explain to the jury what a portable handheld phone is?"

"You should know. You were glued to one during your brother's campaign."

Edward was unfazed. "Explain for the jury, please."

"Sure. But it's really not that complicated. It's a phone that you can bring with you when you travel."

"And you get a separate phone number and bill for that phone, don't you?"

"Yes."

"Were you aware that Mr. Dos Santos took your handheld portable phone when you weren't looking?"

"I was not."

He held the phone bill in the air and waved it. "And acquired the phone bills, which he gave to me?"

"Sounds to me like he may be guilty of theft."

Edward ignored the barb. "The phone bills indicate your call to your father's home at the same time that my father has reported there was an anonymous call to your parents' home—while they were eating with my dad—demanding that my dad go to the rail yards."

"I don't know what you are talking about. I did call my parents that night and explained my paranoia about my wife. They told me to get on the plane and go back to Chile. To pretend nothing happened." Before Edward could ask a follow-up, VJ preempted him. "If you are going to ask me again why I didn't tell the police about the phone call, I will repeat myself – I did not want to embarrass your sister. I didn't want to lose my parents and my wife."

"Bravo again. Outstanding for a C student."

"I thought we were going to leave our personal relationship out of this."

"The problem is, Mr. Petrozzini, that your Uncle Bruno and Gaspar Dos Santos knew that you had not lost your passport after they found it in the fireplace. They became suspicious of you."

"I can't tell you what they thought."

"I will tell you what they thought. They thought they smelled a rat. When your reports back to them started getting sketchier, Mr. Dos Santos came here and followed you."

He looked at Win Gonzalez in the back of the gallery. Gonzalez mouthed the words, "Go for it."

Edward fast stepped to his table and picked up three photos. He gave the prosecutor and the judge copies, and stormed to the witness box. "Mr. Dos Santos saw you go into the hardware store to buy something the day my brother died, and then to the liquor store where you bought a bottle of wine." He slapped the first photo down, in front of VJ. "He took this time-stamped picture of you going into my brother's hotel room, with a bottle of wine in hand, on the day he died." He threw down the second. "He took this one a half an hour later, of you coming out of the hotel room with gray pants and a black leather belt." He laid down the third, as if revealing a poker hand. "And there is this one, a close-up photo of your pants and belt, with a gun slid in the belt."

VJ looked to Straid for help, and got none from the stunned prosecutor.

Edward continued in rapid fire. "You lured my father from your parents' house so that you could kill them and frame him, didn't you? It was you who put the blood stained shovel and plastic bags in my father's trunk. And you forced my brother to write the note and take the rat poison, otherwise you were going to shoot him, God knows how and where."

Straid shouted through the barrage. "Your Honor, I lost count of how many statements Mr. Bennett just made without any foundation. I don't think he even asked a question. Moreover, the three photos purport to address the death of Mr. Albert Bennett, a case which is not before the Court. May I suggest an adjournment so that we can address these issues more efficiently, in fairness to The People?"

Judge Masterson did not answer immediately. Silence hung heavy in the air as the judge pondered, his hand over his gavel. He leaned over and whispered something to his courtroom clerk.

Straid spoke again. "Counsel has presented a lot of new issues, Your Honor, many of which are unrelated to this case, that need sorting out. An adjournment can only help, and will not prejudice anyone."

Judge Masterson replied. "There will be no adjournment. Mr. Albert Bennett's death is before the Court. The People submitted his suicide note, implicating himself and his father in the murders, as a dying declaration at the close of their case. Counsel is entitled to challenge the circumstances and veracity of that note. Being that Mr. Petrozzini is not represented by counsel, I want to be clear with him. The witness will answer what I heard as Mr. Bennett's three questions, or he will assert his Fifth Amendment privilege against self-incrimination." He looked down at VJ.

Straid tried to interrupt. "But Your Honor, Mr. Petrozzini is entitled to counsel."

Judge Masterson ignored the prosecutor and proceeded with VJ. "The three questions that are before you are as follows. Are those photos of you going in and out of Albert Bennett's hotel room on the day he died? Did you cause the death of Albert Bennett? And did you murder your parents? You can either answer or assert your Fifth Amendment right to remain silent and seek counsel. One or the other, Mr. Petrozzini."

Straid pleaded. "Your Honor."

Judge Masterson kept his fix on VJ. "Sit down, Mr. Prosecutor. I may have a few questions for you as well when this is all over."

VJ smiled and looked at Edward. "How many nights' sleep have you lost, Edward, thinking that you couldn't save your father?"

Edward gritted his teeth, his head trembling. "Answer the question, Mr. Petrozzini."

VJ tilted his head, and pitched his voice to a taunting high. "Do you miss your big brother?"

Edward charged the stand, and grabbed VJ by the throat. "I'll kill you right here."

Masterson slammed his gavel violently, causing a shard to fly off it. "Guards, guards. Restrain Mr. Bennett."

VJ spoke through his squeezed windpipe as Edward's clutch tightened. "You don't have the guts to kill someone," he rasped at Edward.

The guards peeled Edward off VJ. Once the scuffle and its echo in the crowd had settled, Judge Masterson demanded an answer. "Mr. Petrozzini, I will only ask you one more time. If you don't answer or assert your privilege, I'll throw you in jail for contempt. Is that you in the pictures? Did you cause the death of Albert Bennett? And did you murder your parents?"

VJ straightened his tie, and lifted his chin. "Yes, yes, and yes." A collective gasp swept the room. "My father. He never believed in me. What kind of father doesn't have faith in his son? He also abused my mother. He didn't deserve to live, and I did not want my mother to continue to live that way. I set her free. I gave Albert what he deserved for being such a pompous prick." He sat back in the witness stand, his right hand gripping the right arm of his chair as if he were on a throne rather than in the dock. "I beat the Bennetts and put my parents out of their misery."

Edward stepped toward the witness box again, shouting. "You sick lying bastard. Your father would never have abused anyone. You just wanted everything for yourself and you didn't think I cared enough about the business to get in your way."

"Maybe if you acted sooner, your brother would still be alive."

Edward stopped dead in his tracks. His eyes opened wide. He had nothing more.

Straid summoned the guards grudgingly to handcuff VJ. As they pulled him out of his seat, he continued to shout, "I beat the Bennetts." When he was escorted out through the stir of the crowd and past his wife, VJ yelled deliriously, "You see, Lisa, I always told you I was smarter than your brothers. I told you."

Like maggots to new raw meat, the mob swarmed their new villain-prey, leaving behind Guy Bennett, his corpse beginning to breathe.

LXV.

❧ ❧

Old Rite

New Meaning

K eeping with tradition, Guy gathered his family at the Bennett home the following October for the annual Autumn Crush. As he unloaded the grapes from the trunk of his car into the backyard, his step was slightly slower, more the pace of his grandfather Stas the day his son Dante left him, or that of his father Dante after becoming crippled shy of his mark.

Waiting to receive the fruit were Edward and his wife Nancy, as well as Guy's daughter Lisa Marie, who would spend her first Crush at the barrel in Albert's place, alongside her father. Edward and Nancy's newborn son, named Gaetano after his grandfather, lay warmly in his bassinet inside the house next to Lisa Marie's newborn daughter, Maria, named after her grandmother. Marie stood watch over both infants, each of them wrapped in white. Albert's children, Albert Jr. and Alexandra, whom Guy and Marie were in the process of adopting over the garbled objection of their daughter-in-law Victoria, were also among the assembled congregation. They each began picking the grapes from the stems and dropping them into the crusher, observing Guy's silence as the stereo played the final scene of Puccini's *Turandot*.

The soprano princess lamented, "*Del primo pianto…Ahhhhhhhhh-hhhhhhhhh. Del primo pianto!*"

Albert Junior looked up at his grandfather. "Grandpa. What's the lady saying? Is sounds like she's hurt."

Guy smiled and lifted a grape to his grandson's mouth. "You're right, champ. The lady is a princess, and she is hurting. She's describing her first tears. In Italian, *primo pianto* means 'first tears.' That's all. She's just crying. Don't worry, she'll get better. But it's nice that you're worried about her." Guy laid the grape on his grandson's eager tongue, content to end the story there.

The soprano's voice at once leapt and turned angry:

> *Quanti ho visto morire per me!*
> *E li ho spregiati, ma ho temuto te!*
> *C'era negli occhi tuoi*
> *la luce degli eroi*
> *la superba certezza…*

> [How many I have seen die for me!
> And I despised them; but I feared you!
> In your eyes shone
> the light of heroes.
> In your eyes I saw the
> proud certainty of victory…]

Young Alexandra took her turn. "Grandpa, is the princess better now? I can't tell. And why would she be crying if she's already a princess? What's she saying? Can you tell me?"

Guy shook his head and looked at his children and Nancy. He now offered Alexandra a grape. "I'll tell you. But you and your brother have to promise me, this is your last question. We have a lot of wine to make, and we'll never get it done if I have to answer all these questions."

Alexandra twinkled her eyes. "I promise. No more questions. What's she saying?"

"Well, she's singing to a prince who wants to marry her. And originally, she told him 'no.' He couldn't marry her unless he solved three riddles. And if he didn't, he would die, like all the other princes that tried." Guy held up a finger. "The determined prince promised he would solve the riddles, and he did. Now she's upset, and talking about the confidence, the victory, she saw in his eyes. The prince won." Guy looked down into his barrel of grapes in despair. "It's just a fairy tale. It's make-believe. It's not important." Guy resumed the crush to alleviate the pain of memories past, when Albert had stood next to him at the barrel.

After another stretch of silence commanded by Guy's melancholy, and while the opera's princess and prince sang to one another in what sounded like a struggle, Nancy demurred. "I disagree, Dad. I think the story is important, and real. Very real."

His hands busy in the grapes, Guy squinted at Edward to get a rise out of him, but Edward did not take. "What's the matter, Edward, you seem out of it today?"

"Just a little tired," Edward answered in a voice barely above a whisper.

Guy cranked the crusher and looked at Nancy. "Well then maybe you can explain the story to Albert and Alexandra."

Nancy continued to pick the stems from the grapes delicately. "The princess is very powerful. But she has no love. As a matter of fact, she is afraid of it. That's why she kills all the others who want to marry her. She has been without love so long that she fears if she finds it, it will disappoint or kill her." Nancy grabbed another bunch of grapes from beneath Guy's sturdy forearm as he cranked away. "I think that she represents power as the absence of love."

Guy slowed his turns. "Okay, but the prince wins. With faith and relentless hope, he wins. That's the point."

Nancy stopped her picking. "You men are all the same! All you can see is the male raising his sword in victory. It's not about him. The prince doesn't win. Love wins. There's power in force and riches, but the supreme power is love." She shifted her look to Edward and Lisa Marie. "You all should know better than anyone. It's not the fancy house or the big backyard that brings you here." She laughed. "And I know it's not the wine, because I've tasted it. No offense."

Lisa Marie smirked.

Nancy continued. "It's love. Love is what kept you together through everything. If you had to, you would be crushing these grapes in a cardboard box in the middle of a battlefield." She paused. "Because of love." She paused again. "And God is love."

Guy pursed his lips and nodded affirmatively.

After another pause, Nancy tapped her ear. "Just listen to the finale, sung by the people, not by some royal prince or princess."

A choir shouted, *"Amor! O sole! Vita! Eternita!"*

Nancy translated *sotto voce*, her lips flush with passion. "Love! O sun! Life! Eternity!"

The legion of singing hearts continued its onslaught. *"Luce del mondo e amore!"*

Nancy stepped into the gap, basking in the sun. "Light of this world and love!"

Her recitation left Guy, Edward, and Lisa Marie speechless.

Albert Junior. puffed his chest and sang as loudly as he could. "Light of this world and love."

Alexandra followed in perfect pitch. "Light of this world and love."

The choir's last exuberant worship needed no translation.

Gloria a te! Gloria a te! Gloria!

His hands soaked in the blood of grapes, Guy embraced his daughter-in-law and children, and whispered "thank you" to Edward through a falling tear.

Through her own tears, Lisa Marie placed her hand on her father's chest, and clenched his shirt in her palm. "I'm sorry."

Guy's wife Marie looked with joyful calm from the kitchen window, her new grandchildren resting quiet beneath her.

And while the orchestral horns climbed to the heavens in thunderous crescendo, Guy looked up. For the first time in countless listenings, he heard in his favorite opera the distant timbre of a clarinet.

So it happened that an exotic beauty, originally spurned, revealed to the Bennett family the meaning of the Autumn Crush.

CPSIA information can be obtained at www.ICGtesting.com
Printed in the USA
BVOW06s2052170815

413697BV00037B/883/P

9 781629 011202